In WOMEN MUST WORK, he adds a third to his bitter and beautiful and compassionate gallery of women.

Etta was doomed to toast her father's Sunday muffins and run her mother's errands until she died or married some gangling, pawing youth in her ugly little seaside town. But she had pride and will and a secret determination to find for herself some reason, some satisfaction for being alive.

This is her vivid, passionate, intelligent quest, as powerful and triumphant a novel as Mr. Aldington has yet written.

In *The Colonel's Daughter*, that savage and brilliant tragedy of a small-town post-war girl which won high and instant recognition, and *All Men Are Enemies*, the profound and passionate love story in which he found a deeper compassion for human beings, Mr. Aldington drew the portraits of two memorable women, Georgie, who could not climb out of the groove of her class and family to find work or love or any significance to life, and Katha, to whom love brought a magnificent fulfillment. In WOMEN MUST WORK, he adds a third to his bitter and beautiful and compassionate gallery of women. Etta was doomed to toast her father's Sunday muffins and run her mother's errands until she died or married some gangling, pawing youth in her ugly little seaside town. But she had pride and will and a secret determination to find for herself some reason, some satisfaction for being alive. This is her vivid, passionate, intelligent quest, as powerful and triumphant a novel as Mr. Aldington has yet written.

WOMEN MUST WORK

Richard Aldington

WOMEN MUST WORK

A Novel

Garden City   *New York*

DOUBLEDAY, DORAN & COMPANY, INC.

MCMXXXIV

PRINTED AT THE *Country Life Press*, GARDEN CITY, N. Y., U. S. A.

And women, too, frank, beautiful, and kind
As the free heaven which rains fresh light and dew
On the wide earth, past; gentle radiant forms
From custom's evil taint exempt and pure;
Speaking the wisdom once they could not think,
Looking emotions once they feared to feel,
And changed to all which once they dared not be,
Yet being now, made earth like heaven; nor pride,
Nor jealousy, nor envy, nor ill shame,
The bitterest of those drops of treasured gall,
Spoilt the sweet taste of the nepenthe, love.

Prometheus Unbound.

CONTENTS

PROLOGUE

A SLIGHTLY PUDGY CHILD, with large grey-blue eyes, thick reddish hair, and a profile like a Lippo Lippi cherub, squatted intently in Aunt Miriam's garden. Occasionally she grunted, for the self-imposed task made large demands on her physical and mental energies. But it was fun to have a whole morning in Aunt Miriam's garden, away from Nurse who, frankly, was a beast, and even from Mummie who had a regrettable tendency to say "Don't, darling."

Owing to the fact that Aunt Miriam's husband was doing pretty well, a builder had been instructed to throw out a bay window; and this he had done with a creditable hideousness. Then the builder had gone away, leaving behind a pile of about a hundred bricks and a trowel. Etta's idea was to build a tower of Babel with the bricks, binding them together with mud strengthened by grass (no straw being available) on the lines recommended by Pharaoh's overseer to the Jews. The whole conception was brilliant and made Etta very happy. Aunt Miriam would be awfully

3

pleased to have a tower of Babel in the garden, and even if the tower didn't quite reach heaven and provide unlimited opportunities of visiting God, still Etta thought vaguely that she might learn an awful lot of languages, and so (hooray!) not have to go to school. Besides, she wasn't allowed to play with mud at home. So everything was perfect.

By the time Etta got to the third story of her impious tower, her shoes and socks were very muddy indeed; there was mud on her blue frock and grey felt hat, and even in her hair, which she frequently pushed out of the way with filthy hands. With the true artist's indifference to personal elegance, she laboured on, as unconscious of her muddiness as she was of the fact that her attitude exposed to view an unconventional amount of lady's underwear. And then, as if God had got frightened and jealous of her progress, she was suddenly seized and jerked to her feet, while Nurse's voice said angrily:

"You naughty child! Haven't you been told over and over you're not to play mud pies?"

The effect was as shattering as if God himself had dropped a bomb in the garden. Etta's heart gave a huge thump, and her aspiring dream contracted to a little point of frightened resentment. But she didn't give way. Wriggling in Nurse's grasp, she put her case with the precise logic of her age.

"I *wasn't* making mud pies. I was building a *tower!*"

"Look at your shoes and stockings!" said Nurse petulantly, ignoring the crux of the argument with grown-up stupidity. "And them filthy hands, dear oh dear oh dear, after I washed your hair and all yesterday. You're a naughty, bad, wicked girl, that's what you are, with your poor mother ill in bed and everybody up half the night."

To relieve her aggrieved feelings, Nurse thereupon slapped her, and Etta set up a fearful howl at this out-

rageous Act of War. So Nurse slapped her again to make
her stop howling, and finding, curiously enough, that this
remedy failed, carried Etta howling into the house to be
washed and brushed up.

As if this wasn't enough shock for one morning, Aunt
Miriam had another one prepared for her as soon as she
was presentable in dull society. Aunt Miriam took Etta
on her lap and said:

"Now, dear, it was very naughty of you to play mud
pies and give Nurse all that extra work. . . ."

With grim courage Etta faced the fact that it was quite
useless to make the distinction between playing mud pies
and building a tower, and Aunt Miriam went on:

"We all want you to be very, very good—Uncle Harry
and I want it, and Daddy and Mummie too, especially
Mummie, who loves you better than anyone in the world.
You'll be good for Mummie's sake, won't you, dear?"

Etta nodded gravely but with no sort of conviction.

"I've got something very important to tell you. What
would you say if I told you you've got a lovely new baby
brother?"

Etta pondered this surprising and not very welcome
item of news in pensive gloom. Suddenly her intellectual
curiosity awoke, and she said, wriggling with interest:

"Where'd he come from?"

"The doctor brought him to Mummie last night in a
bag."

"Where'd the doctor get him?"

"Hush, dear! Your little brother was sent by God to
Mummie. But aren't you glad to have a dear little brother
to love and look after and play with later on?"

Etta wasn't a bit glad. She had a feeling that too much
fuss was being made. Besides, she was jealous. She refused to respond to Aunt Miriam's emotional appeal. She
said:

"Why's Mummie ill?"

"How do you know Mummie's ill?" asked Aunt Miriam in great agitation.

"Well, Nurse said she was!"

"Oh." Aunt Miriam was relieved of a dreadful suspicion and blamed herself for harbouring such a thought about an innocent child. "Yes, Mummie was so happy to have a new little boy that she just wants to lie and rest. Presently you shall go and see her for a minute, and the baby. But you must be very, very quiet and good. You will, won't you, dear?"

Etta was quite still and silent for a moment, then wriggled off Aunt Miriam's lap.

"Can I go and play in the garden?"

"Bless me!" exclaimed Aunt Miriam, amazed at such callous indifference. "Don't you want to see the new baby?"

Etta shook her head, and said simply:

"No."

At an age so tender that it should have excited compassion, Etta was handed over for educational purposes to the secular arm of the Misses Catfield, with the prayer that the child should not be spoiled. These ladies earned a precarious livelihood by running what they called a school, in which infants of either sex but respectable parentage were well grounded in the rudiments up to the age of seven; the advanced course, which included history, needlework, and the peculiar dialect of Anglo-Norman French invented by the Misses Catfield out of Chardenal and Erckmann-Chatrian, with music, Latin and dancing as extras, was reserved for young ladies only. The Misses Catfield were not going to have any scandal, with young Lovelaces of eight and nine busking among the lassies. These venerable ladies (disrespectfully referred to by errand boys as the old geesers) were vastly genteel, and Dortborough knew full well how to honour birth and breeding even when accompanied by financial reverses. This was lucky for the Misses Catfield, for, like many genteel people, their own education was nothing to brag about; so that being genteel was their sole stock in trade. It was also lucky for them that the Board of Education seemed never to have heard of them.

The elder Miss Catfield was lame and wore a dark wig with a black cap permanently pinned onto it. There was no deception about this, however; everyone could see it was a wig, and even the youngest toddlers who had never heard of such a thing soon learned about old Catty's false hair. Miss Catfield's face was sallow and saturnine, marked with furrows which were most charitably said to be the result of study and thinking. She suffered from her liver, and cultivated a stern manner, very frightening to beginners. Miss Betsy Catfield, who couldn't have been more than fifty-five, formed an instructive contrast to her elder and responsible sister. Plump but airy, with a pinky-white complexion, she flitted about inconsequently in youthful blue dressed trimmed with white lace, and set writing exercises—evil communications corrupt good manners—in a beautiful copperplate hand. She played touch-last and here we go gathering nuts and may with the children, while her sterner sister looked on, occasionally reproving some indecorum. In defense of Muncaster House School, let it be said that while these ladies had little to teach, they taught that little well; moreover, they had never heard of the team spirit, so did the children less harm than might be expected.

Incredible as it may seem, the Misses Catfield actually existed in the flesh less than forty years ago, though now, alas, they must be awaiting the general resurrection with genteel and pathetic confidence. They belonged to that type of persons who miss the bus of their own generation, owing to mixing too long and respectfully with domineering elders. They were almost the last survivors of a defunct Dortborough society, which had long before been swamped under a new eruption of tradesmen and professionals. Ghosts of gentility, they haunted a Dortborough which was no longer theirs, consoled only by the Vicar and the sense of their integrity. In the vulgarized false-prosperity-mongering Dortborough of the 'nineties and 'noughts, they were like a couple of bottles of ullaged vintage wine in a grocer's Christmas display. Whatever differences may have existed between the two ladies, they were united in reverence for the memory of the dear Papa who had wronged them so grievously by his crapulous behaviour and having no money to leave them—women often do revere a blackguard father. Even the tenacious memory of Dortborough gossip retained only the vaguest image of Papa Catfield, but apparently he had been a Major in a line regiment, genteel and gallant, but libidinous and alcoholic, and profuse in his spending. That, no doubt, explains why the Misses Catfield were parsimonious teetotal spinsters.

Needless to say, the youthful Etta knew nothing about all this and cared less. The Catfield figures as here presented were built up by her a generation later from the imagination and vague memories of home talk, much as geologists build up some alleged monster from a jaw bone, a tibia, and a footprint. Thinking them over long afterwards, as one does sometimes reflect on the queer lost figures of one's remote past, Etta decided that the Misses Catfield had affected her in a manner which was entirely negative, i.e., with a strong though quite unconscious determination not to be genteel and spinsterish, and, more vaguely, not to live for any such abstraction as the dim social consideration which kept them existing.

Her own impressions were, naturally, entirely subjective. There was Betsy, saying:

"You see, dear, you should have divided by five, and then carry two."

Then, with an encouraging little hand pat, she would frisk away to the next little victim on the hard inkstained bench.

There was Miss Catfield, stern and intimidating, repeating, as if the information were the very core and centre of an encyclopædic knowledge of French:

"Haven't I told you over and over again that 'nopal' forms the plural in 's' and not in 'aux'?"

In the playground, which was an ancient lawn with most of the grass worn away, stood a fine chestnut, under which they played at recess, after a cup of watery milk with skin in it, paid for by anxious parents at the rate of threepence a day. They weren't allowed to throw stones or the chestnuts which fell down so profusely in the autumn with such a rich polish as they rolled out of the husks, or to be rough, or scream, or use slang (hush, dear, don't ever use that dreadful word again), or play conkers, and the big ones weren't allowed to tease the little ones. They played genteel games with Miss Betsy. Recess was always the same —gentle, decorous, and unamusing.

In winter, chilly draughts blew up through the cracks in the uncarpeted and not well-scrubbed boards of the schoolroom floor. Etta blew on her fingers to warm them after doing arithmetic on a frozen slate, and got chilblains. The Misses Catfield hovered round the one small fire at the end of the room and conducted the classes from this point of vantage, like a couple of staff officers. There was a stuffy smell in spite of the cold, an inky, corrosive, musty smell of none-too-clean schoolroom, which seemed like the aroma of Futility itself. In summer, the windows were often open, but the same smell lingered; the chestnut leaves rustled quietly, almost genteelly, outside; a humming drowsiness floated over the copybooks. Every morning, winter and summer, they began by singing to Miss Betsy's waving finger "There is a green hill far away"; and every afternoon they ended with "Now the day is over."

Probably there was less of the element of hatred in Etta's make-up than in that of most people. By nature she was inclined to enjoy the few things which are likable, instead of grousing about the many things which are nasty; and she wasn't vindictive or resentful. But she did hate Nurse. Nurse showed a good many traits of the now ubiquitous proletarian-democratic type. Abject under severity, she was inclined to be more and more uppish when treated with the vague kindliness which permeated the Morison establishment. She was never tired of complaining acidly of her employer's caprices (whams and fancies, she called them) to Cook, who was one of the flaccid, well-I-never, to-be-sure, kind. On the other hand, she abused her delegated authority over the children, particularly Etta, in the vexatious bullying way of petty officials.

One of the ways in which she bullied Etta was by insisting that the official health walk should always be taken up and down the Muncaster Road and never elsewhere by any chance, though she knew Etta loathed it, as a healthy appetite would loathe a prolonged diet of insipid bread-and-butter pudding.

It didn't seem to matter much to Teddy, who made these revolting excursions at first recumbent and then sitting in a perambulator, then on his own strong fat little legs hand-in-hand with Etta, and who was early released on the excuse of games at school. But years and years and years of Etta's young life were haunted by the Muncaster Road. She used to pray:

"O Lord, make it rain hard at walk time, and then clear up and be lovely, for Jesus Christ's sake, amen."

Sometimes it rained, and sometimes it didn't. But even

rain became an impotent ally, when Mummie was con-
verted by a health fiend, and Etta was forced to take her
"constitutional" (with a nurse very bitter on the subject
of whams and fancies) in a mackintosh, umbrella, and
goloshes.

Let us look at the Muncaster Road, for it not only was
(and, alas, still is) a brick and mortar reality, it is a symbol
soaked with threats and omens. Nurse saw no symbol in
it, and only so much of its reality as to wish to goodness
that by a miracle she might be whipped away suddenly
into one of its drawing rooms as mistress of the house, and
be done with looking after other people's ungrateful brats.
And for Etta, at the time when she made that daily dolor-
ous pilgrimage, there was no symbol either. It was the
Muncaster Road. Yet she disliked and resented it, and
rejected it. All unconsciously, she thus rejected what it
symbolized.

At the lower end of Etta's own road, which was an ave-
nue of tall chestnuts, stood a scarlet pillar box, like a very
squat guardsman standing to attention, ready to swallow
anything duly authorized by V.R. Here was the Muncaster
Road, so named from one Hugo de Muncaster, an alleged
Norman knight who had once been seneschal of Dortborough Castle, and whose descendants had possessed an
estate there. At the pillar-box corner, an ordinary street of
red brick villas suddenly expanded to thrice the width,
while the row of villas jumped into pairs, twice as high, of
yellow brick decorated with biscuit-coloured stone and
yellow chimneys. Flights of damp stone steps, like kneeling
housemaids, bent before each front door; and at the side
of each was a humbler portal inscribed in Gothic lettering:
Tradesmen's Entrance. Every garden had a shrubbery of
slightly smoke-blackened evergreens; every façade the
same number of ill-proportioned windows with the same

stereotyped stone ledges, pseudo-classical pilasters and
pediments on which the sparrows dropped little white
splashes. And thus Muncaster Road stretched for fifteen
hundred yards, Dortborough's most ambitious effort at
architectural splendour, the summit of what a century of
Prosperity could offer to satisfy in form and colour the
senses and the spirit.

Yet in spring clusters of snowdrops mourned whitely
over the starved sooty loam, pale, it seemed, from their
captivity behind iron railings and under grim vaults of
laurels. Heroic crocuses pushed up oval bubbles of gold,
which burst gently open into five shining petals. As they
faded, stronger daffodils and jonquils, shaking and bending
in the March winds, renewed their lost gold and silver.
Later, the lilacs suddenly distinguished themselves among
the forbidding frontage of evergreens by decorating their
slender boughs with thick drooping clusters of scented
blossoms. Here and there was more gold from laburnums.
But after that the glory faded, and the garden fronts were
drilled into horrid formations of calceolarias and geraniums
enclosed by lines of plants with no flowers and variegated
leaves.

At first Etta saw them not at all; then, as her small self-
world expanded, saw them as pretty things she was forbidden to pick; and then marked them as distractions to
the monotony of the Muncaster Road. Very often she was
made to read or was read to from a black-bound book in
small type with a gold-leaf top to its pages. And more than
once she read that she was to consider the lilies of the field.
Nobody suggested, and it never occurred to her, that the
daffodils and even the lilacs of the Muncaster Road were
lilies of the field, that they might be considered, that what
they had suggested centuries before might still be true, that
something new even might be learned by considering them.

* * *

Muncaster Road was quiet; Castle Road, where Etta lived, was even quieter under its arch of tall chestnuts; but to the placid inhabitants of those platitudinous dwellings came gleams and rumblings of the distant greater world, placidly accepted as we accept the far-off flash and mutter of a thunderstorm so remote that it can never possibly reach our district.

While Teddy was only a baby and Etta so small she soon got tired and had to be carried, they were taken one morning to the Marine Parade—Teddy in his perambulator pushed by Nurse, and Etta (great treat) carried by Daddy. They lined up with a large crowd on the asphalt promenade, with their backs to the sea and the railings between them and the white road, which was gradually filled after a great deal of trampling and shouting and backing-and-forthing by two long lines of big men in red coats and tightly braced trousers, with funny spiked hats and club-looking things in their hands.

They kept telling Etta it was in honour of the Queen, but she kept forgetting and asking again:

"What are they *doing*, Daddy?"

Until even Daddy got cross and said she was to stop asking the same question when he'd told her already.

There was more shouting, and suddenly all the men in front of Etta waved their arms and there was a long glittering spike on the end of each club, and people were silent and intense, and Etta was a little frightened; and then the men held the clubs in front of them quite still, while another red man on a horse and with feathers in his hat rode by, followed by several others. The first man touched his hat as he went by, but the others didn't, and Daddy said:

"That's the general commanding the garrison."

But Etta didn't know what a general was or what a garrison was. And then the men took the spikes off their clubs, and there was a long wait. Presently a loud voice shouted

"Ready," and people got intense again; the voice said "Present," and the men put their clubs on their shoulders pointing to the sky over Etta's head. She was just going to say again, "What are they *doing*, Daddy?" when the voice said: "Fire!" and there was a dreadful flash and banging noise. Teddy was frightened, and his baby face went all red and the corners of his mouth went down and down, though he didn't cry. But Etta was terrified and threw her arms round Daddy's neck and her head on his shoulder, screaming:

"I don't *like* them, Daddy. Please, please make them go away."

Then she howled like anything. But Daddy said hush, hush, it was only a *feu de joie* for the Queen. Etta didn't understand this either and went on crying. She begged Daddy to make them stop, but he wantonly let the men do the banging twice again. Etta was broken-hearted. She wished there had never been any men with clubs and red coats. But worse than that was the double shock of knowing that Daddy couldn't really do everything and that he didn't love her as much as Mummie said he did.

There came more gleams and mutterings from that perpetual thunderstorm of violence and perfidy which is called the life of nations.

The episode of the *feu de joie* was hidden away in Etta's subconscious memory, and she had forgotten all about red men with clubs, when one night she was awakened by the sound of tramping feet and the roll of heavy wheels going up Castle Road. Actually she didn't really wake up, but heard the noises through a drowse of sleep. Next morning Daddy rustled the newspaper, and kept using the funny word "Fashoda." But nothing more happened.

More months passed by, and again there was the noise of wheels and feet, and Daddy rustled the newspaper angrily and talked about Natal and Ladysmith. This time something seemed to have happened, for he went on talking about them, and they hung up a picture in Etta's bedroom on the wall facing her bed.

This picture was a coloured supplement from a Christmas annual. It represented a fanged, bow-legged, cantankerous-looking bulldog, standing on a Union Jack and snarling at a French poodle, a Russian wolfhound, a German boarhound, and a stately mongrel made to look as like the Emperor Franz Josef as possible. In the background hovered a number of smaller mongrels of dubious but probably dago descent. Underneath the picture it said: Let Em All Come. Why? "Let em all come," Etta murmured to herself as she went to sleep. "Let—em—all—come. Let—em—all . . ."

They took her to Poole's Myriorama, where she saw pictures of the veldt and hospitals and Boer atrocities, and lantern-slide portraits of Buller and Gatacre, Roberts and Baden-Powell, who always got the loudest cheers. Everybody cheered like mad and seemed very happy over the enteric patients in the hospital which dramatically burst into red as a shell hit it. Then a woman came on dressed as Britannia and sang a song about: "Pass the hat for your credit's sake, and pay, pay, pay." Pay they did, and, by the bye, have gone on paying ever since. It proved to be a most expensive entertainment, except for the gold and diamond millionaires and the army contractors. True, Etta only put a penny in the hat, and Daddy gave her the penny; but it was on account, Britannia was merely accepting a token payment.

And that passed away. Etta was standing on the top of the steps leading to the front door, and it was cold, and Daddy and Mummie were talking excitedly but in low voices to Mr. and Mrs. Jefferson, who were leaving. And Mrs. Jefferson bent over Etta and said, very solemnly:

"Always remember tonight, dear. The Great Queen is dead."

Next morning Mummie came to the nursery and changed Etta's pigtail ribbon to a black one and kissed her tearfully, saying: "Be good, always be good like the Good Queen."

PART I

By the time Etta was nineteen, she had made two unsuccessful attempts to get away from Dortborough; and each failure only strengthened the obsession: and since Daddy and Mummie disapproved and Etta had a good deal of determination, the family circle became a battleground. Nothing remarkable in that, you may observe—a stock situation: look at Molière, look at the back numbers of *Punch*. True, but observe this: Etta was not the Molière heroine who at fifteen (life ran high in those days) knew which man she wanted to marry and meant to have him. At that period in all the Dortboroughs of England, and in Manchester, and in South Kensington, there were girls who wanted to get away, not with a man, but *on their own*.

This "on their own" was possible only in a highly industrialized country, where the breakdown of the life ritual, of all living collective inspiration, had reached even the family. All human relationships having been corrupted by Business, no integrity remained but in the isolated individual. In earlier societies the woman on her own had little choice but that of nun, prostitute, or servant; and the servant was absorbed into the family she served, the nun into the family of the convent, the prostitute into the family of the brothel. Hence the instinctive prejudice against the women who wanted to be on their own, because the nun denies her womanhood, the prostitute degrades it, and the servant must subdue it to servitude.

In the twentieth century the women who wanted to be on their own were some of the best, the honest ones, those who instinctively rejected the trash. But here came a tragical dilemma. If they accepted Business and served it, they served the very thing from which they fled, and at best became imitation men. If they rejected Business and lived on allowances or incomes, they were in the anomalous position of hunting with the industrial hounds and running with the agricultural hare. An instinctive sense of this made many of them turn "artist." And so Europe was cluttered up with incompetent English women "artists"— not that a woman is incapable of being an artist, but because the assumed rôle provided an escape. Either situation was impossible, and the solution is not yet found.

The debate about Etta being on her own broke out with especial violence over tea on a gloomy November afternoon.

Tom Morison made a great point of Sunday afternoon tea. At all times he liked to drink quantities of strong Indian tea with plenty of milk and sugar—Sergeant Major's tea, in fact. And at the proper season he derived additional satisfaction from seeing his muffins toasted at the drawing-room fire on a twisted brass toasting fork purchased at the Oriental Bazaar. This task, originally performed by Mrs. Morison, had now been allotted to Etta. There was no practical reason why the muffins should not have been toasted in the kitchen, but Mr. Morison's insistence on the muffin rite and his delight therein may probably be traced to an unconscious symbolical exercise of power—he was asserting the patriarch's right to the services of all the females of his community. At the same time he tasted the only other discoverable reward of the modern family man, which is to contemplate the domestic prison he has given his life and freedom to create, and to believe hopefully that he and his dependents are housed, clothed, fed, and generally provided for a little better and more tastefully than his neighbours.

With the Morison household Sunday was not a day of violent gloom, though a decent air of ennui and overeating enveloped the family, as uninspiring as a twice-read newspaper. This relaxation of an original puritan fervour of Sabbath-keeping was not due to any specially heretical tendency, but only to the fact that every self-tormenting device tends to lose its power with succeeding generations. Churchgoing was no more than a symbol, a guarantee of respectability; and respectability is good for trade.

On this particular Sunday afternoon Mrs. Morison was seated in a small but comfortable armchair knitting a pair of winter socks for Teddy, who was away at school, Mr. Morison was peacefully brooding on the confines of sleep in a large comfortable armchair, and Etta was reading in a sort of recess decorated with white-painted woodwork to which her mother referred proudly as "the ingle nook." Punctually at four-thirty Nelly the maid arrived—black dress, white starched apron, white goffered cap—carrying a white metal cake stand of bread-and-butter, paste sandwiches, home-made rock cakes, and a round uncut chocolate cake. She then placed a six-legged stand before Mrs. Morison, retired, and returned with a large round tray of Benares brass (made in Brummagem) which she set reverentially and carefully on the stand. This tray was crowded with a variety of inæsthetic objects, all polished and shining: a chased and fluted silver teapot with an ebony handle and topknot; a silver tea caddy in regrettable repoussé; an electroplated kettle on a ditto stand with a ditto methylated-spirit heater; a ditto sugar basin with silver tongs fantastically cleft, a ditto slop basin, and a ditto milk jug; two glass jam containers with silver tops; a silver butter dish with glass container and scrolled butter knife; cups, saucers, plates, knives, and spoons from the "best service"; and, last of all, an electroplated muffin dish containing six untoasted muffins.

All these expensive and valueless objects clinked slightly when set down. At the sound Tom Morison sat up, blinked his eyes and seemed as if he rapidly chewed something impalpable several times, and remarked:

"What, tea? Well, well!"

This was said in a tone which seemed to imply great astonishment that tea should have appeared, whereas in fact he had been impatiently expecting it for at least half an hour. Mr. Morison then leaned forward and with unerring instinct placed his hand on the cover of the muffin dish, which he lifted, saying:

"What's this? Muffins! Nothing like piping hot muffins with plenty of good fresh English butter!"

Mrs. Morison, who was placidly counting spoonfuls of tea into the pot, forebore to mention that it was one-and-four a pound Danish; and Mr. Morison, with happy anticipation, lifted the toasting fork from the brass hook on which it hung beside the fire, exclaiming:

"Come along, Etta. Muffins for tea! Here's the fork."

Etta, however, sat down in a small chair as far from the fire as was possible without utterly deserting the family circle.

"I won't toast them today if you don't mind, Daddy,"

she said. "The fire's so hot, it gives one a flushed face and a headache."

"What? Don't talk nonsense. If you've got a headache it's from sitting with your nose in that book all the afternoon."

"Please don't insist, Daddy," Etta said, rather more stiffly than was necessary, but she resented the jibe at her book-reading. "I really can't do it today."

Tom Morison was about to retort when his wife intervened:

"Hand your father his cup of tea, Etta. Or do you feel too superior to do even that?"

"Oh, Mother! Don't be so absurd. . . ."

Etta checked herself and handed the cup to her father, who took it mechanically, still disconsolately holding the toasting fork in his other hand. No muffins! Worse still, not even this petty service from a spoiled girl kept in luxury and idleness! What next! He looked anxiously round the room to reassure himself. Yes, there were the carved cabinets full of knick-knacks, the rosewood upright grand with the silver-framed photographs, the lace curtains, the chintz-covered couch, the pseudo-Jacobean stool, and the two blue Spode plates suspended by metal hangers above the oil painting of Highland cattle fording a burn—all undisputed evidence that his home life was well and truly founded. He put down his tea cup, irascibly spiked a flabby muffin, and began to toast it at the red coals, talking indignantly to Etta over his shoulder:

"I tell you what it is, my girl, you're getting like all the rest of the boys and girls today. Spoiled. There's no other word for it—spoiled. What'll happen to poor old England if we ever get into a war with Germany I don't know. You let your parents work and slave year in, year out, so that you can live in comfort, and you're not even grateful for it. We try to give you the best, and all you do in return is to get high and mighty and discontented. Let me tell you that at your age I'd been earning my own living for two years."

This interesting diatribe, which must already have been a set piece in the early Minoan period, was interrupted by an exclamation from Mrs. Morison and a smell of burning from the muffin which in his agitation Mr. Morison had pushed too near the fire. Mr. Morison readjusted his muffin and remained heatedly silent. Etta sighed. Above all things she hated family rows, unaware that they are merely the expression of an inevitable conflict of egoisms. But she wasn't going to run away from the row she had unintentionally provoked, and had a feeling that she must assert herself now or else go under forever. She took up her father's last remark, ignoring the possibilities of destructive analysis to the other part.

"I don't think you should taunt me with something that happened long before I was born. It wasn't my fault if you had to start work too early. Anyway, you had a place to step into in Grandfather's office, just as Teddy will in yours. I envy you both. Do you think I like to feel now I'm grown up that I'm useless, just an expense to you? I *want* to earn my living, to be independent. I wish you'd take me into the office."

"Impossible," said Mr. Morison shortly. "It'd upset the clerks."

"Well, couldn't you get me into someone else's office?"

"What!" exclaimed Mr. Morison in consternation. "And have it said all over Dortborough that I was so hard up my daughter had to take a job? I'd be ruined. Besides, what could *you* do? *You* don't know anything. You haven't passed the exams."

"But if I'm useless only because I haven't been properly educated, is that my fault?"

"Oh, Etta!" Mrs. Morison almost groaned with reproach. "How can you? If you'd seen the bills Daddy had to pay. . . . We sent you to that expensive finishing school in Paris, and you came home full of airs with a hat like a street woman's and wanting coffee and rolls for breakfast and your head full of nonsense about operas and Louvres and boulevards and reading those horrible French books which I *know* aren't fit for a young girl to look at and I wish you'd burn them!"

"But, Mother," cried Etta, "I thanked you both then for letting me go, and I thank you now. And was it ungrateful of me to try and learn the best I could in Paris?"

"Umph! The 'best,' you call it? *I* call it a pack of unhealthy nonsense, and if I'd known then what I know now you'd never have gone. And to think that a daughter of mine should bring into my home a photo of a naked woman with a pot on her shoulder!"

"But I've told you over and over it's an Ingres, Mother," Etta pleaded.

"I don't care what they call it. I know what *I* call it: sheer disgusting filth! And I wrote and told that Paris woman so."

"Oh! You didn't really write that to Mrs. Cleveland?"

"Didn't I! And I'm proud of it—it was my duty as a mother!"

For a moment Etta put her face in her hands in an agony of shame. So that was why her repeated letters had received no answer from the one person she respected and loved, the one human being who had awakened all her enthusiasm so that she had believed Mrs. Cleveland was the ideal of what women could be in the world! And to have lost her in a manner so petty and shameful! Mrs. Morison's voice went on with placid relentlessness:

"And as if it wasn't enough that you persuaded us to waste all that money on a wild-goose chase which might have landed us all in disgrace and I don't know what, you hadn't been home five minutes before you were pleading and pleading to go to that music school in London. I'm sure I was against it from the beginning, but your daddy always would spoil you, and after all our trouble and paying all those fees, you only stopped one term. I suppose because I took care that you shouldn't come in contact with any of that Paris filth there, it wasn't good enough for you."

Etta thought of the South Kensington home where her virtue had been guarded with such ferocious care and life had been so dull; but it had been London, and there had been escapes, there had been concerts and the other students and, above all, the happiness of living her days with music. Then came the day when she asked her master to tell her frankly if she had a chance of a musical career, and very kindly but frankly he had said that she had appreciation but not the gifts to make a first-class executant; and after the first few days of pain and revolt, she had accepted his verdict, and had gone quietly home with a deep sadness at her heart. And it would have been so easy to deceive her parents, who thought her playing wonderful, so easy to have had three years in London and perhaps have found some other way out. But it wouldn't have been honest or fair to them; and after the three years she would still have been a failure. But it was a little hard to hear from her mother's lips this distorted version of the bravest and least selfish action of her life.

"It wasn't that I thought I was too good for the Academy of Music, Mother," she said quietly. "I found out, when I got among people who were really pianists, that I wasn't good enough for it."

"Stuff and nonsense!" cried Mr. Morison. "I bet there wasn't one of them as good as my girl. *I* never heard better playing in my life!" Which was not surprising, considering he had seldom been to any musical display more elevated than a smoking concert.

By this time Mr. Morison had toasted himself red and three muffins brown, and chewed himself back to good-humour. A kind-hearted man, even when offended by her, doesn't like to see his daughter pressed too heavily by his wife. Dimly he perceived that Etta could make no adequate defense against the attack of her mother's jealousy —a jealousy which was not personal, but the jealousy of the static, contracted life for the life which is trying to expand. He went on:

"Besides, I don't see what all this is about. Don't you worry, Etta. *My* daughter won't starve. Drink up your tea and give us a tune."

"Yes, but don't play anything but *sacred* music," said Mrs. Morison, who included in the term "sacred" all music which would now be called highbrow. "The neighbours don't like anything too rattling on Sundays."

"Pooh," retorted Mr. Morison, "an Englishman's home is his castle."

"Not on Sunday," she replied firmly.

"But, Daddy," Etta intervened, "am I to live all my life as a parasite on you and Teddy? Am I never to have a life of my own?"

"What d'you mean 'a life of your own'?" said Mr. Morison gruffly.

"Of course we hope that one day you may have a nice *home* of your own." Mrs. Morison gently insinuated a possibility which her husband was not fond of contemplating.

Etta's mind dwelt for a second on a rapid series of mental pictures of the middle-class male youth of Dortborough, all of them desirable young men riding upon bicycles. A house in Dortborough, in the Muncaster Road if the man were rich enough, evenings of playing him soothing tunes (sacred ones on Sundays), servants and bills, sending another Etta for constitutionals on smooth flagstones between iron railings, timidly and jealously holding back another younger self from life by telling her that one day she would have a nice home of her own. . . .

"I think I would rather die than live all my life in Dortborough," said Etta, looking thoughtfully at the fire.

"Why, what's wrong with Dortborough?" cried Mr. Morison in honest amazement. "It's one of the most go-ahead towns on the South coast."

"You're allowed to come to every At Home with me," said Mrs. Morison tartly. "It's not *our* fault if you prefer lounging in your bedroom to decent society."

"You've had several invitations to dinner this autumn," said Mr. Morison.

"And to three dances," added his wife.

"And when the snow comes you can go tobogganing," said Mr. Morison, who could seldom remember that Etta was no longer fifteen.

"And skating," said Mrs. Morison.

"There's a sixpenny pop every Saturday night," said Mr. Morison. "You ought to be able to pick up all the catchy new tunes."

"I shall want you to help with my stall at the bazaar in aid of the Orphanage Funds," said Mrs. Morison. "And you may thank your lucky stars you're not an orphan."

"You've got a bicycle, too," said Mr. Morison. "That's good healthy exercise, though I won't have you wearing bloomers."

"And Teddy will soon be home for Christmas," added Mrs. Morison in a tone of doting possessiveness.

"And Christmas pudding, hurray!" exclaimed Mr. Morison enthusiastically. "Mother'll want you to help her make them this week."

"There'll be plenty for you to do. You can start hemstitching the new sheets tomorrow."

"So there's nothing much wrong with Dortborough, eh?" Mr. Morison wound up, rubbing his hands, though there was something a little doubtful in the glance he gave at Etta's cold expression. She was wondering how to parry this double onslaught, how to excuse herself from this deluge of delights, how one acquires the difficult art of expressing unpopular sentiments and insinuating different ideas. She said:

"I still feel as if I would rather die than spend all my life in Dortborough. Perhaps I ought to feel as enthusiastic about these things as you do, but—well, they bore me."

"I suppose your parents and brother bore you too?" remarked Mrs. Morison sarcastically.

"Oh, Mother, how unfair you are!" Etta exclaimed. "But how can I love you properly if I'm unhappy in myself?"

She said that thinking she believed it, but as she spoke a sort of inner voice was saying: That's the first false thing you've said so far. You know you don't love them as you love Teddy, as you loved Mrs. Cleveland, as you might love other men and women who were at one with you, above all as you might love a man. They're your parents, but they're not really your sort; and you know it.

"Now, look here, Etta," said Mr. Morison apoplectically, "what the diggins *do* you want?"

Etta swiftly swallowed down a small lump which was beginning to rise in her throat at all this hectoring, and fought off a disposition to cry.

"I want to go right away from Dortborough," she said as firmly as she could, though her voice trembled a little. "I want to live for a time quite by myself, very simply, and think things out. I should like to shape my own life as far as a person can in this world, without having it all moulded for me. I don't want to spend my days sitting back and saying 'Hurray!' to everything my men relatives think, say, and do. I don't want to be just a dependent on Daddy and Teddy. If I marry a man, I want to marry him

as an equal, not as a parasite. I want to respect myself.
And I want to find out other girls and women who think
and feel as Vera and I do."

"Vera?" said Mrs. Morison sharply, pouncing on the
one unguarded reference in Etta's words, "Vera! Dear,
dear, I *wish* you wouldn't always be running round to her,
filling your head with all that Suffragette nonsense. One
of these days she'll be arrested by the police, I know she
will, and then think of her poor mother."

"Suffrage does mean something, I believe," said Etta
quietly. "You don't understand it, you just believe what
the newspapers say. But it's not just to get a vote I want
to go away."

"Votes for women? Blokes for women, that's what they
really want, I always say," interjected Mr. Morison heartily. "But every Englishman knows women'll never get the
vote in this country—they don't really want it. But that's
neither here nor there. The point is, how're you going to
carry out all this high-falutin stuff you've been talking?
How're you going to carry it into practical effect? That's
what I want to hear."

"It *is* difficult," Etta agreed humbly. "Perhaps it's
difficult because it's worth doing. Perhaps it only seems
difficult. I've thought a lot about it. Sometimes I feel so
desperate I think I'll run away and be a servant or a
nurse. . . ."

"Well, I never. . . !" Mrs. Morison interjected, scandalized.

"But then I realize that's only running out of one prison
to another," Etta went on recklessly. "There seems only
one way . . ."

She hesitated.

"Well, what's that?" asked her father heavily.

"I've hoped . . . I've sometimes thought . . ." Etta hesitated timidly, "that I might ask . . . that you might perhaps

give me a small allowance . . . just for a time, of course . . .
only until I could find some congenial work. . . ."

She stopped, flushing with shame at having to beg.

"Allowance indeed!" exclaimed Mrs. Morison. "You've
got an allowance, which I'm sure I never had when I was
a girl."

"Only ten shillings a week, Mother," Etta pleaded.
"And I have to buy clothes and books and music with that.
I've tried so hard to save from it, and there's so little saved.
But if Daddy could give me two pounds or even thirty
shillings, for a year or so, I'd . . . I'd try so hard . . . I'd
repay it some day . . . I'd . . ."

She had to stop to fight back the tears. Mrs. Morison
was about to speak, probably tartly, but her husband intervened:

"If you *please*, Mother. As head of the household, this
concerns *me*." He turned to Etta. "I take it that your
proposal amounts to this, Etta—you're discontented with
your home life, we're not good enough for you. You've
been getting ideas in your head, but you don't know what
you want to do really. I won't say anything about how
you've hurt us both by your attitude. I leave that to your
conscience. Perhaps it's been my fault for giving in to you,
and letting you go to Paris and that music hall in London—" Mr. Morison sincerely believed that music and
indeed all the arts must be inevitably connected with
vice—"but I won't go into that either. You ask me for
two pounds a week, so that you can give up your home
duties and go off gallivanting about where we can't look
after you, and the Lord-knows-what might happen to you.
That's the proposal, I take it?"

Etta didn't answer. She couldn't. She just sat nervously
plaiting a fold of her dress between her first and second
fingers—nice slim fingers, by the way, with delicate oval
nails.

"I won't say I can't afford to give you two pounds or even three," Mr. Morison went on, with the heavy pride of a man who knows his bank balance is on the right side. "I daresay it could be done for any sensible proposal, but not for a wildcat scheme like this. And let me tell you this, Etta, I have to provide for this household; I've got to think about the days when I shan't be able to work, and to provide for your mother in the days when I shan't be here; and I have to fork out pretty liberally to give Teddy a chance in the world. You've got all a girl has a right to expect, and a jolly sight more than most girls ever get. So don't let me hear any more of this nonsense."

Etta swallowed twice, and then she said in a voice which even she recognized as a beaten person's voice:

"So your answer is 'no'?"

"Flatly, no. Emphatically, no. And I'm ashamed to think that a daughter of mine should think so little of her home and of the love that's given her. Now, do as your mother tells you—go and give us a tune, but don't play anything which'll upset the neighbours."

Mr. and Mrs. Morison exchanged glances of mutual approbation with perhaps a trace of uneasiness in them, as Etta walked slowly to the piano. She sat down and began mechanically to play one of the least happy of Chopin's Preludes. From where they sat, they could not see her tears falling onto the keys.

2

ETTA'S PARENTS HADN'T SEEN her tears at the piano, she took good care of that. Suppose they had seen, they would have thought them tears of petulant resentment and self-pity. And they would have wounded her still more deeply by patronizing compassion, a blundering sympathy. But the tears were of humiliation and fierce self-reproach. Etta wasn't feeling sorry for Etta anything like so much as she was calling her a fool and a weakling. How silly to lead up to this terrifically important request by putting Daddy into a temper over his old muffins! And she hadn't even led up to it; on the contrary, she'd let herself be pushed into making it at the worst possible moment. After so much thought, after so many imaginary dialogues, how her wits had deserted her, how she had allowed herself to be intimidated, how awkwardly she had put her case, how feebly defended herself!

So Etta bent forward at the piano and the tears fell on the keys, as she went on playing Chopin, refusing herself to the music's appeal, coldly and exactly reproducing what the emotional Pole had written and cruelling debunking its romantic emotionalism. Mrs. Morison, listening, said to herself that the girl hadn't an atom of real feeling either about her parents or her music, and Mr. Morison, listening and digesting his muffins, fell asleep. Watching her moment, Etta moved quickly from the room and didn't come back until she was quite sure they wouldn't be able to see she'd been crying. All that evening she was the most composed of the three, enduring perfectly the ambiance of hearty and self-conscious *détente* which inevitably follows a family row.

For a few days they watched her, and after the midday meal one day exchanged impressions when Etta had gone out. Mr. Morison brought the matter up suddenly, rather like a cow bringing up a ball of grass for careful chewing.

"Well, Mother," he remarked cheerfully, "how do you think our little girl's looking?"

"Perfectly well, though I must see she doesn't get bilious at Christmas," said Mrs. Morison, ignoring his obvious meaning.

"I don't mean that. I mean how do you think she's

taken this allowance business? Doesn't look to me as if she's laid it to heart."

"It was only a girl's whim," Mrs. Morison explained. "Part of that Paris nonsense."

"I was wondering," Mr. Morison said thoughtfully, "if maybe we hadn't been . . . well, a bit hard on her?"

"Certainly not."

"As a matter of fact," Mr. Morison said timidly, "the Town Clerk was in the office yesterday, and I mentioned the matter to him. Course, he was too polite to say anything, but he seemed to think we are wrong. It appears his own girl is at London University. . . ."

"I wish you'd keep family affairs to yourself, Tom," she retorted, "and not go tattling them all over the town. I know my own daughter better than the Town Clerk does. Let him mind his own business and look after his criminals or whatever he does out of the rates we pay to keep him. What use would London University be to Etta I should like to know? We sent her to that music place, and she wouldn't stay. If it wasn't for me you'd spoil that girl completely."

"And if it wasn't for me you'd spoil Teddy—a nice old bill I have to pay every term because you would have him go to a swagger school."

"He's different," said Mrs. Morison complacently. "He's a boy, bless him. And he's got his way to make in the world."

"I want to be fair to both my children," said Mr. Morison quietly.

"And so you are! I'd like to know where they'd find a better father. You're giving Teddy a good education, and Etta has a nice comfortable home with home love. What more does she want? One of these days she'll marry and settle down. You mark my words. Don't pay any attention to her tantrums."

"Tantrums?" Mr. Morison protested. "She seemed quiet enough to me."

"Young girls get silly ideas in their heads and bring them out when they're not feeling well," said Mrs. Morison crisply. "They learn better later on."

"You think so?" he said doubtfully, but letting Etta's cause slide. "Perhaps you're right."

"I know I'm right!"

And there they left it, Mr. Morison consoling himself with the thought that there are times when all women are hysterical. No doubt about it, hysteria. Sort of maggot in the brain, poor things—makes them silly and cantankerous. For their own good one mustn't give in to women when they're hysterical.

Puffing calmly at his pipe, Mr. Morison felt aimiably superior in the conviction that *he* would never be hysterical.

Meanwhile Etta was walking through the streets of Dortborough in a manner so unhysterical as to excite no comment. She cut across the Muncaster Road towards High Street, partly from instinctive dislike, partly that she might have an alibi to oppose to the spoken or unspoken accusation that she had been to see the disapproved-of Vera who lived there. She bowed to the Vicar of St. John the Divine, who fortunately passed by on the other side of the road. As she turned into High Street, she bowed to Mr. Grant, the editor of the Dortborough *Messenger*, founded 1875, who was cycling—a heavy man, with a moustache like a wave of asphalt, wearing a black overcoat and a bowler. High Street lacked the *belle ordonnance* of the Muncaster Road—it was not straight but crooked. In fact, as soon as you were fifty yards past the Town Hall, you became aware that it had been a mediæval street, in spite of the shop fronts, the yellow trams and dull green

tram standards, the bicycles, the posters, the baby carriages pushed by mothers anxious to fulfil the rite known
as "looking round the shops," and the unmerry people.
St. Mary's Church crouched at least three feet below the
road level, as if greatly ashamed of her inability to do
anything about Dortborough.

The market place was encumbered with a small metal
forest of tram standards and a cab rank, but no market.
Instead of a market there was an enormous grocer's shop
behind a façade of plate glass set in brass, the distinguished
proprietor of which had just been knighted. A little farther
on all traces of a superseded past had been obliterated to
make way for an asphalted square of tall sombre houses,
which looked as if meant for a race of respectable troglo-
dytes. Possibly the square had been built to commemorate
the Charge of the Light Brigade, for in the middle stood a
squat grey granite column of displeasing and heavy pro-
portions, to which were clamped sundry pieces of iron
work, held by the learned to symbolize the gallant feats of
Her Majesty's forces in the Crimea. Beyond that were the
black asphalt promenade, a grey-brown pebble beach, and
the grey-green Channel, or as much of it as could get inside
the breakwaters of Dortborough's new harbour.

Etta turned and walked along the almost deserted front.
A damp cold wind blew off the sea under a ceiling of low
ragged clouds, and chilly-looking waves bounced themselves into icy foam on the pebbles. Etta bowed to a red-
faced man who was stamping heartily along the quay in
a vaguely locomotor-ataxia manner. This was Commander
Briggs (R.N. retrd.) who, as he crossed Etta's bows, shot
out a breezy broadside of words: Keeping-fit-eh?-that's-
right-sort-of-day-makes-you-feel-glad-to-be-alive-what?

A little farther on Etta sat down in one of the damp
deserted "shelters," feeling more miserable than ever in

her life before. She heard the heavy clop-clop, clop-clop, of a horse and the slow grind of wheels, as one of the Dortborough growlers crept along the road. Then it turned up a side road, and she heard only the swish of the wind and the unfriendly crash of waves, distant metallic noises from tramp steamers unloading, and the harsh near crying of kittiwakes. The ennui of Dortborough life quenched her inner sunlight like a ragged sea mist. Her spirits fell with unhappy rapidity as she thought hopelessly of the impalpable walls and bars which kept her imprisoned in Dortborough and in so narrow a segment. Sterne's starling was a happy bird in comparison with Etta at that moment.

Her misery was too acute for her to formulate it exactly and face it. She found herself wondering what was the mysterious process by which Dortborough invariably got her down? What was the secret of its genius for devitalizing? Etta likened herself to one of these motorcars everyone was wanting to buy. When she came back from Mrs. Cleveland she had felt as if inside her was a little life-engine, running smoothly and swiftly and happily. Dortborough hadn't done or said anything, hadn't criticized, hadn't even noticed apparently; it had just been innately discouraging. Under a régime of slow stares, unsmiling lack of response, bromide remarks, Bœotian pleasantries and disapproving silences, the machine had faltered, run slower, and then with a sort of groan stopped running.

There could be no doubt about it, the Dortburghers were masters of the art of getting you down. Etta clenched her hands in a useless rage as she thought of it. They get you down, they get you down. In revenge she tried to think of an adjective which exactly expressed the Dortborough quality she found so discouraging. *Mesquin*, she decided, was the nearest. But it wasn't savage and comprehensive enough—she needed some tremendous portmanteau word.

. . . Not finding it, she tried to imagine what deity, what
local god presided over Dortborough, something more
exact and up-to-date than the symbolism of the town arms.
It would have to be something ambiguous, an undertaker
posing as Robin Goodfellow, or the Devil disguised as a
churchwarden, carrying a heaped offertory plate and remarking "Jesus gets them all."

Ignorant of Newton's first axiom, she was unaware of
how the modern world had come into existence, or even
that an enormous increase in knowledge and power had
been misappropriated by unscrupulous impresarios. Etta's
repulsion from Dortborough was instinctive and irrational,
a conviction that the quality of life which Dortborough
had to offer was not really worth accepting. Shivering with
cold on her damp bench, not far from tears, her hands
clenched, Etta affirmed once more her rejection of Dortborough. Female, life transmitter, essential and irreplac-
able link in the long series of living beings, potential source
of every possibility within Mendel's law, she unconsciously
refused Dortborough her womb. Not that she put the matter in any such portentous terms. She only said aloud:
"I would rather *die* than live in Dortborough."

Saying this made her feel better, though obviously it
brought her no nearer any practical solution. Yet it gave
her energy to continue her walk, instead of remaining in-
definitely in the damp shelter. As she emerged she came
face to face with Vera Wraxall.

This meeting was not quite so much of a coincidence as
it looks. Etta had certainly avoided passing Vera's house,
so that if questioned (as she probably would be) she could
say truthfully that she had not been in the Muncaster
Road. On the other hand she knew perfectly well that
Vera, a person of punctilious habits, generally took an
afternoon walk along the promenade. And she did want to

talk things over with the one sympathetic person in Dort-borough.

"Whatever made you sit in that half-open shed on a day like this?" Vera exclaimed in her clear, decisive voice, taking Etta's hand. "Why, gracious, you're frozen! Come straight home with me and have some tea. Walk briskly, now, and start your circulation."

"I'd rather not . . ." Etta stammered.

"What do you mean?"

"Oh, well, you may as well know," said Etta desperately. "But Mother disapproves of our friendship because you're working for suffrage, and if she finds out I've been to tea with you, there'll be another row, and after what's happened I just can't stand it."

Nobody likes to be considered an evil influence, even by imbeciles, and Vera was naturally a little incensed by this revelation. However, she was decent enough not to turn her resentment against Etta, and said:

"We'll go to a tea-shop, then, and you can tell me what's happened."

"If you're sure nobody'll see us . . ." Etta hesitated.

"Heavens! Why shouldn't they see us? We're not doing anything wrong, and this isn't Siberia."

"It feels rather like it," Etta shivered.

"Don't stay here arguing or you'll catch pleurisy or something," said Vera peremptorily. "Come on."

And Etta went, not unwillingly. It was a relief in her state of confused wretchedness to let Vera take command for a while. She felt grateful for any kindness. Not that Vera was altogether the ideal woman Etta would have chosen as friend and confidant. Sometimes, indeed, when she thought of Mrs. Cleveland, she felt a little ashamed that Vera was all she had been able to discover—a thought promptly suppressed as unworthy and disloyal. Vera thought of herself as a very practical person, and so she was if it is practical to see nothing in life but immediate obvious action of a rather insignificant and subordinate kind. She was born to be one of life's camp-followers, because she was loyal and, within her limits, efficient. She had acquired her convictions painfully, and clung to them with the fanaticism of one who does not intend to go through the discomfort of thinking twice. Her faith in the splendour and righteousness of human machinery was incorruptible, and she was a zealous member of the Dortborough Woman Suffrage committee, with the distant hope that she might one day sit in the larger mixed committee at Westminster. Unluckily, even in the smaller and preparatory Parliament of Dortborough, Vera's zeal was wholly at the service of the smaller and more militant section of ladies, so that a committee meeting with Vera present resembled Ouida's celebrated description of the rowing crew—all talked fast but none faster than Vera.

The bun shop to which Vera now took Etta was called the Oriental Café. After passing through a small outer shop where they sold exotic teas and coffees in dainty packets, you passed through an oriental bead curtain which rattled in the Eastern fashion, into the Divan or Tea Lounge. The four corners were occupied by superb papier-mâché inglenooks, copied at vast expense and considerable distance from the Alhambra of Granada. These and the rest of the floor space were occupied with English tables and chairs, but there were a number of inlaid Turkish stools (not to sit on), and the walls were decorated with imitation Persian scimitars, imitation Saracen helmets with mail cheek-pieces and Japanese prints. The tea things were Japanese of the pinky sort, and they gave you a paper napkin with a geisha on it. At one time the waitresses had been dressed as geishas (just after the Japanese exhibition), but Dortborough had decided that it was a bit too thick, so they went back to caps and aprons. But everything else was oriental right enough, except perhaps the tea and coffee, and certainly the buns and toast. . . .

"So you see," Etta said, winding up the narrative of her defeat over the teacups, "I'm in a complete blind alley. They won't help me to get away. I've not been trained to do a single thing to earn a living, and yet I'd rather die than live in Dortborough."

The repetition of this exaggerated phrase of heroic resolution failed to comfort Etta this time. Vera disapproved.

"Dortborough's all right," she said firmly. "The cause is making good progress—this week we shall have ten women selling the paper in the streets. We shall make ourselves heard at the next election."

"Oh, Vera, you are funny! Of course, I believe in suffrage and all that, but if every female down to the she puppies had a vote, I'd still hate Dortborough and long to . . . to be alive."

"That's where you're so wrong," Vera retorted intensely. "Can't you see that . . . ?"

"I can see it all!" cried Etta. "And you've told me often enough. But I can't live on voting once in five years. Don't let's argue, Vera dear—it makes me think of Daddy and Mother."

"They're very much to blame in denying you independence," said Vera severely, "especially your father."

"He's not so bad," said Etta, "except when he gets pompous about the firm being the oldest-established chartered accountants in Dortborough. Of course, I don't think he's really noticed anything much in the last fifteen years. If I had him to myself I could manage *him*. It's Mother. She always thinks, if she doesn't say, 'Mother knows best,' but she always seems to do her worst."

"I can't believe one woman would so betray another,"
said Vera solemnly.

"Believe it or not," retorted Etta, who was getting a
little intoxicated and giggly with tea, "woman is woman's
worst enemy. Look at the beastly tricks girls play each
other to get hold of a man."

"Etta!" Vera seemed pained. "How can you say such
false and vulgar things? What would Mrs. Cleveland have
said if she'd heard you?"

"I believe she'd have said I was right and advised me
to do a little better myself," Etta replied.

"She'd have done nothing of the sort!" Vera cried. "A
splendid woman like that. . . ."

"Well, perhaps she would have squelched me," Etta interrupted. "But does it matter? Please, please, Vera, don't
sit there disapproving me and talking at random. I shall
have to go soon. Try to think of something to help me."

She looked appealingly into Vera's face. At a first glance
it seemed a naïve sort of face, more round than oval, with
a very clear virtuous skin, large childish eyes, and fluffy
yellow hair which always looked very fluffy in spite of
Vera's despairing efforts to screw it into a practical bun.
Closer inspection was less reassuring. There was energy in
that straight, rather narrow nose—so different from Etta's
with its slightly Florentine tilt—plenty of determination
("confounded obstinacy" Vera's father called it) in those
large blue eyes which an infatuated Dortborough youth
had idiotically likened to pansies, which aren't blue anyway; while an almost puritanical lack of what used to be
called the softer passions was indicated by her thin, delicate lips, which the same sentimental youth had described
as a Cupid's bow, in spite of the obvious fact that they
were nearly straight. Vera isn't pretty, Etta thought to
herself, but she certainly makes the worst of what looks
she has—whatever makes her wear those floppy tweeds

and that mannish-looking blouse and collar and that awful old hat?

Not being able to read Etta's private thoughts, Vera responded to her last words. Anything which gave Vera an opportunity to mount the "practical" hobbyhorse was fairly sure to win a response. She said:

"It isn't easy to make any really practical suggestions, but if you're serious I'm sure we can find some way out. Look here, we're frightfully hard up for voluntary suffrage workers in Dortborough—why not make a start here? It could easily lead to something else."

"No, thank you," said Etta decisively. "To be quite frank, I've no love of work for work's sake, unless of course I could find something which was fascinating. Working is only a means of getting away from Dortborough."

"It *is* a shame your father won't give you an allowance," said Vera helplessly.

"Mother won't let him. I might try being a chorus girl —I've got rather nice legs."

"Don't be beastly," exclaimed Vera. "Fancy showing yourself half-undressed to a lot of pigs of men! You're really not fit to make a stand for equal rights and independence, Etta."

"Now you're being disapproving again," Etta complained, "and I thought you were so practical."

"I am practical, but you don't give me much encouragement to be serious." Vera's sternness was quite awful. "But there is just this possibility: Our organization in London is constantly expanding, and though our funds are very small, some of the leaders can afford to have a paid secretary. But then you're quite untrained."

"What's a secretary have to know?" asked Etta hopelessly.

"Shorthand and typing, to start with; then she has to know how to deal with correspondence, keep notes of her chief's engagements, help to organize meetings, and perhaps be able to act as a spare speaker—the secretary's job is to relieve the chief from all routine details."

"It sounds like playing Red Indians when you keep talking about chiefs," said Etta languidly. "Is it hard to be a secretary?"

"You need to have your wits about you and work hard," said Vera, ignoring the frivolity of Etta's last remark. "But it can be done with determination. The trouble is you're so utterly untrained."

"I might learn. But how does anyone learn anything in Dortborough?"

"That's just where you're wrong about Dortborough," Vera exclaimed triumphantly. "There's the Technical School which has night classes for adults. I know they have a course in shorthand-typing and general secretarial training."

"Why shouldn't I go there?" Etta was suddenly excited. "I think I'd go to prison if it meant an eventual way out. But," and her excitement suddenly dropped, "I suppose it's frightfully expensive."

"Not more than two pounds a term. Could you afford that?"

"Yes, I think I could," said Etta, sacrificing books, music, and new gloves with a pang.

"And you'd work seriously?"

"Desperately."

"Well, then, I'll give you a typewriter for Christmas, and you can practise typing at home."

"Oh, Vera, you're a darling. How wonderful!"

"And when your shorthand is advanced, you can come to some of our meetings and report the speeches, and then later on I'll try to get you an introduction to someone really important. Think, Etta, you might even become secretary to Mrs. Pankhurst!"

But Etta's face was not irradiated with the joy which should have appeared at so glorious a prospect. In fact, it went a little pale and very tense.

"Shush, shush!" she muttered. "Be quiet. I can see Daddy coming in. O God in heaven, this means another rumpus!"

Mr. Morison observed with surprise the presence of his daughter in the Oriental Café. Being a broad-minded man, he had no objection—absolutely no objection whatsoever —to his daughter's taking tea in a café, however oriental. But, after all, there was tea at home for her, and going out with Vera in this clandestine manner had a look of rebellion—Etta'll be wanting a vote one of these days, he thought, good Lord!

"Hullo!" he said, coming to their table. "What are you two doing here? Plotting mischief?"

"Yes," Etta answered, inventing feverishly. "We've been talking over Christmas presents. I can't think what to give Teddy, he's getting such a big boy. Do sit down and help us."

"Ah! So that's the trouble?" Mr. Morison was already fumbling in a memory well stocked with standard jokes on the interesting topic of the incompetence of women in giving presents to men. He sat down. "I suppose you know the story about . . ."

Vera sat in silence, stunned by the revelation of Etta's duplicity and outraged by her gross flattery of her father. Must Woman always be abject before the domineering male? Her indignant soul seemed to lift small hands to matriarchal heaven, praying for the ballot box to vote the brutes down.

Etta's daughterly attentions put Mr. Morison into excellent humour, there was such a jolly ripple in her laughter at his prime jokes. With bluff good-nature he exasperated

Vera to suffocation by paying for her tea and insisting on giving her his escort home—not quite the thing for a girl to be out alone after dark even in sex-repressed Dortborough. Only Etta's pleading glances enabled Vera to throttle down her rage, and to say good-bye with what looked like common civility.

Etta and her father proceeded arm-in-arm along the Muncaster Road.

"Rum sort of girl, Vera, can't think what you see in her, sort of fishy and dull-witted," said Mr. Morison, who had not failed to notice that Vera had not laughed at one of his jokes. "She hasn't an ounce of what I should call feminine charm."

"I suppose she must seem rather stupid to you," said Etta hypocritically. "But then she's an old school friend, and it doesn't do to drop people, does it, Daddy?"

"Certainly not," said Mr. Morison virtuously. "I wish I could get hold of old Wraxall's accounting work, though. It's a good business."

Mr. Morrison seemed lost in admiring contemplation of the excellence of old Wraxall's business, and Etta did not interrupt the silence until they passed the pillar box and turned into Castle Road under the damp bare chestnut boughs.

"Daddy!"

"Yes?"

"D'you mind not saying to Mother I was with Vera?— it always makes her cross. And it was all an accident— I met Vera on the parade, and we started talking and then she made me go and have tea."

With a sense of enjoyment at being privy to his little girl's Christmas conspiracies, Mr. Morison answered:

"Right you are, but don't see too much of her."

Two days later Etta went to bed with a violent cold,

and when she recovered, the Technical School had closed
down for the Christmas holidays.

3

IN CHILDHOOD ETTA HAD FELT deeply hurt that the Disposers of Events had made her birthday only two days before Christmas. In the matter of presents, her funeral
baked meats had to do duty at the wedding. Thrifty relatives—and most of Etta's relatives were thrifty in this
respect—artfully timed their parcels to arrive on the evening of the 23d, labelled inside: "For darling Etta, wishing
her many happy returns of the day and a merry Christmas." Even Teddy, wrapped in the superb selfishness of
young males, had been known to remark carelessly that
it was rotten luck.

But that year, when the invisible but inexorable time-
taximetre we all carry with us had ticked up "20" for her,
Etta had more serious matters to consider than presents.
In a sombre meditation, which could only be adequately
rendered in the gloomy eloquence of *Urn Burial*, Etta
accepted the fact that she was now *old*. At twenty-three a
girl was on the shelf; at twenty-five middle-aged. So she
had only five years in which to live: a tragical thought none
the less poignant for being absurd. Not that Etta felt any
distress at the idea that she would soon be far too aged to
think of anything so frivolous as matrimony. Her problem
was to get her own life straight. The various youths and
young men who had tried to interest her in holding hands
and kissing, or even attempted vague passes at her person,
had failed miserably. The temperament which was obviously in her slumbered or found normal derivatives. And
she had been no more than agreeably fluttered by the two
proposals of marriage she had received at dances, one from

a bald-headed solicitor in pince-nez who "begged to submit" a contract in re bed and board, and the other from
a blushing young man sweatily ill at ease in his first suit
of evening clothes.

The problem remained the same—how to get away from
Dortborough, how to turn her empty days and months
into full ones. And now it was complicated by this hideous
menace of age. Think of it! Twenty and nothing done.
Life, Etta reflected, is like a complex game of chess where
you don't know the moves properly and every mistake is
a disaster. If you pondered too long over the board, age
had you by the neck; if you moved hastily and unwisely,
you came a cropper and had to go back to Dortborough.
And when you had got a plan, you had to start by moving
a pawn, in the hope that it might lead five moves later to
an opening for making the first real advance. Discouraging.

Vera's shorthand-typing-secretary suggestion had
seemed to open a way for new moves on the chessboard.
But in a month (what with the cold and Christmas coming)
she hadn't got far—about three pawn moves. She had
bought a shorthand book, entered herself for the next
session, and Vera (good friend!) had yesterday brought her
an enormous second-hand Remington, much to the disgust
and scorn of Mrs. Morison and the amusement of her
husband. Now she had to pass in shorthand and typing
to qualify for the secretarial course; having passed that,
she had to find a job in London; then succeed at that.
And this was only the beginning! She would have to go
beyond that to reach something really interesting—she
had no idea what—or her efforts would be wasted. And
with age creeping on like this, she had only about two years
to do it in—certainly it mustn't be later than 1915.

To persist needed a good deal of resolution. Perhaps
the best sign that her resolution still held was that she said

nothing about it to her adored Teddy. It would have been so easy to get his sympathy, and so nice to share the great secret with him; but not wise. Teddy had a habit of blabbing out everything to his mother. Moreover, Etta had a dim feeling that a resolution advertised loses half its force. She would waste her energy in daydreaming with Teddy, instead of getting on with the job. Still, it was hard not to feel impatient and discouraged.

Only those who have attempted it know the discouragements of trying to learn shorthand. You begin by learning a number of signs which seem insensately arbitrary and then try to combine them, after which you are pleasantly surprised to find another set known as "grammologues." In learning these you forget the others. You then start all over again. Having, as you think, at length mastered the beastly thing, you ask a friend to read from a newspaper—and find yourself hopelessly at sea. More work. You try again, and this time manage to report what is read, only to find that you cannot read your own shorthand. At this point strong men weep and women faint. Most people give up. The dogged ones start all over again. Even when you can report a friend reading, you are apt to be flummoxed by the eloquence of the Mayor after a public dinner; and that is child's play compared with the job of making a neat sensible letter from the ramblings of an illiterate boss who can't compose a grammatical sentence, who hesitates, repeats himself, changes his mind, answers the telephone, forgets where he was, and prides himself on his style.

For months Etta struggled through all these stages except the last, for there was nobody to employ her. Typewriting she found simple, as indeed it is—even novelists learn to play the instrument with one finger. Daddy allowed her to copy documents for him and paid her, until

Mummie discovered that "crouching over that machine" was bad for Etta's health. Both marvelled at her persistence; neither suspected her plan, though on general principles of home love Mummie felt there should be at least a modicum of thwarting.

Teddy returned for the Easter holidays, superb in stick-up collars and brilliantine (Lower Fifth), with his wrists and ankles sticking out of a suit which had seemed ample in January. Etta longed to confide in him, but didn't. She struggled on for more months, and Teddy came back for the summer holidays, having performed the same remarkable feat with another suit. By this time Etta felt she was competent to be confidential secretary to anybody, and had indeed reached a point of efficiency where she might have been accepted as a beginner by an easy-going firm. What was the next step? Etta had heard her father say that "we advise you to take in the *Daily Telegraph*" was a formula used to tell a clerk that he had to look for another job. Vera, therefore, took in that valuable paper, and Etta answered advertisements, using Vera's address. In most cases she received no reply; once or twice a curt letter arrived bidding her call with references at 9 A.M. on the day she received the letter. High hopes fell to low hopes, to no hopes at all, as it gradually became evident that you had to be on the spot and pretty quick to get any job at all.

Baffled but not defeated, Etta again took counsel with the loyal Vera, who wanted to throw her neck and crop into the suffrage movement. Possibly it was Vera's insistence which determined Etta not to do anything of the kind. At any rate, together they evolved a plot, which was complicated in its details but simple in outline; i.e., Etta was to run away to London and start the career which would lead to—what? Etta couldn't exactly say—something at the centre of life, something that would seem worth living, something at any rate that wasn't Dortborough. But be-

fore she went Teddy had to be told, and arrangements
made for him to write—she couldn't bear to be quite out
of touch with him. The only doubt was whether he would
"understand," for even Etta realized that Teddy was at
that ungraceful hobbledehoy stage where a barbaric
schoolboy is awkwardly at odds with a young man.

To the east of Dortborough lay a waste of sand dunes
and marsh intersected with dykes. Flowering rush grew
in the water courses, and there were lovely patches of blue-
purple bugloss on the edge of the sand; at night you might
hear the strange cries of curlew. To the west there was a
long ridge of broken chalk cliffs with mysterious lines of
dark flint. On top the turf was kept short by sheep and
the strong winds, and in it grew harebells, dwarf scabious,
bird's-foot trefoil, and "hardheads," which opened surprisingly into purple flowers.

About a week before he went back to school in September, Teddy graciously agreed to spend an afternoon with
Etta, walking over the cliffs. Etta chose the cliff walk—it
looked more arduous and determined. They climbed the
long hill past the barracks, and came to the open treeless
down with its jagged seaward break. Large white clouds
floated gently through the pale blue sky and dappled the
wide Channel with dark blue shadows. About two miles
farther on they came to a field of red clover with a thick
hedge of thorn which threw a little shade. Etta felt her
heart beating with something more than exercise as she
suggested they should sit down and rest—how would
Teddy take her fearful revelation? For a minute or more
she sat silent, watching the flicker of butterflies over the
brilliant scarlet flowers. Then she made her plunge.

"Teddy!"

"Um?"

"Can you keep a secret?"

"Of course I can."

"I don't mean a silly secret like Christmas presents or a party, but a real secret, something that nobody else knows but Vera, something you mustn't let anybody know, especially Daddy and Mummie."

Teddy had been lying on his back, chewing a stalk of grass, with his straw hat pulled over his eyes. Something in the tone of Etta's voice made him sit up and look at her. His round face and clear eyes looked rather comically solemn.

"You haven't got yourself into disgrace, have you?"

"No, of course not." Etta laughed.

"There was an awful row at one of the fellows' homes last hols," said Teddy solemnly. "I don't know if I ought to speak of it, but, as a matter of fact, they found out his sister was going to have a baby, and she wasn't married. Ghastly for him, you know."

"What about her? But don't worry—it's nothing of that sort."

"Have you got engaged?" asked Teddy, still pursuing scandal.

"No. I'll tell you what it is if you'll give me your word of honour not to tell a single person, not to let it out to anyone. Promise?"

"Yes, I promise. What is it?"

"I'm going to run away."

"Run . . . What for? Where to?"

"After you're back at school, I'm going to London without telling anyone, and I'm going to look for work."

"Love-a-duck!" said Teddy in amazement. "Whatever for?"

"Listen, Teddy. Oh, I wish I knew how to tell you! It's so hard to find words—but I simply must get away from home and from Dortborough. If you knew how dull, how pointless it all is. If I hadn't found things to do on my own, my life would have been nothing more than pottering about the garden and housework, eating large meals, and sitting in armchairs afterwards. That's really all Mother and Daddy want to do, and they don't seem to realize we're grown up. It's not so bad for you, because you have more freedom at home, and anyway, you get months away at school."

"That's where you make a mistake," Teddy interrupted. "I hate school."

"But I heard you telling Mother the other day that you liked it!"

"Oh, her," said Teddy. "What's the good of telling her the truth? It only starts another jawing."

"What don't you like at school?"

"Oh, everything—being cooped up, and rotten grub, and chapel every morning, and having to learn a lot of Latin and stuff that's no good to anybody in life, and all that."

This was news to Etta. She had imagined Teddy as happy at his school as she had been with Mrs. Cleveland.

"What do you want to do when you leave?" she asked.

"Oh, I don't know, go into Dad's office, I suppose."

"And live all your life in Dortborough?"

"Why not? It's as good as anywhere else, isn't it?"

"Not to me," said Etta quickly. "I feel if I don't get away the place'll squash me to putty. But, you see, there's room for you in Dortborough. There's none for me. Daddy wouldn't let me try to get work there, and of course he could stop anything I tried to do. I'm rather glad in a way, because it means I have to go farther away, to London first, then perhaps Paris or Berlin."

"What do you want to do?"

As he said this, he shocked her by lighting a cigarette. She was about to remind him that this was forbidden under fearful penalties, but instead reminded herself she was treating him as "grown-up."

"I don't know, that's what I want to find out," Etta answered. "It's not so simple. I can't say I want to be a hospital matron or an actress or a London hostess or a doctor. I've got to find what I can do. But I do know now what I don't want to do. Perhaps you haven't thought that I've either got to live all my life dependent on Daddy or you or else marry somebody in Dortborough, unless I do something for myself."

"But Dad'll leave you some of his money."

"Don't be beastly, Teddy! It would be dreadful if Daddy died—I don't want him to die. He may live till I'm frightfully old, thirty or thirty-five, and then what good would money be? Besides, from what Mother says, I believe he spends everything he makes, so one of these days the whole burden will fall on you. Why should it?"

"I don't know about that," said Teddy philosophically. "A man has to look after his family nowadays, you know."

"But why?"

"Because it's the right thing."

"It isn't the right thing. Suppose when you're much older you marry, and Daddy should die, you'd have Mother and me and a wife on your shoulders. Besides, how do I know you mightn't be as mean as Daddy? Do you know he refused to give me an allowance even of thirty shillings?"

"Old people are mean," said Teddy wisely. "They've got tons of money, and they never shell out. I wouldn't be like that."

"What would you do if you had money, lots and lots of it, all you wanted?"

"I should buy a motor and some horses, and go shooting and fishing in Scotland, and go to the theatre and . . . and have a good time. What would you do?"

"I don't know," said Etta thoughtfully. "Yes, I do! I should go straight to Mrs. Cleveland and spend a year with her in Paris, then I should go to a university, and travel every year—I want to go to Spain and China and everywhere—and I should have a lovely old house somewhere with a garden and a music room, and I should help girls to get away from their families."

"Don't you want to get married?"

"No, I might have lovers, but I shouldn't marry."

"Etta!"

"Don't say 'Etta' in that tone of voice! You think you're quite sincere when you feel shocked and angry with me for saying that, but you haven't thought what your real feelings are or would be. You believe you would be disgraced if I do anything which isn't considered 'virtuous.' Don't you?"

"Well, hang it, Etta, a man has to defend his sister's reputation."

"No, he hasn't—he's got enough to do if he looks after his own. I won't be your moral responsibility any more than your material responsibility. But don't get it into your mind that I'm going to elope with a man, or that I'm going off for *that* sort of thing. Clever men make experiments in science—I'm making an experiment in living. To see if a woman, starting from little enough, can stand alone in life. It'll be hard, and I'll get some knocks and perhaps fail, but I'm going to try. I think that perhaps everybody has at some time to be alone, quite, quite alone, in solitude. Think how we live at home, neither to ourselves nor to each other, but in a kind of blur. I want to get the outlines clear. Do you see?"

Teddy said, "Yes," wondering in himself what all this rigmarole was about.

"A blur," said Etta, thinking aloud more than addressing Teddy. "Do you know how Mother really thinks of me, for all her talk about love and home and all the rest of it? Of course you don't. A bit of a child, a bit of a servant, a bit of a nuisance, and with all that a bit of herself —doing and thinking exactly as she wants—she's all sweet and amiable. But directly I'm the tiniest bit different, something that after all is myself, she instinctively thwarts. And do you know why she does that?"

"No," said Teddy.

"Because she was thwarted herself. Families will make an effort for sons, especially an eldest son, but daughters . . . All they can think of for a daughter is to marry her to a man who has some money or keep her at home if she can't get a man. I've tried to talk to Mother about it. Cut out all the frills about love and duty, and what she says comes to this: 'Do all you can to please men, and be sure you're a virgin when you marry.'"

"I say!" Teddy protested.

"It is so. And in a way she's right—that's the way the world's run."

"Perhaps the world's right," said Teddy.

"Perhaps it is and perhaps it isn't. I think it isn't. For one thing, I believe it isn't sensible to keep half the human race in ignorance and subjection."

"I say, that isn't true," Teddy objected.

"Yes, it is. My education was a farce until I went to Mrs. Cleveland, and I only heard about her through Vera, and had to beg and pray before I was allowed to go. And then what happened? Mother got jealous of my having something she hadn't had, and took me away, and made a scandal, so that I was cut off from Mrs. Cleveland. What I say is true, Teddy. Women *are* left ignorant, and men complain they haven't brains; they're purposely kept away from the realities of life, and men say they're silly; they're always treated as subordinates and then sneered at for not being able to run things. Oh, there's so much to say if I could only say it!"

Etta was silent, consumed with feelings she could not express, angry even with Teddy for not understanding. After a long and rather awkward pause, Teddy said:

"What are you going to do in London?"

"I'm going to look for work," said Etta hesitatingly, rather brought down from her wrongs-of-women heights by this direct question.

"What sort of work?"

"I hope to get a secretary's job," said Etta, feeling it sounded very feeble. "I expect I shall have to start as a shorthand-typist and then work up. I'm quite good at shorthand and typing."

"I don't think you ought to be an *office* girl," Teddy objected, "coming from a family like ours."

"Don't talk rot! We're just an ordinary middle-class family like thousands of others, and I'd rather be a wage earner in an office than a servant at home."

"You won't like it."

"Then I shall try for something I like better."

"You'll be home within three months."

Etta made no reply and stood up. The talk had gone wrong somehow. Instead of getting Teddy's sympathy, she had alienated it; instead of putting her case clearly and logically, she had talked wildly and stupidly. She said:

"I think we'd better start back now."

They walked towards the crest of the hill without speaking. Suddenly Etta said:

"You'll keep my secret, Teddy?"

"Yes."

"Promise?"

"I promise."

She squeezed his arm affectionately and added:

"I shan't tell you any more of my plans, so that if you're asked, you won't know. I'll write you from London and give you an address. You will write, won't you? Remember you're the only person in the world I really love—much more than Vera, more than Mrs. Cleveland."

"All right, don't bother, I'll write when I get time." Teddy was embarrassed by the emotion in Etta's voice. He knew it was bad form to show emotion.

Etta dropped his arm and sighed. When they came to the top of the hill, she paused. To the north the chalk wave sank down into a long green valley and then swept majestically up once more to a long treeless ridge. Three farmsteads, sheltered by clumps of old elms, stood in the valley, which was broken into fields by hedges. There were cattle in the soft green pastures, and the stubble wheatfields were pale and yellow. In one field Etta noticed they were carrying the last stooks. To the east stretched the wide marsh, hazy and silver with heat, which made the white spire of a distant church tremble. South lay the Channel, quiet and blue, splashed here and there with the intense white spots of the sails of a yacht race. Further out were the dark steamers with their widening trails of black smoke. A threshing machine droned in the distance, and there was a shrill crying of gulls.

Quite suddenly Etta realized that she might never look on all this again, that she was making her first break with all the old life. She said softly:

"However far I may go, whatever I may see, it will never be just like this. How beautiful it all is today."

"Um," said Teddy indifferently.

"In twenty years I haven't been here twenty times, but I've been twenty thousand times up and down the Muncaster Road."

"What's the matter with the Muncaster Road?" asked Teddy grumpily.

"Nothing—except that it exists. Come on, I'll race you to the next stile!"

4

A FORTNIGHT LATER Etta stood at the window of the smallest and cheapest room of a Bloomsbury lodging house, watching the fading light of an October evening. The window glass was rain-specked and not very clean, and the view was not extensive. At her feet was a piece of ground, not much larger than the garden at Castle Road, divided into small rectangles by high and sooty walls of dingy brick which had once been yellow. These "gardens" looked from above like a set of prison cells with the roof off. The prisoners in Etta's "garden" were three or four nearly leafless trees mournfully waving thin black fingers in the wind, some stunted shrubs, an abandoned dog kennel, and a broken statuette streaked with rain and soot. There were also two wire clothes lines and a large zinc dust bin.

So far as she could see in the fading light, the other gardens were laid out in the same classical style minus the statuette and the dog kennel. One, plainly in the possession of a demented romanticist, appeared to have some grass in it. Opposite, like a short but dirty cliff, rose the backs of another row of houses, each with the same projecting bathroom (added on), the same winning design in outside water pipes, and probably exactly the same number of bricks. Here and there the gloomy cliff was miraculously cut by a small square of soft nostalgic yellow. The horizon was a flurry of chimney pots and lurid-looking clouds.

To an unbiassed eye (Etta admitted) it was considerably worse than Dortborough, with an additional encrustation of filth and soot. Slightly depressing to the morale on her first night of "being on her own" to reflect that this would be her main outlook for how many months? As she drew the roller blind down, she reflected that the only way to live in London was to forget you had eyes and ears and touch.

Etta lit the gas and looked round the room which was to be the first stage in a thrilling career. Admittedly it was not large—five steps one way and four the other—and, as in most attic rooms, the sloping ceiling came down rather low on one side. In fact, she realized at that moment that whenever she lay in the small iron bed, with its cotton sheets and thin blankets, she would be able to touch the ceiling with her hands. Etta hoped it wouldn't give her Poesque nightmares. Jammed in between the bed and the window was a chest of drawers, and on the other side a small writing table with a wooden chair—the kind used in lecture halls. And there was an armchair with the stuffing coming out of it. But by far the most conspicuous article was the bright red, shilling-in-the-slot gas meter which stood blatantly on the worn linoleum beside the gas fire. It was beyond disguise; you couldn't even label it "Eve Iroquis" and pretend it was one of those Futurist sculptures of which Etta had vaguely heard. The books she had arranged in the hanging bookcase, and the four reproductions (Ingres, Raphael, Turner, Rossetti) she had pinned on the green wall paper, failed to overcome the squalid oppressiveness of this miniature gas works.

No, it wasn't exactly inspiriting, Etta admitted that frankly as she made her frugal tea. Not exactly affluent, either. On the contrary, a bit lonely and (the Dortborough adjective) *mesquin*. She tried to recapture the thrill of escape by telling herself that she had got up that morning a good domesticated daughter in Dortborough and was now a bold bad hussy on her own in Bloomsbury. But the thrill wouldn't come. Questions came instead. Suppose she couldn't find any work before her fourteen pounds was spent? Suppose she had condemned herself for life to clerking at a pound a week—year after year growing slowly older and duller and sadder in the cheapest room of Miss Millingham's cheap house in Bloomsbury? Suppose . . . suppose . . . suppose? Suppose Dad and Mother, after reading her farewell letter, had pursued her to London, and should burst into the room, irate and virtuous, insisting on her going home? It was a slight comfort to feel sure she would refuse. . . .

A crude rap at the door made Etta start to her feet in a panic. They *had* come! How awful! Before Etta could speak, the door was flung open, and the pasty face of the servant girl appeared.

"Miss Millin'am says yer to go down and see er," she remarked; and disappeared with a slam.

Etta thought this a very rude method of summoning a tenant, but after patting hair straight, she started off downstairs, a little timorous but also a little resentful, and determined not to stand any bossing from Miss Millingham. She went down the worn wooden stairs to the first floor, where a couple of voices—male and female—were violently arguing, and then down a once opulent-looking stone stairway to Miss Millingham's room on the ground floor. A gentle quavering voice said, "Come in," and Etta found herself in a large dimly lit room with a good coal fire, so crowded with relics of Miss Millingham's better days that it looked like a mid-Victorian museum. The only jarring note was the muted echo of the quarrelling on the floor overhead.

Miss Millingham came tremulously towards Etta, winding a devious way through the clusters of furniture. She was a middle-aged little woman with grizzled untidy hair and a red nose like a bullfinch's beak, dressed in a princess robe of worn wine-coloured silk with white ruching on the sleeves and bodice, and a necklace of large green beads. She was devoted (secretly) to port and (admittedly) to celebrity and suffrage.

"How kind of you to come!" she quavered garrulously, taking Etta's hand. "I didn't send you up a note—so absurd and formal in one's own house, don't you think?—and I like my guests to feel at home. I told Gertrude to see you were quite comfortable and had everything, and to say that I should be so happy if you could spare a few minutes to call on me.. I hope she gave the message correctly? Do sit down. Would you like a fire screen? No? Would you like me to ring for tea?"

"No, thank you," said Etta, a little overcome by this polite volubility. "I've had tea."

Thump, thump, sounded on the floor overhead. Etta looked apprehensively at the ceiling and the shaking gas chandelier, but Miss Millingham went on with the serene poise of the perfect lady:

"I do hope Gertrude behaved herself properly? Believe it or not, Miss Morison, maidservants today are not what they were in *my* young days, and I can assure you Gertrude is far from being the *ideal* maid. It's this London street life, not, in my opinion, a proper environment for girls, though of course we're all more broad-minded about everything nowadays, aren't we? But it's my settled and unmovable opinion that nothing can be done about the servant problem until all we women have the vote. As I say, we alone understand the problem and therefore we alone can deal with it. Only the other day I was discussing it with one of our local leaders, Mrs. Walton, such a distinguished woman and an *intimate* friend of Mrs. Pankhurst, and I said to her: 'Do believe me, my dear Mrs. Walton, the servant problem ought to be in the forefront of our agenda,' and she promised me faithfully it should be looked into!"

"How very interesting," Etta managed to murmur, listening at the same time to the trampling and thumping overhead.

"Yes, *isn't* it! Some day you must meet Mrs. Walton,

and I feel certain you'll find her impressive. *Such* an intellect, my dear. She carries masses of statistics in her head, all about dairies and child welfare and bacon and that sort of thing. And her husband is such a nice man, with us heart and soul, though of course his wife's intellect *towers* above his."

The disturbance overhead had suddenly ceased while Miss Millingham was talking, and was succeeded by a dead silence so appalling that it seemed to creak. Had somebody been murdered? Taking no more notice of the silence than of the din, the old bird went on chirruping:

"I hope so much you will be comfortable, Miss Morison. You must tell me if there is anything at all you need. Of one thing I am certain—you will find us *interesting*. I pride myself on the fact that everybody under my roof *does* something. On your floor there is a Mr. Tomkins, such a distinguished man, a scholar *and* a gentleman. Day after day at the British Museum, poring over books of *the* most abstruse kind, making extracts and notes, you know, for one of our leading biographers. Then there's Miss Blatterthwaite, who *paints*, quite the loveliest talent, I assure you. She'll be going to the Riviera soon now for the winter— every year she goes, and brings back such exquisite vignettes and thrilling stories about the interesting people she meets. Her room is always kept ready for her. And Mr. Snell, the poet—I'm told one of his lyrics recently appeared in the *Thrush*. Have you seen it?"

"No, I'm—I'm afraid I haven't . . ." Etta stammered.

"Oh, but you should—such distinguished work. And then on the floor above live Mr. and Mrs. Clagger, theatrical people—she's Cecily Periford, you know. She had such a good part in *Five Mice*, or was it in *See How They Run?* I forget which. But they're extremely interesting too, temperamental, of course, temperamental. But as I say, we ordinary people must be prepared to make every allowance for those who *do* things. But here I've been chattering away and not giving you a chance to say a word. So thoughtless of me! I'm longing to know what you *do*. Miss Wraxall said you are a musician. I always think that such a wonderful gift, such power, such elegance. Dear Beethoven! Such expression! So like Shakespeare, don't you think?"

"Vera was exaggerating if she said I am a musician," said Etta apologetically. "It's true I did study the piano for a time, but I soon found I wasn't really good enough and gave it up, except for my own pleasure."

"Now there," Miss Millingham interrupted, "I feel that you are wrong, Miss Morison. Music is a talent, and talent leads to celebrity. I used to sing myself, but my voice is not what it was—da, da, da, da, dee, dee, dee, Deeee, Deeee, Deeeee. The high notes are so tiresome, aren't they? But I hope you'll sometimes let us hear some of your renderings. I have an excellent Broadwood, left me by my dear father—such a distinguished man, he held the post of Crown coroner for thirty-seven years and then died universally regretted—a little out of tune, the piano I mean, but we can have that attended to. It will be delightful to hear a little *good* music. A real intellectual treat. May I offer you a glass of port?"

"No, thank you," said Etta politely.

"Oh, do, please do, just a little drop," and before Etta could protest again, Miss Millingham had whipped out a bottle and two glasses, into which she poured a little drop for Etta and a whacking big drop for herself, rattling away all the time: "This is quite *special* port, my dear, my wine merchant imports it specially from Portugal for me. You'll see it's marked on the label: Produce of Portugal. Such exquisite flavour, and only three and six a bottle. But, apart from your music, Miss Wraxall mentioned that you had other plans—may I venture to ask, are they for the Cause?"

"Well, not precisely," said Etta, feeling she couldn't dash all Miss Millingham's hopes and illusions about her latest "distinguished guest": "You see, for a long time now I've been working hard to qualify myself as a secretary." Miss Millingham nodded sagely and approvingly, and Etta went on: "Vera wanted me to try at once for a post with one of the suffrage leaders, but I want to get something which will give me wider experience. . . ."

"Now there again I feel you are wrong," Miss Millingham interrupted amiably and persuasively, holding her wine glass with great elegance. "We women of talent, of distinction, have an obligation to devote ourselves to the Cause. Quite recently I was saying to Mrs. Walton. . . ."

Two hours later Etta returned to her room, a little dazed by Miss Millingham's eloquence and distinction, but certainly more cheerful and confident than when she had received Gertrude's version of the message. True, Etta realized that a little of Miss Millingham would go a very long way, but still the chirruping old bird had changed the house from a tomb to an aviary of "distinction." The doors she passed no longer seemed blank, but entrances to the nests of queer birds. Here was the door of the temperamental histrions, dead silent—probably out; here above dwelt the fashionable painter, the warbling thrush, and the erudite Tomkins. Etta was *rather* impressed, in spite of her inclination to laugh at Miss Millingham and her "guests" —nobody was a lodger with Miss Millingham, but a guest, an honoured, a distinguished guest, with whom certain financial transactions privily took place at stated intervals, failing which the guest incurred Miss Millingham's displeasure and left.

Before she went to bed that night, Etta wrote a letter:

DEAREST TEDDY:

This is my first evening all on my own in London, and I want my first letter to go to you. It's been such an exciting day and so much seems to have happened already, I can hardly believe I only left Dortborough this morning. I told Dad and Mother I was going over to Brighton for the day, and then posted them a letter from the junction where I had to change, so that they wouldn't worry when I didn't return. But I told them pretty straight that I'm not going back. I'm of age, and I won't.

I had a lovely journey up in the train, too excited to read, so I looked out of the window and thought how marvellous life is, though it was raining. Vera met me at Victoria, with my typewriter and the two bags I got round to her, and she brought me to the house where I now am. We had lunch together at a Lyons and looked at the shops until Vera's train went. After I got back here alone I got a bit panicky, but I talked to the funny old lady who runs this place and felt better. I seem to have got into a house full of freaks, though some of them sound rather important and distinguished— anyway, thank heaven, they're not Dortborough.

Don't worry about me. I'm going to be very energetic and not waste a minute of time, and I've got some introductions from Vera, and I shall look up the people I used to know, so don't imagine I shall be lonely.

I hope you're all right at school. Write when you can, and address Poste Restante, Western Central District P.O., London. Don't forget me.

With love,
ETTA.

5

QUITE RAPIDLY Etta became acquainted with the realities of poverty in one of its loneliest forms—that of the poor middle-class girl looking for a job. Only youth can engage in this struggle and survive as a vital human entity. For the older ones it is death, death of the spirit, because the pittance, the bit of bread and drink, the wisp of clothing, the flicker of fire must be begged of Business, not even as charity, but as a gracious boon in exchange for the best waking hours. It is always your money *and* your life. Not that Business is intelligently ruthless, don't think it. Business is like a huge cretin, scuffing its great feet over the flower-beds of life while it thinks itself the most wonderful puffing billy, self-invented into the bargain.

The loneliest. The young man who has a suit of evening clothes and a suit of correct behaviour will be asked out, so long as he isn't married. But invitations are given by women, and they're not fond of penniless pretty girls except in spasms of charitable self-righteousness. As a rule, the hostess feels she must protect her males from this type of adventuress, unless of course she has some interest in palming her off, which changes the situation entirely. So Etta didn't get many invitations. The loneliest. The girl is barred from her own class by poverty; but her class bars her from the poor. Good-nature and good-will can leap the class barrier, but not abolish it—at least, not yet. However hard Etta tried, she could win no real response from Gertrude, because to Gertrude Etta was one of the bosses, and therefore the enemy, and therefore to be mistrusted. Yet Gertrude was a girl on her own, and not so poor as Etta, for she had a job (a rotten one) while Etta as yet had none. But the bond of being girls on their own didn't seem to bring them any nearer.

Yet poverty is an essential experience, an essential discipline, which is why the wise rich rear their children in artificial poverty. Not to be able to go without is to be the slave of commodity, the abject comfort worshipper. Utter penury makes us abject, we "lack the common privileges of humanity." But great wealth makes us abject too, because the privileges are valueless when unearned.

And poverty when it lasts too long makes us mean and pinched and envious. It turns the noble anger and indignation which live in every complete man and woman into the snarl and whine of the starved cur. But poverty is a great master.

Poverty taught Etta with intelligent ruthlessness. It was not quite the ultimate ruthlessness which presses on those —the many—who have simply no way of retreat, who simply must sell their souls to live. Faced with the despair of starvation, she could always have betrayed her pride, abandoned her struggle, and have gone humbly home to Dortborough, forever defeated but not starved. From poverty Etta learned to clean her own shoes and to wash and mend her own clothes, to buy food carefully and prepare it herself and eat sparingly, not carelessly or grudgingly, as she might have been made to do any of these things at home, but seriously, in earnest. Poverty acquainted her with the cheap chain restaurants where the common food is served alike to thousands with a rattle of plates on marble tables, as in some awful phalanstery. She learned that poverty must walk where others ride, or if it must ride, then it must bundle in with the multitude and wait in the crush for its place. No more cabs or taxis. And she learned to stay outside the theatres and restaurants which others entered, to be cut off from the comfortable luxurious life of London which goes on almost secretly behind its dull grimy façade. Above all, she learned to do this without envy, for envy is the slave's vice and kills the heart. But she did not learn without pain and humiliation.

During those first few weeks Etta brooded a great deal, alone in her room or walking alone in the damp streets thronged with people and traffic, where the air was heavy with choking mist, brooded often in doubt and distress but nearly always with a subtle underflow of exultation, an instinctive certainty of impulse. She was hurt by the scorn and anger and repudiation in the letter she received from Daddy and Mummie, still more hurt by the indifference in Teddy's letters, his blunt acceptance of the home attitude that she was merely being silly and perverse and had better beg everybody's pardon immediately. Teddy also complained that he hadn't any pocket money. Etta left the home letters unanswered and sent Teddy a postal order for five shillings she couldn't afford to give. Not answering those exasperated, rather unkind home letters (naturally they thought her silly and ungrateful) meant a certain cutting away from them. Not a final cut, though. She knew she might have to go back, and on terms which even though unspoken would be bad ones, a sort of domestic slave; and now she knew that once in their presence again the old dominion would easily be renewed. But as long as she could keep away, the cut was valid. As for Teddy and his five shillings, that wasn't a cutting off. It was putting him in his place—the ally who had failed her. She felt hurt inside when she thought of Teddy.

Dressed in an old tweed skirt, country shoes, and a long raincoat, Etta liked sometimes to wander about the streets and squares after dark. Coming out into the quiet road she saw the huge glare over London and was drawn down into the great thoroughfares, fascinated by the streams and eddies of people, the throbbing traffic of the rush hour, the sharp or glowing lights with their dim waving reflections in the wet mud. Men sometimes touched her or spoke to her and tried to follow her, but she passed on scarcely noticing, discouraging them by her indifference. When the big Atlantic winds and rains had passed over the town, sweeping away some of the corrosive soft coal soot which is always at our lungs, she could smell and taste the sea. She was as sensitive to this salty quality in the air as she was indifferent to the men who in their crude way tried to obtrude their vulgar sex on her. Not yet, her body seemed

to say to them, and put them proudly aside. But the salt
air was exciting and frightening. In the imagination she
saw all the cliffs and sands of England, dim in the winter
darkness but alive with the rushing wind and the sea, the
dark land ringed by the white fire of foam.

It was so hard to know which way to go; not in the
streets but in life. You might lose your way in the streets,
but it was easy enough to find the right way by asking. But
there didn't seem much use in asking people the right way
in life—they had nothing but platitudes to give and little
to recommend but a routine. If she demurred, the remark
always was:

"Oh well, if you've got plenty of *money.*" This always
made her angry, probably because she knew she hadn't
money and needed it badly. Etta admitted that if you had
money many things were easier, you went through life
with a first-class ticket. She wondered whether it wasn't
more fun to go third class. In any case, she had handed
back her second-class Dortborough ticket gaily enough.
One thing to avoid, she decided, was routine, and yet most
of her efforts were concentrated on getting into a paid
routine so that she could continue to exist. She felt like
a bird which flutters hopefully out of its cage, only to discover that it is tied by the leg; and in her case the string
of comparative freedom was getting daily shorter, as she
had to spend from her little store. . . .

Etta might have lost herself entirely in these vague emotions and musings, if she had not been hard pressed by the
need for action. Somehow London had to be persuaded to
yield her thirty shillings a week, and seemed wonderfully
reluctant to do so, even if she accepted the routine. She
dived once more into the dreary and humiliating business
of answering advertisements. Sometimes she was inter-
viewed after long ignominious waits in outer offices, where

other girls and office boys stared rudely at her, and was invariably turned down. She had the courage to refuse a couple of miserably inadequate offers, which even she could see were attempts to exploit her under the pretense of "gaining experience" and a vague promise of better wages "later on." Once she thought for a brief moment that she had found the ideal job. She answered an advertisement for a private secretary, and was told to call at an address in Regent's Park, where she found herself in the studio of a prosperous portrait painter.

He was a tall man of about forty, with thick hair and a beard. He had flashing brown eyes and very delicate hands, and might have been considered handsome but for a fleshy nose and rather flabby mouth. After a few minutes of shyness, Etta found herself getting on amazingly well. He treated her more as an acquaintance on a call than as a possible employee, talked to her about music and pictures, listened to what she had to say, and laughed at some of her remarks. There was a courteous, almost caressing quality in his attitude which charmed her the more from its complete contrast to the offhand brutality of business employers. He said nothing definite about engaging her, except that in an aside he apologized for the smallness of the salary—he could "only afford a couple of hundred a year, but of course you would live with us." It seemed to Etta too good to be true. It was. Just as she was trying to bring him to the point of clinching the matter, the door opened, and Mrs. painter appeared and was greeted by her husband as "Mousie." She was a mouse—a shrew mouse. She took one glance at Etta, who was still glowing with the animation of talk, and began to nibble at her with offensive questions. Etta tried to keep her temper and to answer politely, but each remark she made was interrupted rudely with another question. The painter hung about miserably in the background, smoothing his beard and agitatedly buttoning and unbuttoning his brown velvet coat. Finally, Etta was told unceremoniously that she wouldn't do. As she left the studio, resentful and humiliated, she heard the woman say:

"I won't have that sort in the house again—remember what happened before."

The painter's feeble expostulations and her sharp replies were abruptly lost as the door closed.

Etta walked rapidly home, aflame with anger and annoyance, but when she was alone in her room, threw herself on the bed and cried with disappointment and shame at the indignity.

So the dark October days moved on to the darker days of November, and life was far, very far from being the gay adventure she wanted. With that harsh anxiety of the dwindling purse, it was hard, sometimes impossible, to create her days into living things. If it hadn't been for the underlying sense that she was moving towards something, life "on her own" would have been as discouraging as life in Dortborough. She wrote to Vera about this discouragement, and Vera wrote back that she ought to "see people" and sent introductions to suffrage women. And Etta, who with all her independence, was really very suggestible and docile, did try to see people.

As was sensible, she didn't neglect the people nearest at hand. The dramatic couple repelled and frightened her; their lives seemed so turbulent in an aimless and slithery way, so untidy with drink and quarrelling and imitating the mannerisms of successful actors. And Mr. Snell would have nothing to do with her. He consorted only with thrushes, and let her see plainly that a miserable little hedge sparrow like herself was an intruder in those groves of melody where he lounged and smoked exotic cigarettes and chirruped interminably with other thrushes about "the poetry of the future"—which of course was going to be sung by the thrushes, one of these days, when they got going. So she was pleased when she received (through Gertrude) a formal invitation to take tea with Miss Millingham at four precisely, "to meet Mrs. Talbot."

Punctually at four Etta descended and found Miss Millingham dressed all in green and stateliness. Miss Millingham drew Etta's attention to the dress almost at once:

"I hope you approve of my frock, Miss Morison? I know it's a little *old* for me, but I prefer dignity and simplicity. The colour is intended as a compliment to Mrs. Talbot— the nearest shade of green I could find to the green of the W. S. P. U. banner!"

Etta said it was charming and a charming idea, and fortunately Mr. Tomkins came in and had to be introduced, and then Miss Blatterthwaite. They sat about primly and made conversation while they waited for Mrs. Talbot. They told Etta how wonderful Mrs. Talbot was, such a magnificent mind, such strength of character, and yet with it all so gracious, so womanly. Miss Blatterthwaite told a serious anecdote of Mrs. Talbot, Miss Millingham a laughable one, and Mr. Tomkins recollected that he had seen her "doing research" at the Museum. Everything was beautifully prepared for the dramatic entrance of Mrs. Talbot, but she didn't come.

"She'll be here any minute now," said Miss Millingham. "I know her well. Some important business always crops up for her at the last moment, and has to be dealt with before she can get away. How interesting her life must be—always at the heart of things."

But the minutes ticked by, and still Mrs. Talbot didn't come. At half-past four Miss Millingham rang the bell for tea, remarking that Mrs. Talbot must have been detained by *very* important business and would prefer them not to wait tea. At the third cup—"not weak, my dear, and

no sugar"—Miss Blatterthwaite suddenly responded to
caffein intoxication and became talkative. Etta had imagined her a small exquisite person delicately bowed over
her water colours, whereas in fact she was a huge gawky
creature with a flat pasty face and hands like bath-chaps.
She was brother and bob with the aristocracy, and saw no
reason why the world shouldn't know it. Miss Blatterthwaite's aristocracy consisted of Lady Gunter. For nearly
an hour, to the appreciative accompaniment of Miss Millingham, she played variations on the theme of the distinguished Lady Gunter—Lady Gunter's place in Sussex,
Lady Gunter's villa on the Riviera, Lady Gunter's taste,
Lady Gunter's *chaaarming* children, Lady Gunter's this,
that, and the other. Miss Millingham was enraptured
(she had heard it all many times before) and remarked
how distinguished it all must be. She only "ventured to
differ" in the matter of suffrage. Lady Gunter, it appeared,
was *not* in favour of woman suffrage, saw no need for it,
believed women should be womanly; and Miss Blatterthwaite (oddly enough) agreed entirely with her. To end
the dispute to which this led, Miss Millingham (always the
distinguished hostess) threw the ball of conversation to
Mr. Tomkins.

But Mr. Tomkins was a butter-fingers at that game. He
could talk about nothing but books, British Museum
books. He, poor devil, made a pound or so a week by devil-
ling for a genealogist who was then writing the family history of a retired Bradford wool merchant. A curious form
of fiction. Mr. Tomkins babbled a little of charters, parish
registers, tombstones, and heralds, and then perforce they
returned to Lady Gunter and Mrs. Talbot. Etta gazed at
him with pity and horror—such a dry, bowed, hopeless
creature, seedy-looking, with his pale myopic eyes hide-
ously magnified by thick glasses. He wore a greasy black
ribbon to his glasses in a futile effort to meet Miss Milling-

ham's demand for the "distinguished-looking scholar,"
and the tea on an empty stomach made him belch apologetically. The Reading Room derelict.

Mrs. Talbot didn't come after all, and Etta went back to
her room sadder than when she came down. These three
elderly people, all "on their own" in life, were far from
encouraging. She had heard about the battle of life, and
perceived she had been taking tea with some of the casualties. Looking from her window at the grey fog, she shuddered. How dreadful, how dreadful if their fate were to be
hers.

Etta tried farther afield and went to three or four gatherings of her old South Kensington acquaintances. They sat
about in costumes meant to be distinctive, mostly on
cushions on the floor, drinking pale milkless China tea
from small bowls, eating beechnuts and candied fruits, and
talking and smoking. They argued vociferously and omnis-
ciently. They were Wagnerites against Debussyites;
Maeterlinck fans against Shaw-Wells fans; London group-
ers against one or two wild men who burbled of painting
in Paris and the Russian Ballet. Flirtations went on below
the talk, and everybody felt very emancipated and as if
something extremely exciting would shortly happen. It
struck Etta as a bit factitious and up in the air, but then
they were young, and there was plenty of laughter. There
was a ferment of life in them, and Etta felt tempted and
a little wistful. Only—and it was an important "only"—
they all seemed to have small incomes or to be inheritors
of incomes. That cut her off from their amusing play lives.

No such feeling of futility and pleasant waste was suggested by the women she reluctantly went to see after
much urging from Vera. True, they unintentionally made
her feel ignorant and provincial, but she didn't mind that.

Their enthusiasm, their conviction that they were engaged in a contest of tremendous importance, moved her. Etta could not help feeling that their cause was essentially hers. The vote was a mere symbol. What they were really seeking, she felt, was a revaluation of women's share in human life. They had an almost mystic faith which she found thrilling.

One evening Etta was taken to a large meeting in a public hall, where she had a reserved seat near the front and listened to several speakers. Before the speeches began, Etta was struck by the different types of women present and by the absorption in a purpose which wiped out temporarily all the barriers of class and age. Wealthy and poor women, girls and mothers, sat together united by a common sense of wrongs to be righted and aims to be achieved. Etta was particularly interested and moved by one speaker, who came after the recognized notorious leaders and a fiery little cockney woman who denounced the male world with the unscrupulous energy of a Hyde Park orator and of course was immensely popular.

This woman spoke calmly and evenly and gradually imposed herself on a slightly restive audience which wanted more fireworks. She began by talking of the status of women under Roman law, which recognized them only as daughters, wives, and mothers—a male always had to be responsible for them. This had been perpetuated right down to the eighteenth century, even if the rigours had been softened. The women of Provence, of Renaissance Italy and eighteenth-century France had attempted to create something better, but all failed. Yet in the pre-industrial world women had certain privileges and compensations now lost. They were undisputed mistresses of the household, and the men gave their consciences over to the women's keeping—they lived their lives as men, but rarely behaved in such a way as to alienate or destroy the women's lives. Moreover, women were not then cursed with idleness—even queens worked at the distaff. The men fed the world, but the women clothed it. There was a balance of the sexes, both materially and spiritually; and if men might rightly be proud of their share, so might women. Neither could exist without the other.

This delicate balance, she went on, was destroyed in one respect by the rapid introduction of machinery. "Spinster," instead of meaning a woman who span, became a sort of joke. Women were defrauded of a large part of their most interesting work. So far as working-class families were concerned, the job of producing was dumped entirely on the men, and the women were left to be household drudges —the men now never thought of sharing this work as they had done. In the well-off classes it was even worse. The middle-class lady was invented. She was forbidden to do anything useful or sensible. Her job was to lie on a couch and be sexually attractive in a clinging please-protect-me way. She was instructed in "accomplishments," not for her sake or their sake, but because they were supposed to charm men. And these futile accomplishments plus a little household management were often her only preparations for the realities of marriage and maternity. Was it any wonder, she asked, that sensible and self-respecting women of all classes were in revolt against a state of affairs which made them parasites or drudges? Wasn't it reasonable to ask that the balance should be restored, that one half of the human race should not be defrauded of the right to its share in human activity?

This speech was not very well received. Etta heard a working woman behind her say:

"What's she talking about? We've got too much work as it is—we don't want no more."

"Ah," was the reply. "I've got four and me old man and meself to do for on thirty-two bob a week, and go out charing three days a week. She don't know what work is, she don't."

Etta wanted to turn round and argue with them, but couldn't pluck up courage. At the same time, she wanted to ask the speaker several questions. Etta thought that she hadn't quite made her points and had left out a lot, and yet so much of what she had said crystallized what Etta had herself dimly felt but had been unable to express in words. At any rate, she agreed whole-heartedly in the revolt against the lady, or rather the pseudo-lady, such as she had been brought up to be.

After the meeting the women in the audience gradually dispersed, in a babble of talk. The girl who had brought Etta said:

"I've got to go to the committee room. Is there anybody you'd like to meet?"

"Yes. One of the speakers—if it isn't an intrusion."

"Which?"

"The tall handsome woman who spoke about the balance of the sexes."

"Oh, Ada Lawson? Yes, if you want. But she's not of much importance, you know. We don't take her very seriously. But come along, I'll introduce you."

As they made their way slowly through the moving crowd, Etta asked:

"What sort of a woman is Ada Lawson? Is she married? How does she live?"

The girl laughed.

"We call her the happy-go-lucky. She's been so lucky in life, and she's so good-natured and cheerful about it. She inherited money and married a rich man who adores her, and she's got two lovely children, a grown-up boy and a girl. She's been everywhere and knows everyone. They live in Knightsbridge, looking over the park, and they've got a big country house on the Thames. Everything."

"I feel rather frightened of her," said Etta smiling, "but I did like her speech."

A few minutes later Etta, in some confusion, found herself standing opposite Mrs. Lawson under the scrutiny of her dark, vivacious eyes. The other girl left them almost immediately after the introduction.

"You wanted to ask me something?" Ada Lawson said kindly.

"It seems such cheek," said Etta, blushing and hesitating. "But I *did* like your speech. It said a lot of things I've felt and couldn't express, only . . ."

"Only what?"

Etta blushed more deeply but continued to meet Ada Lawson's gaze frankly.

"I'm so ignorant," she said humbly, "and it's so hard to find words, but . . . you said . . . you spoke about the balance of the sexes in the past . . . the men having their lives and the women theirs . . . and working together . . . did that really happen?"

"If you want historical proofs, I can't give them. My only 'authority' is my old nurse who used to tell me stories she had heard from her grandmother when she was a child, stories going back to eighteenth-century England. I daresay she saw it all *couleur de rose*. But even if such a life didn't exist, do you think it wrong to assume it did? As a kind of parable, I mean. It seems easier to work towards something which you believe has existed then towards something quite new and untried."

"I see," said Etta thoughtfully. "Yes, I think I understand. But then we can't possibly be real 'spinsters' again, can we?"

"Of course not. But if we agree to the principle, we ought to be able to adapt it to modern life. At any rate, I don't think we should think of men as enemies, though they've treated us shabbily enough, the brutes!" Ada

Lawson laughed and went on: "There's too much merely negative in this very fine movement, too much blind man-hating. Don't be a man-hater."

"How can we help it?" cried Etta. "Men have so much and we so little. It's a world made by men for men, and most of us just have to submit or . . ."

"Or what?"

"Or be lost and unhappy," said Etta, her lip quivering.

"Not necessarily," she replied, quickly but kindly. "We all have to go through growing pains, and they're not anybody's fault. Being young's a desperate business. I tremble for my own children, but what can one do? There must be suffering. But one mustn't fall in love with one's own pain. And we can save ourselves a good deal of unnecessary suffering if we make up our minds not to expect too much of life."

Etta was about to reply, but a fresh male voice at her side exclaimed:

"I *say*, Aunt Ada, do you know the time? We shall be late for dinner and the theatre. Do come along. I've been searching madly for you."

Etta was so wholly absorbed in conversation and at the same time so *émotionnée* that she started at this interruption. She dimly heard Ada Lawson say something about "my nephew, Ralph," and then add:

"Here is my card with my address. Will you come to see me—say, next Thursday, any time between four and six?"

Etta took the card and tried to say "Yes" and "Thank you," all the time conscious only of the young man's presence. She felt angry at his interruption and at his manner —the rather insolent, rather self-conscious swagger of the wealthy young Englishman who knows it isn't the meek who inherit the earth. During those brief seconds she was aware of his good-looking face and hazel eyes laughing down at her a little insolently, and at the same time there

was another unexpected feeling quite away from her anger
and distress, a peculiar sort of tension. She stood startled
and shy, unaware of time, part of her angry with him, and
part of her vibrating in this curious unexpected tension.
Then her eyes lost his in a little panic of shame, and she
heard Ada Lawson say: "Good-bye, and don't forget—
Thursday," and her own voice say: "Yes, yes, good-bye,"
and the tension was over, and she found herself standing
alone among the groups of people talking.

As she made her way towards the door she found she
had something in her hand—why, of course, it was Mrs.
Lawson's card. She put it in her purse, and got through
the door into an unfamiliar street. She walked at random,
wondering why that brief talk with Ada Lawson had made
her feel so trembly. And that vibration, like a dim rather
frightening glow inside her—it must be because she hadn't
had tea. Or perhaps it was because she felt so angry with
that insolent-modest young man for *commanding* his aunt
away. "Rafe" she had pronounced his name, "Rafe."

6

ON TUESDAY EVENING of that week, Etta found a couple
of letters laid out for her on the large ugly marble table
opposite Miss Millingham's door. They were commercial
envelopes, and she knew at once that they were replies to
her advertisement-answering—the first she had received
for over a week. Annoyingly each asked her to call the
next morning at exactly the same hour. She looked at the
two addresses. One was in Holborn, quite near; the other
far down in the city almost at Aldgate. Etta decided to go
early to the Holborn address, and then, if she failed there,
to rush down to the other.

At twenty to nine the next morning, Etta was in Holborn, looking for Thirlby & Co., Exporters. She found she

had to go under an archway with a lot of name plates on it, through a short, very dirty passage to a small flagged court, with offices and the backs of warehouses all round it. There were rain puddles among the uneven flagstones, and all the lower windows had reflecting mirrors in the faint and dismal hope of increasing a light which wasn't there. Thirlby & Co. were at the far end, on the ground floor of a house painted strong tea colour, with a couple of iron Ionic columns forming a pseudo-porch.

Etta went timidly into the outer office. It would be an error to suppose that this timidity came from any sense of awe and reverence. The young men of half a century earlier had perhaps really "entered business" (at five bob a week) with the conviction that they were becoming privileged initiates in the great new religion of getting-on. The tradition still lingered with employers, but not with the employed. In Etta's case, which no doubt was like a good many others, she went because she had to. But the timidity came from an inner shrinking, a kind of spiritual nausea, a dread, as if she were going to be hit.

The outer office was empty, except for a row of chairs and an office boy on a high stool at a desk. He looked up inquiringly.

"I have an appointment with Mr. Drayton," said Etta, holding the letter.

"About the job?"

"Yes."

"Well, you're too early. He won't be in till nine."

"I'll wait."

"You'd better go away and come back again," he said rudely.

"Thanks," said Etta, "I prefer to wait." And she sat down on a chair. The boy stared at her, sucking his teeth audibly. Presently he lounged into the inner office, and came back looking disappointed, but still sucking his teeth.

He stared again, scratched his head, whistled a few bars of Mendelssohn's "Spring Song," and returned to his job of sorting letters. Every now and then the front door swung open, and a young man or woman hurried through, with a nod to the boy and a brief stare at Etta. Exactly at nine, three other girls arrived about the "job," and took their seats beside Etta with hostile glances. They seemed to know each other, and talked and giggled, looking at her from time to time in a jeering way.

A few minutes later a bulky man, wearing a dark over-coat and a bowler and carrying a rolled umbrella, came in and stood looking at them. The office boy said, "Good-morning, sir," and feigned intense industry. The man's eyes moved from one girl to another and rested on Etta. Something in his gaze made her feel abashed and resentful, it was so impertinent, such a violation, as if he were able to look through her clothes and see her sitting naked. He seemed almost to handle her with his eyes, like a farmer handling an animal in the market. Then he turned away and went through the inner door.

They waited. The girls whispered and giggled, and from time to time the boy sucked his teeth with hideous power and shrillness. Suddenly a bell rang sharply over his desk, and he darted off, then reappeared and went up to Etta with a grin, saying:

"You've clicked. He wants to see yer. Come on."

Etta stood up with a nervous jerk, much more aston-ished than glad that she had been selected for the first in-terview. As always, when she had to face the business man, she felt uncomfortable and nervous. Her throat felt dry, and she couldn't control a slight shivering of her leg mus-cles as the boy led her into the inner room. It felt cold in spite of a large fire at one side. She noticed it had four painted iron pillars like those on the porch, and that round the sides were a number of built-in pens with glazed doors and between the pillars girls were seated busily preparing their typewriters. One began to click, as the boy opened one of the glazed doors with "Mr. Drayton" painted on it.

The room was larger and more comfortable than Etta had supposed, with a gas fire and a bookcase with commercial reference books. An almanac from a shipping company with a picture of an ocean liner was nailed on the wooden wall. Then she saw the man who had looked at the girls outside seated at a roll-top desk. He was a little bald and looked rather jowly as he sat there opening letters which he placed in different piles after reading

"Here," he said sharply to the boy. "Take those letters to Mr. Thirlby—and don't dawdle."

The boy fled, and the man looked at Etta, again in that divesting way she resented so much. He told her to sit down, asked her name, looked up her letter, and began asking her questions, in a tone part overbearing, part gross deference—as if he were uncertain whether he meant to play the boss or the cheeky masher. It was unpleasant, but she felt she had to endure it. He asked for references, and Etta with trepidation presented the letters written by Vera and two other suffrage women.

"Dortborough," he said, merely glancing at them. "How did you come to be there?"

"My home is there."

"You're not living with your family?" he asked, narrowing his eyes.

"No."

"I see." He paused, watching her, began another question but broke off to say: "You've no commercial experience?"

"No, but . . ."

"All right. There's a pad and pencil—take down this letter and then type it on that typewriter."

He rapidly dictated a brief letter, which she took down

rather shakily but accurately, and then typed and handed him the sheet.

"H'm," he said. "You must use single spacing and a wider margin, but you've got it down all right except that you left out f.o.b."

Etta stared at him, not understanding, as she hadn't understood what he dictated.

"Don't you know what f.o.b. means?"

"No."

"Good heavens, what do they teach you at school? It means 'free on board.' But never mind, you'll learn. I'd rather have an intelligent beginner than a fool who thinks she knows everything. But are you sure you want a job of this kind? You're not the usual type of office girl—and you'll have to work hard."

"I do want the job, and I'm ready to work," said Etta quietly, though her heart was thumping and her head beginning to ache with nervousness at this cross-examination and the man's furtive repeated stares.

"All right. Now listen. Mr. Thirlby and I both need competent private secretaries. He's got a good one, and I can't find one. You'll have to learn a lot about the business and my ways in a very short time. Think you can do it?"

"Yes," said Etta as confidently as she could, though she felt the very opposite.

"Very well. Beginners usually start at fifteen shillings, but in your case I'll make it a pound. If you're a good girl and do what I want, I'll pay you more. But you'll have to be quick and obedient."

"I'll do my best."

"You're not used to calling your employer 'sir'?"

"No—I mean, no, sir."

"Try to remember. When can you start work?"

"Now if you wish—sir."

"Ah, that's the right spirit, but your predecessor doesn't leave until Saturday. Be here, in this room, ready to begin work at nine sharp on Monday."

"Yes, sir."

"Now go, I'm busy. Oh, tell those other girls they can go away, and send that office boy to me sharp. Good-morning."

Etta said, "Good-morning," feeling a little dazed, and as she turned away had the sensation that Mr. Drayton's eyes were pulling the clothes off her back. She almost ran out of the room.

Such is the wantonness of human nature that Etta had no sooner got her job than she wished she hadn't. She didn't like Mr. Drayton—he made her feel uneasy. She didn't like the office of Thirlby & Co., which seemed to her dirty and disagreeable; and she felt numb at the thought of spending all her weekdays there from nine to six, with a lonely Sunday and Saturday afternoon for youthful frolics. The underlying exultation at "being on her own" disappeared entirely, leaving her grey and colourless to face a succession of bad quarters of an hour. The chess board, however much she pondered, allowed only three possible moves—home, Thirlby & Co., starvation. She admitted frankly that she didn't want any of them, with a rueful footnote to the effect that while it might be useful to know what you didn't want to do in life, it would be vastly more satisfactory to know what you *did* want to do and to do it.

When Thursday afternoon arrived, Etta cheered up a bit. She tried to forget the dreary certainty that as a nine-to-six wage slave she would never have another opportunity to go to any of Ada Lawson's teas. And though it didn't seem either sensible or possible, she did rather desperately want to have some touch with Ada Lawson's world.

Etta dressed carefully in the best clothes she had and took a bus to Knightsbridge to keep her shoes clean. The entrance to the Lawsons' house was a little intimidating, the steps were so meticulously white, the green door so freshly painted, and the brass so dazzling—clearly, everybody who pulled the brass bell wore gloves. Still more intimidating was the footman who opened the door, and who by his servile-contemptuous manner seemed to know at once that she was a nobody. There was a large hall entry with a bright fire over an immaculate hearth, and on the wall two of the fifty thousand authentic Romneys which belong to England's upper-class homes. Before she could pull herself together, the footman led her to a door, announced her name in portentous tones, and Etta, hesitating in panic on the threshold, found herself facing a large room full of chattering people.

In her simplicity Etta had imagined herself quietly taking tea with Ada Lawson and continuing their talk alone together. Well, perhaps she had rather hoped that the interesting "Rafe" might come in, but only after she had had time to ask Mrs. Lawson's advice about what she should do. . . . With an effort she crossed the room, shook hands with Ada Lawson, and then shrank away to a seat by herself, angry that she had succumbed to this bad attack of *mauvaise honte*. Perhaps six weeks of solitude, worry, and under-feeding had something to do with it. She noticed that most of the men were dressed in black tail coats and striped trousers, while the women wore expensive Paris gowns and enormous hats. In her Dortborough dressmaker's frock she felt as out of place as a shabby frog in an aviary of humming birds. She was so much absorbed in looking at their curious social contortions that she started when a voice said:

"Your tea, Miss Morison. Will you have sandwiches or bread and butter?"

The voice belonged to Mr. Ralph Lawson, who looked very smart and slim in his morning clothes. Etta took the tea and a sandwich, and presently he came back and sat down beside her.

"Are you very anti-men?" he asked, smiling.

"No. Why?"

"You looked vipers at me on that suffragette platform the other evening."

"Did I?" Etta laughed. "I'm so sorry. But, you see, Mrs. Lawson was talking to me so sympathetically I was disappointed she had to go."

"Oh, is that all?" He seemed relieved. "Aunt Ada knows so many suffragettes who seem to think a man is a noisome reptile that I'm scared out of my life. So's Uncle Randolfe."

"You don't look very frightened. Are there many reptile haters here?"

"Lord, no. This isn't the weekly suffrage beanfeast, or I shouldn't be here."

"But who are these people, then?" asked Etta curiously.

"Don't you know them?" He seemed surprised. "They're only a few specimens of the scum of London— the scum being the cream on the pot you know. You see that poetical-looking man with the Vandyke beard and noble brow talking to those two rapt damsels?"

"Yes."

"He's Mogenheim, the Anglo-German-Jew millionaire. He's got the worst pictures and the worst cellar in London, and everyone's afraid of him."

"Why?"

"Because he's rich enough to smash anybody and lends money to royalty. You see that very dapper old gentleman, with a face like a withered apple, the one telling improper stories to Lady Clipsby?"

"How do you know he's telling improper stories?" said Etta, blushing a little.

"He always does when he gets alone with a woman. He'll tell 'em to you if he gets a chance. That's Professor Wren, the greatest living authority on medieval Romance languages. The man with a moustache and a particularly vacant look—ah, he's brightened up, he's caught sight of himself in the mirror—that's Major Jervyns of the Coldstreams. That little shrimp with the falsetto voice is Lord Pellingham, a great friend of Oscar Wilde's. He paints and collects Sicilian shepherds. That offensive old hag in the enormous hat, blaring away at poor Jimmie Slough, the poet, is the Duchess of Crewkerne. I loathe her."

"Why?"

"Oh, she's always running after me, and I have to dance with her, and she treads on my toes."

"Are you making fun of me," cried Etta, "or is this true?"

"All sober truth, I give you my word."

"Then who is that very distinguished man with grey hair and a fine profile your aunt just spoke to?"

"Who? Oh, that's the butler."

"And are you the kitchen boy?" asked Etta, laughing again, and quite uncertain whether he was in earnest or joking at the expense of her ignorance.

"Very nearly. I'm in disgrace. I've been progged so often I've been rusticated for a term. So I'm rusticating in London, and then I'm going abroad for a few weeks."

Etta didn't know what progged and rusticated meant exactly, but she knew they had something to do with universities and implied trouble with authority. Already she had forgotten about being angry with him, and his light-hearted chatter abolished all present sense of women's wrongs. And now he had the additional merit of being persecuted by dreadful old men in mortar boards.

"Did you do anything very bad?" she asked, but in a tone which seemed to imply that you couldn't prove to her that Ralph would ever do anything really bad.

"Oh, it's a long and squalid story, involving bump suppers and smashed windows and leading to a climax of impertinence—not on my side, of course, but from the dons. They're a malevolent set of eccentric old owls, besotted with port and intellect."

"I should have thought you would enjoy going to a university," said Etta reproachfully, rather scandalized.

"So I did until I went there."

"And where are you going abroad?"

"Monte Carlo—but I shall run over to Florence for a week-end. They'll feel gratified if they think I've been pursuing culture in the city of Dante, though personally I think Dante's a bore, don't you?"

"I haven't read him."

"Neither have I, so we're both fully qualified to be English Dante scholars. By the way, where shall you be this winter? It'd be awfully pleasant if you could come to Monaco."

"I'm afraid I shall be working in an office," said Etta shyly, but quite determined not to get into this little world of luxury on false pretenses.

"What!" Ralph was evidently amazed. "Why ever are you doing that?"

"Because I have to."

He gazed at her with large incredulous eyes, which, she noted, had flecks of green in the hazel. Plainly, he had never before met a girl who *had* to work in an office, and didn't know what to say.

"You see," Etta tried to explain, "it's what you would call a long and squalid story, but—I ran away from home, and since my parents cast me off, I naturally have to earn my living."

"I say, that was plucky of you," said Ralph admiringly. "But what made you run away?"

"I told you it was a long story. Shall we say that it might be founded on the same sort of discontent which got you into trouble at your university?"

Ralph laughed.

"Well, I don't know about that, and I'm pretty sure I shouldn't have the pluck to run away from home and earn my own living."

"I'm quite sure you wouldn't," said Ada Lawson's voice. "Has anybody you know done such a thing?"

"Yes," said Ralph, "Miss Morison."

Ada Lawson smiled as she looked down on them—quite a handsome pair, if the girl had been a decent match, which obviously she wasn't. Ada Lawson was a kind-hearted woman, otherwise she would never have followed the generous impulse which led her to invite a penniless pretty girl to tea. But, as every decent-thinking person will allow, there are limits to generosity—a penniless-pretty has no right to absorb more than a few minutes of an eligible young man's time, especially when he's a near relative.

"Go and talk to the duchess, Ralph," said Ada Lawson, still smiling. "You haven't spoken to her or even looked at her since she came in."

"Why should I? She's nothing to look at, and she makes me feel uneasy."

"Do as I ask you, Ralph. Your mother would never forgive me if I let you offend the duchess."

Etta heard Ralph murmur, "Hang the duchess," but he got up and went over to her all the same. Etta got up to leave.

"Don't go," said Ada Lawson quickly, wishing to atone for her manœuvre. "I want to talk to you. Everybody will be gone in a few minutes. Do please wait."

Etta sat down again. She was far too innocent to notice what had happened and was guiltless of any designs on Ralph. Perhaps Ada Lawson's instinct was quicker than hers. But then Etta hadn't been able to see her own face grow animated as she talked to Ralph. For the moment she sat there quietly, watching the guests disperse, thinking how handsome Ralph looked as he talked with the duchess, hoping that Teddy would be as charming in a few years, and discovering with surprise that she felt quite happy and cheerful—it *was* a nice change to listen to someone rattling off high-spirited nonsense.

There is a feeling of ease and security in a well-warmed, softly lighted, expensively furnished room of a wealthy house, even if you're the death's head at the feast, one of the penniless who've no right to be there. The servants move with such discreet dexterity, and the guests talk so wittily and naughtily about the dear friends who are not present. Such a room broadens the mind. If you keep quiet and listen, you can learn a lot you'd never find out in an A. B. C. bun shop or a doss house. You'll learn about the finer feelings and the subtler soul. You'll learn about how wicked it is for Calabrian peasants to snare thrushes to eat with their dry bread and olives, and how fine it is for the gentleman to shoot partridges for fun. You'll learn how important humane feelings are—in the case of birds and animals. But don't mention the unemployed. If you do, you'll learn that they're lazy and prefer to live at other people's expense. Don't, Etta, please don't say that a pound a week is too little for a girl to live on decently, unless you want to hear that your work isn't worth a pound a week, whereas you ought to realize—little duffer —that the leisure of those about you is worth at least a pound an hour, sleeping and waking. And don't mention income tax, unless you want to get the fright of your life by learning that The Whole Country will be ruined if it isn't halved next budget.

Unfortunately, Etta neglected the opportunity of instruction. She sat dreamily in that rather light-headed daze which comes to people who haven't eaten enough for some time. Ralph had forgotten to offer her another sandwich, and ungenteelly she could have eaten a plate full. But it was soothing to sit there, very still, and to look at the rosewood cabinets filled with Chinese ivories, the tall Renaissance cabinet of ebony inlaid with silver, the old pictures, the firelight glinting so sharply from the polished silver on the tea tray, and the dark ample curtains which seemed so solid and were so fragile a barrier against the outside world. It was seductive. And yet, subtract the taste, the opulence, and the duchesses, and this was the very same thing from which she had fled. And yet again it was seductive—Etta thought of her cold little room. . . .

Nearly all the guests had gone. She noticed Ralph going away with the duchess, for whom he opened the door. But instead of following her, he came quickly back to Etta.

"I've got to go off with her," he said petulantly. "Aunt Ada let me in for it. Isn't it awful! I say, I do hope I shall see you again."

"I hope so," said Etta, feeling the hope was pretty fragile.

"Make Aunt Ada invite you. She will. Good-bye. I must rush."

When everyone had gone, Ada Lawson came over and sat beside Etta.

"What is this wild story Ralph has been telling me?" she asked. "Is it true that you have run away from home and are going to work in an office?"

"Quite true."

"But—forgive me if I seem intrusive—do you think it wise? Have you no parents?"

"Yes. I think my parents meant well, but they held onto me too closely. I had to live their life, not mine. Of course, I could have stayed on or perhaps have married somebody, but . . ."

"But what?"

"I believed I could make my own life. And then Dortborough, where I lived, is so ugly and depressing."

"Isn't London ugly and depressing?"

"Yes, but after Dortborough it seems wonderful, and then I am on my own, it is an adventure."

"Do you think you will like your work?"

"I'm sure I shall hate it," said Etta frankly. "But it is only a beginning. I have to start at the bottom and work upwards."

"I'm afraid that in the modern world those who start at the bottom don't as a rule get very far. The world is not so much cruel, as utterly indifferent, especially to a girl by herself. Is there any way I can help you?"

"Not now, but perhaps later on. It's very kind of you. Perhaps, when I've a little experience, you might be able to think of something better for me to do, but I've got to learn first."

"It's brave of you. I hope you won't be disappointed or suffer too much. You must let me know how you get on."

"What I most fear is falling into a routine for the rest of my life," said Etta thoughtfully.

"But for nearly everybody life *must* be a routine or things couldn't go on. We can't all be pioneers."

"Women have got to be, in these days," said Etta determinedly. "I exist. And there must be thousands of other girls like me. We can't or we won't go on in the old way,

so we've got to try and find a new way, even if we get horribly lost."

Ada Lawson was going to say, "Isn't that a little conceited of you?" but checked herself and said:

"Will you come to tea on Tuesday? I shall have other
friends here, and one or other of them might be able to
help you."

"Thank you, but you see, I shall be at the office until
six at the earliest—I shan't have time."

"How tiresome!" Ada Lawson seemed to feel aggrieved
by this spoke in her plans. "Well, leave me your address,
and I'll arrange to see you some evening. Are you free
then?"

"All my evenings are free," said Etta simply.

The footman condescended to show Etta out with
affronted dignity, but showed his displeasure by slamming
the door. Things, he realized, were not as they had been
in the old days, when those who had carriages were never
visited by those who hadn't. Here was Mrs. Lawson receiving a female who didn't even call a taxi. He shivered to
think how Socialism was gnawing at the nation's vitals
and decided to give notice—there must still be a few decent
families in St. James's, a few gentlemen of the old school
round the Burlington Arcade.

7

"*Esa muchacha gana poco, pero siempre va muy bien
puesta.*

"That girl earns very little but is always well dressed."

Some of the transactions of Thirlby & Co. related to
South America. Moreover, their system of paying employees was based as far as possible on the venerable and

perennially successful principle of the carrot in front of the donkey's nose, paying with hopes and not in cash. When Etta had been at work for a month she ventured, such is the ungrateful avarice of employees, to point out that a pound a week was too little and asked Mr. Drayton for a rise. Bitterly hurt in the tenderest point of his honour, that honest gentleman replied that it was impossible, impossible—why, girls who had been with the firm two years were only drawing thirty shillings. To which Etta replied that thirty shillings was better than a pound, and that the girls in question did not have to do the extra work and take the responsibility of a private secretary.

At this Mr. Drayton leaned back in his chair and frowned. That talent for acting which made Elizabethan drama is now devoted to Business and promoting the elegant fiction that honesty is the best policy. Mr. Drayton acted injured honesty and wounded benevolence vividly, and with a fine imitation of stern rectitude said again that it was impossible, impossible—nothing could be done before Christmas. Then, in despair, Etta played a desperate stroke—she said she was afraid then she'd have to leave. Now Mr. Drayton had his own ideas about Etta, and had no intention of letting her leave. He got into a little panic at the thought that she might slip through his fingers. So he rapidly assumed the part of the *faux bonhomme*, the gov'nor who's a decent chap and human and all that, and after a lot of palaver, agreed that in January she should have twenty-five shillings—the principle that nothing could be done before Christmas was cast-iron.

At the same time he produced one of the carrots which experience had shown was very efficacious. He talked about the importance of the South American trade; he drew a warmly tinted picture of the benefits which were showered on those who studied it; pointed out that the foreign correspondence clerk earned a full Three Pounds

a week. Since Etta wished to better herself—he commended the ambition—why did she not study Spanish
and qualify herself for the dizzy financial altitudes of
Three Pounds a week? Etta took the bait like a hungry
codling.

Thus it came about that on Christmas Day Etta was
seated alone in her room, wrapped in her overcoat and a
blanket from the bed, poring over a phrase book of idio-
matic Spanish. And then she came upon the sentence:
"That girl earns very little but is always well dressed,"
which diverted her attention from the problem of Spanish
to the problem of herself.

Her reflections had no cast of the pathetic, and had nothing to do with a lonely and presentless Christmas. As a
matter of fact, Etta felt rather pleased with herself for
making a solitary Christmas dinner of tinned herring,
bread and butter and tea, when at that very hour—it was
about two-thirty—large numbers of people were surfeiting
themselves on food and domesticity. She shuddered as she
thought of the family circle, to which she had been invited
by an epistle from her mother, full of injured forgiveness,
subtle malice, and the spirit of Tiny Tim. And she didn't
regret having refused the Lawsons' invitation to the country—it would have cost far too much in tips and fares.

The Spanish phrase about the girl who earned little but
looked well dressed brought her up with a jerk. It was true
that with the clothes she had brought from home, she was
better dressed than the other girls in the office; but how
long would it last? Etta had discovered that most of them
lived at home, which meant that they paid over ten or
fifteen shillings a week and had the rest of their wages
as pocket money. They went to matinées and skating rinks
with young men, and if their office clothes were shabby
they had plenty of finery for week-ends. And they were
quite content. Sooner or later most of them would marry

out of office work. That was what Thirlby & Co. had discovered—girls were cheaper and more docile and conscientious than young men, and in this new rush of "emancipation" the supply was abundant.

Etta wasn't content and didn't see how she could be.
Not only had she bound herself to the dreaded Routine,
but it was a most dreary one, and, moreover, a routine
which didn't even pay. Cutting out Saturday afternoons
and Sundays—which also formed themselves into a stereo-
type—one day's routine was very much like another. At
seven-thirty each morning the alarm clock awoke her with
a start—one of her dreads was that one morning it
wouldn't go off, and she'd be late and lose her job. She
had to jump up at once in the dark, light the gas ring and
put on a kettle; then still in the dark and shivering with
cold make her way down to the one bathroom. There she
lighted the gas, put a penny in the gas meter, and in trepidation turned on the geyser.

This geyser was another terror. It was old and cumbrous,
and the brass parts which Gertrude never condescended
to polish were green with verdigris. Etta was convinced
it would one day explode and blow her to pieces. In any
case, it always lighted with such a thunderous bang that
she jumped with fright. The bath was old, too, and where
the paint had been chipped or worn away showed the black
metal, so that Etta could never feel it was quite clean;
and a pennyworth of gas didn't make a very luxurious
bath.

Then upstairs, still in the dark and still shivering, to
light the gas in her room (she couldn't afford to put on
the gas fire), which she swept and tidied, to make her bed
and breakfast on Quaker Oats and tea. By the time she
had washed up, put on her shoes (cleaned overnight) and
got ready to go out, it was twenty to nine, and she had to
hurry to get to the office in time.

Followed four hours of office routine, with Mr. Drayton sometimes genial, but more often in a bad temper, and always making her work at top speed. Etta was thankful that he had ceased looking at her in the odious way she detested so much—in fact, he scarcely ever looked at her or met her eye—but it did seem to her that he drove her harder than anyone else, piling work on her. Before she had well started typing out her shorthand notes of the letters he had dictated, he would send the office boy to tell her to bring him the correspondence files about So-and-so and So-and-so, which wasn't really her job; and long before she had finished the first batch of letters he would send for her and hand her five or six letters from other firms, saying: "Just answer these letters for me, Miss Morison, you know all about the matters involved." Which meant looking up the correspondence files and doing his work for him.

At twelve Mr. Drayton went out to lunch, usually at the Holborn Restaurant—dropping casually another dollop of work on Etta as he passed. At one Etta went out to lunch, invariably at an Express Dairy, where she had a poached egg, a roll, and a cup of coffee. At two she was back at work. Mr. Drayton strolled in about three, and was very much shocked in all his moral fibres if Etta had not finished the work he had left for her, and still more shocked if she had finished and was doing nothing. Occasionally the austere form of Mr. Thirlby, who wore a top hat and a look of incalculable avarice, passed through the room, leaving a trail of awed industry behind him. But, as Mr. Drayton's "private secretary," Etta had very little to do with him.

At six the other girls began to leave, but the "private secretary" often had to stay on later. Mr. Drayton didn't dine until eight. So it was often seven or later when Etta got back to her room, after walking through muddy and wind-swept streets. Sometimes she was too tired to eat at once, and lay on the bed in the dark until the cold made

her move. Sometimes she was so cold that she had to light
the gas fire to thaw her fingers enough to get her porridge
supper. After that she hadn't the strength to walk about
the streets in the wet and cold; she couldn't afford the
cheapest music hall or the new moving-picture places; she
had no friends to go to at that hour. So she stayed in,
trying to learn Spanish, then washed up, cleaned her shoes,
put everything ready for breakfast, and went to bed after
carefully winding the alarm clock. . . .

And that was life on her own. Etta looked again at her
Spanish book—"*esa muchacha gana poco.*" Too true. Although Etta by now knew her budget by heart, she took a
pencil and an old envelope and wrote it down once more:

Rent	8/–
Gertrude (stairs)	1/–
Seven breakfasts	2/–
Six lunches @ 8d.	4/–
Six suppers @ 6d.	3/–
Sunday	1/–
Gas	7
Bath	7
Five teas, office	5
Total	£1 0 7

This looked almost like solvency, but wasn't, since ne-
cessities like soap, tooth powder, blacking, anything beyond daily subsistence had to come out of the few pounds
she had left. Out of her wages she couldn't even afford a
penny stamp for a letter. Impossible to get any more
clothes; and yet already her shoes needed repair, her gloves
were getting old, she wanted a new hat, and one day she
would have to get new stockings and a frock. Twenty-five
shillings would barely keep her going; even thirty shillings
would be a struggle. The future looked pretty desperate.

If only they would give her ten shillings a week from home
—but they wouldn't. They were being hard and trying to
starve her into submission. She could hear them saying to
each other, comfortably replete with muffins on Sunday
afternoon: "Etta will learn her lesson in time and come to
appreciate a good home and family love." Cruel to be kind.
Well, damn family love that isn't worth ten bob a week.
Damn family love that wants to keep me an overfed servant and sycophant or to get rid of me by mating me with
a coarse fool.

The joke is, if there is a joke, that they don't really care,
Etta thought. In a way, they're much more separated from
me than I am from them. I can't ever get free from them,
because they made me direct all my childish emotions on
them. They wanted to be "loved," which meant they
wanted me to live only in and through them. How beastly
love is, what a lot of cant! Even the catechism doesn't tell
you to love your parents, it only tells you to "honour"
them, whatever that may mean. Because of that absorption of my childhood, they still have power over me, while
I've none over them. Daddy has a lot of old man's senti-
mentality about his "little girl," as if I were a sort of
platonic sweetheart. He's quite prepared to be amiable so
long as I pretend to think he's the biggest thing that ever
happened in humanity. I really believe he seriously thinks
that the height of felicity for me ought to be toasting his
rotten old muffins for him. Anyway, he's furiously jealous
if I prefer anything in life to humouring him. And Mother's
worse—she's jealous of my learning or doing anything she
hasn't done or couldn't do. Oh Lord, here I am going over
all this again, and it's no good. But how well I can see
through her! Of course, she doesn't know how I'm living,
but if she did, all she'd care about is to keep the Dortborough people from knowing it. I wonder what lies she
tells them?

She returned to her budget. Where could she cut it down? Rent? Well, doubtless in the outer suburbs she could get a cheaper room, but there would be daily fares, and she would not have the freedom of being one of Miss Millingham's "distinguished guests." Baths? She couldn't go dirty. Gertrude's shilling and the fivepence for office tea were perquisites. Food? For three weeks now she had eaten no fresh meat, and she was ashamed at realizing how greedily hungry the thought of it made her. But, no, it would have to go, and the tinned things she had been extravagantly buying would have to go too. There was only one thing to do—give up all middle-class luxuries and try to live like an Irish peasant. Or rather, a mixture of Irish and Scotch. Etta had heard vaguely that the healthiest people in the world lived on cereals, milk, and potatoes. If men could do hard physical work on that diet, surely she could do her paltry office work. Anyway, she could but try. If she bought margarine instead of butter—hateful necessity!—she could get more milk. And then, in an ecstasy of Spartan frugality, she decided that the daily egg was a luxury. By allowing forty minutes of the lunch hour to walk to and fro, she could have twenty minutes at home to get herself tea and as much bread and margarine as she could eat. Altogether she could save three or four shillings. Splendid.

She worked at her Spanish until it was dark, and then lay on the bed wondering how she could get out of Thirlby & Co. to something better.

8

UNNATURAL HISTORY tells us that chickens always bully speckled hens; and hence any person in a community who is unpleasantly conspicuous and therefore pecked at by everyone is popularly called a "speckled hen." Not bad, but untrue, as anybody who has looked at a farmyard with a philosophic eye will know. It isn't being speckled which invites the farmyard pecks. But pecking there undoubtedly is among both hens and humans. The difference is worth noting as an illustration of the habits of the dreary and ferocious animals we have to associate with. Hens are all against failures on the part of whatever makes hens. Healthy eugenists, in fact. What they go for is the under-sized, bedraggled, moping, misbegotten, ill-hatched speci-men, which would obviously be better dead.

Humans feel otherwise. Most of them are no particular credit to any creative force, and therefore are only too pleased to discover an even worse specimen which they can patronize with pity and exult over with charity. What humans unite to peck at is superiority, natural superiority, when it is unaccompanied by power. Release unto us Barabbas.

Etta was the speckled hen of the staff of Thirlby & Co., at least, among the other hens. She was prettier than any of them, and her body more beautifully formed. She was so healthy that even semi-starvation had so far only had the effect of making her skin clearer and fining her face until prettiness had become delicate though not vivid beauty. Uneducated as she was, she was better educated than they, and had better manners. They decided she was uppish, and that she must be rich, and that she was taking-the - bread - out - of - the - mouths - of - them - that - needed-it, and that she secretly received large sums for being the mistress of Mr. Drayton. So they pecked at her, and she naturally pecked back. Being quicker-witted (another offense) she pecked better, and that also was held against her. The only peck she couldn't retort to was the sneer:

"Going out with Mr. Drayton tonight?"

This seemed to her so silly that she merely shrugged at

it. Who on earth would want to go out with a boor like
Drayton, especially after having to put up with him all
day? And she was so innocent that she entirely failed to
see the insinuation in the words.

Etta belonged to a type, now apparently diminishing in
numbers, which was incurably conscientious. When she
undertook a job, however distasteful, she did it as well and
energetically as she could; and didn't expect to be thanked
for it. When the other girls complained that they were always being driven, Etta injudiciously retorted that they
asked for it by always slacking on every possible occasion.
This was doubly injudicious, since it proved to their minds
that she was in league with the bosses and therefore *must*
be Drayton's mistress.

She was particularly exasperated by the way they staged
their regular absences, and the amount of unnecessarily
low drama they introduced. Officially these absences were
not recognized (that would have been indelicate, as every
bishop and employer knows), but in fact they couldn't be
prevented. A girl would turn up with a wan countenance
which she made no attempt to disguise. There would be a
twittering among the others of "Isn't it a shame?" and
"Take it easy, dear," and "It didn't ought to be allowed."
At a suitable moment the girl would clutch her brow and
exclaim, "Oh, my head," and seem to swoon. All the girls
except Etta, who would go on energetically with her work,
would immediately crowd round with tragical exclamations of pity and terror, and the sufferer would be conducted staggering to the hat-and-coat room. Mr. Drayton
would emerge angrily from his office, demanding to know
what was the matter and be greeted with reproachful cries
of "Miss Beaufort's taken ill, sir!" Whereupon he would
look rather gratified and hurry to see how she was, pack

her off, and drive the others back to work. But, anyway, these unseemly episodes provided a few minutes' break for all, fifteen minutes for the conductors (who took it in turns) and a couple of days' miking for the sufferer.

The stiff back and barrage of typing which Etta invariably turned on these scenes did not make her more popular. They loathed her for it. Here they were skilfully and successfully playing off one of the classic tricks on the eternal and stupid enemy, Man, and she refused to aid and abet. Traitress! Vamp! Villainess! Unwholesome creature, probably not made right, my dear! And how she hated them for it all! They ruined everything. As she saw it, the whole point of their lives of drudgery was to prove that women are not helpless creatures who have to be protected and periodically helped off the stage of life, that they can do a lot of the work which the enemy, Man, arrogantly pretended he only could do. And here they were playing straight into the enemy's hands and demonstrating that they couldn't stick it and inviting inferior wages into the bargain. So her back grew stiffer and the typing barrage more insistent, and they hated her more. However much her head and insides ached, however limp she felt, Etta wasn't going to beg an hour off. No, sir. You think we can't do a job as well as a man or better? I'll show you.

Owing to this propensity for not giving in, Etta was at the office on the first pay day in January. As usual she went to the cashier, and as usual received one sovereign.

"This is a mistake," she said quickly.

"What d'you mean, a mistake?" he said in a surly way. "It's what you always get, isn't it?"

"Yes, but Mr. Drayton agreed last month that I was to have twenty-five shillings, beginning this week."

"I can't help what he said, I haven't had any instructions."

"But he promised me."

"I can't help that."

Like most people of sensibility, Etta very seldom allowed herself to be angry—it hurt too much. But this made her angry, and when angry she was very angry indeed. Moreover, she was hungry. For weeks she had schooled herself to being more or less permanently hungry, but she promised herself that out of that first additional five shillings she would buy herself one of the small meat pies she had seen in a shop window. Certainly, it was not the sort of food Mr. and Mrs. Morison would have considered a treat, but Etta wanted it, and she meant to have it and her five shillings. But even in her anger something in her was laughing at the ridiculousness of being angry about five shillings a week and a meat pie.

If she listened to that inner chuckle instead of to her anger, she knew she would be lost. In a flash she was back in the main office, tapping sharply at Mr. Drayton's door. He looked up as she entered, startled by her furious eyes and cheeks flushed with rage.

"What does this mean?" she demanded, holding out the sovereign contemptuously, and forgetting to "sir" him. "The cashier says he has no orders to pay me the advance you *promised*."

"Oh." He looked embarrassed. "I should have told you earlier. I mentioned the matter to Mr. Thirlby, and he said . . ."

"I don't care what Mr. Thirlby said," she interrupted. "You promised me on behalf of the firm, and it's dishonourable on your part, dishonourable."

"I can't disobey Mr. Thirlby," he said sulkily.

"It's not a question of disobeying. You know perfectly

well the whole payment of the staff is left to you. I know it too. How can you break your word like that?"

Mr. Drayton fumbled in his pockets and produced two half crowns which he held out to her, saying:

"Oh, well, if you feel like that about it, I'll pay you out of my own pocket. Here you are."

"I don't want you to pay me out of your own pocket," Etta retorted disdainfully. "I want the firm to keep the promise you made for it. Let the cashier pay me. I don't want to be associated with dishonourable people."

"You're a nice young fury, aren't you?" He laughed. "I didn't know you had so much spirit. But it would mess up the books if I gave the order now. Take my five bob this week—I'll get it refunded—and I give you my word that the firm shall pay you twenty-five hereafter."

Etta still did not take the money. He got up and put the two coins in her hand, which he held, saying in a caressing voice:

"You look ill, Miss Morison." Etta had indeed turned very white. "Why not take a day off?"

"Thank you, I don't want a day off," she replied, trying to disengage her hand and feeling rather faint.

"I think you do." He took her other hand and squeezed it. "You know if you were very nice to me, instead of being so stand-offish, I could make things a lot easier for you, get you a substantial rise, perhaps."

Etta didn't see what he meant, but she hated him being near, hated the touch of his hands, the hypocritical voice, and instinctively suspected this offer of favouritism. She jerked her hands free.

"Thank you, Mr. Drayton, I don't want anything I don't earn. I work hard for the firm. You won't get more work from me by underpaying me. You might get more if you paid me decently. Good-night."

As she went out, she saw he looked disconcerted and

annoyed. She didn't care. But the scene upset her so much she wasn't able to eat the pie, after all.

The monotony of routine was broken by a visit from Vera, who spent a Saturday in London. Half-humorously Etta noted how humble her scale of life had become. After all, it was only old Vera. Six months earlier an afternoon with her would have been a pleasant release from home dullness, nothing more; now it seemed like a visitation of the gods.

That day Etta had been kept later than the others, as usual, and found Vera waiting impatiently and sniffingly in the outer office. At the sight of Etta her indignation changed to horror.

"Etta! How *ill* you look!"

"Do I?" said Etta, opening the door for Vera to pass. "I'm all right. It's the end of the week, you know."

"I know. But do you know what you look like?"

"A bit shabby and rather hideous, I'm afraid."

"Nonsense!" Vera's indignation made her stride along at a pace Etta found too fast for her. "You look fagged out and terribly thin and unhappy."

Etta turned away her head and then tried to laugh.

"I'm all right," she said lightly. "But would you mind not walking so fast? It puts me out of breath."

"I'm so sorry, but that only goes to prove how ill you are. It's working in that awful office. Office they call it! It's a cattle shed. They ought to be reported to the authorities and prosecuted. They wouldn't dare keep factory workers in such conditions."

"Don't let's talk about it," Etta pleaded. "This is a holiday. Would you—would you like to lunch at an A. B. C.?"

She hesitated as she spoke, wondering if she could afford to stand Vera a lunch. But Vera brushed aside any idea

of A. B. Cs., or of Etta standing her lunch. She bustled
Etta into a taxi and to a restaurant, where she insisted on
ordering delicacies Etta could scarcely eat. All through
lunch Vera chattered about non-personal things, occasionally glancing at her with a look of consternation and self-
reproach Etta found rather entertaining. Finally, when
Vera found she could not persuade or force Etta to eat,
she said:

"What would you like to do now? Rest or go to a theatre
matinée or a concert?"

"Oh," exclaimed Etta, "if only I could hear some music!
But it's too extravagant . . . I can't afford . . ."

Vera's mouth set in the straight line of determination
Etta at one time had resented so much. They decided on
a symphony concert at Queen's Hall, and with some difficulty managed to find seats. It seemed queer but great fun
to Etta to be back in the familiar ugly hall, with the huge
red lamp shades and the organ pipes. But from the first
few bars of the Jupiter Symphony she forgot all about the
hall and the people, sat back with her eyes shaded under
her hand, listening. It was all so familiar and yet entirely
new, a new revelation, as if she had never really understood
music before. How divine a grace was Mozart's, how exquisite a sensibility! Etta didn't criticize the performance
as she would once have done, for criticism so often is the
unlovely privilege of satiety and ingratitude. She lived in
the music, deeply moved. It was like being suddenly trans-
ported from a London winter to an unhoped-for spring
in a strange land—flowers coming out as the snow melted
under blue sky.

Then they played the Unfinished Symphony of Schubert,
and Etta felt ashamed to think that in her student days she
had scorned it as hackneyed and commonplace. She hum-
bled her spirit before it and confessed her foolish conceit.
Those long cadences hadn't the loveliness of Mozart, who

seemed almost nonhuman in his unearthly quality, the Kappelmeister of some heaven where there were no Christians, but Schubert was easier and warmer, more like a full summer bending to autumn fullness. She could hardly breathe for the tightness at her heart and throat; she wanted the music to go on, never to cease, to hold her forever in this trance of beauty.

At the interval Etta was too much stirred to be able to speak. She sat in silence, with her eyes still hidden, and Vera gracefully did not attempt to speak. Gradually, the hum of talk and banging of seats subsided to a silence broken only by the coughing of the inevitable few who will impose their colds on public entertainments. The conductor waited for perfect silence; and then her life merged with the Fifth Symphony of Beethoven. It was too much. The others had been lovely, but this majestic tragic beauty —also so familiar, and yet fresh and poignant as if never heard before—washed over her like an irresistible sea. Human life was not merely squalid and petty; it had nobility; and profundity of feeling raised it to tragedy. Those violins, those violins tearing at her heart. They were playing the second movement, and her heart was breaking. Impossible to resist—*le cœur se bronze ou se brise*. The ice of suffering melted, and quite silently she wept, not with sobs or resistance to sorrow and the sense of spiritual failure, but with quiet tears streaming under her sheltering hand.

The last chords died on the air, and there was a clamour of hand-clapping. Etta knew that the last item was "The Ride of the Valkyrie," and she felt that she could not endure the vulgarity of Wagner's brazen emphasis. Still crying, she turned to Vera, and said:

"May we go? Do you mind?"

Vera took her by the arm and led her out gently. Etta

held a handkerchief to her face, and didn't see the people staring at them or read the contemptuous "hysterical woman" in their eyes. The street outside seemed curiously empty and unreal, still more unreal the fool's-cap church tower at the corner. Vera said:

"Where do you want to go?"

"To my room—please, please forgive me."

Vera squeezed her hand affectionately and silently held it in hers as they drove along in a taxi.

The commonplace activity of making tea for Vera soon brought Etta back to the usual world and to her self-control. The emotional discharge cheered her up, and she had the feeling that her own petty grief and humiliation had been wiped out through this brief touch with universal tragedy. Her tears had been given to something greater than herself. Vera thought that Etta had merely "broken down." She wanted Etta to leave Thirlby & Co. immediately, return home, and wait until "something better" could be found. Etta refused.

"I'm not going to give up now," she said, "or at any time, unless I collapse completely. It would be ignominious defeat."

"No, it wouldn't. It would only mean you realized you'd made a false start, as you have, and that you meant to try something better."

"No." Etta shook her head. "If I went back now, I should never have the energy to get free again."

"But surely we ought to be able to find you something which wouldn't leave you starved and ill."

"Find it for me, and I'll go to it. But running home won't find me anything. And if I got tired and didn't eat properly, it was out of ignorance. I had to work very hard at first because I knew nothing. And I'm learning how to buy food more sensibly."

"Well, you don't look like it. How much longer are you going on like this?"

They argued for some time over Etta's plans and the possibility of help from Mrs. Lawson. Vera said she would write to Ada Lawson, whom she knew slightly, and Etta begged her not to. Finally, Etta said:

"You know, Vera, we were very ignorant in those Dortborough days when we used to talk about what women should do in the world. It isn't so simple. One of the things we didn't know is how the world is run."

"It's run badly," said Vera decisively, "because it's directed almost entirely by *men*—in their own selfish interests and against ours."

"That may be," Etta replied. "But merely saying so won't alter anything, and women voting even won't alter much. The human world is frightening, a dogfight pretending to be a justly ordered community. You've got to snatch what you can get from the dogfight, but keep inside the rules."

"But when we get political power and begin to organize . . ."

"But you haven't got it," Etta interrupted. "And meanwhile I've got to live. What's the use of waiting for a perfectly just state of affairs to be created, especially when you're pretty sure it won't be? Thirlby & Co. treat me like a dog. So I am, an under dog. But I'm not going to remain one. Drayton's idea is to get as much as he can from his employees for as little as possible. That's business. Most of them retaliate by doing only what they're driven to do. That's slave mentality. I've worked hard. I've learned as much in ten weeks as most of them learn in two years. Already I know more than Drayton thinks I know —for instance, that the business is slowly declining. And he also doesn't know that I'm reading and replying to some of the South American mail."

"I don't see——" Vera began.

"Well, I do. I see, among other things, that Drayton believes he's got someone to do a lot of his work for him for a pittance. I also see that in a few weeks' time I shall be fairly competent at this sort of office job. If Thirlby & Co. give me a proper wage, I shall stay for a time. If not, I shall go somewhere else. You think I've been silly to go without food, but I had to keep those few pounds intact so that I can really threaten to leave and be able to, and I have to keep my clothes decent, so that I can see people like the Lawsons without looking a fright. If I once let myself get too shabby, I'm done."

"You sound rather hard, Etta," said Vera, a little perturbed.

"One has to be in some things. An hour ago you thought I was soft—confess it—to be so much moved by that music. But, Vera, we've got to be hard to the hard side of life, without letting it kill our sensitiveness to the beautiful side. You wouldn't have me indifferent to Beethoven and yielding to Thirlby?"

"I don't want you to get hard and mercenary and to lose sight of our ideals."

"But I have to deal with realities! And apropos realities, there's another point. . . . I think Mrs. Lawson is right in saying we shouldn't be man-haters. There are decent men as well as rotters."

"I've always thought you'd marry one day," said Vera reproachfully.

"I don't mean marriage. Why should I get married? I don't want a man to keep me. But if I'm independent, as I mean to be, and if I fall in love with a man——"

"Etta!"

"Why not? Why should we cut ourselves off from an essential experience? It's part of life."

"But suppose you had an illegitimate child?"

"I've heard you rage against men having the sole right over children. If I ever wanted a child, I should have it, on my own. But nowadays a girl needn't have a child if she doesn't want. I know where to find out."

"Etta!"

All Dortborough was in her reproving voice. Vera was so scandalized she choked over her tea.

"Don't be so prudish, Vera! We're made as women, aren't we? Why should we be ashamed? I don't believe in 'Love' as it's handed out to us by our parents and library novels. It strikes me as a sham. Yet I do believe one might find a man . . . perhaps that might be worth more than anything else in life."

Vera, still coughing, made no reply, and soon after had to catch her train.

9

IF ETTA HAD her plans with regard to Mr. Drayton, so had he for her; and both sets came to maturity about the beginning of March. The blank monotony of her life had gone on, except for one most welcome diversion. Vera had written to Ada Lawson, and in consequence Etta received an invitation to supper every Sunday the Lawsons were in town. These evenings helped her to endure her life, and she enjoyed them the more since they were informal— the servants were away, and the guests helped themselves. It was pleasant to put on clean clothes, carefully ironed by herself, and her best dress; to go out feeling she looked nice, and to spend a few hours with people who could afford to take life easily and gracefully.

In spite of the air of determined confidence she had assumed to Vera, Etta found her heart thumping and her legs a bit wobbly when she finally tackled Mr. Drayton. She hated doing it, hated the fencing and bargaining, but drove herself ruthlessly. As she walked towards his office, she noticed a last gleam of March sunlight through the dingy windowpanes and found herself thinking of the crocuses in the gardens along the Muncaster Road. Mr. Drayton nodded in answer to her, "May I speak to you a moment, sir," and watched her as she made the little set speech she had rehearsed. He noticed her pallor and nervousness—obviously getting near the end of her tether. And if she got any thinner she'd begin to lose her looks. Etta wondered why he looked away and smiled in a curious manner.

"That's all very well, Miss Morison," he said, playing with a ruler. "You seem to forget that you had a rise less than three months ago."

"It was never adequate. I do more work and have more responsibility than any girl here, and I'm paid less than any of them. Is that fair?"

"You accepted the wage offered when you came, and you've had a rise before you were due for it. The firm has its rules and can't make exceptions. You can mention the matter again in the autumn."

Etta flinched a little at the cruelty of his voice, but kept her control. She played her next card.

"I don't remember your exact words, but you told me that if I learned Spanish I should be worth three pounds a week. I don't know Spanish, but I've learned enough commercial Spanish to read and answer letters!"

Mr. Drayton looked surprised; here was a donkey actually trying to grab the carrot. He handed her a letter in Spanish, which she read easily; then told her to write the reply, which was also easy to do since she had herself composed the answer he had signed.

"I see you've been working," he said. "Very commendable, very commendable indeed. But look here, we've already got a foreign correspondence clerk, and we don't need another. Are you suggesting that I sack Watson to give you his job?"

Etta was staggered. In all her planning she had over-looked this very simple fact. For a moment she felt frozen. But she managed to answer quite calmly.

"Not at all. I don't want to take anybody else's post from them—all I ask is that you should recognize I am efficient by giving me an adequate salary."

"I've already given you my answer to that."

The room seemed to waver, and Etta was surprised to hear her own voice saying deliberately:

"But you would not refuse to give me a reference honestly stating what efficiency I've reached?"

Drayton looked at her intently. Etta had such a feeling of defeat and humiliation and was so scared at having virtually given notice that she didn't realize he was not looking at her in his official way, but in the impudent manner she had resented so much at first. She expected him to tell her she could go; and to her astonishment he put on his genial, caressing voice.

"Look here, Miss Morison, it's getting late and I must be off. Come and have dinner with me tomorrow night at Frascati's and we'll talk the matter over. I'll think about it in the meanwhile and see what can be done. Meet me there at seven-thirty. Now I must be off. Good-evening."

It all happened so quickly, Etta had no time to protest or refuse. Before she had time to say a word, he had gone, leaving her acquiescing by her silence. Well, she needn't go if she didn't want. Yet, after all, why not? Why shouldn't she go out to dinner with her business employer? That was the business way of doing things—have a meal about it, put forth an ostentatious sprat to catch a shy whale. Though in this case it was a whale to catch a sprat. It seemed so ridiculous, she half persuaded herself that the proposal had never been made. If somebody had told her she had dreamed it, she would almost have believed, for what remained with her was the sense of ignominy and defeat—her work wasted, and the careful plan so easily thwarted. She felt exhausted and that she had made a fool of herself into the bargain.

She dreaded going to the office on Saturday morning, almost expecting Drayton to say to her harshly:

"What are you doing here? Didn't you dismiss yourself yesterday?"

But he did nothing of the sort. On the contrary, he was particularly amiable and smiling. Instead of piling work on her as usual, he lightened her tasks and sent her away early.

"Don't forget," he said, "Frascati's at seven-thirty."

She found Drayton waiting for her in the lobby, dressed in a dinner jacket. The neat black and white made his face look redder and showed up the grey hair at his temples. The bald patch on his head shone like a heliograph, and the black waistcoat bulged slightly. He greeted her effusively, and began to compliment her, not with any grace or subtlety, but yet not so fulsomely that she need actively resent it. Yet she always did resent this inane complimenting of men, which was really such an insult, treating women as if they were conceited fools easily subjected by a little insincere flattery. But why should Drayton take the trouble to flatter one of his underpaid clerks? Etta asked herself this as she was leaving her outer things in the cloakroom. She remembered again the sneer: "Have you been out with Mr. Drayton?" Perhaps this dinner invitation was a stroke of business, a method of staving off a demand for proper treatment. That must be it, she decided.

Drayton fussily escorted her to a reserved table in a cor-

ner, where they could look out on the other tables and
yet scarcely be seen through the palms and pots of little
shrubs. Etta found a bunch of red carnations on her plate
and put them quietly aside without looking at them or
smelling them.

"Don't you like your flowers?" Drayton asked reproachfully.

"They are beautiful," she said calmly, but did not touch
them.

The waiters brought a bottle of champagne in a frosted
ice bucket and served caviare. Etta took a little.

"Don't be afraid!" Drayton exclaimed. "There's plenty
more where that came from. Here, let me help you."

And he put a large spoonful on her plate.

"Thank you, but it will be wasted," said Etta impas-
sively, but she couldn't resist adding: "Recently I've
grown quite accustomed to doing without luxuries and
large meals."

Drayton ignored this and began talking about other
things, from time to time urging her to eat and making her
drink more of the wine than she wanted. He drank a good
deal himself. Etta listened almost in silence to his talk,
wondering what on earth he was getting at. He began by
talking about life in London—after all, whatever they
might say about Paris, London was the greatest city in
the world and had the most to offer. But even in London,
especially in London, you were quite impotent without
money. Take the shows, for instance: splendid shows in
London—he described a turn at the Tivoli, screamingly
funny—but after all, you couldn't get in without money.
What he meant to say was, you're impotent without
money. Take the restaurants, again—Frascati's was pretty
good, one of the best, in his opinion, good food and no silly
frills, but there were better ones, expensive, though.
Whether it was a question of going to Hurst Park for a bit

of a flutter or to Wimbledon for the tennis, buying a new
ribbon or taking a taxi, you'd simply got to have your hand
in your pocket. He realized Miss Morison had been decently brought up and was used to decent living and all
that, and an intelligent girl like her would see at once that
you're impotent without money.

Etta felt like saying, "Well, why don't you pay me a
decent wage, then?" but merely murmured a noncommittal
acquiescence. She wondered vaguely what one really does
want money for. But then most of her attention was concentrated on trying not to overeat and not to get drunk.
She was horrified by the gruesome collection of luxuries
he provided. Lobster à l'Armoricaine was followed by a
huge mixed grill, with which a bottle of Beaune was served,
and that by a bombe with a great deal of cream. Through
a slight muzziness she watched with fascinated disgust as
he ate solidly through heaped platefuls and swallowed large
mouthfuls of wine.

Meanwhile Drayton went on talking. He switched off
money onto himself, a subject he contrived to see in a
pathetic light. He'd married early, too early. A mistake.
And the wrong kind of woman. Another mistake. She had
no brilliance, no intelligence. Just wanted to sit about at
home night after night and darn the boys' stockings. He
was fed up with it. A lonely man, that's what he was, with
some of the best years of life before him, and nobody intelligent to share his interests and hobbies. Incredible as
it might seem, Mrs. Drayton had never been to the races
in her life, and on the one occasion when she went shooting
—two very important men on the Stock Exchange and
their wives—she'd made a hopeless fool of herself. Well,
he asked her. But then—a pathetic sight—there were the
kids. Can't let the kids down. They must have a home and
proper education, and damned expensive too nowadays.
But for the kids he'd have got out long ago. And there he

was, a lonely man, only asking for a little affection and someone with a bit of life in her, and could he get them? No. Girls nowadays were just hard and selfish, no real feeling in them at all. A lonely man, weighed down with responsibility, he often envied his employees their happy, care-free lives.

Coffee was served, and Drayton took a double brandy, insisting that Etta should have a crème-de-menthe. She said frankly that she hated it, but he seemed to think it was the right thing for her to have; so the little full green glass stood before her with the nearly full red glass and the half-empty yellow glass. Drayton was by now so intent on his discoursing that he hardly noticed she wasn't drinking. Etta watched him with absorbed frightened eyes, wondering whither all this rigmarole was tending, amazed by the spectacle of this gross creature posing as a sentimentalist. She wished her tummy didn't feel so full and her head so muzzy.

He switched back again to money, growing confidential and even more caressing. She wouldn't know it, but on the strict q. t. and she mustn't breathe a word, Thirlby & Co. were not doing so well as they had. German competition. Their line of export trade had been a good thing in the past, but it was going down. As a business woman herself, Etta would realize that in business you've got to look after Number One. And he didn't propose to go down with Thirlby. Time to get off that sinking ship. Metals. Metals were the thing. In his opinion things were blowing up in the direction of a war on the continent, and of course "we" should do the financing and supplies. It would be a splendid opportunity for business all round, and those who didn't do well out of it would be m.u.g.s. In any case the metal market was due for a rise, and even if there wasn't a war, which of course would be a godsend in its way, there'd be a rising demand for metals for industrial expansion.

At last he came to the point. He said he'd been surprised to see how well Etta cottoned on to business methods. Never in all his experience, which was pretty extensive, he might say, had he seen a girl get down to brass tacks so cleverly. He admired her gumption. And he didn't say that in any idle spirit of flattery. He meant it. And he also meant it when he said he'd honestly never known a prettier or a more ladylike girl. She could take it or leave it, but there you were, a man couldn't help his feelings, and he didn't mind admitting he was pretty far gone on her. That being so, he proposed to be fair and square, open and aboveboard, and see her through, if she was agreeable.

He suggested they go into partnership and see how it worked out. A nice little comfy flat in Maida Vale to begin with. He'd pay the rent and allow her seven pounds a week to run it. Admittedly, this wasn't much, but it was better to walk before you ran, and of course she'd get her money from Thirlby's, which might conceivably be knocked up to thirty bob or a couple of quid. Naturally, he couldn't be with her all the time, but there'd be week-ends and odd nights and plenty of evenings. And it stood to reason that he'd pay for all jollifications, such as the present little spread, which he flattered himself was quite a *recherché* little meal. Then, when he left Thirlby's, he'd take her along to organize his office, only a small affair at first, two or three clerks. Personally he was all in favour of women taking their place in the world and saw no earthly reason why in time she shouldn't come in on a few deals and make a good thing out of them. He could see her head was screwed on the right way, and he knew she could see which side her bread was buttered.

Well, there it was, and she'd only to say the word now,

or take a few days to think it over and come to terms. He was perfectly willing to meet her in any reasonable way, but thought she'd admit he'd put all his cards on the table. Perhaps she might think, being young and romantic, that he was putting business first and sentiment after. Nothing of the sort. He yielded to none in his appreciation of sentiment and was prepared to state that you couldn't get on without it. But as a man of the world he didn't believe in trying to get round a girl unless you were prepared to do the handsome thing, as he was. It was a unique opportunity for her, and looking at it from a business point of view alone, he thought she'd be a fool to let it slip. Into the bargain she'd have a decent straight clean Englishman to fill her life and show her what's what. And then, as he'd mentioned before, there was the matter of sentiment, which no doubt appealed to her as much as it did to him. Well, what about it?

For a long time Etta had listened to Drayton's voice in bewilderment. Such was her simplicity that she didn't guess his meaning until he arrived at the nice comfy little flat in Maida Vale. But at that point even a pure fathead could scarcely have failed to understand the nature of the proposal. What was to be done? Etta saw, or thought she saw, the situation quite clearly—this erotic fool had to be humoured, at least to the extent of getting rid of him quietly. But all efforts at trying to make plans to grapple with the situation were lost in the very uncomfortable feeling that she was going to be sick. In his anxiety to stimulate her senses Mr. Drayton had miscalculated the effect of his foods and drinks on a half-starved organism. True, "keeping her on short commons" (as he would have roguishly put it) was part of his game with Etta, but then, as he had never experienced it himself, he couldn't be expected to know what its effect would be on another.

He was therefore surprised and not a little hurt when she
said in reply to his last query:

"Do you mind if I go home? I'm not feeling very well."

"Not feel well?" Mr. Drayton was indignant. "Nonsense! You feel perfectly well. Trouble is you don't eat
enough to keep a sparrow alive. You girls are all alike nowadays, turning up your noses at good food and wasting
your money on frippery and gewgaws."

"I'm sorry, but I'm afraid I must go at once," said Etta
firmly. "I—I can't discuss anything now . . . next week
. . . good-bye."

She had an idea that she ought to say, "Thank you," but
what for? A vulgarly ostentatious dinner which had made
her feel sick? Or for his kind proposal to set her up as his
nice little whore? Thank you, Mr. Businessman. She
turned and walked away. In the cloakroom she felt so ill
she had to sit down, fighting against her nausea. The
woman attendant fussed round, irritating her by a sentimental assumption that Etta was enceinte. This intrusive
sympathy was the more annoying since it cost Etta sixpence she couldn't afford. Outside in the lobby she was
dismayed by finding Drayton. Under the bright electricity
he looked rubious and congested; and if Etta had been
more sophisticated she would have known at once that he
was pretty drunk. He had a taxi waiting and truculently
insisted on her getting in, stumbling over her legs as he
followed. She noticed that he was breathing heavily.

Before the taxi had gone fifty yards his truculent mood
suddenly evaporated, and he went all amorous and sentimental. Muttering something about "You be nice to me,
and I'll look after you," Mr. Drayton put an arm round her
waist and tried to kiss her. She tried to push him away,
but a swerve of the cab threw all his weight on her, and at
the same time he tried to force her knees apart. Etta was
frightened and revolted, yet half paralyzed by a queer

sensation of inertia, as if something in her wanted to submit to this violence. In her panic she hit Drayton in the face with the handle of her umbrella, rapped madly on the front window, and as the taxi-driver abruptly drew up she jumped from the moving vehicle, fell on one knee in the mud, and then, recovering, ran frantically through the Saturday night crowd.

Her hat was awry, her hair coming down, her skirt torn and muddy. People stared in surprise at her white terrified face, but in her panic she scarcely noticed them, obsessed with one thought—to get away from Drayton. She was convinced he was following her, and that if he caught her she would never be able to get free from him. She turned up a side street and ran, still clutching her umbrella, then turned again and, still running, came to a large empty square with a railed-off garden in the centre. Trembling all over, she clutched at the railings, feeling she was going to faint. Then she was violently sick.

When she recovered, she was icy cold and still trembling. Something made her knee smart badly. Another panic swept over her as she imagined herself being arrested for drunkenness in the street, and she began walking again as fast as her shaking legs allowed. Presently she came to a street she knew, and in a few minutes was in front of her own door. Etta felt infinitely thankful that she had a latchkey—how on earth could she have faced Gertrude or Miss Millingham in that state? As she silently closed the outer door, she noticed a ray of light under Miss Millingham's door and heard a murmur of voices—one of the distinguished parties, obviously. Etta tiptoed upstairs in the darkness, and felt safe only when she had shut and locked her own door.

With shaking hands Etta drew her curtain and lighted the gas and then turned to look at herself in the mirror. A horrible feeling of ignominy and shame flooded over her as she gazed at herself. That scared-looking, dishevelled, pale, trembling creature was the girl who had rejected Dortborough as not good enough, the girl who was going to live on her own and show what a woman could make of life. Crumpled up in helpless panic. She turned away in disgust. With the distress of the very poor, she realized that she had lost one of her only pair of gloves, that her skirt and petticoat were badly torn. She began to undress, and then noticed that her left knee was bruised and cut. Rather savagely she washed the wound in cold water, punishing herself by treating it roughly. She bound it up with a clean handkerchief, put on her nightdress, turned out the light, and lay in bed, miserable, shivering, and bitterly ashamed.

10

WAKING UP IN THE MORNING after one of the numerous little Waterloos which occur in most lives is never very pleasant. It wasn't at all pleasant for Etta to wake on the Sunday morning after her *sauve-qui-peut* flight from the enterprising Mr. Drayton. She lay quite still under the bed-clothes in her drab, chilly little room, facing the situation, admitting she had been a failure, and rather a squalid one. She had failed utterly to realize what Drayton was planning, and on the very first occasion when she came up against the predatory male she made a fool of herself. All her work and energy and privations were wasted. She had dismissed herself from her job, and in such a way that she couldn't even decently ask for a reference, so that after several months of effort which had almost exhausted her, she was exactly at the point where she had started, except that she had lost strength and hope.

Blowing her nose miserably, Etta pondered over the social structure as it had been revealed to her during this short period "on her own," and wondered what place it had for her and why on earth she wanted one. It struck her that the universe of men, which was supposed to be so godlike and interesting, was distinctly less majestic and orderly than the stellar universe to which she had heard it likened. There was the grand galaxy of business, a Milky Way of Thirlbys and Draytons of various magnitudes, with their clusters of overworked and underpaid staffs. There were the "youth" satellites of South Kensington, children of various brands of Thirlby and Drayton, who could afford to play at the artistic life. There were Miss Millingham's distinguished guests, dreary little erratic comets somehow managing to describe parabolas on the fringe of the galaxy. And, of course, there were the splendidly decorative stars who clustered in Mrs. Lawson's drawing room. But what on earth it was all for and what sense there might be in this complicated and peculiar mess, Etta couldn't imagine. Dropping her stellar metaphors, she remembered she had told Vera that life was a dogfight. Well, it was. And she had come out of the first round scratched, bitten, and beaten.

She got up and began preparing her frugal breakfast, still cogitating. What was to be done? There was no use yelping like a wretched little bitch after the bone which had been snatched away from her. *Soyons réaliste*. In her position, it was obviously ridiculous to waste energy in criticizing the social structure. She had to accept it as it was. Building Utopias was a hobby for people with leisure, or a safety valve for the discontented. She had to earn a living. Etta smiled as she remembered how confidently she had informed Vera that one had to be hard to the hard things of life, and soft to the beautiful things. She hadn't been very successful in applying that maxim to realities. Stirring her porridge abstractedly, Etta decided that it was useless to go on answering advertisements—it would be Drayton and slavery all over again. There were only two possible lines—appeal to the Lawsons or go home. If the Lawsons failed, home or starvation.

She cleared away the breakfast, washed up, then cleaned and mended her petticoat and brushed the mud off her torn skirt. Then she sat down and wrote a short letter to her parents, not telling them anything about herself, but writing in a neutral-friendly sort of way. It went horribly against the grain, but what else was there to do? At eleven she went to the public telephone box at Russell Square Station, rang up Mrs. Lawson, and got permission to go and talk to her an hour in private. She then took a long walk through the park and Kensington Gardens, and pondered over the nature of things for a long time in the Dutch sunken garden near the palace.

Ada Lawson received Etta in a room which looked like a boudoir in a small library. The bookshelves were filled with books, mostly French expensively bound in leather. There was a large writing table, with a confusion of opened letters, where Mrs. Lawson had been writing.

"You wanted to discuss something with me?" Ada Lawson asked. "Tell me what it is. You look worn out. Have you been overworking?"

Etta paused. She had been rehearsing this scene most of the day and had determined to be cool and unemotional but entirely frank. Quietly, as if she were talking about somebody else, she began to relate her life during the past six months. Ada Lawson listened but did not interrupt except for an occasional question and exclamation. Etta felt rather proud of her self-control, but when she came to the scenes of the night before and remembered her own distress and humiliation, she found her voice and lips quivering and nervously bit her handkerchief to keep back her tears. Ada Lawson walked angrily up and down the room.

"What an appalling brute!" she exclaimed. "He ought to be punished. He *shall* be. Tomorrow I'll go with you to my lawyer. We'll make a public example of him. It's disgraceful that women should be exploited and insulted by such blackguards."

"Please don't do that!" Etta implored. "Remember, I have no witnesses, so he could easily deny it all. Even if he admitted it, I don't think he has done anything for which he could be punished by law. And then think what a ridiculous and ignominious figure I should be if this were made public—the half-raped girl. Think of me pilloried in the witness box by some unscrupulous lawyer in that atmosphere of legal cynicism and lechery. Think of me served up at every Sunday breakfast table in England as the victim of a criminal assault in a taxi. No, no! If you don't want to make me a figure of disgusting ignominy, you mustn't go to a lawyer, you mustn't ever speak of it to anybody."

"But you have been shamefully treated!" exclaimed Ada Lawson. "This man takes you into his office, underpays and overworks you, with the deliberate intention of bringing you to such a state that you will be almost compelled to accept his—his abominable lust, and you can do nothing about it! Is there no justice?"

"Not from the law and law courts. Besides, I blame myself. There was ignorance on my part, but also conceit. I ought to have guessed what he was thinking, and I should have known that in an office of that kind no utterly inexperienced clerk would have been given my job unless there was something behind it. If I hadn't been blind, I should have understood what the other girls were hinting at. But I was so determined to get on and so confident of my ability, I thought I could prove to any employer that I was worth a decent salary. Curiously enough, I succeeded. But it didn't help me. Being a business man, Mr. Drayton merely altered his plans so that he could make use of my mind as well as my body."

"All business men are not like that," said Ada Lawson quickly. "My husband is a business man, entirely scrupulous and honourable."

"I beg your pardon," said Etta humbly. "I know there must be exceptions. Perhaps Drayton is the exception. I only speak of the business man as I've observed him. In any case, I can see it from his point of view too. In his way he meant to be generous, and was."

"He was unspeakably mean!"

"Not from the point of view of that sort of man. Why, he even vaguely promised that I should 'come in on a few deals.' From his point of view, could he offer more? And don't let me get your sympathy on false pretenses, Mrs. Lawson. It wasn't his proposal that I should live with him without being married which shocked and frightened me. It was because he is utterly repulsive to me physically, and because I despise his character and his whole conception of life—he represents the very thing I want to get away from. If he had been the kind of man I could respect, I might have accepted. And if he had been the kind of man who could make me fall in love with him, I think I should have accepted with gratitude."

Ada Lawson sat down and looked at her thoughtfully.

"I understand you," she said. "And of course there are plenty of girls now who would agree with you. But don't you think you are all of you taking great risks if you enter on these unlegalized unions?"

"Of course we are," said Etta confidently. "And we must be prepared for them. But are there no unhappy and disastrous marriages? And if the woman's movement means anything, we ought to refuse to marry as things are now. For women marriage mostly means slavery."

"Not necessarily," said Ada Lawson, thinking of herself.

"But I see why you want to avoid any legal action about
this outrage, and I promise not to speak of it to anyone.
Since that's out of the question, what do you want me to
do?"

"This," said Etta, trying to be precise and businesslike
and feeling how bitterly hard it is to have to ask favours.
"I've told you the truth about myself and my adventures
in trying to earn my living. I've only got enough money
to last me for a very few weeks, and when that's gone I
shall have to go meekly home and confess myself defeated
and live a home parasite the rest of my life, unless in the
next fortnight or so I can get a job with decent people
who'll pay me a decent wage."

"What do you consider a 'decent wage'?"

"Two pounds a week. I can live on that and buy myself
clothes, so that I don't look like a frump or a beggar. When
I first came to London I spent more than was necessary,
because I was ignorant. . . . There must be many firms
where they are not Draytons. Mr. Lawson must know
them. Would he recommend me? I can't give a reference:
you know why. But I'm willing to work a trial month for a
pound a week anywhere decent, if they'll promise me a
proper wage when I prove myself competent, which I
know I can do. That is what I ask."

Etta drew a deep breath and felt the blood flushing in
her cheeks. She wondered if she would ever grow hard
enough to be able to ask for things without feeling abashed
and miserable. She glanced imploringly at Ada Lawson,
who gazed silently at the fire, smoking a cigarette. Etta
misinterpreted the silence, and told herself she had merely
wasted her time in making this appeal—as if a rich woman
could ever really sympathize with a pauper!

"It isn't easy," Ada Lawson's voice startled her by its
suddenness. "And I don't want to promise what I can't
fulfil. I know several people who have private secretaries,

but they invariably employ men. I'll talk it over with my husband and then write to you."

"Thank you," said Etta tonelessly, taking this as a polite put-off. She got up to leave.

"Don't despair," said Ada Lawson kindly. "I promise you I'll do my best. But I can't carry out what I have in mind until I've discussed it with my husband. Won't you stay and have supper?"

Etta hesitated. She wanted very much to stay, but she had the poor person's dread of being importunate, and in her present mood she couldn't face talking to people.

"Thank you very much, but—I was upset last night and didn't sleep well. I think I shall go straight back to bed."

"Very well. And cheer up. I'll write to you early in the week, and I hope I shall have good news for you."

Etta thanked her again and then walked back to her room, very close to despair, so close that she found herself wondering whether throwing oneself in the Thames would be a very cold and horrible death.

Nor did this mood of despair evaporate; on the contrary, it was intensified. Again and again Etta pondered the chess board of her life, and each time she was forced to admit that the position was hopeless, that she was defeated.

In an agony of self-depreciation she turned and rent herself. What a fool, what a pompous, ignorant fool! What a romantic idiot! Looked at dispassionately, what was Etta? The daughter of a provincial accountant and his wife, with no traditions but those of respectability and getting on, no grace, energy, or passion of living, no aspirations beyond gross comfort—an existence as platitudinous as the Muncaster Road, at once the creation and the symbol of them and their like. However much she might revolt

against all this, was it possible to deny that she was their
creation, that their environment had marked her forever?
Made in their image, could she escape their fate?

She remembered what Ada Lawson had said to her at
their first meeting—that almost everybody must be content to live in a routine, because in no other way could the
human world continue. Everybody couldn't be a pioneer.
Granted her make-up, what she came from, and what she
was, it was surely the mere female romantic folly men
laughed at, to suppose that she could make an interesting
and valuable life—show people an example of the modern
woman creating a career.

Unwilling to let Miss Millingham know she had lost her
job, Etta got up and left the house at the usual time and
wandered about the streets and parks, lacerating herself
fiercely with scornful self-reproaches. She sat on benches
in the Green Park, hardly noticing the clusters of crocuses,
equally indifferent to the people passing and to the exotic-
looking birds on the artificial lake, lost in a dismal introspection. It was cold in the east wind under the dull sky,
and tired as she was, she had to go on walking to keep
herself from shivering with cold.

Once, as she got up to move, she passed a shabbily
dressed woman pushing an old shabby mail cart with a
baby in it and dragging by the hand a shabbily dressed
little girl. The woman was hurrying, and the child whim-
pered and protested, but the mother only jerked its arm
and scolded; and Etta noticed that the woman's face was
a squalid mask of anxiety. In a second they had gone by,
and Etta could not bear to turn and look after them,
though she could hear the child wailing as it was dragged
along.

Etta used even that to torment and reproach herself,
thinking of the millions of women who tried to rear families
on no more than the wretched pittance she had found so

inadequate, women who had no middle-class fathers and brothers on whom they could fall back when the world was too hard for them. What a poor tool was Etta Morison! A very few months of work and hardship, comparative only, had made her a despairing wreck, ready to run home whimpering to beg for the protection she had despised. And she was one of the fortunate few, for her childhood had at least been fed, clothed and carefully protected. But these others—undernourished and ill-trained, slaves mocked by the illusion of freedom, slaves being everywhere ousted by machines from the little they had, spending all their days in labour with no hope of emancipation, or subsisting on the bitter mercies of public charity. . . . What cruel imbecile of a god had brought them into being? What delusive instinct kept them from mass suicide? And yet they went on breeding; and yet comfortably housed criminals exulted over the high population of England and wrote pompous letters to the newspapers deploring a mere percentage decline in the birth rate. An inner voice mocked her—one must be hard to the hard things of life: be hard, for you cannot afford to be pitiful.

By midday on Tuesday, Etta was exhausted by these dismal emotions and by continuously walking about in the cold. As she dragged herself back to make her meagre lunch, she decided that she must stay in and rest that afternoon, whatever Miss Millingham might think. What did it matter, anyhow? The true situation wasn't altered whether Miss Millingham knew or not. In any case, life "on her own" would come to an end in a few days or weeks and what Miss Millingham thought or knew would have no more influence on Etta's life than the habits of infusoria.

Three letters for her lay on the marble-topped table. She looked at the envelopes as she went upstairs; one was from Teddy, one from her mother, and one from Ada Law-

son. Etta tore open her mother's. It was exactly what she
had expected. The letter was garrulous, offensive, and in-
exact; it drew a would-be pathetic picture of the poor old
folks at home brooding over a desolated hearth, and con-
trasted this with Etta living in luxury in London and ca-
reering about in contempt of her parents' broken hearts.
The only thing for Etta to do was to come home at once
and care for her poor father (by toasting muffins?), for he
was visibly declining owing to her cruelty.

Etta laid the letter down with a sigh; it was only too
vivid a reminder of what she would have to return to and
endure for a good many years. She perceived very clearly
that the chief result of her bid for freedom would be to
provide her mother with an inexhaustible theme for dis-
paraging remarks and a knock-down argument against
anything. She opened Ada's letter and read:

On Sunday I failed to tell you how much I admire your
courageous efforts at independence and how sorry I am that
you should have been treated so vilely. You have made me
feel I must redouble my efforts to bring about a better state
of things for women. After you had gone I couldn't help crying as I thought of what you have to suffer.

Sympathy is not much use without practical help. I talked
about you with my husband—of course, keeping your secret
—and for various reasons he is against offering you a post
in his own office. One reason is that if you were there I couldn't
ask you here as a friend without causing all sorts of jealousies
and complications. However, he will make inquiries, and may
find you a post where you will have a chance, and where in
any case you will be free from the odious persecution you
endured from that creature.

Meanwhile, if you care to accept, I can pay you two pounds
a week to act as my secretary, and you can live with us, here
and at Dymcott. I haven't invented this merely to help you.
For some time now I've wanted a secretary, and since Edith
is at school and no longer has a governess, I think I may

afford it. I should want you to deal with some of my social correspondence and engagements, various charities, and all W. S. P. U. work. This will give me time to do some writing (you can help me here too), and I shall have more time for speaking. So you will be indirectly helping on the cause we both have at heart.

I know there is no future for you in this sort of work, and I only suggest it as a temporary arrangement. As soon as my husband finds you something better, you will be free to leave. But it seems a way of tiding you over a difficult period. No doubt you would like a few days to think this over, but perhaps you could let me know by Saturday, and if you accept, you could come to us on Monday.

Yours sincerely,
ADA LAWSON.

P.S.—Of course, you will live with us as a friend.

Holding the letter in her hand, Etta went over to the window and looked out. Spring had not softened the grimy desolation of the prison cell "gardens"; there was still not a leaf on the sooty trees, not a flower in the acrid soil, although here and there weeds and sickly grass were heroically struggling against a hopeless destiny. A dirty white cat sneaked in a predatory way after sparrows along one of the walls. Etta looked at her room, the truckle bed, the worn linoleum, the little armchair with the stuffing coming out, the ugly red gas meter. "No doubt you would like a few days to think this over!" She laughed—how little the fortunate few know of the lives of the many. Think over what? The chance to exchange squalor for elegance, solitude for cultivated friends, semi-starvation for luxury, hard work ill-paid for easy work, a hunted despair for hope?

She read the letter over and over again to make sure it was true. Again she looked round at her miserable room, and her eyes filled with tears. Be soft to the beautiful things. She had not felt so deeply moved since she had listened to Beethoven with Vera. But instead of the passionate upheaval of emotion she had felt at that impersonal tragic experience, she felt only a quiet thankfulness. Through Ada Lawson the gods had given her a chance, and standing at the window between the squalid room and its squalid outlook, she promised herself she would not be ungrateful.

To answer Ada Lawson's letter was more difficult than she had thought. She began letter after letter and tore them up—some seemed so hopelessly inadequate, others hysterically exaggerated. At last she contented herself by writing a short note of acceptance, adding:

> I find I have no words to thank you for what you are doing for me. I can only say that your offer seems to give me back life and hope; and I can only prove my gratitude by action. I shall never forget that you have saved me.

It seemed a poor acknowledgment, but Etta feared that if she said more she would say too much and merely embarrass. To make up for this reticence, she poured herself out in long letters to Vera and Teddy. Afterwards she added long postscripts warning them ferociously not to dare to mention what she was doing to her parents. Even this seemed dangerous. Suppose either of them did let it out, and her mother sent some dreadful insult to Ada Lawson? She deliberately tore up the letters and wrote again, leaving everything vague. She was beginning to learn.

That night Etta slept with Ada Lawson's letter under her pillow, and twice in the night woke up and lighted the gas to read it—she wanted to be quite sure that the peace and hope which had come to her were not a delusion.

PART II

THE SPRING SEEMED to come suddenly into flower.

In her bedroom at Knightsbridge Etta was awakened at dawn by sparrows twittering and fighting on her window ledge. From a distance came the shrill fine notes of blackbirds singing in the park shrubberies. Then she fell asleep until the maid brought morning tea and drew the chintz curtains. Even when it wasn't sunny, Etta couldn't stay in bed, she had to make sure it was real—the garden with its thick clusters of daffodils and jonquils, the tall privet hedge, the screen of budding trees which muted down the noise of traffic, and through which she could see the park lawns bright in the sun or hazy in rain. Ada Lawson filled the rooms with bowls of freesia, hyacinths, tulips, and long sprays of yellow mimosa and early lilac; so that the whole house was scented, but kept fresh with open windows. Etta was allowed fresh flowers in her workroom and bedroom.

Her own life seemed to come into flower too. During the weeks at Thirlby's, numerically not so many, but in the living of them so long and hopeless, Etta had sometimes felt that life would never be essentially different for her— always a squirrel's cage routine of daily working to live to work to live to work forever. But life went on and was entirely different, so changed that when Etta went out she was surprised to find the same streets and shops and house fronts, the same policemen and buses. It seemed incredible that she could be living in the same world, the same town, not a mile from Miss Millingham and not many days removed from Drayton.

The work was slight, and after the first few days very easy—so easy that Etta felt scruples about taking so much for doing so little. With the aid of a filing cabinet Etta introduced order into Ada Lawson's chaotic arrears of correspondence; after which everything went quickly and smoothly. Ada Lawson was pleased, and surprised at the alteration in her own life. Instead of passing her days in an anxious frenzy over neglected letters and lectures put off until the last moment, appointments forgotten for which she had to apologize endlessly, and social engagements seldom enjoyed because she ought to have been doing something else, Ada Lawson found she had plenty of time.

Every morning the maid brought her the list of her day's appointments which Etta had typed out the night before; and if she lost it, Etta had a duplicate. When she came to Etta's workroom a little before lunch, she found the replies to her morning letters ready for her signature. She was made to dictate lectures and articles in plenty of time and found them immediately typed in duplicate. When she couldn't remember what a letter referred to, which was pretty often, Etta could prompt her or could turn up the filed reference immediately.

Etta couldn't help smiling at Ada Lawson's repeated exclamations of wonder at the ease with which everything

was now organized. After the grinding work and the rush
and complication of a busy office, it was all so easy. And
such a blessed, blessed change to peace and good-nature
and friendliness and courtesy that Etta felt she could go
on her knees to Ada every day to thank her.

One morning, about a fortnight after she had come to
the Lawsons, Etta had finished her morning's work before
eleven and was looking through the shelves of French
novels for something to read until Ada Lawson came to
sign the letters. She rejected Balzac. He was far too close
to the bitter realities of daily life, which she wanted to forget. She wanted somebody like Shelley, who would take
her out of the ordinary world into a world of beauty which
would yet seem convincingly real. It wasn't easy to find, a
bit on the impossible side in fact—rather like hoping for a
midsummer night's dream in Pimlico. She was still hesitating when Ada Lawson came in.

"I'm not disturbing you?"

"Not in the least," said Etta, feeling guilty at being discovered idling. "The letters are ready for you. Is there
anything else you would like me to do?"

"Already! How quick you are! No, there's nothing else.
I only wanted to speak to you."

Ada hesitated and looked embarrassed. Etta felt her
heart stand still and then start pumping with fright. She
gazed at Ada with terrified eyes. She was certain she was
going to be dismissed.

"You don't find this work too much for you?" Mrs.
Lawson asked abruptly.

So that was the line she was going to take. Etta determined to fight hard not to be sent away. She laughed and
tried to make her laugh sound happy, in spite of her apprehension.

"Too much! Why, of course not. It's very easy. If you

would like me to help with the house or anything . . ."

"Oh, I wasn't suggesting that. How sensitive you are! I was afraid you might be overworking and that you have no time to yourself or to go out."

"But I have plenty of time, more than I need, and I go out nearly every afternoon! I would gladly do far more, if you wanted."

"We seem to be at cross purposes," said Ada, laughing.

"You think you are not doing enough, and I think you may be doing too much. I am more than grateful to you, my dear, for the way you have organized my very disorderly life. I actually have time to do everything, and I haven't had to apologize to anybody all this week. I was thinking about it last night, and feeling I ought to pay you more."

"Pay me more!" exclaimed Etta. "Why, if you let me live here and gave me five shillings a week pocket money, I should be entirely contented. If you knew—but you can't know, you think the life here is everyday and commonplace. You think you know that other people live differently, but unless you have been forced to live in it, you can't know the monotony, the dullness, the stupid cruelty of the world from which you saved me. You can't know the loneliness and emptiness of all one's life that isn't distasteful work. You can't know how every instinct and aspiration and hope are checked and blasted all the time. It isn't only or even chiefly the material comfort, though God knows I'm grateful for that. You use money, even if you're extravagant with it. You're not just trying to get richer and richer at other people's expense; you don't bully and starve people to get the last farthing out of them; you don't respect some damnable scoundrel because he is unwholesomely rich. You haven't a horrible attitude that to be able to spend money lavishly, no matter how vulgarly and destructively, is the summit and apex of human achievement. You make life gracious and vivid and intelligent."

"You mustn't flatter me like that, you'll make me vain," said Ada, trying to smile at Etta's intensity.

"Flatter you! It's less than the truth," Etta retorted, too excited and *émotionnée* to check or watch her words. "You've never made me shed tears of humiliation or exhaustion or utter misery. You've never made me feel I want to kill myself. If I've cried here, it was from relief and gratitude. Nothing would be too much to do for you. So don't speak of paying me more. I am overpaid if you are satisfied!"

Ada took Etta's hands, saying:

"There! Since you feel like that, I won't speak of payment. There are things which cannot be paid for. Remember, though, if you need more money, you mustn't hesitate to ask for it."

"I have all I need."

Ada kissed her forehead and then released her hands.

"I wish you hadn't had to suffer so much. And yet perhaps . . . It's easy to feel that other people's sufferings are inevitable and the price for what we are all forced to learn. You must forget them, and not let them make you bitter."

"No," said Etta decisively. "I must remember them. I mustn't forget that others are suffering many worse things than the little things I found so painful. And it isn't bitter to know and tell the truth. It isn't bitter to love what's good in the world and in people, and to hate cruelty and bullying and grossness."

"That's true enough, but I wasn't thinking of it in that way. You know there is a deal of bitterness in our movement, and though I know it's more than justified, I think it a mistake and a pity. Men may have wronged all women, but mere resentment is useless and self-maiming. There are nice men as well as nasty ones. Don't get to hating all men just because they *are* men."

"I don't think about then," said Etta smiling. "I'm too much interested in my own life. But you'll admit that Mr. Drayton was no recommendation to his species."

"Oh, well," said Ada, falling back on the inevitable *cliché*, "it takes all sorts to make a world."

"Yes, but how much nicer the world if some sorts could be gently eliminated!"

It was quite true, as Etta had said, that in her life at the Lawsons' she valued other things far more than the mere well-being. She spent very little from her wages except to get the clothes she thought necessary so that they wouldn't be ashamed of her. Except when they entertained, the Lawsons lived simply, more simply but more fastidiously than her own family. What Etta valued, or thought she valued, was the opportunity to reshape her own life. She was encouraged to use the piano which stood in the tranquil music room; she had the run of all the books; her presence at all dinners was taken for granted. When the Lawsons were dining or lunching out, she was allowed to ask her own friends to meals. Ada Lawson took Etta to concerts and theatres and let her have tickets she couldn't use herself. She introduced Etta to people, always speaking of her with high praise, and among them Etta made friends.

All this Etta found exciting and delightful; she responded to it like a young tree to rain and spring sunlight. Now life seemed springing up in her. The pallor and harried look left her face. She found herself singing quietly and gaily as she dressed. Sometimes her conscience grew a little frightened at this tranquil happiness. How long would it last? How would she feel when Mr. Lawson discovered that new office job? Could she ever endure to

work in an office again? And then more insidious whisper-
ings—wasn't all this pleasant life based eventually on the
sufferings of others, wasn't she as much a parasite, in spite
of her nominal work, on the Lawsons as she would have
been on her family if she had remained at home? Sometimes at a dance among the scent of flowers, the music
and light, the chatter and laughter, the voice of her partner
making pretty compliments; or at a concert room after
music had moved her; or even when she was reading, she
would think of the people at Miss Millingham's, the clerks
at Thirlby's, the woman she had seen in the Park. And
she felt guilty, as if her happiness were stolen. She invented
answers, defended herself to herself; and as the full, pleasant days passed, these visitings of conscience grew rarer
and almost ceased. Etta had managed to snatch her bone
from the dogfight.

Oddly enough, her conscience didn't register the change
in herself. Etta had fled from Dortborough on instinct,
a passionate dislike for its ugliness and smug nothingness,
and a passionate delusion that somehow, by living differently, she could do something about it. Now she fought
for her own hand. Without perceiving it, she had become
a little ruthless, more than a little calculating and wary.
She thought her eagerness to please Ada Lawson came
from gratitude and devotion; and so it did, but there was
a grain of calculation—Etta wanted so much not to be
sent away, and what better means of avoiding it than
making herself indispensable? Long before, she had determined to meet people and be friendly with them; but now
she selected, unconsciously trying to please those who
might be useful to her. It was the same in everything.
Even the ardour she put into music and reading—never
missing a moment—was not the result solely of pure
enjoyment; she was getting everything she could.

The parsimony so implacably forced on her during those

miserable months became a habit. She was terrified of spending money on herself; and this made her ungenerous to others. If Ada offered her the use of the car for her own purposes, Etta always refused—it might mean tipping. She opened a post-office savings account, and every week paid in thirty shillings, keeping the rest sacred to clothes. She tended to brood over these little savings, watched them slowly grow with almost morbid pleasure, calculated what they might become in a month, in two months, in six months. It was almost miserly. Yet if anyone had suggested to her that she was becoming mean, she would have been shocked and indignant.

Each small saving was another tiny raising of the defense against being pushed back into the Thirlby-Drayton world. When Ada Lawson sent Etta on some fairly distant errand, she invariably gave her a taxi fare. At first, Etta tried to refuse; then accepted silently, went by bus or tube, and saved the balance. She did feel guilty about this, but sometimes in a week it gave her six or eight more shillings' protection against Thirlby-Drayton. She sent no pocket-money to Teddy—not that she grudged it, oh no, but she was certain he would only waste it. And there was Vera, who had been so staunch a friend, to whom she owed that Beethoven afternoon which had saved her from despair. Well, Vera sometimes came to London, and Etta always put everything else aside to be with her. Usually, Etta managed to have theatre tickets given her, but Vera invariably paid for buses and meals. Etta protested and argued but always yielded. After all, Vera had a private income, Vera was only too glad to pay. *She* hadn't been forced to work for Thirlby's and had to live in Miss Millingham's boxroom on bread and margarine. . . .

And she was wary with people, not especially with men **any** more than women, but just wary. Without knowing it she mistrusted people and reserved herself; she watched them and played up to them. The one person among all Ada's guests whom she disliked so much that she couldn't be nice to her was the Duchess of Crewkerne. Etta couldn't imagine why, but she detested the old woman with her raddled face and commanding manner and inevitable escort of young men.

In the Lawson household there was no need for wariness, though Etta was always careful to have an imaginary personal appointment when she knew some particularly important dinner or luncheon was arranged. Except at meals and gatherings, she saw little of Ada's husband, and still less of her son Robert.

Etta liked Mr. Lawson. He looked more like a country gentleman than a business man, although he had the bald patch on his head Etta had come to associate with all successful Business. Do they scratch the hair off their own heads in perplexed calculations, Etta wondered, or do they scratch it off each other in frenzies of defeated cupidity? Mr. Lawson, it is true, seemed remote from frenzy. He emanated grave dignity which seemed to have no particular foundation except that he did everything very slowly. His movements were slow, his voice was slow, and to Etta's rather swift mind his mental processes seemed uncommonly slow. He spoke rarely at meals, but when he did it was almost more tedious than listening to Henry James. Apart from business and a little mild killing of small animals to prove he was a Man and a Gentleman, he seemed to have no interests but his son and wife. In his slow, entirely inarticulate way he was passionately devoted to his wife. Whatever she said or did seemed to be right. Sometimes Etta imagined that his whole life was passed in a dream of amazement that a woman so admirable as Ada had consented to marry him.

Robert Lawson was unlike either of his parents. He

had a pale long face, with hard eyes, a thin disdainful nose, and narrow, tight mouth. His manner to Etta was almost pure insolence; and at every moment he let her feel that he thought her an inferior and knew her to be a dependent. He was at Sandhurst, and wanted his father to give up business even though it meant giving up the town house and living in the country—it was a handicap in good society, Robert thought, to have active trade in the family. Yet both his parents were devoted to him and appeared not to notice his faults. Etta was very careful to conceal her dislike for Robert and never to resent his insolence. So far as she was concerned everything changed for the worse when he came into the house. Mr. Lawson was indifferent and slower than ever, Ada offhand, a little distant, always in a slight flutter about what would please Robert.

2

ETTA HAD JUST FINISHED dressing for dinner and stood gazing from her window as she absently pinned on some flowers Ada had given her. It was pleasant to linger, looking out over the park with a clear green-blue afterglow beyond the pattern of tree boughs and young leaves, and the thrushes and blackbirds calling over the rumble of traffic. The evening rush was almost over. Etta noticed that a few people still kept the old two-horse landaus, looking already lost and out of place among the high-built taxis and the electric broughams. A queer new world— where there would be no horse or horse traffic.

At that moment a man came through the French window into the garden. Robert! From that height she couldn't see his face—only the hair and the foreshortened body with jerkily moving legs attached. But it must be Robert. How annoying! Her contentment disappeared. Now, instead of a quiet, easy dinner, there would be constraint, and she would have to sit mute and despised like a nursery governess in a snobby house. How beastly! Curious and rather degrading these survivals of primitive murderousness, which made some people hate you and want to crush you out as far as they dare, while you had to hate them too. Impossible to pretend another engagement now. One thing was certain: she couldn't afford to have any kind of quarrel with Robert.

Going downstairs, Etta wondered if she ought to take off her flowers—they might give him an opportunity to make one of those frigidly contemptuous remarks she resented so much. But no, that was being over-fussy. She went into the drawing room as quietly as possible, almost apologetically. Robert was there all right, she could see his back; but for a moment everything else vanished as she found herself looking across the room into the eyes of Ralph Lawson. It was no more than a glance, and yet quite decisive. Etta made no pause in her movements, no slightest gesture, no dramatic start; but there was a deep surge of her blood, a sudden tremor at her womb, and her legs seemed strengthless. She heard Ada say:

"Here she comes."

And at the same moment of time Etta was pierced by the meaning of the glance, knew she had fallen in love with Ralph, that she must unconsciously have been in love with him from her first meeting, realized why she disliked Robert and the old duchess, and knew or almost knew that Ralph was in love with her.

It was a moment of pure intrinsic happiness, but also of disintegrating embarrassment. Of all the people in the world, the three present were those whom she least wanted to guess what had happened. Fortunately, only Ralph had seen her entrance, only he had noticed the swiftly passing look in her eyes. But it was the most terrifying test in social dissimulation she had ever endured; and she met it perfectly. She accepted Robert's limp cold hand-shake and met his contemptuous aloofness with a light, unconcerned smile. Ralph, disappointed, felt no response to the warm pressure of his own hand. She made no answer to his boyishly overeager: "I *am* glad to see you again," though all her body wanted to whisper, "And I too, my dear, I too." Then she sat as far from Ralph as possible, and in a position where he could not see her face. All this she did with a surface consciousness which left no record in her; she remembered nothing he had said or done between the moment of entrance and the moment when she gradually reëstablished self-dominion as she sat silent in her chair—nothing except the touch of Ralph's hand and the fact that she had dared neither to look at him nor to answer him.

As the blood slowly sank back from her hot cheeks and the almost unbearable heartbeats faded to normal, Etta's one thought was that she must have betrayed her-self abjectly, that all of them must have seen. She heard Robert's voice saying spitefully:

"I think you must be getting very lazy, Mother, or is it now the fashion to have someone to send out invitations to tea?"

"Not at all," Ada answered in her brisk voice. "I'm much more occupied than you know, Robert. I should be lost without Etta, who rescued me from dreadful con-fusion. She's cured me of my bad habits, or rather makes her efficiency seem mine."

"Oh, if it's a new whim of yours . . ."

And he dismissed the subject with a contemptuous tightening of his thin nostrils, as if it were not worth dis-cussing. Etta received and winced at the wound of his unkind intention, although Ada had been swift to shield

her. She felt very much outside this family circle, altogether in a false position, and could only respond feebly
to Ada's well-meant openings for her to enter the general
conversation. Etta longed for the moment when she could
be alone to think over this perilous revolution within
herself and decide how to quell it.

As they went down to dinner Ralph said to her:

"You're very distant. Aren't you at all pleased to see
me?"

"Of course," said Etta, trying to be light and indifferent.

"When you came in just now I thought you looked
lovely in that dress."

"Did you?"

"Yes. And those flowers suit you so well. I wish . . ."

He didn't have time to say what he wished, for Etta
turned away from him, how regretfully she alone knew,
in the dining room. But, as Ada placed them, she found
herself seated beside Ralph with Robert opposite. Etta
divined rather than perceived that Ralph was a little afraid
of his cousin and influenced by him, the harder, stronger
will easily dominating a more sensitive nature. Robert
began chaffing him in a way which annoyed Etta, it seemed
so crude and unnecessary. She longed to defend Ralph,
but dared not, and had to sit silent, suffering far more for
him than he suffered for himself.

It appeared that Ralph now had "rooms" in London,
and after a not too distinguished university career was
being crammed for the diplomatic service. Robert attacked
him on his choice of a career—a life of inglorious verbiage,
without action or discipline, where he would spend years
of his life dangling after the whims of some senile ambassador and his wife.

"Oh, well," Ralph retorted, trying to defend himself, "I suppose the nation must have a few brains as well as an army."

"Brains! What an acquisition you'll be to the nation! And I'm none too certain that you'll be able even to pass the examination. You waste all your time over pictures and theatres and novels, which are all very well in their way, but I despise people who give too much attention to frivolous amusements."

Ralph coloured and, ignoring him, asked Etta if she had heard any music recently, and in her anxiety to back him up she began too enthusiastically to praise a concert she had been to. Through their talk she heard Ada saying:

"I don't think it quite just to say that Ralph's artistic interests are frivolous."

"For a man who will have his position in life they are," Robert said coldly. "Such things are better left to people of the schoolmaster and governess class."

That at the moment when she was talking music with such youthful earnestness was so insulting that Etta's impulse was to leave the table. She resisted that, but couldn't prevent her voice faltering. Ralph, more intent, did not hear him. The remark seemed to Etta more incredible since a little earlier Ada had said that Etta would help to look after Edith during the summer; moreover, the two or three officers she had met at the Lawsons' had delighted Etta with the ease and urbanity of their manners; and whatever his faults, Robert had always seemed to her to have the army polish. She thought Robert must have guessed her feeling for Ralph, and hated her for it.

Ada managed to get Robert talking to her, and Etta tried to devote her attention to Mr. Lawson, leaving Ralph to do as he chose. Unluckily, Mr. Lawson was in one of his most sluggish conversational moods—it was like talking to a Madame Tussaud's figure. Etta wished she were a

ventriloquist, to make his answers for him. But Ralph
refused to talk to Robert and was determined not to be
silent. He was annoyed with his cousin for trying to
disparage him (gratuitously, he thought) before a girl
he particularly wanted to think well of him. While Mr.
Lawson was ponderously searching for a phrase, Ralph
very neatly cut him out and forced Etta to listen to what
he was saying.

But there was another embarrassment. Partly because
he wanted to show Robert how small an effect he had
made, but chiefly because Ralph was anxious to make a
good impression on Etta, he talked to her in a much more
friendly and intimate way than seemed judicious. Every
moment Etta felt he was foolishly revealing her—perhaps
their—secret to three hostile people. Somehow she
managed to reply through the interminable minutes of the
meal, a most exquisitely painful ordeal. The irony of it
was that the things Ralph said and the tone of his voice
would have made her wildly happy if only they had been
alone. In her mood of hypersensibility Etta believed
that even the impassive servant moving silently about
the room was disapprovingly conscious of her feelings.
Horrible to have Coleman discussing her in the servants'
quarters!

At last the agony was over, and they left the table. Etta
made a pretext that she had a headache and in spite of
Ada's protests ran quickly upstairs. Get away, at all costs
she must get away by herself. By the time she reached the
landing her legs were quivering under her, and she was
forced to walk slowly. She snatched open her door, locked
it behind her with a trembling hand, moved blindly across
the darkened room to a chair, and sat with her hands
pressed against her aching forehead, covering her eyes
against her shame.

Her disarray was complete and overwhelming. Etta had never experienced such shattering confusion of mind and sensibility. She could not recover from the shock of this abrupt plunge from balanced tranquillity into what seemed like a mad cataract of emotions where she vainly struggled for a resting place. Her whole life seemed to be involved in her present sharp misery of shame, humiliation, and failure.

Her hot cheeks grew hotter as she imagined Ada, good-natured kindly Ada, to whom she felt such devoted gratitude, saving her nephew from a wretched entanglement by telling him the squalid story of Etta and Drayton. She saw his face going cold and contemptuous, like his cousin's, as he listened. She made herself flinch with pain by imagining that Ralph had asked her to tell him about her life; in her imagination saw herself truthfully telling him, and saw him turn from her in pain and disappointment. How could he be anything but disappointed and faintly disgusted by a life like hers? And what had she to offer him but a young body and a humble devotion and a passionate gratitude and longing to please him? He'd want more than that from a woman, and even if he didn't, his relatives would fight hard to save him from her.

What misery to be a woman, and how right were those peoples who filled with lamentations the house when a female child was born! Only because she was a girl, they had scamped her education, thwarted her friendships and ambitions, denied her liberty, compelled her to scramble ignominiously for a living. Only because she was a girl, she had been underpaid at Thirlby's, and Drayton had tried to buy her. And after that, the bitterest of all. Just as life was opening out to a happier prospect, hope was quenched—because she was a girl, because she had attracted one of the three men it was madness to think of in her position, had let herself fall utterly in love with him, and had lacked the wit to conceal it from those who must be the enemies of such a love. Well, there was not much sense in worrying. In a few hours it would all be settled by Ada sending her away, and after that what did anything matter?

For a long time Etta sat motionless in her chair, watching her thoughts move across the faint glow of the window blind, where the light from a street lamp entered the room. At last she sprang up, hurriedly undressed, and huddled shivering into bed. She couldn't sleep, and lay there brooding wretchedly. She remembered how often she had dreamed of her first love, how she intended to plan it all so that it would be a triumphant consummation of life. And what a failure she had made of it! There was no way out—she'd simply have to go away and renounce Ralph forever. And yet if only . . . If only things had been different. . . . If only he would kiss her once, just once. . . .

3

IN A SLEEP MADE RESTLESS by incoherent dreams, Etta found herself transferred to a scene she had read of long ago in a historical novel. There was a sharp knocking of hammers building a scaffold for somebody, she didn't know for whom, but—knock-knock-knock—it was sinister and unhappy. People were going to be executed, and somehow she was involved and Ralph, and it was the end of everything pleasant in life. Knock-knock-knock; and then she awoke with a start to realize that it was the maid trying to get in with her morning tea. As she put the tray down on her table, she noticed that a note addressed in Ada's large dashing hand lay beside the cup.

She lifted the envelope, and then without opening it slowly laid it down again. The dismissal. It would be

polite and considerate, and there would be some perfectly
valid excuse in it, but none the less it would be dismissal.
Farewell to hope, all hail Dortborough! Etta poured out
some tea, and, leaving it to cool, drew her window blind
and opened the lower sash. In the night there had been
rain, which had left heavy clouds with blue rifts; there
was a faint scent of earth and wet greenery even in the
dank London air. It was a dismal thought that she would
never again wake to look out on that bit of London park
which had already become familiar and dear to her.

With a sigh she turned away and caught sight of her
face in the mirror. She looked a wretched fright, what
with the headache and the broken sleep and the worry, but
that didn't matter now. Perhaps if she could only manage
to look permanently ugly she might be able to get a job
she could keep. In a spasm of energy she dragged out one
of her bags and began to pack, but soon wearied of it and
went down to her bathroom. By the time she had dressed
and had drunk all the tea she could squeeze from the
pot, she felt better, almost strong enough to face a very
unpleasant day. She decided she had better find out
what Ada wanted her to do and tore open the envelope
to read:

> I'm so sorry you had a headache last night. Robert and
> Ralph wanted to say good-night, but as you'd gone to bed
> I wouldn't have you disturbed. Do stay in bed today and rest.
> Ring for anything you want. May I come up and see how
> you are before lunch? ADA.

What did this mean? Etta read the note again carefully.
Well, of course, Ada was too good at heart to send her away
if she were unwell. And then Ada's pride would make her
delay a little, she would want not to connect the dismissal
too closely with last night and Ralph. How long would it
be? Etta determined it should be over as quickly as

possible. Miserable to linger on from day to day. She was tempted to take advantage of the note to go back to bed for breakfast and avoid meeting Robert. But no—get it over. As soon as the second bell rang, she went down —to discover Robert was not there. Ada gently scolded her for getting up, Etta protested that she was perfectly well, and the remainder of breakfast passed in an unbelievably tranquil and normal way. Etta could not but admire the poise with which the Lawsons concealed what they must be thinking of her. Ada even referred casually to both Ralph and Robert. Amazing self-control, but Etta felt that for once she would have preferred worse manners and her *coup de grâce*.

As they were rising, Ada said:

"By the way, Etta, haven't you arranged for me to speak at the Willsden meeting on Thursday?"

"Yes."

"Robert wants me to go out with him. Will you write them a polite letter of excuse and say I'll come next time? And don't forget I shall want you to be with me."

Sitting over her typing in the workroom, Etta puzzled over these last words. It seemed needlessly elaborate and unkind to make such a point of a vague future appointment when she would certainly be gone by then. Perhaps Ada wanted to keep her on until her successor was found— but was all this needed? Surely Ada could see or at any rate guess. . . . Oh, well. As the typewriter rattled away, Etta began to feel ashamed of her tragical reveries of the night before. After all, nothing had been said or done that was irrevocable. Perhaps she had imagined all she thought she had read in Ralph's eyes. Probably he didn't care tuppence about her, whatever she might feel about him. So it was all about nothing at all. And she made the typewriter rattle away like a miniature machine gun, trying to forget it all and of course thinking about it all the more. She was just finishing her first unhappy morning's work at Knightsbridge when there was a tap at the door and a male voice said:

"May I come in?"

Between dismay, astonishment, and a hurt happiness at seeing him, Etta was unable to speak as she found herself gazing at a very cheery and fresh-looking Ralph. What did this mean? Was there to be some awful scene, after all?

"May I come in?" he repeated, as she didn't answer. "Am I interrupting you?"

"No—yes. Does Mrs. Lawson want me for anything?"

"Not that I know of. She said you'd probably be here. I say, I was awfully sorry you had a headache last night. Is it better?"

"Yes, thanks."

"May I sit down a moment? I won't interrupt the work for long, but I want so much to talk to you. I *was* disappointed last night. Look here, I've got tickets for a piano recital tomorrow afternoon. Will you come? Do say you will."

"I—I'm afraid I can't—I may not—be here," Etta stammered, so bewildered she hardly knew what she was saying.

"Oh, what a pity! Is it anything important? Aunt Ada said you wouldn't be doing anything for her. Can't you put it off?"

"Does Mrs. Lawson know you're asking me to go to a concert?"

"Why, naturally. I had to ask her first, hadn't I? I do wish you'd come. She said you ought to, you don't go out enough, and that she'd be delighted."

"Did she really say that?"

"I shouldn't say so if she hadn't."

Etta gave up trying to understand. It was all too complicated and incomprehensible. What on earth did Ada mean? However, in any case, she would have to refuse. But somehow—alas for good midnight resolutions —she didn't in the end refuse. What with the hope that after all she mightn't have behaved so disgracefully, that perhaps after all Ada hadn't seen, and her queer behaviour meant there wasn't going to be any dismissal, and the thought of how wonderful it would be to hear music with Ralph, and Ralph himself pleading with astonishing energy and determination—she finally said Yes, yes, she would go. Astonishing how hard it was to resist his persuasions, especially when he looked into her eyes in that indescribable way.

"That's all settled then. Splendid!" exclaimed Ralph. "And look here, I'm going to get tickets for the Russian Ballets. There's going to be a season soon, and I must see as many as possible with you. I'll give you the dates as soon as I know them, so that you can keep them free. Do you like the Russians?"

"I'm afraid I've never seen them."

"Not seen them? Whatever have you been thinking about? But that settles that too. Why, it's part of your education."

"I don't think I ought to go with you," said Etta, miserably fighting herself in the interest of prudence and her own resolves.

"Why not?"

"Because—well, because, I'm the secretary here, and I've work to do, and Mrs. Lawson might object. . . ."

"Don't you worry about that. I can fix it up with Aunt Ada—anyway, I told her about it. So promise."

And weakly, blaming herself one moment, feeling blissfully happy the next, Etta promised. Ralph talked excitedly about the ballet and presently interrupted himself:

"I must be keeping you from work! I suppose I ought to go?"

Now Etta really did intend to say: "Yes, you must go," but what her voice said, and said quite happily, was:

"Oh, no, I can finish it in ten minutes."

So Ralph stayed and went on talking, and as he talked he looked at her, and she was *almost* sure that his eyes were trying to say again what they had said the night before. And this started the whole confusion all over again in an even worse complication, although in spite of fears and worries it made her blissfully, blissfully happy. And then she grew afraid of it all and said he must go. Ralph stood up obediently but regretfully. After they had said good-bye and shaken hands he turned back from the door and said hesitantly:

"I say, Robert was awfully unpleasant to me last night. Please don't be influenced by what he said about me. I'm really not such an ass as he made out."

"Oh, I wasn't influenced. He was all wrong, and very unkind. I thought he was hitting at me."

"At you! Why, doesn't he like you?"

"Very much the opposite."

"He must be mad! Hasn't he got eyes in his head? But, look here, don't pay any attention to him. It's only his beastly jealousy."

"Jealousy!"

"Yes, didn't you know? He's jealous of everybody Ada likes. At any rate, he's jealous of her liking me, and he can see she's fond of you. When you came down last night, he was furiously jealous because Ada had been saying how charming you are, and how much she likes you, and wishes you never had to go away. That's why he made that perfectly disgusting remark when you came in—I wanted to knock his head off. Then, because I glowered at him he went for me."

"Are you sure about all this?"

"Quite sure. I know Robert. Didn't you notice that as soon as he got all Ada's attention to himself at dinner, he left us alone?"

"I think so . . . yes, I did."

"There you are. Don't let that worry you. And for heaven's sake, don't let a miserable redcoat like Robert put you off me. Let us be friends. Why not?"

Etta could think of no answer which would not betray her too far or—good resolves to the contrary—not be needlessly cold. Instinctively she held out her hand again to him, but instead of merely grasping it, he bent and kissed it very gently and respectfully, and was gone.

"Why not?" His last words echoed in her hearing. "Why not?" Etta softly closed the door and walked slowly up and down the small room. Why not, indeed, why not? Why shouldn't she be friends with Ralph Lawson? She knew perfectly well why not. When he said "friends" and she acquiesced by giving her hand, hadn't they both known that they both meant "lovers"? When she was face to face with Ralph, and he looked at her with that quick deep gaze, perplexity and shame and wretchedness disappeared, leaving only happiness and confidence that they were right, essentially, eternally right to be in love, whatever the complications and contingencies of life. And when he talked, no longer trying to be witty, but speaking in eager stumbling phrases, the most ordinary words glowed with lovely meaning. Not what he said, but the tone and look were so persuasive. They seduced her resistance, and when she ought to say No, when she meant to say No, they made her say Yes.

But when he was no longer there, how quickly the confidence died away into cold ashes of uncertainty and self-reproach and hopelessness! Etta tried to keep alive the little flame of happiness, but it was quenched by the unavoidable torturing questions. Suppose Ralph asked her to marry him, could she say Yes to that? Impossible for a hundred reasons, but if for no other, because it would wreck his career and life. She had a faith to keep with Ada; that violated, Etta was forever dishonoured. And wouldn't the same faith be equally violated if she said Yes, yes, they could be lovers? Yet was it really Ada's concern what they did, so long as the blame was all Etta's and she didn't betray Ralph into legal and social chains?

Hopefully Etta tried to persuade herself that Ada wouldn't care, that it was nothing to do with her. If Etta chose, why shouldn't she be Ralph's mistress? And she answered herself: Not while you are under these obligations to Ada; not while you sleep under her roof and eat her food and take her money; not while you are virtually a servant in her house and your very intimacy with him depends on that. Never under those conditions—it would be like the housemaid seducing the young master. But Yes, if you hadn't those obligations, if you were really on your own, if you had a place to which you could ask, and could give yourself and take him as an equal, a free woman who can freely dispose of herself! And to that there was no valid reply.

Must I always be thwarted by this helplessness of poverty? Etta said bitterly to herself. Is there nothing lovely in the world that must not be purchased by money?

4

THE DAYS WENT ON, but Etta didn't cease worrying. The result of these long and painful soliloquies was always the same—the conviction that she oughtn't even to see Ralph again until she had really solved the problem of living on her own. But, as Etta found, it is one thing to make a virtuous and *tranchante* decision in theory, and quite another thing to put it into practice, especially when some of your deepest instincts have no intention of letting you do so. In any case, it wasn't in her power to prevent him dropping in unexpectedly to lunch or dinner or at any time he liked, since he had the freedom of the house. So she couldn't avoid seeing him. Here, no doubt, virtuous resolution should have called a halt, but it didn't. Seeing Ralph meant that she fell more in love with him, and therefore her efforts to refuse his invitations became weaker and weaker, and then each time she went out with him she came back a little more in love.

So, in the end, Etta abandoned even the pretence to herself that she wouldn't see Ralph again, and allowed herself to glide through the weeks on Mr. Gray's allegorical shallop—Youth at the prow and Pleasure at the helm. Indisputably they were both young, and there could be no doubt that they took pleasure in each other's company. It was very pleasant to them, especially to Etta, to go out together to theatres and concert halls and picture shows, and to agree or to argue about it and about, in the earnestly hopeful manner of the period. Best of all was the Russian Ballet, which they agreed was the summit of all art, the perfect expression of the coming age of perfection. For days Etta's whole life was coloured by the sorrow of Petrouchka or the tragical splendours of Scheherazade; the minutes danced like lovely Kharsavinas to the music of Stravinsky in a Bakst world where there were no typewriters and letter files and penniless girls.

They were both vaguely but ardently devoted to Socialism, though they knew rather less than nothing about it. Their favourite adjective of depreciation was "Victorian," despite the fact that this deplorable age had in its favour the production of themselves. In music their opinions began to diverge, and in painting positively differed.

Ralph had what were known as modern tastes. Having had some musical education, Etta could not agree that music began with Wagner; and she took no joy in the coloured spaghetti designs of Picabia which made Ralph so happy (so he told her) he had reproductions of them pinned on his walls. In the matter of woman's suffrage, it was just the opposite. Etta was the modernist (she had reason to be), but Ralph believed the woman's problem would best be solved by a revival of chivalry—a Tennysonian opinion not very consistent with his other views.

But whether they agreed or disagreed, they were equally happy. Sometimes Ada, occasionally Ada and her husband, came with them, but usually they went out alone. Etta still puzzled herself occasionally about Ada's attitude. There had been no hint of dismissal, and gradually it dawned on Etta that her fears and woes had been products of her own disordered intellect. Nobody had suspected anything. Still, she knew Ada wouldn't like a love affair; and yet she encouraged them to go about together. Etta couldn't forget how Ada had steered Ralph away from her when they had first talked together at the tea party. Then suddenly one May afternoon as they sat over tea something Ada said to another woman gave her the solution. Ralph now knew exactly Etta's status—Ada was therefore certain he wouldn't propose marriage. She was equally certain he wouldn't attempt anything else, because Etta was under his aunt's protection. But it was much better for him to be interested in a girl who was ineligible both ways than to get himself entangled elsewhere. In other words, Etta thought ruefully, I'm the safety valve, the nursery fire guard to keep the valuable nephew from burning himself —women *are* kind to each other.

The London season of 1914. Long after it had dropped into oblivion, the mere words evoked for Etta a special

mood, which the most Proustian subtleties would fail to
create for those who did not live it. Etta lived those weeks
in a dream which seemed entirely real, if only because she
believed it was only the beginning of a happy life; whereas
to her after-memories it became the more dreamlike
because then she knew, or thought she knew, that it was
impossible to be so happy again. Perhaps being young
and in love is sufficient explanation of Etta's feeling that
she had then lived in enchantment; but she was also intoxicated by the strong waters of a general hopefulness
and gaiety all about her. For, while many elderly people
shook their heads dolefully over the degeneracy of everything, as invariably happens, the young were mostly of an
excessive hope. They were so hopeful that they were
even "extraordinarily happy" (the words are Rupert
Brooke's) about the declaration of war. What now seems
extraordinary is the happiness.

Yet it is not given to everybody to be personally happy
in a time, however short, which believes itself happy.
Etta at least had that experience. Whatever ugly wounds
she had taken seemed miraculously to disappear. The
squalor of her first months on her own was as much forgotten as the winter darkness in the June sunlight. She
ceased to worry about her relations to Ada and Ralph and
all the possible complications and distresses, living only
for present happiness. Her work—how did it happen that
what had seemed so important in her life was now a bore,
a piece of meaningless ritual which had to be gone through
daily with impatient efficiency? She broke recklessly into
her small savings to buy new clothes. She wanted to look
pretty for Ralph. As to the future, she was very hopeful.
It seemed impossible so kind a world could be unkind to
her. Later on Mr. Lawson would find her a suitable post
with a salary of five or six pounds a week (her minimum
had risen), and she would have a flat on her own, where

Ralph could come to see her, and where they would be happy together. For the rest—it is ridiculous to look too far ahead in life.

Such being Etta's mood, she wanted nothing except that life should go on exactly as it was. And indeed she seemed to have stepped into a timeless world. Mornings and evenings came and went; Ada's letters arrived and were answered, appointments were made for Ada, kept, and then crossed off; the "May" on the calendar became "June," and every day Etta tore off a number; from her window she saw the spring flowers fade, but others took their places, and the leafier trees cut off more of the park from her view and quite obliterated her glimpse of the Serpentine, but they did not shut out the sky. Why should the spring end? No need that sort of spring should end.

The number below the "June" on the calendar was "18." The flood of "season" letters and engagements for Ada was just as heavy, and Etta was working away furiously to get through them, to have time to read the latest Anatole France which Ralph had given her. Ada so rarely interrupted her in the morning that Etta apprehensively guessed at some calamity when Ada came in, frowning a little, and holding the usual typed list of her engagements. Was there some error? Etta remembered, conscience-stricken, that she had dashed it off quickly, not to keep Ralph waiting. The fear was confirmed by Ada's first remark:

"Is this list correct, Etta?"

She took it guiltily, checked it with her own notes, and felt relieved that she could answer:

"Yes, quite correct."

"Have I really promised to do all this? Why, I shan't

have ten minutes to myself from eleven until after midnight. It's impossible!"

"I can look up the files, but I know you told me to make those appointments."

"And I suppose tomorrow and the next day are equally full?"

"Very nearly, I'm afraid."

"I can't go on like this!" Ada exclaimed. "It makes a goblin of the sun. I shall be ill. Could there be anything more ridiculous than this turning the pleasures of life into a mad, exhausting day? Make no appointments for me after the 25th. Refuse everything."

"You already have some," said Etta looking into her diary register.

"Then cancel them all by telegram. We'll go to Dymcott on the 25th—you must be tired out too, my dear. Send a wire to Robert and write to Edith's school to say that when they break up she's to come to Dymcott, not here. And make any other arrangements needed. I must have a long rest in the quiet after all this racket of London. Get ready yourself. You'll love Dymcott, Etta. Now I must rush—I'm late already."

A sense of disappointment and disillusion came over Etta as she took the block of telegraph forms from a drawer of her table. Strange that she should feel like that when far back in those March days she had looked forward so much to Dymcott. From what Ada said it sounded like the real country Etta had always wanted to know, and Ada had said there would be very little work, and they could spend long summer days in the garden and orchard and on the river . . . and now, through some inexplicable perversity, Etta found she didn't want to go, that her eyes were filling with tears at the thought of leaving London—London, which not so long ago she had mentally denounced as Dortborough on a large scale. It was very queer.

Scrupulously Etta had always let Ada know when and where she was going out with Ralph, directly or by implication asking a permission which was never refused. But for some reason she forgot to mention that Ralph, after much persuading, had her promise to dine with him on her last night before going to Dymcott. Ada was in a vortex of last-hour engagements and was going out to dinner, and Etta had been busy all day packing. Perhaps that made her forget. She only remembered when Ralph came to call for her, after Ada and her husband had left.

As she stepped down the stairs, taking care not to let her train trip her, she saw Ralph standing in the hall, gazing up at her. He looked very handsome, she thought, with the soft white silk scarf at his throat, the neat black of his dress suit, and the evening hat in his hand; and she wished she had another evening gown besides the one he had already seen so often. But that was quickly forgotten in the pleasure of greeting him, and so too was the slightly trepidant feeling that she was being very daring and advanced in dining alone with a young man—an emancipation which was still not permitted to most girls in those days. Now she was a woman on her own Etta could throw off these *Victorian* prejudices. Still, there was all the excitement of the unusual. She never once thought of her parallel evening with Drayton.

The taxi Ralph had waiting took them to a small West-End restaurant at that time fashionable among young men from the universities. Etta saw he had planned it all carefully to please her. A table was reserved, and there was no fussing over menus—the dinner had been ordered. It was quite simple but very well cooked—a consommé;

fillets of sole with a sauce Etta thought wonderful, accompanied by a little very cool white wine; then a poussin, with half a bottle of old Bordeaux; a superb basket of fruits; and then coffee. Of course, it was pure waste to give a young woman vintage wines, and not until years later did Etta appreciate the dinner's artistry. But in Ralph it was pure plagiarism from a gastronomic uncle. At any rate, Etta appreciated the intention. So unsophisticated were the young of those days that she would gladly have shared an eggs-and-bacon dinner with Ralph.

English scarcely allows the half-ironical, half-sympathizing succinctness of *"ils étaient bien naïfs, mais beaux."* They were indeed inexperienced but very natural, and it is always pretty to see two handsome young people in love. A couple very natural and loving—but unfortunately the remote sea cave which sheltered the loves of Juan and Haidee was not at their disposal. Nothing in human life is ever quite perfect, and this otherwise perfect dinner was shadowed by a mundane, slightly ridiculous, but crushing problem. They had nowhere to go where they could be securely alone together.

For weeks now they had been telling each other the state of their feelings as plainly as may be without downright words or kisses; and Etta's coming departure staged the crisis. Only the impotent and the piously vindictive (upon whom be prayer and peace) will deny that there was only one logical sequence to this agreeable little dinner. But no Polynesian couple, contemplating defiance of their complicated sexual customs, were ever so much embarrassed by invisible taboos as these two civilized young whites.

Under their gay talk each felt the suspense of the situation. Something decisive ought to happen, but how? It was the moment for Ralph to declare himself or else forever hold his peace, and being a sensitive young man he didn't want to declare himself in a public restaurant or amid the instabilities of a moving taxi. The hanging gardens of Babylon would scarcely have been adequate as a setting to the scene he imagined. So he said nothing, and their talk became more and more artificial, and they avoided meeting each other's eyes. They promised to write, and Ralph said he would come to Dymcott, and they made vague plans about rowing and walks and tennis, and even for the distant autumn when Etta would be back in London. But the tension only grew, and as time passed Ralph could do nothing but fidget and look mournful.

Etta was in a mood to accept any barely possible solution Ralph offered, but when at last even she had to admit that he hadn't got one, she cut short a meeting which was becoming painful. She said she must go home. Ralph protested, but, confronted by his own incapacity, had to give way; and they sat in silence, but hand in hand, as the taxi swiftly took them to Knightsbridge. Until the last moment Etta still hoped he would think of something, but he didn't; and she had to find the way out, on the flimsiest of pretexts, but still a pretext. As they stood in the silent hall, Etta said hurriedly:

"What did you say your address was? I'm sure I'll forget it. Would you mind coming up to my workroom and writing it down for me?"

Flimsy indeed, but Ralph acquiesced eagerly. Etta listened as they ran upstairs—there was no sound from the drawing room or Ada's boudoir, they were not back. Before she could turn on the light in her workroom (perhaps she was in no hurry) Ralph had seized her hand and had closed the door, and a moment later had her in his arms and was kissing her lips. Now of all the many splendid words Ralph had meant to utter when this moment arrived he remembered none, and only murmured incoherently: "Etta, Etta, I love you." But Etta did not answer. Words, words . . . why break the spell by speech? They were not acting something from a wordy book or play, but living in the living body. She wanted the touch of Ralph's lips, not their sound. She swayed to him in the darkness, for the touch of his kisses went deep, deep, until her blood quivered, and they stood in silence, in a timeless ecstasy.

But to his male overconscious sensibility her real response, her real acquiescence were not enough. It was not enough that in the living body she accepted him, that with the unconscious pathos of women her head was bowed to his shoulder submitting to him. He wanted to be assured; to be told, almost to have in black and white what she felt towards him. He whispered restlessly:

"Etta, Etta, do you love me? Do you? Do you?"

In the darkness she could not see his eyes, but knew they were pleading, using that dominion of persuasion he loved to exercise over her; and something remote in her knew she would love him more deeply than he could love her. And still she did not speak, but took his hand and laid it on her left breast.

"How your heart beats!" he exclaimed. But before he could speak again, she put her mouth to his, deliberately, the answer to his question; then slipped from him and switched on the dazzling light.

"Go now, my dear, go quickly. It would spoil it all if you were found here."

Ralph lingered, protesting, but Etta was almost panic-stricken in her eagerness to have him gone—not for anything must those moments be spoiled. Awkwardly he presented her with a small white box, saying:

"This is for you. I meant it in case we couldn't . . . Wear it for me."

As he turned to go, she unaccountably changed her

mind and wanted him to stay. She followed him to the stairhead, caught his hand, and whispered: "Yes, I love you." And fled swiftly to her room.

In the little box was a love-letter wrapped round a thin gold chain with an amber pendant.

5

DURING THE FIRST DAYS at Dymcott Etta was too much agitated by mental conflicts to feel the beauty of the place. The night after her dinner with Ralph she scarcely slept, but through all the night hours lay motionless, living in the lovely borderland between sleep and waking, the limbo of wish-fulfillment. In that delicious haze of half-consciousness she relived over and over again the emotions and sensations of the evening, and projected them on the future, as if all life to come was to be the delicate morning of a first love. With all self-criticism suspended in her dream state, even the memory of what had happened became more beautiful than in the reality; while the dream future was fancifully delicious. Yet, in the illusions of the mysterious Heraclitan flux we call living, who is to say that this dream happiness was any less "real" than our convention of reality? At any rate, there was no bitterness in its memory.

This mood lasted into her first waking hours, when the high pinnacles of her castle in Spain were still clear and shining. But directly she met Ada by the car the dream castle collapsed to its foundations, and the mood was lost forever. The mere sound of Ada's voice giving an order to the chauffeur sounded hostile and a condemnation. Etta dared not meet her eyes and was thankful Ada was so weary that she dozed most of the way. All that had so recently seemed so beautiful now looked ugly and furtive.

Etta condemned herself ruthlessly: she had broken her
faith to Ada. She had helplessly failed to direct her own
life. Worst of all, she had herself provoked the final scene,
so had not even the miserable excuse that Ralph was to
blame. Yet the "renouncing" of Ralph had become all the
more difficult and painful.

All this was complicated by the arrival in quick succession of three long and extravagantly worded letters from
Ralph—he couldn't eat, sleep, or work for thinking of her,
he must see her soon or he would go mad, might he come
the next week-end? The mere receiving these letters
seemed to her another treachery to Ada, and Etta was
terrified of what might happen if Ralph suddenly arrived.
She wrote him a long wild letter, full of self-accusation
and (unconsciously) of her passion for him, beseeching him
not to come, not to make her feel she had ruined his life.
She felt out of harmony with the country and its slow deep
life rhythms; she missed the swift staccato rhythm of
London, and the dark silences of the country nights frightened her.

Gradually and then quite rapidly Etta grew accustomed
to Dymcott, then liked it, and at last came to love it
deeply, so that her dream of felicity was to live at
Dymcott, with Ralph, "forever."

And indeed it was a pleasant place. Ada had searched
for months before she found it, then waited a year to get
possession, and had spent more money than the old house
was worth to make it what she wanted. The E-formed
Elizabethan manor had degenerated into an insanitary
farmhouse; Ada restored it, and modernized the upper
floor. Etta particularly liked the old hall, which had been
repanelled and turned into a combined library and music
room. The windows looked over the sloping lawns and
flower beds to the river and the wooded water meadows

beyond, with their lines of poplars and aspens, elms and sycamores. The low hilly bank on which the house was built sheltered it from the east wind, and except for the orchard and one small field was covered with beech copses among which stood tall individual trees.

A passion for solitude sprang up in Etta. Where the high ground suddenly sloped to the north of the house a small tributary ran into the river. Here was a covered boathouse, and a little higher up a small wooded island connected with the land by a Venetian-arched foot bridge with a locked gate. On the far side of the islet was a bathing pool. Etta had keys to the boathouse and bridge, and spent the days bathing and on the river or lying under the trees, sometimes reading but more often lost in reverie. The swift lapse of quiet water was very healing, and she loved to watch the aspen leaves quivering over her head and the white clouds moving over the sky beyond them. The river banks were lacy with meadowsweet, and she gathered the scented water mint, loosestrife both gold and purple, and the tall rose bay. The scent of hay drifted over from the shorn water meadows, and the summer air was moist with sweet river breath. In that charmed interlude of peace Etta forgot shames and cares, past, present, and future, called a truce to the mortal strife in herself and with the world.

Every week-end Randolfe Lawson came down, but it made little difference to Etta's days of solitude. The last Thursday in July was warm, tranquil, and sunny. Etta bathed before breakfast, and afterwards explored the tributary in a canoe, going farther than she had ever been, until she was halted by a weir and mill race, near an abandoned mill. For a long time she watched the water trickling over the moss-grown broken wheel, and the broken shadows of the trees on the glinting river. She bathed again when she got back, and promised herself a long afternoon under the aspens on the island. But at lunch Ada said:

"You haven't forgotten that Edith will be here by the three-twenty?"

Etta *had* forgotten, but she said:

"No."

"Would you mind going over in the car to meet her? This heat makes me so languid."

And, of course, Etta had to give up her afternoon. She had dreaded Edith's coming, thinking how awful it would be to have her solitude invaded by a young female Robert. To Etta's relief, Edith turned out to be a tall girl of sixteen, with all her mother's sweetness and a good deal of her father's reserve. Etta hoped that her river loneliness would be saved. But when they arrived back from the station, there was more disturbance—a telegram from Mr. Lawson to say he was bringing Ralph for the week-end.

"What fun!" exclaimed Edith. "Will he be here long, Mother?"

"No, his examination's on Monday, he'll have to be back for that. I suppose he wants a little rest, he's been working very hard."

"Oh, well, he can come back," said Edith. "The holidays won't be holidays without Ralph."

"You don't mention Robert," said Ada reproachfully.

"He's so stiff and silly," said Edith petulantly, "and he never has any fun like Ralph. Ralph's a darling."

Was that sharp little pain she felt really jealousy, Etta wondered, or was it just the reminder that she was only a nobody, an interloper in the family? She hadn't time to decide, for Ada, ignoring Edith's last remark, said:

"Etta, would you mind telling them to prepare Ralph's room? And see they do it properly. Really, this heat is as trying as London."

"Is that how it feels to be jealous?" Etta asked herself, as she went on this errand; but how absurd, of course other people love him, he's lovable—and jealous of a schoolgirl, his own cousin! Still, she couldn't help wishing that Edith wasn't quite so pretty and so entirely eligible, even though she was only a cousin. A feeble line of Tennyson's—"Trust me, cousin, all the current of my being sets to thine"—kept maddeningly repeating itself in her brain as she gathered flowers from the garden for Ralph's room. And it went on as she arranged by his bed a small extra vase of her own wild flowers and mint, as she selected a few books she thought he would like, and even when she remembered the ash tray the servant forgot. Etta stood at the door, looking back at the pleasant chintzy room to make sure nothing was forgotten, and then sentimentally kissed her fingers to the place where "he" would sleep.

The newspapers always arrived a day late at Dymcott. Etta seldom bothered with newspapers, and while she had been at Dymcott had never looked at one—she didn't want to spoil the lovely peaceful mood with crimes and stupidities. But the next morning at breakfast, while she and Edith talked, Etta noticed in a casual way that Ada neglected her food, so absorbed in reading the centre pages of *The Times* that she appeared to forget everything. Twice she looked up and gazed from one to the other, seemed about to say something, but paused and returned to her reading. After breakfast Edith got up, saying she was going out by herself, and Ada folded up the newspaper and began discussing week-end plans and telling Etta what she had to do. Suddenly Edith bounded back into the room.

"Mother! I can't find the keys of the bridge and boathouse. Where are they?"

"Aren't they on the usual nail?"

"No, and I've looked everywhere."

Etta found herself reddening, as she was obliged to say:

"I'm so sorry—they're in my room. I'll get them."

"Leave them on the nail while the others are here," said Ada kindly as Etta rose. "Then you'll know whether they're in use or not."

A trifle, but as Etta ran up to her room she knew it was another reminder that she was an interloper—*her* solitude wasn't hers, it belonged first to Edith or any of the Lawsons who wanted it.

The meeting with Ralph was much easier than Etta had imagined. She didn't go to the station with Ada and Edith and kept out of the way until tea-time. When Etta came in she found them all talking eagerly. They were so much interested in what they were saying that Ralph, who appeared to be very excited, did not seem even to notice her much: which made her feel more of an outsider than ever. Ralph kept saying:

"I wish I'd gone to Sandhurst instead of into the diplomatic."

Etta listened to the talk, and gradually discovered that a war had started in central Europe, that all England except herself knew about it and wondered if England would be involved. Mr. Lawson thought not, it would be unbusinesslike; but Ralph, who had brought a splendid collection of rumours with him, was convinced to the contrary. He vowed it would come—it would be just the thing England needed to wake it up, and then, what a splendid chance for Robert! At Robert's name, Mr. and Mrs. Lawson grew silent, but Edith said she knew Robert would love it, but anyway, he wasn't even commissioned yet.

"But he soon will be," said Ralph enviously. "And I'm not even in the Territorials, and it'll be all over before I can get out."

"I hope we shall not be in it," said Ada gravely.

And that started Ralph off all over again. To Etta their excitement was incomprehensible. What did it all matter to them? She had long ceased to think of her childhood, of the men whose clubs made such a banging to frighten her and Teddy, of the tramping and noise of wheels, of the picture "Let Em All Come." And if she had thought of them then they would have meant nothing. Wars were things which happened in far-off places and interested newspaper readers, not ordinary civilized people.

That night they dressed for dinner in Ralph's honour. After much hesitating and inward conflict, Etta finally clasped on the chain and pendant he had given her and ran quickly downstairs before she could change her mind. He saw it at once, and his quick glance made her evening happy.

During the week-end Etta hardly saw Ralph alone for a moment. Part of his time had to be spent with Mr. Lawson, and then Edith was always exclaiming: "Shall we go on the river, Ralph?" or some other proposal, from which, with unconscious cruelty, Etta was tacitly excluded. And when Ralph tried to bring her in, she either refused or, if she accepted, felt uneasy and disappointed.

After dinner on Saturday Etta went out alone into the garden and walked slowly up and down the lower terrace lawn. The house was hidden from sight by the rock-garden wall of the upper lawn, but occasionally she heard the faint tinkle of a piano. Etta liked this lawn, with the scent of invisible roses in the darkness and the river gently swirling below. At one end was a thick row of tall rhododendrons, and from the other end she could look down on the dark tree-tops of the islet. It was her favourite place in the warm dusky evenings, but that evening her own thoughts veiled all the beauty from her. She had determined to

break with Ralph and be done with vacillations and
hypocrisies. . . .

She started violently as she turned and found Ralph
close behind her—the grass had made his footsteps
noiseless.

"How you frightened me!"

"I'm so sorry."

He took and kissed both her hands and then tried to
kiss her lips, but she held him off.

"The others? Where are they? What are they doing?"

"In the library. Edith is showing off what she hasn't
learned at school. But never mind them. I've been longing
every minute to be alone with you, my beautiful one."

Again he tried to put his arms round her to kiss her,
and again she resisted.

"Not here, not now. Besides, I—I want to talk to you.
Shall we walk?"

In silence they walked on the smooth turf. Ralph tried
to take her hand, but that too she refused—it made an
agonizing difficulty more difficult.

"You wanted to say something?" he asked, a little hurt
by these refusals.

Words wouldn't come to help her, and he repeated his
question more gently.

"It's all so hard for me, so difficult," she said miserably.

"What is hard? What do you mean?" he asked.

"It was all such a mistake. I shouldn't have allowed
it. I'm a weak fool. Sometimes I wish I'd never seen
you."

"Etta! What has happened? How can you be so
capricious and cruel when I've been living on the thought
of you and your last words to me in London all these
dreary weeks? I insist on your telling me what has happened."

In their agitation they paused under the dark shadow of

the rhododendrons. Etta stamped her foot in vexation and distress.

"What has happened?" she exclaimed. "Can't you see? Can't you guess? Must you have it all in words? Must I always be shamed and shamed? What would Ada have thought and said if she'd seen you trying to kiss me?"

"Ada? What do you mean? Our love is no business of hers. We're both free."

"Oh, Ralph! How can you talk so childishly? We're not free. We're held from each other in a dozen ways."

"I don't see it," he said sulkily.

"Must I speak my humiliation, then? Don't you know I'm Ada's dependent, her servant, that I live on her food and her charity?"

"But you work!"

"Work! Do you really think I earn what Ada gives me?"

"Of course you do—she says——"

"Ada would say anything that was kind. My God, how ignorant of life you are! There are thousands of girls, far more competent than I, who would leap at the chance of my so-called work."

"But, my darling, my darling, even if this is true, what does it matter?"

"Listen, Ralph. If I'd stayed at home you'd never have known me. I ran away, and by chance met you with Ada. Then I was an office hireling, a creature you wouldn't have looked at, and I dismissed myself because my employer got drunk and tried to make love to me. From that misery Ada saved me out of her pure loving kindness to another woman in misery and distress. Would she approve of your making love to me? If she would, why are we so secret? It's hateful."

"Let us be engaged. I'll tell them."

"Engaged! Are you mad? You're too young. It would ruin your life and your career. What do you suppose would be your fate when it was whispered and then openly said that you'd married a servant from your aunt's house?"

"But you're not a servant."

"Oh, don't quibble! It's the same thing. You're generous to make the offer, and I believe you mean it, but it's insane. I wouldn't accept such a sacrifice from you. I love you, I don't conceal it, but I'm proud enough to want to give to my love, not take from him. I never meant that you should even speak of marriage, but if I were really free, if I could really meet you as an equal, I'd—I'd—you wouldn't need to ask the registrar for permission."

"Etta!"

"But not here, not now."

"Etta, Etta, what are we to do? There's nothing wrong in our loving each other, and how do you know Ada would be angry? Why are you so unreasonable? Can't I do anything?"

"Yes. Often and often I've told myself I ought to renounce you forever, but I know I can't. You say you love me, then I'm your mistress and you must obey me. You must go back to London and pass that exam, and pass it well—for me. Let me stay here alone with Ada for the summer. Don't come down—it's too hard; and I must get strong again."

"Oh, my darling, you're crying. Don't, please don't. Let me——"

"You mustn't kiss me until you've promised to do what I ask, and I'm not crying . . . only a little, women are silly. In the autumn I'll get other work, and then have a place you can come to freely, where nobody can reproach us

with ingratitude and duplicity. You'll be bound to nothing
and by nothing but your love, as long as it lasts."

"But this is fantastic."

"I'm promising to give you all I have to give. Won't
you promise to do this for me?"

"But all those months—the autumn—I want you
now."

"Ah, you think *I* shan't have to wait? You think I
don't want *you?*"

She stepped back to avoid his embrace.

"Not until you promise."

"Oh God! You're hard. But yes, yes, I promise."

For a long time they stood closely embraced, and
Ralph's lips felt the tears from her wet cheeks and eyes.
Then at last she whispered: "Go back to the house now,
don't follow me. Remember I love you, and remember your
promise."

Then she sprang away into the darkness. The gate on
the bridge to "her" islet was open, and she passed over and
lay down under the trees, sobbing, and shedding many
tears, but feeling peace in her heart. Presently the tears
ceased, and she half sat up, looking at the grave stars
through the night-darkened foliage, listening to the small
night sounds—the rustle of leaves and the river whispers,
the plop of a diving water-vole, the breathless churr of a
nightjar, the shrill musical crickets. On a sudden impulse
she stripped off her clothes and stood naked to her waist
in the cold water, bathing her hot tear-stained face in
splashing handfuls. Then she returned to the bank,
feeling the dead leaves and grass crushed under her feet,
and shivered a little in the cool air as she rubbed herself
dry. She turned and stretched out her arms to the invisible
house, whispering to herself:

"Tonight my body could have been his. If I've done
wisely or foolishly, who can say?"

6

ON TUESDAY ETTA WAS LEFT alone for most of the day.
Ralph and Mr. Lawson had gone back to London; Ada and
Edith motored over to see Robert, who disliked Dymcott
so much he very rarely came there.

Theoretically she ought to have been entirely happy.
To have Dymcott to herself, if only for a day, was exactly
what she wanted. And in a way she was happy in the still,
cool house and the green lawns, in the orchard with its
ripening fruits, and on the river where she spent much of
the day. In the long quiet reaches between the villages
Etta kept telling herself how heavenly it all was, how good
to be alive, with the larks endlessly singing far overhead
and the strong growth of coloured flowers along the banks,
the iris line cut by a kingfisher in flight, the strange piping
call of redshanks, the lines of pollarded willows throwing
green shadows on the water. . . . There were so many
things to delight in, so much that should have given her
that golden peace of the lovely non-human world; and yet
she was restless and uneasy. The ecstasy was not quite
true, the peace was troubled.

As she worked her way steadily up against the stream,
keeping close to the bank to avoid the strong current, Etta
thought of Thirlby's office, the rattle of typewriters, the
fusty air, the termite activity. It was an easy transition
to self-reproach, to accuse herself of having betrayed all
she had set out from Dortborough to vindicate. In nearly
five months there had been no further mention of the
"real job" Ada Lawson's husband was to find for her, and
Etta had never once brought it up. She had let herself
be seduced, like so many women, by comfort and ease
of living and the minimum of responsibility. She was
funking the responsibility for her own life. If she really
wanted to be independent, to be free to have a lover of

her own, and, if she wanted, a child of her own, without anyone having the right to interfere, then she couldn't go on dreaming away life as a dependent of the Lawsons. These things wouldn't come to her if she merely gave out that she wanted them and then sat down and did nothing.

This was bad enough, but when complicated by the Ralph situation became a maddening set of problems. In trying to clear up the position and to free herself, she had very possibly made it worse. How absurd to tell a man you love him and are ready to be his mistress, and then order him to go away! Besides, it hadn't removed any difficulty except her own sentimental and unimportant objection to being made love to by Ralph under Ada's roof. A question of honour, was it? Well, if honour decided that it was wrong to have an affair with Ralph, then wrong it was, always and everywhere. And if it was right, what on earth could it matter where they consummated? And if Ada would hate them to make love at Dymcott or Knightsbridge now, why should she be complacent if it happened somewhere else in six months or a year? Ah, yes, but the point was that on her own she would be free of obligation to Ada. Yes, but if she owed to Ada the job which enabled her to be on her own, that was an even greater obligation. . . .

And thus, on the last day of peace, the last hours of the old fool's paradise this century will never see again, Etta worked herself into one of her "states" and missed serenity.

Ada and Edith were half an hour late, and arrived in such a pother of excitement Etta almost thought they had gone insane, as indeed they had. Edith had a small Union Jack in her hand which she waved enthusiastically.

"Hurray! Hurray! We've come in!" she shouted.

"They've invaded Belgium," Ada explained.

"Robert got a telegram from London," shrieked Edith, dancing wildly.

"It was a question of national honour, and thank God we've done the right thing," said Ada.

"Robert's going to fight," shouted Edith. "The army's mobilized, and he's going to be commissioned, he'll look lovely in uniform."

"It will all be over long before he gets out," said Ada.

"He's going to bring me one of those spiky German helmets. It's war, war, war! Hurray!"

"Hush," said Ada in annoyance. "Don't be so noisy, Edith, you bewilder Etta. Behave yourself, and remember that your business is to try to be worthy of the fine men who are going out to fight for England."

"I don't understand," Etta stammered. "What has happened? Is it like the Boer War?"

Both began explaining, but they talked so fast and interrupted each other in a way so unusual in that quiet well-bred household that Etta was more astonished by their sudden attack of bad manners than enlightened by their words. She saw that Ada had a bundle of special editions under her arm. Etta pointed to them and said:

"May I see a newspaper?"

They left her to get themselves ready for dinner, and Etta was alone in the very silent room. Most of Europe at war, millions of men marching—and a queer, cold uneasiness came over her. It was men who were marching, not women. Except for that one thought it all seemed remote and unreal, another newspaper scare. . . . Edith came rushing back into the room:

"Come on, Etta, dinner's ready. Isn't it all *ripping?*"

It was curious, Etta felt, that in spite of this momentous news life seemed to go on exactly in the same way. But not quite. Like the first, almost imperceptible edge of an advancing wave of poison gas, restlessness percolated into Dymcott and spoiled Etta's pleasure in its solitudes. Now they waited eagerly for letters and newspapers, people were always dropping in to talk in lunatic gravity or enthusiasm about what was happening, Ada rushed about in the car as if this constituted valuable aid to her King and Country. Ada indulged in a sudden outburst of private and secretarial correspondence, which occupied more of Etta's time; and somehow Etta found herself drawn into the circle of excitement.

The spirit of "Let Em All Come" inflamed many bosoms, although as a matter both of fact and mixed metaphor the boot was on the other foot—it was a glorious and universal dogfight, with the bold bulldog grinding his little teeth in the background. Etta, more or less indifferent to the whole thing, wondered why there was so much cheerfulness about what looked to her like an awful mess; even the agricultural labourers to whom she said "Good-morning" replied in tones which implied this-is-a-bit-of-alright-this-is. Why? She decided that human beings are so bored with their own lives that they eagerly welcome anything that looks as if it would brighten them up. They loved vicariously living in horrors, and this war was better than a spicy society scandal or a murder in a bath.

Even Mr. Morison seemed to be affected in the same way, for Etta received a letter from him saying that they must all do their duty, as indeed they would, the last man in the last ditch, and her mother was very poorly, oughtn't Etta to give up idling about with the aristocracy and come home and look after her mother? Etta paid no attention to this news, and the hint, thinking it merely one more clumsy attempt to get her home. Meanwhile, as August went on, the bulletins could no longer conceal the fact that the French armies were in full retreat and the English divisions with them. All sorts of rumours of defeats and fearful casualties began to be whispered, and the wiser sort pinned their faith on the navy.

Ada's excitement suddenly evaporated, though she still loyally repeated the phrases about honour she had taken from Robert. She went about looking a little pale, and one day appeared in half-mourning. Etta discovered that the sons of two of Ada's friends were reported killed. A little later she heard from Edith that Robert would certainly be commissioned immediately, instead of waiting to complete his course. Etta tried to be hard about it—after all, Robert had chosen his career, what did Ada expect? But the uneasiness came a little nearer. How fortunate that Ralph was not a soldier! She felt very sorry for Ada. And at times a little sorry for herself—Ralph had not written to her.

Most of this was at least temporarily overlaid by a different anxiety and a new problem. Etta received another letter from her father, a short one this time, merely telling her that her mother was very ill after a heart attack, might very likely die. He ordered Etta to come home immediately—how would she feel, how would they all feel, if she heartlessly abandoned a dying mother? This was perturbing, but Etta would still have thought it highly overdrawn in the usual home style, if this letter had not been followed the next day by one from Teddy. His account confirmed her father's—the doctor was coming twice a day, they had a nurse in the house, everything was at sixes and sevens with nobody to look after the housekeeping. They'd be in an awful jam if Etta didn't come and look after things until Mother was better.

On reading this, Etta's impulse was to take the next train home. She believed Teddy; and here was something real to be done. But the old parent-child dilemma came up again. If she did her "duty" to them, what about the "duty" to her own life and beliefs? Going off like that might be construed by Ada as a tacit release from her promise to help. If she went home and her mother died, how could Etta avoid being roped in as housekeeper for the two men? And if her mother didn't die, there would still be the old battle to fight over again. She temporized, and wrote that it was impossible to get away at once—she would perhaps come later or if matters were very serious. As she posted the letters, she wondered if she were being very sensible or very selfish.

The crisis occurred a couple of days later at breakfast, after Etta had been rather upset by reproachful letters from Teddy and her father. Ada said:

"I've good news for you, Edith. Ralph writes that he'd like to come here for the remainder of our time. Doesn't that please you?"

"I don't care if he comes or not," said Edith ungraciously. "He's got so solemn and priggish about something or other, he's no fun any more."

"Probably he was worried about his exam. He says he has private but quite certain information that he has passed well enough to get an appointment, and that he's tired of London heat. I think he deserves a holiday. I wonder what will happen about his appointment if he gets the commission he's applied for?"

Nobody could answer that question, and Ada took up the newspaper. The rustling of the sheets as she tried to unfold and refold it got on Etta's nerves. A loathing for all human beings surprisingly took possession of her. She wanted to leap to her feet and run away from them, all of them, away from the infernal worries and situations always being sprung on her by them. How lovely to get right away from all civilization to an island in the Pacific somewhere, to live a perfectly healthy, natural life with peaceful savages, bearing them savage children, swimming and gathering fruit and making meals, and worrying not at all about this complicated and destructive European exist- ence. And under that thought she instinctively made up her mind—to go, and go back to Dortborough. Ralph had broken his promise, and Etta was determined not to live through the hell of having him in the same cottage with herself and the other Lawsons.

She went upstairs and grimly packed her bags. Going, going, gone. This was the end, finis, of that particular ad- venture. She'd tried hard enough and failed. But one thing was certain—Etta was not going to repay Ada's kindness by having a clandestine intrigue with her nephew. Taking her father's second letter in her hand, Etta went down to Ada and found her still poring drearily over the newspaper. She looked up enquiringly.

"I have very bad news from home," said Etta, holding out the envelope. "Would you mind reading that?"

Ada read the letter hastily and looked at her. The pallor of Etta's face, her nervous movements and tightly clenched lips were attributed by Ada to natural anxiety about her mother.

"I'm very, very sorry," Ada said kindly. "What do you want to do?"

Etta bit her lip in desperation—it wasn't a question of what she wanted to do, but of what she was being forced to do.

"I think I—there seems no alternative," Etta stam- mered. "Could I go for two weeks?"

"Don't set any period to it, stay until your mother is quite well again."

"Thank you, but that will be enough—may I go to- day?"

"Certainly, I'll have the car for you."

"I wouldn't go unless it seemed absolutely necessary,"

said Etta deprecatingly. "But I feel I must go. You do
understand, don't you?"

"Why, naturally."

"I hope it won't inconvenience you?" Etta said, trying
to get Ada to say something about coming back. "There
isn't much to do while you're in the country, and anyway
I shall be back before you return to London."

"Not in the least. But I've decided to put Ralph off—
perhaps you wouldn't mind sending the telegram for me—
and go back to London immediately. With this war going
on, I feel restless here—and I shall be nearer Robert."

Etta made no comment, for none seemed possible. She
sent the telegram from Dymcott station, and then sat in
the corner of an empty third-class carriage, looking at the
gliding landscape through tears. It was nearly dark when
she got to Dortborough, and the air was stiflingly hot.

7

THERE ARE, ON AN AVERAGE, 1440 thunderstorms a day
going on over the earth, most of them quite harmless. The
human tempests known as wars are less frequent but more
destructive, and Dortborough, where the international
barometer had stood at "Peace" for so long a time, woke
up one morning and found there was a war on. Like Dymcott, Dortborough was delighted, thereby giving one more
proof of the soundness of the classification which flatters
us with the description *sapiens*. Dortborough wasn't afraid,
not it. A hard-headed business community standing no
nonsense, Dortborough immediately performed the extremely rational feats of hating a lot of people it had never
seen, going frantic about a symbolic totem of three coloured crosses, and getting an emotional kick out of several
indifferent popular songs.

At any rate, the fact remains that Dortborough was well inside the international storm area, though not as yet in the danger zone. Hence perhaps the cheerfulness. But so far as Etta was concerned, the storm was very distant— she was mildly patriotic, but cumbered with much serving. On her arrival she found her mother was ill, but not so ill as all that. There had been a slight heart attack, for which the doctor had counselled rest and a modified diet. The "nurse" turned out to be an old body whose chief jobs had been to pity the poor invalid in tones of whining and hypocritical solicitude and to make a devilish good thing out of the housekeeping bills while keeping Teddy and his father on short commons. After a short but demonstrative scene, in which Etta most unwillingly played the part of the returned prodigal, she took matters in hand, discharged the "nurse"—and found herself deep in domesticity.

Like some other elderly ladies with nothing much to do, Mrs. Morison enjoyed her illness thoroughly. Doubtless she had been alarmed at first, but her own feelings and the doctor's repeated assurances soon convinced her that this was only a very preliminary tap on the shoulder from the fell sergeant. But she kept this conviction to herself, and went on being ill while constantly asserting that they were "keeping something from her." In an uneventful life a malady was too fruitful a source of diversion not to be exploited, and then, since it had proved so efficient in howking back the naughty Etta from a life of sin and shame, it might be equally so in keeping her. The only snag was that it rather prevented her from enjoying all the fun of the war, but that was compensated by the increased number of visitors only too anxious to discuss it and by the leisure to read all the horrors in the newspapers.

"Just listen to this, isn't it *dreadful* . . ." were words Etta came to fear, as portending some further atrocity,

with infinite comments thereon. Mrs. Morison daily as-
serted that the conduct of the Germans made her feel sick,
which perhaps explains why she loved reading about their
atrocities. Meanwhile Etta had to run the house and at the
same time be in constant attendance on the invalid, who
gave her a good run for her money. By her bedside Mrs.
Morison kept—appropriately enough—a muffin bell, which
she rang whenever she thought Etta was getting too much
time off. Etta obeyed it promptly and uncomplainingly,
and Mrs. Morison congratulated herself on the success of
her astute maternal discipline. She couldn't see what was
going on in Etta's mind.

One day in the old home and one walk down the Muncaster Road were sufficient. Etta admitted that her own
life was a tangle, and that so far as dealing with contem-
porary society went she had so far been a childish failure;
but in all the uncertainty and confusion one thing was
definite—she wasn't going to stay at home in Dortborough.
The place itself looked uglier, dingier, pettier, and more
platitudinous than ever. And in comparison with the Lawsons and their circle, the people she met were common and
dull. One person only awoke her interest and affections,
and that was Teddy.

In a few months he had developed exceedingly. He was
changing from a huge hobbledehoy of a schoolboy into a
tall, good-looking young man, very self-conscious but nice.
Etta spent much tact in modifying his clothes and trying
to give him some hint of the manners she liked so much in
Ralph, but without much success. Although he was barely
eighteen, Teddy was so anxious to "get on" in business
that he had already started in his father's office, and was
mightily self-important about it, though in fact he was
little more than a privileged office boy—Mr. Morison had
no intention whatever of handing over his command to

Teddy. For the rest, Teddy was most excited about the war, and had in his bedroom a map of Europe bristling with pin flags which he moved daily. From the care he bestowed on his appearance and his self-consciousness about what he did when he was out, Etta suspected that he had a girl. She tried to warn him against early marriages.

"Do you think you'll like to live always in Dortborough?" she asked him as they walked down Muncaster Road.

"Well, I'm in business now," Teddy said loftily. "And Dortborough's a prosperous little place. Besides, all my friends are here."

"Have you many girl friends?"

Teddy blushed a fiery red as he tried to answer indifferently:

"Oh, yes, quite a lot."

"I wish you could have seen something more of the world before you settle down in Dortborough, but if you're happy, that's all that matters."

"Oh, I'm happy enough."

"Still, you mayn't always want to be here—you may change your mind in a few years. I don't want you to tie yourself down here too completely."

"How do you mean?"

"It would be a mistake, I think, if you married too soon."

Teddy blushed again, and Etta judged from his confusion that there *was* a girl somewhere.

"I've no intention of doing that," said Teddy rather blusteringly. "But a man ought to marry sooner or later, and I don't see why two people should waste the best years of their lives."

"Neither do I, but I'm not sure a premature marriage isn't wasting them. Marrying means making yourself responsible for a girl, and children if you let yourself have them. Girls are rather unscrupulous, Teddy, especially

if a young man has any sort of position, as you'll have
with Daddy."

"I don't agree with you," said Teddy stiffly but plainly
very uncomfortable. "Marriage gives a man something
to work for."

"Say rather it keeps him chained to his work. Oh,
Teddy, my dear, don't commit yourself too soon. I know
you're a man now, but surely there are other ways—I don't
mean street women—but couldn't you—I mean, surely it's
possible for you to have what you need without getting
married until you're much older and know really what
you want?"

He turned on her in a fury, his face red and distorted
with prejudice and angry shame.

"Look here, I don't want to hear anything of that kind.
If you like to be beastly and immoral with the beastly
immoral people you pick up in London, that's your look-
out. I intend to live a decent clean life."

Etta shrank away, amazed by the violence of his utter-
ance. He looked exactly like a frightened animal. She felt
acutely sorry for him, without any anger. Poor lad, struggling against a terrifically powerful primal impulse with
nothing but ignorance and prejudice to help him. Naturally the instinct would win, and as soon as he was twenty-
one would fling him gleefully into the social trap. A year's
honeymoon, then the first baby, and a struggle for the
rest of life to provide for them through Business. No
wonder life was a dogfight. Etta felt thankful that at least
she had saved Ralph from that, however clumsily and with
pain to them both.

This episode was unfortunate because it made an
estrangement of confidence and thereby deprived Etta of
her one consolation in Dortborough. She felt no resentment against Teddy's violent rudeness. After all, the con-

flict was the old one of superstition against informed reason. Just as her parents accepted without criticism the common superstitions about the status and requirements of girls in human society, so Teddy accepted the current superstitions about sex.

Ten days after her return home, Etta wrote to Ada, saying that her mother was much better, and adding that she would be back at work on the following Monday. By return of post came the answer. Ada had evidently acquired by contagion that peculiar theory of wealthy people that in moments of national crisis the right thing to do is to sack as many employees as possible and virtuously save the money involved. Of course, she didn't put it that way. What she said was that most people didn't realize what the war meant (unhappily only too true) and that on account of the number of casualties among Guards officers and the gravity of the situation, she felt that she ought not to afford herself the luxury of a secretary any longer. A cheque for ten pounds was enclosed. She said nothing about Ralph or about the post which Mr. Lawson was to have found.

The shock of this was almost more than Etta's courage could bear. In all her weighing of possible chances she had never foreseen the chance of Ada's defection. And how bitterly ironical the whole situation was! From the best motives of scruple and gratitude, Etta had denied Ralph; from the same motives she had seized the excuse of her mother's illness to leave Dymcott and avoid Ralph—that sacrifice also proved to be unnecessary as well as useless. And the final result was that Ada deserted her. How did one learn to act sensibly in life, to square interests with standards of honour? Suppose she had acted with crude cunning, had accepted Ralph's offer that they should be engaged, had encouraged him to write her compromising letters, and had allowed Ralph to get her with child? How easy for her to play the part of the seduced maiden, and to plant herself on the Lawsons as an obligation for life! Yes, and how utterly odious and self-degraded she would have felt for the rest of that life.

In the bitterness of her soul, Etta's first impulse was to return the cheque with a stiff, formal note of acknowledgment. She had sealed the letter up and was on her way to post it when she suddenly changed her mind and decided it was foolish to gratify a momentary anger at the expense of losing her one powerful friend. She did not post the letter. If only it had been possible to consult somebody, but one result of independence and trying to live on your own was that you had no friends. Teddy had loyally kept her secret a year before, but in his present mood she was afraid to trust him, and though she longed to tell Vera all about it, Etta had determined that nobody must hear anything about Ralph. And, as she ruefully admitted, the last bundle on her poor little camel's back was the undeniable certainty that she was more in love with Ralph than ever and that she would do almost anything to see him again.

After a couple of days of weary hesitations Etta wrote a warmly worded little note, understanding perfectly, et cetera, thanking Ada for her kindness, and asking if Mr. Lawson could now find her the promised post. Back came the answer that "things in the City" were so chaotic and uncertain, it was impossible to do anything at present, but that later on Ada would see what could be done. Etta digested this last disappointment and then wrote again politely. After which was silence; nothing from Ada, nothing from Ralph; the whole Lawson episode seemed over.

8

FOR MANY WEEKS Etta now abandoned hope, and her days passed in apathetic misery. There were moments when she

even regretted the days at Thirlby's, when at least she had
some hope, however delusive. It struck Etta as remarkable
that nobody seemed to notice her misery or to have the
slightest suspicion that she was not living in bouncing
merriment. If she had broken her leg they would all have
showed instant sympathy; but she had merely broken her
heart and her spirit, and they were not even aware of it.
Her apathy was mistaken for having "learnt her lesson."
Half-unconsciously they exploited this, with an air of
triumphing over her foolishness; and because she didn't
care what she did, the family very easily slid into the habit
of making use of her.

This was not the only respect in which Etta came to
realize that she had worsened her position. On the credit
side she could only claim that she had proved she could
do a job of work and that she had about £20 more money
than when she left. That was something, but a pretty
meagre reward for her toil and suffering. She had yet to
learn that by running away she had jeopardized her moral
reputation. Dortborough didn't judge hastily or unchamit-
ably, oh no, but still it was a queer thing for a girl to go
off like that, wasn't it? And then her own mother had
dropped some pretty strong hints about impropriety, and
there must have been something behind them because,
after all, the mother would be the first to try to conceal
things, and even she hadn't been able to avoid letting it
out. And so on and so on. However, as the girl obviously
wasn't pregnant, Dortborough decided to watch and wait,
meanwhile giving her the demi-cold half-shoulder.

For a number of weeks Etta remained in complete ignorance of this, partly because of her absorption in her own
misery and partly from a very real indifference to what is
known as public opinion. The first hint came when her
energy and hope so far recovered from the knock-down
of Ada's letters that she ventured to ask her father once

more if she might not work in his office or elsewhere in
Dortborough. He immediately became very angry.

"Certainly not. I've told you before I won't have it.
Why can't you put this nonsense out of your head? Women
aren't wanted in business, except as shop girls and—and—
and that sort of thing. I suppose you'll want to be a bar-
maid next. Let me tell you that you ought to be very grateful that we took you back and forgave you for disgracing
us."

He went on for some time on this theme, and Etta saw
it was hopeless. She didn't understand his full meaning,
interpreting the word "disgrace" as meaning no more than
local disapproval of a girl going "suffragette." Nor did
she notice that Teddy was frequently invited while she was
ignored. The truth only hit her at a dance given by Vera's
family in the one large hotel ballroom of Dortborough.
Etta had recognized a girl friend of her school days, and
they were talking together when the girl's mother came
up. Etta smiled and uttered some conventional greeting,
but the woman took no notice and almost snatched at her
daughter's arm:

"Come with me, Eileen, I want you."

As they went away Etta heard the mother say:

"Haven't I told you to have nothing to do with a girl
with a reputation like that?"

Eileen's protest was lost in the general movement. Etta
saw the implication in a flash, and between anger, surprise,
and contempt was unable to move. So *that* was it! She
pulled herself together, found Vera and said that she felt
ill, and went home at once. As she walked through the
dimly lit streets, Etta raged at them. What a set of
idiots! What inane prejudice! They could only imagine
a "wicked" sexual motive for what she had done, and
their only standard of judgment of a woman was what they
imagined her sexual conduct to be. So long as a girl was

reputed to be physiologically "pure" all was well, however
stupid, malicious, and dishonourable she might be. A
woman might go through life making everyone near her
miserable and ruin a family, and yet so long as a court of
justice could pronounce her "pure" she was a "good"
woman. Another woman might be Nature's masterpiece
of amiability, intelligence, and character and yet be
shunned and despised as "impure." What stupidity, and
what cheek! And what real contempt for womanhood un-
derlay it all! The joke was, though it was rather a bitter
one, that she was as physiologically "pure" as any of
them. In her contemptuous rage she thought of getting a
doctor's certificate of virginity, handing it round, and then
cutting them all wholesale. That made her laugh at her
own violence and restored her equanimity. All the same, it
was hard to put up with such twaddle.

Winter enveloped Dortborough, and the dull days slowly
dropped away until they brought the dreary hilarities of
another Christmas. If Etta had been asked, she could
scarcely have explained how she managed to keep sane
and alive during those weeks. They were spun out in a
flat sameness of routine which was suicidally depressing
from its having no particular object so far as she was concerned. The war even had got stuck in the mud like herself.
The only break in the routine was an occasional tea with
Vera at the Japanese shop and a renewal of good relations
with Teddy. In her hunger for affection, Etta almost abjectly flattered Teddy's tastes and prejudices. She was
rewarded by hearing from him that she had "improved a
lot" since getting back to Dortborough and "dropping
the airs" she was supposed to have acquired illicitly in
London. The only sign that Etta still cultivated a flicker
of hope was that she kept up her typing and shorthand.
The only outward event which came like a brilliant star

into her firmament was an utterly unexpected letter from
Ralph, which arrived about the middle of January.

This letter puzzled Etta: it was and it wasn't a love
letter. Its news was interesting enough—Ralph had passed
his examination and had been appointed, but after less
than two months his application for a commission had been
passed and he was going into camp to train. This was put
in quite an offhand way, and then the tone suddenly
changed—he must see her before he finally went overseas,
would she promise to meet him in London during his final
leave? The last words were: "There is something I must
know from you before I go." If Ralph still cared for her,
why had he allowed her to suffer for months through
his silence? And if he didn't care, why want to see her?
How mysterious is the life of another person, how impossible it is to follow subtle changes of mood and
impulse.

Though this letter seemed enigmatic, it had an immensely stimulating effect on Etta's ambition. Under the
pressure of monotony and the will-against-her of the family,
Etta had become almost resigned to a perpetuity of Dortborough—but not quite. Ralph's letter not only stirred up
her yearning for him, but made her almost frantic to get
away, to stop this futile waste of days, to be doing something. She didn't admit to herself that Ralph had anything
to do with it. And this turmoil of thwarted desires showed
itself in a more violent loathing of Dortborough. Sitting
over tea with Vera a few days later Etta inveighed against
the place in good set terms:

"If only I could get away finally and completely from
this pestilential abode of fools!"

"Oh, Etta!" Vera's common sense was offended. "It's
silly to talk like that. It's conceited."

"Quite right," said Etta smiling at her own violence.

"It does sound conceited. Let's say I'm not good enough for Dortborough people. *They* don't like me, and *I* don't like them. It's a misfit."

"Wouldn't it be more sensible to try and fit in?"

"Yes, it would, if I absolutely despaired of ever getting out and fitting in somewhere I liked more. But I don't— at least, not always. I believe I shall get out eventually, but how and when, I can't imagine."

"If you want to go so much, why don't you just leave as you did before?"

"Because this time it must be final. I can't crawl home defeated again. For one thing, they probably wouldn't have me. And I'm not going to throw myself recklessly on the world. I suppose it's risky even for a man, but it's madness for a woman."

"I don't see that it's so different. . . ."

"Yes, it is. You're protected by having an income of your own. You don't, you can't know. There aren't many jobs for women, and most of them are rotten ones. They aren't easy to get, but it is easy to be starving or half-starved if one just rushes away from home at random. And if you're on the misery border long enough and still look presentable there's a pretty obvious danger. A woman has got one commodity she can sell—herself."

"Etta!"

"Don't be so shockable, Vera. Don't be like everyone else here and refuse to see unpleasing realities. Can't you see how weak and cowardly that is, how it plays into the hands of rogues and scoundrels, how it makes people unconscious hypocrites? Prostitution exists; and most of those in it are pushed in by poverty. I don't intend to be pushed in, but I shan't keep out by being shocked at the mention of it or by despising my luckless sisters. I shall keep out of it by understanding men and the world, and by using my wits."

"It sounds rather hard and calculating," said Vera uneasily.

"Of course it's hard and calculating, but what's the good of being a witless softy? I've learned a lot in the past year, and I've thought about it. God knows what I thought was going to happen when I left here, but I got a number of unpleasant surprises, I can tell you. It's useless for me or any other woman to go out blindly and expect to make a success without facing the realities."

"But, Etta, you used to have such high ideals. Do you remember when we talked once in London I begged you not to lose them?"

"Did you? What I do remember is that you were very kind to me when I'd almost lost heart. That I won't ever forget. There *are* nice people in the world. Unfortunately the niceness doesn't seem to penetrate far into business or any of the ways of earning a living. As for ideals—it depends what you mean by the word. I've come to think the word should often be spelled 'self-indulgence.' Ideals! Daydreams of ignorance and presumption. I want the realities."

"I can't bear to have you talk like that, Etta! Don't you ever now have any aspirations to something more than gross materialism? Take care! Already you're growing harder and harder, and you'll end up by becoming like the very people you most despise."

"Shall I?" Etta laughed. "And whose fault will that be? You told me to fit into Dortborough. How if I 'aspire' to fit into something better? I'm not a nun or a poet, so I don't 'aspire' to a life of contemplation or rosy raptures. I'm an ordinary woman, but without being conceited I think I can say I'm a little more intelligent and energetic than some are. The realities I want are not all 'gross materialism,' even though they are the desires of an ordinary woman."

"Well, what *do* you want?"

"Let me think," said Etta, reflecting. "First, I want a life that is full and interesting. I should like to work at something which had a purpose beyond mere money-making. I should like to mix with people who would make my life fuller. I want to live with or near a man I love and who would love me, and I think I'd like to have a child; but I don't want that in squalor and misery. As jam for it all, I'd like to live part of the time in London and part in a lovely place like Dymcott—Mrs. Lawson's house. Yes, if I had the right occupation and friends, and could own Dymcott and live there part of the year with a lover and a child, yes, my life would be all I could desire. Of course, I should want music and books and flowers and so on, but all that would be naturally included."

"And you wouldn't want more? Owning Dymcott and having all the rest would be enough?"

"I think so. If I had Dymcott and—but what's the use of talking about all these things when I'm a million miles from ever getting them?"

"Yes, but, Etta, don't you think that's very selfish? Surely you want to do something for humanity, for other people too?"

"Well, I should do something for a man and his child. Altruism should begin at home. And, yes, I would try to do things to help other women, as Ada Lawson tried to help me. But nobody can play fairy godmother to other people's lives—you can only give them a leg up. I don't want to be given those things, I want to earn them. If I got a leg-up I believe I could do it. What I hate so much is droning about here without interests and without work. I want to *do* something."

"But here it is right under your nose! Aren't you interested in the war, can't you work for it?"

"I'm not patriotic like you, Vera, and I simply couldn't

persuade men to go and suffer and be killed where I can't
go myself."

"Oh, Etta, you're not a pro-German, you're not a
pacifist, are you?"

"I haven't thought about it," said Etta carelessly. "Of
course I want us to win the war, and I wouldn't mind
working for it if there was anything I could do, but there
isn't. They only want men."

"That's just where you're wrong."

"Why, what could I do?"

"Do? Help make bandages and swabs for the wounded
for one thing. There's a group of us doing it. Why not
join us?"

"Why, yes, I'd like to," said Etta brightening, "especially if it's doing even the teeniest bit of real good. But
d'you think they'd have me? I'm not supposed to be respectable now, you know—I told you about Eileen's
mother at the dance."

"Oh, *her*," said Vera scornfully. "We wouldn't have a
creature like that. No, they're nearly all the W. S. P. U.
women you used to know."

"Right. If they'll have me, I'll come. The sooner the
better."

It can't be said that Etta enjoyed these swab-making
bees, but at any rate they made a break, they were better
than afternoons of mournful brooding. The party was presided over by a bustling widow of an officer killed in the
South African War. Her patriotism had the ferocity of
Huitzilopochtli demanding blood sacrifice—having lost
her own man she wanted to thrust every other woman
into the same position. Every volunteer was cross-
examined as to what her men were doing. Etta had a
pretty good alibi—her father and Uncle Harry were over
military age, and Teddy was under.

"Ah, well," said the widow comfortingly, "he'll join up on the first day possible, won't he?"

Etta didn't like this. For a moment the war ceased to be something in the newspapers and became a personal reality—the reality of Teddy a soldier. Quickly she put that aside: it would be over long before he was old enough. She contrived to sit as far from the widow as possible, and listened vaguely to the talk as she made swabs from lint and gauze. The talk was of things which are now so dead and boring and unreal (and will remain so until they are revived in different terms by the next effort to make the world safe for dictatorship), talk of surplus generals and gun shortage, of battles and sudden death, of how right "we" are and how wicked "they" are, of the million more men called for, of how wonderful life will be "after the war."

This last topic gave Etta an idea. As she walked listlessly home one evening about the end of February, she was wondering if the others had noticed how strangely deficient in manual skill most of them were; and if they imagined, as she did, how their innocent-looking snowy piles of lint would soon be dyed blood-red and then chucked away. A million men. She suddenly halted as another startling thought came to her. If a million men were going, if there was such shortage that work by "ladies" was not only tolerated but, bewilderingly enough, encouraged, then . . . Why, then, might there not be a place for her in the world a little better than amateurishly making swabs in Dortborough?

Etta almost ran home in her excitement. Eagerly she rushed to her bedroom, found notepaper, and began writing a wild appeal to Ada. She described her loneliness, the futility of her days, the intolerable ennui of her routine, her subjection, the nullity which was imposed on her. She reminded Ada of the promised hypothetical job, and that Ada herself had thought her efficient. Would Ada recommend her, find her something possible to do, whether it directly concerned the war or not? Without hesitation she sealed and stamped the letter and ran out at once to post it.

Several days passed, during which high hopes faded to discouragement. Ada had forgotten her. But an answer came—Robert had gone to the front; Ada had been unwell; but Robert was *so* happy to be out; she would do all she could to find Etta something. Etta replied immediately, and then came another dismal silence. She counted the days—ten days, a fortnight, three weeks, and nothing happened. All useless. Etta decided that there was nothing else for it, she'd have to take Vera's advice and try to fit into Dortborough: a bleak and painful prospect.

It was raining heavily, but there was a whiff of spring in the air as Etta quickly opened her bedroom window one morning. She couldn't wait to enjoy it, because she was late for breakfast. She found the others already seated, the two men manfully getting through their eggs and bacon, with Mrs. Morison (who had regretfully got better at last) not a bad third.

"Two letters for you," said Teddy between his munches, as she sat down.

Etta grabbed them eagerly and read them before eating a mouthful, laid down the envelopes on the table, and rested her hand on them lightly and gratefully. The way out at last, and not as a slave of private greed, but as a servant of England. It was a moment of pure triumph. She could feel her cheeks flushing with excitement as she looked from one to the other of her family. The way out at last. But how would they take it? Etta felt she couldn't bear a scene which would wreck her mood of happiness;

yet she had to be in London that night, and if she wasn't to sneak off, they would have to be told before the men went to their office. Her eyes turned wary as she calculated the best method. She cleared her throat nervously and said:

"I have to go to London this afternoon."

"Oh, indeed," said Mrs. Morison sharply. "And what for?"

By way of answer Etta handed one of the letters to her father, who so far had showed no interest in either the letters or her remark. He glanced at it indifferently and then sat up sharply.

"What's this, what's this? Interview at the Admiralty!"

"What? Who?" asked Teddy and his mother simultaneously.

"Etta, if you please! For a temporary clerkship. Who'd have thought it?"

"Well, I'm blowed," said Teddy.

"Perhaps it's all a mistake," suggested Mrs. Morison sweetly.

"It's not a mistake!" exclaimed Etta, suddenly flaring up. "Why must you always try to disparage and thwart me, Mother? I have another letter from a friend, who says it's certain, and moreover, I'm invited to live there."

"Don't get ratty," said Teddy. "You needn't be so swanky about it. Let's have a look at the letter, Dad."

"May one humbly ask who your friend is?" asked Mrs. Morison sarcastically. "Young ladies don't *usually* go to live with their gentlemen friends."

Etta flushed again, this time with annoyance—here was the scene coming.

"It's only Miss Millingham," she answered, lying calmly. She wasn't going to tell them that she had been asked to stay with Ada—no repetition of the Mrs. Cleveland scandal.

"Well," said Mr. Morison, "I congratulate you. Doing your bit. How much are they going to pay you?"

"Three pounds a week, to start."

"Umph. Shouldn't have thought you were worth it, but I s'pose they know their own business. Good luck to you!"

"Thank you, Daddy," said Etta submissively.

"Three pounds a week!" said Teddy. "Well, I'm dashed —that's twice what *I* get!"

"You'll get more when you're worth it," said Mr. Morison austerely. "At present you're a liability, not an asset."

"I'm sure he's worth every penny of three pounds," said Mrs. Morison, on the defensive at once for Teddy. "And anyway, he sticks to his home and his father's business and doesn't go trapesing off with strangers and admirals and unnatural things for a young girl."

"Don't be silly," said Mr. Morison. "It's an honour to have our little girl working for the old country. Here . . ." He fished a couple of five-pound notes from his pocketbook and slapped them on the table before Etta. "Take that. I daresay they'll give you your uniform, but you may have to pay for it. Money's always useful. And if you want more, there's more where that came from."

Etta gazed at him in bewilderment—why was it so immoral to want to earn a living in peace and so virtuous to help men kill each other? And then for some reason she burst into tears.

9

To be back in london was exciting, so exciting that Etta overlooked the real nature of her employment and the means of obtaining it. The feeling of triumph which had moved her to tears had been personal: it seemed a justification of herself. And so, in a way, it was. But she quite forgot that without the Lawsons she would never have thought of this kind of work, and that she would have been a very long time getting it without their support. More-over, Etta never thought of the price others were paying for her emancipation. Why should she? A merciful self-preservation hides from us the sufferings of others, or we should go mad. It was so pleasant to be in her "own" room again with another spring just stirring in the park, so de-lightful to settle into the rhythm of life with the Lawsons, that for a time she hardly noticed how, when Robert's name was mentioned, a strange expression altered Ada's face, while her husband grew more silent than ever.

Etta started on her new work with awe and timidity, soon grew confident, and then disillusioned. There was no Drayton atmosphere, for which she was grateful; and her men superiors were entirely unbusinesslike, i.e., imper-sonal and to the point.

Three months later, when another batch of newcomers arrived, Etta was one of the four girls from the first set who were given slightly more responsible posts, with a small increase in salary. But in spite of her pleasure at this, the feeling of disillusion remained. Not much was required of her but docility and exactness, a precise carrying out of rules. Very rarely did she understand the purpose or mean-ing of what she was doing, and gathered the less she thought about that the better. Stick close to the rules and you'll be all right, was the principle.

One obvious result of this was an inhuman disjunction between the activities by which Etta earned her living and the activities which made it worth while to go on living at all. Her own life faded every morning as she entered the office, and she left it at night as willingly as a child leaves school. She only wished she could forget it all as easily as a child forgets its lessons. Yet the only way to "get on" and to realize the ambition of being "on her own" was to force herself to a concentrated interest she didn't feel. How identify herself with the navy? Her working life and her personal life were completely opposed and mutually destructive.

In most lives, Etta reflected, there is a sharp contest between the job and the person; and the job, reinforced by inexorable necessity and social practice, usually won. Those who refused to give in became adventurers, mostly criminal ones, whether they got into jail or were knighted. The great mass became just bits of personality, feeding their vital impulse on every shoddy and sensational substitute. Etta lost herself in vague dreams of a perfect society where these conflicts would be ended and human beings reconciled with themselves. She returned to her old habits of hoarding all she could save. Money, that was the way out, money. With money one could really live. Meanwhile, fierce concentration on the job.

But, as Etta found, life is not so easily put off as that. Man is a consciously life-seeking animal. No matter how crude or perverted the "instinct," it is always there. Even the suicides are life-seekers; they are *les délicats;* what is offered them seems not good enough. All religions promise more life. Three hundred generations ago men gathered cowrie shells because their sexual shape made them life-givers; later they hoarded coins because they symbolized cowries, and gold is another life-giver, a double potency; now the mere written symbols of cowrie coins thrill us because we live in the age of words and ballyhoo. And still we have not discovered that "life" is in ourselves and nowhere else, that we receive back only what we give out.

Man is also the most instable of animals. Compared with the sea urchin, hoary echinus, we are the parvenus of a day. Apart from their superstitions, men cannot make up their minds what they want to achieve. Perpetually menacing themselves with the fate of the ant, they perpetually get frightened, destroy their ant-hills, and avoid ant-dom. The variety of their activities is terrific, from Osiris-Pharaoh to a mud-eater, from the monstrous selfishness of Trimalchio to the monstrous self-abnegation of a juggernaut victim, from Jesus to a London intellectual. Some want to be utterly identified with their collective function; some want to have no function at all but that of a copepod on humanity. But the object is always the same —more life. Astonishing *sapiens!* long may you live indeed, perpetually self-defeated and perpetually tightening your belt for the next round with nothingness.

Etta was no more free than anyone else from this instinct, its errors and consequences. At Dymcott in the summer she had reached a point of exaltation when she could sacrifice her "life" for Ada and Ralph, but during her miserable winter in Dortborough she had tormented herself with longing for the very thing she had sacrificed. At first she had suffered agonies of yearning for Ralph, but his absence, his silence, the pressure of Dortborough had slowly damped down that clear flame of desire to a hidden smouldering. Etta believed the flame had gone out—it had all been a mistake—they were young and foolish then— she had been terrifically in love with him once—but it was all over—and anyway he'd probably forgotten all about her.

So, naturally enough, during the spring of 1915 Etta's life-seeking turned chiefly to the job, until she sprang the "disjunctive" theory on herself, which was only another way of noting that a temporary clerkship in the Admiralty didn't interest her deeply and didn't satisfy her. Nevertheless, she stuck to it and even managed to do fairly well. The war hung over her life like an imperceptibly thickening cloud, but remained distant and impersonal. She thought, not unjustly, that because of it, the spring of 1915 was less beautiful and happy than the spring of 1914. Ralph,

of course, had nothing to do with it. Nothing whatever.
Etta made up her mind she was going to have nothing
more to do with men—it wasn't worth the price one had
to pay. And that in spite of certain symptoms, not uncon-
nected with the life instinct, which might seem to imply
if not to demand some different solution.

In May Robert came home on short leave, sterner and
more cold-eyed than ever, with a fanatical contempt for
everything and everybody not directly engaged in the
war. Entirely reticent about his own experiences, he raged
against the government for not forcing the whole nation
into war service. He seemed surprised when told what
Etta was doing, but his approval—if any—took the form
of contempt that men could not be found for the purpose.
Then he was gone again; and even Etta noticed that Ada
looked haggard under her seeming cheerfulness.

One afternoon in early June Etta left her office as usual,
carrying her attaché case, and as usual walked back
through the Green Park. In the distance she could see a
column of men in khaki marching along, while a crowd
waved and shouted to them. But such sights were already
becoming too common to attract her attention. She was
thinking that it was almost summer. If Ada and Edith
went to Dymcott, would she be allowed to stay on, or
would she have to find a room? And if she herself had a
holiday, where could she go? Every week the figure of her
savings bank book increased; she hated the idea of having
to lower it. Perhaps she ought to go and see Miss Millingham again soon.

On the upper landing Etta saw a servant going into one
of the guest rooms, carrying clean linen. Without stopping
to take off her hat, Etta turned back to look for Ada, whom
she found sitting alone in her room with her face hidden in
her hands.

"Ada! What is it? What has happened?"

Etta never forgot the strange look in Ada's eyes as she lifted her head, a doomed look of pain.

"Ralph now," she said tonelessly.

"Ralph! What about him?"

"He's coming tonight for a couple of days, to say good-bye to us, and then back to his parents."

"To say good-bye? I don't understand."

"He's ordered overseas, on active service."

Etta felt herself growing pale with terror as she stared into Ada's eyes. Active service. Ralph. Perhaps not come back. But he must, he *must* come back. Because she loved him he must come back. Quickly she turned away her eyes —what was she allowing Ada to see there? She said:

"But I thought there was soon going to be a big push to end the war?"

"That is why he is needed."

"Oh, well," said Etta, trying to reassure herself, "it'll soon be over, and then he'll come home again."

"Robert may be in it too."

Etta didn't know what to say. She put her arms about Ada and kissed her cheek and held her, saying at last:

"He'll be all right, I'm sure he will."

Ada shook her head.

"Ever since he went I've been afraid," she whispered. "Afraid every day, almost every hour. I daren't let him know—he wants me to be brave, a soldier's mother. And now Ralph. So much of my life is in those two boys, they're both like sons to me. Help me to be brave, Etta, for my heart's dread is that they may neither come back."

From that moment the war for Etta ceased to be something only "in the papers."

But when Ralph appeared about an hour later, he made all their sadness and forebodings seem ridiculous. He was in the highest spirits, absorbed in his new life, about which he chattered continuously—stories about the men and other officers, the absurdity of army regulations and so on, but above all about how fine the men were and how splendid it was to be all going out together. Etta thought he looked very grown-up and handsome in his smart uniform. Ralph told her how to distinguish an officer's rank by his badges, and explained the devices on his cap and coat lapels and on his buttons. Etta had never noticed them before, but after this she nearly always looked at a man's badges, just in case he might belong to the Royal Artillery.

The evening passed pleasantly. Mr. Lawson returned from his office and insisted that Ralph should come to the cellar with him to choose the dinner wines. Mr. Lawson enjoyed the wines, and the others enjoyed his good intentions in serving them. After dinner Ralph struggled valiantly with one of his uncle's choicest and longest cigars; no doubt it was pure enjoyment which caused him to lay it down half smoked and to remain rather silent for a time. He refused to go to a theatre, said he was quite happy where he was; and they all sat round and worshipped him, and he accepted their worship with charming innocence. Altogether, Etta felt it was by far the happiest evening she had spent since—oh, since last year, since a certain dinner party of two, in fact. Of course, she told herself as she went to bed, she wasn't in love with him, nonsense, that was all over. And her shock of emotion when she heard he was on active service? Pure friendship for Ada's nephew.

She didn't see him in the morning, for Ralph wallowed in the soldier's luxury of a late breakfast in bed with nobody sounding reveille. And in a dull routine life it was natural she should think of that pleasant evening during her work. And she still thought about it as she walked home. Ada and Ralph were sitting over tea talking and laughing.

Etta tried to excuse herself, to leave them alone, but Ralph said he fancied a walk in the park, wouldn't Etta come? And yes, strangely enough, yes, she would love to go, and they were soon walking together by the Serpentine. The sky was cloudy but full of afternoon light which glimmered on the lake surface and glinted from the shaking leaves. There were a few skiffs on the water, people lounging along the walks, children feeding bread to the ducks; from time to time a man in khaki saluted Ralph smartly, and he acknowledged it. Etta felt pleased that Ralph was so important a person. In the distance was a camp, and men were drilling on the wide lawns.

Ralph found a couple of green-painted chairs, and they sat under a rustling sycamore, looking over the water. They were silent for a time, and then he said:

"Did you get my last letter?"

"I think so. Which was it?"

"I said I wanted to speak to you before . . ."

"Yes, oh yes, I had it."

"You didn't answer."

"Because there was nothing to say. At any rate, here I am, and you're speaking to me."

"Tell me why you left Dymcott so suddenly, without a word to me. Why did Ada put me off and come to London?"

"My mother was very ill, I had to go."

"Was that all? Had I nothing to do with it?"

Etta hesitated. She had only to say "No," and then so far as Ralph was concerned, the nuisance of a working woman's having a man in her life would be over. Say "No," she prompted herself. "No," her lips formed, but they said:

"Yes."

"Tell me what it was."

"Must we go over all this? Isn't it all dead and forgotten?"

"Not by me. I *must* know why you did that, why you led me on to think you loved me and then threw me over."

"I didn't! I did love you, but you promised me, and you broke your promise."

"I didn't."

"Yes, you did."

"Well, how could I go on like that? I knew I should be going into the army, and I wanted those last days with you. We should have been lovers by now. Why did you cheat us of that? Why did you go away and then not even answer my letter?"

"Why?" Etta asked herself. It did seem rather absurd and heartless now.

"I told you why at Dymcott. I won't, I can't let you be my lover, Ralph, under these conditions. It seems hopeless for me to struggle any more for what I want, so we'd much better not think about it any more. I *won't* be dishonourable to Ada."

"But, Etta, aren't you sacrificing me and yourself to your own pride? Aren't you quibbling? Is it at all essential? As for Ada—her world is dead. Suddenly, much sooner than we thought, it's our world, our responsibility."

"Why are you in the army?"

"Because it's my duty!"

"And you think women have no duties?"

"You're doing your bit."

"I don't mean that—that's nothing. I've got a duty to myself and to other women. Unless some of us make a stand, our sex will go on being a misery and a servitude to us. Can't you see I should be betraying our love if I didn't stick to my principles?"

"Then you do still love me?"

Etta was silent. She hadn't meant to say that.

"You do love me," he insisted.

She moved her head from side to side in distress.

"Why torment me?" Etta asked. "Haven't I suffered enough? But it's all hopeless. We can't have each other, and so it's better we should part and forget."

"But I can't forget, and I don't believe you can!"

"You didn't write to me. I thought you'd forgotten."

"Don't let's argue, my sweet. I don't ask anything of you now. But look, the war will be over this year or early next year. Won't you wait for me that long? I'll gladly wait for you."

"What do you mean?"

"It'll make all the difference to me, Etta, if I can go out knowing you love me and that I shall come back to you. By that time you'll almost certainly be in the position you want, and I promise you I'll agree to any conditions you like. Do you understand?"

"Yes."

"I know in a way it's asking a lot to ask a girl to bind herself to a man who . . . you know what I mean?"

"Oh, Ralph, don't, don't. You mustn't be hurt, you shan't be."

"Of course I shan't. But you see what I mean, if you'll write to me, your letters'll mean a lot, and I shall see you on leave, and then afterwards . . . Will you?"

"Will I what?"

"Write to me."

"Yes, of course I will."

"And go on loving me?"

"Ah, Ralph, how can one promise that? I've tried not to love you, and you see how I've succeeded. But I promise I won't try to stop loving you."

"That's all I ask. Oh, Etta, I wish I could kiss you now."

"Too many people, my dear."

"There always *are* too many people."

As they walked back through the park, Ralph said wistfully:

"I wish you'd let me tell my parents and Ada that we're engaged."

"No, no!" Etta exclaimed. "You mustn't do that. Keep it to ourselves. And don't think of marriage. There'll be your career when you get back."

"I don't care tuppence. . . ."

"Then you ought to. If you can't think for yourself, I must. You can't marry me. Anything else, but not that."

Ralph pondered a little and then said:

"It seems to me you must love me very much. How about your own life, how about your disabilities, if—if we . . ."

"Don't you worry," said Etta gaily and triumphantly, "I'll look after that."

When Etta came down to dinner she was wearing Ralph's pendant, and before he left very early the next morning he came quickly into her bedroom and kissed her good-bye as she sat up in her nightdress, half frightened, half happy, and wholly desolate that he was going. The buckle on the cross-strap of his Sam Browne belt bruised her undefended breast as he held her tight in young arms which did not know how strong they were.

10

WHEN THE GLOW of Ralph's presence faded and sorrow at his going was overlaid by time, Etta's life fell upon another arid stretch. It is dreary to live a life of waiting, worse still when you don't know how long you must wait, and again worse when every minute holds a deadly threat. Time dragged. Etta concentrated on her work in a desperate attempt to forget and to make the time pass. She assured herself that she *must* not think of anything else, that work was her life; but in fact she lived for the white

envelopes addressed in indelible pencil, marked "B. E. F."
at the top, and signed "R. Lawson 2d Lieut." in the left-
hand corner. She learned to know the wild anxiety of
waiting when they were delayed, the passionate relief
when one or perhaps two or three unexpectedly arrived,
the killing thought: What may have happened since they
were written? Every morning and evening she read the
official communiqués.

Ada did not go to the country that summer—it would
have wasted valuable hours if Robert unexpectedly got
leave. In August Etta had a holiday and went with Vera
to New Radnor, where they lived very cheaply in a cottage
and spent their days taking long walks over the treeless
hills of Radnor Forest. In that solitude, where in narrow
glens they came upon full-grown lambs which were so tame
through having never seen human beings that they could
be patted, it seemed impossible that only a few hundred
miles off, men, Ralph among them, were in deadly strife.
And yet they couldn't wholly forget it. On their walks
Etta told Vera about her work and also a little about herself and Ralph—not much, but enough for Vera to know
that Etta had a very special reason for wanting the war to
end. So by way of hastening that desirable climax Vera
suddenly decided that she also must do real war work,
instead of amateur work in Dortborough. They planned
that Vera should get a job something like Etta's, take a
room at Miss Millingham's, and that Etta should come to
stay there too when she had to leave the Lawsons'.

Yet even that brief respite could not be left untroubled.
Etta received the news from her parents that Teddy had
joined up. Although he was under age, he looked older because he was tall. A girl had given him a white feather in
the street and had made some contemptuous remark. They
hadn't seen him since, but he had written from a training
camp, which he didn't like very much. Still, it was the

right thing to do, and of course they were all proud of him.

Vera was sitting opposite at the table and gazed in astonishment as Etta damned her hat for not going on properly.

"Are we going out at once? It looks like rain."

"Do you mind if I go alone?"

"Oh no, of course not," said Vera a bit huffily.

"Here," said Etta, throwing her the two letters, "read
those. They've got my brother now."

For hours Etta tramped over the uplands, raging and
crying. Rain showers swept over her, drenching her and
soaking the grass and bracken so that her shoes squelched
with water. Robert and even Ralph, yes, they were men
and somehow belonged to the military class. But Teddy!
A boy who was so easily swayed and, in spite of his airs,
still such a child! What would happen to him in that dire
rough-and-tumble? Why, she herself would make as good
a soldier as he. Poor Teddy, dear little brother! Etta
damned the war and the War Office and damned herself
for not having been nicer to Teddy. She arrived back at
the cottage in the evening, wet through, without having
eaten; and all the good it did was to give her a heavy snuf-
fling cold, which Vera soon caught. They returned to
London rather a sad pair.

Back to the routine once more. Every week Etta wrote
regularly to Ralph in France, and to Teddy in camp, always putting in a postal order for Teddy. It seemed incredible to her now that for so long she had felt indifferent
to the war. Quite impossible, she thought, to be more
deeply involved than now. She had yet to learn what in-
genious surprises in the way of mental and emotional
torture the monster could devise. Coming home as usual
one evening towards the end of September, 1915, she found
Ada, white and tragical, pacing up and down, while Ran-

dolfe Lawson sat helpless and silent in his chair. Etta looked from one to the other enquiringly, but neither spoke. At last she ventured to ask:

"Has something happened?"

"We started the big push this morning," said Mr. Lawson.

Etta's eyes met Ada's in startled pain. For a moment there was no veil of pretence between them. Each of the women knew what the other was feeling, and each accepted the other. The wealthy woman and the poor dependent were for that moment two females, each with a dagger of anxiety in her heart.

"We expect a great victory," said Ada hurriedly, turning away her eyes.

"Oh, it's sure to be!" said Etta.

"Our men have been waiting for this," said Mr. Lawson. "Now they're unleashed there'll be no stopping them."

"How soon can we expect official news?" asked Etta nervously.

"Not for two or three days, perhaps not for a week," said Ada, giving the right interpretation to the question.

"What do you mean?" interrupted Mr. Lawson. "It'll be in tonight's communiqué, or tomorrow's at latest."

"It's hard to have to wait," said Etta aloud, while a voice inside her head was saying: "Let him be saved, O God, let him be saved, and Robert too for her sake."

"Perhaps you'd both like to go to the theatre after dinner," suggested Mr. Lawson.

"No, thank you," said Ada.

"How did you hear about this?" asked Etta.

"Privately. I'm told the War Office are delighted with the preliminary results. If we've broken the line, they'll soon be rolled up."

"It's what we've all been waiting and working for," said Ada, nervously clasping and unclasping her hands.

"Yes, of course," said Etta, going to the window to blink her eyes without being seen.

"A great moment in the history of England," said Mr. Lawson solemnly.

They made no comment on this remark. Presently Ada said:

"I must go up and dress."

"It's early yet," her husband objected.

"So must I," said Etta, following Ada to the door. Outside her room Ada paused and, with her head averted, held out her hand. Etta took it quickly, and they stood thus for a moment; then parted without a word.

At breakfast Mr. Lawson was eloquent over the morning's news—great British victory official, said the headlines, prisoners, guns, advancing, some units held up. It was discussed excitedly or condescendingly at her office, where nearly everybody had a special bit of secret news or rumour of his own. But the news Etta and Ada wanted was not among them. One, two three, four days passed. Etta couldn't have believed days could go so slowly if she hadn't lived them. Every morning, when she met Ada, they each asked hurriedly, almost furtively, but with a pretence of indifference:

"Have you heard?"

And each silently shook her head.

Every evening when Etta came in breathless from rapid walking she glanced eagerly at her letter rack, and then looked for Ada to ask the same question and to receive the same answer. Five days, six days. Etta's spirit writhed under the torment. She wondered if her own face looked as pallid and drawn as Ada's. How could they go on enduring this?

The torture relaxed as suddenly as it began. Etta found in her rack (rather appropriately so named) two Field Service cards—"I am quite well"—and a letter, brief and rather incoherent but reassuring—the date was five days after the opening of the battle. Etta rushed upstairs to the room where the Lawsons were sitting, and exclaimed:

"He's safe!"

"Yes," said Ada, a little distantly. "I've had two letters from Robert. It appears he wasn't in the action at all."

"I'm—I'm so glad," Etta stammered, trying to hide the post she was carrying.

"I knew he would be," said Ada, knitting calmly at a sock and refusing to look at Etta. "The mail was delayed for some reason, that was all."

"Yes," said Etta, turning to go. "The mail *was* late, wasn't it?"

Etta went and sat at her bedroom window, looking out at the trees which were already flecked with the gold and bronze of autumn. From time to time a leaf eddied to the ground. She could guess what had happened. Ada must have seen the cards from Ralph, and was offended that in the stress of battle he had thrice sent messages to Etta and none to her. Hence the cold attitude and the intentional omission of Ralph's name. Now that the anxiety was over, they were no longer two women equally suffering, but patron and dependent. Ada wasn't going to admit that Etta had any right to take a special interest in Ralph. It was quite reasonable, quite understandable, but hurting. Etta decided that she would have to leave the house as soon as she could and not overstay her welcome.

Life went on in the same routine. In November Vera got a small job with the Department of Munitions and was installed at Miss Millingham's in the room which had belonged to the poetic Thrush, now warbling on the western front. Miss Millingham was delighted to see Etta again and was very strong on the war.

"My dear," she said, "what thrilling times we live in! So different from the old humdrum days. My only regret is that my dear father, the distinguished judge, you know, did not live to see them. *How* interested he would have been!"

Etta murmured something appropriate, interested to find that Miss Millingham's patriotism had led her to promote the deceased gentleman from coroner to judge.

"And the women," Miss Millingham pursued, throwing back her head. "How splendidly they're behaving. They can't long refuse us the vote now, my dear. We've *proved* and will prove all we can do in any and every field of national service. Are you working with Miss Wraxall?"

"No," said Etta. "I'm a temporary supernumerary clerk at the Admiralty."

"At the Admiralty! How distinguished! How well I understand your choice. I've always had a passion for the sea and seamen, the foundation of our empire. But do let me ask you one question, in the strictest confidence, of course. How is it that our fleet has not long ago sunk— scuppered is, I think, the right nautical term—all the German ships?"

"I really don't know," Etta replied, trying to hide a smile. "I have nothing to do with questions of strategy."

"Well," said Miss Millingham firmly, "I think you should make the suggestion. England expects it, and the sooner the better in my opinion. By the way, Miss Morison," she sank her voice to a confidential whisper, "why do not you and Miss Wraxall occupy the suite immediately above? You would be very comfortable, I'm sure, and under *my* protection. I must tell you in confidence that I'm gravely disappointed in my present guests, the actors, you know. *He* should be in the army, and *she* drinks, and I have every reason to know that their finances are in a deplorable state. Any time you want the suite, it is yours."

"Why, it's very kind of you," said Etta, "and later on I think I may want it. How much notice would you need?"

"A moment's, my dear, a moment's. They are here under notice and merely on sufferance. I shall be happy to be rid of them. But now, tell me . . ."

Gradually Etta formed her plans. She heard from Vera that the Munitions Department was constantly expanding, and also saw that she had little chance of promotion at her present work. After much discussion, it was arranged that Vera should try to have Etta asked for by Munitions, if possible as a personal secretary to one of the numerous new chiefs of sub-departments, and that when the time came they should share Miss Millingham's "suite." Privately Etta had fixed for herself when she would leave the Lawsons'. By the beginning of December she had saved £80. She wanted to have £100.

The transfer came more quickly than Etta had expected. The application was made by a personal friend of Vera's (Etta had seen him several times) after Vera had refused the post for herself. The Admiralty made no objection, and it was arranged that Etta should be transferred immediately after the Christmas holiday. Etta wondered why she felt so unelated by this success. Wasn't it exactly what she had wanted—a responsible job with a good salary, where she could use her own wits? She tried to persuade herself that she felt ashamed because Vera had given up the post for her sake; but that was absurd, because Vera herself admitted she was incompetent to hold it. Etta didn't like to admit the real truth—that while the war lasted, while this menace hung directly over Ralph and indirectly over Teddy, she couldn't feel happy, and nothing seemed worth having.

Robert came home on leave for Christmas, but Etta saw little of him, since she spent the days, rather unwillingly,

at home. Teddy had been one of the unlucky ones, and
got no leave. Ralph also wrote to say he couldn't have
leave, but that he was on the roster and hoped to come
"in the spring," and hinted very clearly that *then* . . . Etta
was glad to go back to her work. Her parents depressed
her, they were so utterly and complacently blind to the
threat over Teddy's life, only congratulating themselves
on the fact that he was doing his bit, and more concerned
at his not getting leave than at his possible fate.

At first Etta was very nearly happy in her new post.
King, Cawdor, Glamis, thou hast them all, the Disposers
of Events might have whispered ironically. Not that ambition was satisfied, but it seemed to her she had made
the decisive advance. Hitherto she had been handicapped
in work because she was forced to function below her own
level, in the sense that only part of her potential ability
could be used. Now she had her chance. She liked her chief.
It was so much easier to work for and with someone who
took for granted that she had a sense of honour and a
little judgment. Instead of drilling her to a mechanical
schedule, he put her on the basis that there was so much
work to be done—things that must be remembered, situations which had to be dealt with promptly and intelligently
—assumed she would do it. Mistakes were dropped on
swiftly and ruthlessly but without acrimony or useless
nagging. She liked his intelligence.

At the same time Etta enjoyed the freer manner of her
new surroundings. There were many more civilians, most
of them amateurs like herself. And instead of the formal
rigid discipline, there was a more friendly attitude of get-
on-with-the-job-in-your-own-way. It was pleasant, too,
working with people she could really like. The pettiness,
the intrigue, the departmental manner inseparable from

all bureaucracy did not at first strike her attention. Nor did she at all suspect that her comparative freedom was an illusion, that she was still nothing but a replaceable bit of human material in the vast industrial machine which was also the war machine. Absorbed in the immediate, she forgot the end to which the machine worked, and merged her own life in the routine. These minutes, these contracts, these schedules, the correspondence and appointments, seemed at first to have but the vaguest connection with the rifle Teddy was holding on parade, the shells soaring over Ralph's head. She was staggered by the magnitude of what was being organized, and it wasn't mere vanity which made her feel her job was more important than theirs. In the age of words the paperworkers always feel superior to the men of action, until the men of action accidentally or intentionally squash them.

In her bureaucratic haven Etta was dealing with realities at second hand with great satisfaction; but the realities themselves were waiting for her. A little more than a fortnight after her transfer, Etta returned as usual to the Lawsons'. It was January, and she had put off her moving until February—she wanted so much to have enough money to make everything perfect when Ralph came. She meant it to be the perfect love affair. Wool-gathering these soft erotic anticipations, Etta hardly noticed that a doctor's car was parked outside the Lawsons' gate, but she did observe with surprise that one of the maids stood at the front window making hush signs. So unusual a proceeding prepared Etta for something—she couldn't conceive what. The girl met her in the hall, plainly explosive with sensational news.

"Oh, miss, oh, Miss Etta," she exclaimed, her eyes goggling.

"What's the matter, Emily? Are you in trouble?"

"We're all in trouble, miss."

"In trouble! What do you mean?"

"Haven't you heard?"

"No, I haven't heard anything. Don't keep me waiting like this. What is it?"

"Mrs. Lawson's ill!"

"Ill! Oh! Is it serious?"

"I don't know, miss, the doctor and Mr. Lawson's with her now. It all come on after she got the telegram."

"What telegram?"

Emily began to whimper in sniffling breaths while she shed tears abundantly.

"About him, miss. He's dead. Mr. Robert's been killed in action."

Killed in action, Etta's hearing said to her brain, killed in action. She had often seen the words in print, but now for the first time they applied to someone she had known, whose hand she had shaken. Killed in action, nice bureaucratic words such as Etta herself had often copied for My Lords to concur. Killed in action, My Lords concur. She pushed almost roughly past the weeping girl and went to her room. Ada ill because Robert was dead and nothing to be done about it. Etta took off her outdoor things and sat staring out at the dim foggy blackness. What was to be done? Nothing, My Lords concur.

After a long time she got up and walked softly down, listened, heard nothing, and went on. She saw a light under the door of Mr. Lawson's private room, tapped and entered. He was sitting crouched in a large leather chair, flaccid and clumsy.

"Mr. Lawson!"

He looked up at her uneasily, and she felt frightened by the vacant animal misery of his face. The red flesh occasionally shivered with a slight undignified twitch, and his grey hair seemed to her pitiful. He tried to rise to his feet, but Etta seized his hand and pushed him back.

"Don't move. I'm so sorry, so sorry. . . ."

"Ada? Did she send for me?"

"No. I only wanted . . ."

"You heard about . . . about . . ."

"Yes."

"Yes. He would have wished to die . . . a soldier."

"Yes."

"We must accept . . . for England . . . his mother . . . she suffers."

As if he were not suffering! And she adding to his suffering by importunity. Etta made up her mind.

"Mr. Lawson, I can do nothing here. I'm only a nuisance. You must be alone. I shall go at once. If Ada wants me, if there is anything I can do . . . send for me. . . ."

"Thank you."

"If I could do anything . . . But, you understand, I'm going to relieve you of a stranger . . . not from ingratitude."

"Stay, if you wish. Ada . . ."

"No. If I could do anything . . . I shall leave my address downstairs and tell Emily where to find me. Later I shall write, and hope to see Ada."

"Yes."

"Tell me now if I can do anything, any errand you want done?"

"Yes? No."

Obviously he wasn't listening, obviously she was merely once more the interloper. She couldn't say: "Because I'm in love with Ralph, your nephew, I've a right to thrust my unwanted consolation on you." She squeezed his hand tightly.

"I'm sorry, I'm *sorry* . . . you understand? . . . but I can't *do* anything!"

II

ROBERT'S DEATH would have haunted Etta more deeply if
she had not been absorbed by her work and by the excitement of getting installed in the "suite." After all, Robert
hadn't meant much to her, and in those days the death
of one more young man wasn't much of an event. For a
week or two Ralph's letters reflected his grief, but he too
seemed to forget quickly. People did. Only Ada seemed unable to forget. Etta called several times, but was told Ada
would see nobody; she wrote, and received no reply; and
then heard that Ada and Randolfe had gone to Dymcott.
Consolation, Etta felt, was futile; and, though she longed
to do something for Ada, she couldn't do the only thing
Ada wanted—bring Robert back.

And this disappeared under another blow. In February,
Teddy went overseas. In her distraction, Etta wrote a wild
letter to Ralph, beseeching him to "look after" Teddy;
and was offended when he pointed out that a gunner subaltern attached to "X" Division stood as much chance of
meeting an infantry private in "Y" Division as of getting
a month's leave out of his turn. (The question of leave was
a sore one with Ralph—he had been put off once more.)
Etta sank into despair about Teddy and reproached herself for being callous. She had to believe that Teddy and
Ralph would be all right, or go insane. She dared not think
about possibilities, any more than she dared face the ever
more insistent questionings about the righteousness of the
war which forced themselves on her. Once more, *le cœur
se bronze ou se brise*, and in self-protection she had to be
hard.

Weeks passed, and nothing of what Etta dreaded happened. Sometimes it seemed as if the only difference was
that she addressed two sets of letters "B. E. F." instead of

one, and that instead of postal orders she sent Teddy
francs. Spring of 1916 dawned slowly in London, the battle
of Verdun raged monotonously; and Etta lived for two
human lives.

Suddenly Ralph's letters became more frequent and
ardent—everybody was going on leave, he was certain to
come, it would be in three weeks, the Adjutant had given
his word. This news galvanized Etta from apathy into a
violent physical and mental activity. He was really coming
at last, and this time nothing could keep them apart. She
had satisfied the self-imposed conditions. She was free and
independent; she needed to ask nothing of Ralph. They
were equals, and if anybody had to suffer it would be herself, though she had no intention of advertising what she
intended to do either at home, at the office, or to anyone.
She made her plans.

Vera was calmly told, and willed into acquiescence. It
was agreed that while Ralph was on leave she should live
in a hotel, for which Etta insisted on paying. That point
carried, Etta made a belligerent attempt to improve Miss
Millingham's "suite." She bought a pot of enamel and
repainted the bath; she got a new bath mat, and polished
up the antiquated copper geyser until it would have satisfied a sergeant major. Then she turned to the rooms. Vera
had her bed, with a large screen round it, in the outer room,
where they mostly lived. Etta arranged that the bed was
to be taken down, polished up Miss Millingham's battered
furniture, and bought brightly coloured materials to hang
on the walls.

The inner room, where Etta slept, had a double bed,
which had belonged to the theatrical couple. She was determined that it should be purified of their presence. A
whole Saturday and Sunday were spent in repapering the
room. She cast back the bed in Miss Millingham's teeth,
bought a new one and a complete new set of bedding. She

bought two pillowslips, one embroidered with "R" and one with "E." A small lumber room leading off the bed-room was cleared and cleansed and made into a dressing room for Ralph. She got new curtains and a new carpet and more hangings. She bought new dresses and under-clothes. She even bought the cigarettes she knew he liked, and hunted for hours to discover the wine he had given her in 1914, in case he wanted her to make lunch or dinner for him. She intended to buy the flowers he liked on the day he arrived.

By the time Etta had done all this, she had spent nearly fifty pounds of her savings; and there was only a week to pass before Ralph arrived. She looked at her handiwork and saw that it was good; and she had done it all herself. She was satisfied. Following impulses far older and more profound than she knew, she had carried out ancient ritual in her own way. It was right, it was good, to sacrifice part of her harvest—the patient saving of months of labour —in the great feast. She had decorated the cave of Miss Millingham's "suite" as handsomely as she could for the coming of the sun god, the lord, the life-giver, the proud-stepping son of heaven. Matriarch, she had chosen, she had won back the lost female pride. Not for him, the far-wanderer, Odysseus, to build round the olive the bed for patient Penelope; but for her, Isis on her crescent moon, to lift him to her throne.

"It does look pretty," said Vera, running from one room to the other. "You've done marvels, Etta. I shouldn't have dreamed these old rooms could look so gay and sunny."

Etta didn't answer but began to dance round and round the room on the tips of her toes, lifting her arms and sing-ing, "He's coming, he's coming, soon he'll be here." Round and round, lightly on quick feet, chanting her spell, until Vera begged her to stop, stop, it made her giddy. But Etta went on, until at last she dropped into a chair, laughing and dizzy with turning, and exclaiming:

"Silly Vera!"

"It's you who's silly," retorted Vera. "Cavorting about like a mad heifer. If you knew how ridiculous you looked."

"Silly Vera, poor Vera, who isn't happy," said Etta.

Every day she wrote to Ralph, and every day received a letter from him. How charming of her to let him come and stay with her, how happy they would be! He had planned his fortnight exactly. The first three days would be sacred to Etta; then he must give a week to his parents and Ada; but the last four days should be hers too. A week, a whole week. Never mind the going back, don't think of it. She had a small pocket calendar and put a red border round the 1st, 2d, and 3d of June, and the 11th, 12th, 13th, and 14th. All that came after didn't matter, it was too far off. Every day she scratched out one of the ugly twenty-four hours of May which stretched between her and the sunrise. She found out the time when the leave train came in and wrote that she would be there to meet him.

The hardest thing was to get through the office hours. It is difficult to take a so-called intelligent interest in official documents for destruction when you are living in the golden dawn of the creation mysteries. If her chief noticed her lack of diligence, he said nothing; perhaps he had observed before in young women that unconscious rhythm of step and the eyes absorbed by something far off. And indeed Etta was living in the contemplation of things beyond the immediate. Not until her luncheon hour on the day before Ralph's arrival did she recollect that she had made all these arrangements without consulting Miss Millingham. It would be awkward if the old girl objected, and beastly to sneak in and out.

Courageously, as soon as she got home, Etta prepared to tackle the Millingham dragon at the entrance. Vera had already gone, her bed was removed, and the room looked lighter and larger. Etta changed into the dress she was going to wear for Ralph—it was absolutely necessary to make sure it was right by wearing it. She turned from side to side in front of the long mirror, looking critically over her shoulder at her image; and, yes, it really was a nice dress.

It wasn't so easy to come to the point with Miss Millingham—suppose she turned catty and horrid? They talked of the war and what women were doing until Etta was nauseated with her own cowardice. At last she plunged.

"I want to ask you something, Miss Millingham."

"Indeed?" said Miss Millingham, cocking her head. "I shall be most happy."

"We've often talked about what women should do in the world, but you've never told me what you think our relations to men should be."

"My dear, I think the less we have to do with them, the better. Men are conceited, ill-behaved children. Always smoking such strong tobacco, quite overpowering, and the way they eat!"

This wasn't encouraging. Etta persisted:

"But we can't put men entirely out of our lives. After all, men and women fall in love. Don't you think that is inevitable and right, and that we should have a new attitude towards it?"

"Any woman who falls in love has my sympathy and regret," said Miss Millingham firmly. "It leads to nothing but misery, and I'm not sure it isn't positive downright treachery to The Cause."

"You don't encourage me to say what I must say, but the fact is—well—a friend of mine, a young officer, is coming home on leave from the front—and—I thought you wouldn't mind—I wanted to ask you—if he might stay here—a few days—we shall not disturb . . ."

"A young officer! Of what regiment?"

"The Artillery."

"The Artillery," said Miss Millingham amiably. "How very distinguished! Here, there, and everywhere is their motto, I'm told. Such brave men, firing off those unpleasant guns. The noise is inconceivable. I was once present when a royal salute was fired for the late dear Queen—I was with my father, the well-known judge—and the guns were just behind us. I assure you, Miss Morison, that I actually screamed when the first one BANGED! Positively I—jumped—out—of—my—skin!"

"But," asked Etta, "have you any objection to Lieutenant Lawson's coming here?"

"Not in the least," said Miss Millingham, who seemed suddenly to alter her views about males. "The Artillery, most distinguished. In my humble opinion we cannot do too much for these gallant fellows. But for his high functions my dear father would have been a soldier, he longed to measure himself with the Zulus. Personally I have never associated intimately with soldiers, although in my young days I assure you the house was literally thronged with the most eligible *partis*. I refused them all for my dear father's sake and——"

There was a knock at the door, and the servant came in.

"Telegram for you, Miss Morison. He's waiting for an answer."

From Ralph, of course. Was it to confirm his time of arrival or—let it not be so!—to say he couldn't come? She tore open the envelope and read:

TEDDY OFFICIALLY REPORTED WOUNDED AND MISSING LAST WEEK GO IMMEDIATELY WAR OFFICE ASK INFORMATION WIRE HERE BOTH DISTRACTED DADDY.

Etta sat staring at the carbon pencil words, unable to comprehend. Teddy wounded and missing. What did they mean, what were they talking about? Wounded and missing. Wounded and missing. She heard the girl's voice saying rather impatiently:

"Any reply, miss?"

"No," Etta said calmly. "No reply."

"Not bad news, I hope?" asked Miss Millingham, with pleasant curiosity.

"I think," said Etta, rising, "if you don't mind, I'll—I'd better go upstairs."

12

GRADUALLY, as Etta walked up and down her room in the long twilight, she understood what the words meant. Wounded—that meant that Teddy had been hit by a bullet or a piece of shell, the kind of thing she worked to help make; and missing—that meant that nobody knew where he was. Her brother, her near flesh, was lost and in pain, perhaps dying, perhaps dead. Oh no, not that. He mustn't be dead. But he might be dead. Now she knew how Ada had felt about Robert, but this was worse—there was a torture of hope in it, and the torture of fear. Nobody knew, nobody could know the truth.

The darkened street lamps in the street outside flicked into a dim glow. She heard taxis pass, one or two railway horse wagons, and laughter from a group of young men and women coming back from dinner. She couldn't eat, but from time to time she felt her way into the dark lead-smelling little scullery, drew water from the tap and drank. Then returned to her tiring up-and-down, the iteration—wounded and missing. At last she huddled into bed and tried to sleep; but in the darker sleepless hours more agonizing images tormented her. She saw Teddy wounded in the head and in the body, now with an arm shattered, now with crushed legs. She imagined him crying, as he had done in childhood, for her to help and comfort him. Sometimes he lay in the desolation of no-man's land with the star shells overhead, sometimes in a trench when he was trampled by cruel feet. Impossible to sleep; you couldn't call that fevered nightmare sleep.

With morning came a little energy and the necessity to act. She was early at the office, haggard and miserable-looking from her night's sleeplessness, impatiently waiting for her chief. As soon as he arrived, she said to him, calmly but insistently:

"Mr. Reynolds, I must ask you to help me, please. My brother is wounded and missing. Could you ask the W. O. for information, please?"

He looked at her attentively a moment and then said:

"I'm awfully sorry. Ring up the W. O. and say I must speak on urgent business to Colonel Walter."

Etta got through, switched the line to Reynolds's desk, and put down her own receiver. She heard him explaining and then: "Hold on a moment." He looked up:

"Your brother's full name, rank, and regiment, Miss Morison."

"075391, Private Edward Morison, 9th Fusiliers."

Reynolds repeated it, and she heard him say: "What? Yes, I know, but I'm personally interested. I can't help that. Do the best you can, and inform me at once. Right you are, thanks."

He stood up and took Etta's hand.

"They're wiring immediately to Geneva, Miss Morison. The Spanish ambassador will ask the Germans for information. Your brother is probably a prisoner, you know. We'll just have to wait. Now, I think the best thing for you to do is to take the day off and rest. Are you on the telephone?"

"No."

"Well, give me your address, and I'll wire you or send a messenger if there's any news. Now, go home and lie down, you look rather ill."

Etta tried to give him thanks, but he shooed her away —she could take a couple of days if she liked. It was no good protesting that she wanted to work, that she could work. Reynolds wouldn't listen. And, really, in herself she knew he was right; she couldn't work. For the moment there was no room for anything but the image of "wounded and missing" in all the shapes of mental anguish. She walked the streets, looking at the red buses and at re-cruiting posters and newspaper placards, wondering at the strange indifferent people. Even the men in khaki didn't seem to mind about Teddy. For a long time she forgot all about Ralph, that he would soon be on a boat in the Chan-nel thinking about her, and that this was the day they had wanted to come for so long. She ate something in a restau-rant at lunch time and then went home feeling very tired. The rooms seemed still and empty without Vera, and gaudily mocking in their new cleanness and colours. She lay down on the bed and went to sleep.

When she awoke she could see from the light that it was already late afternoon, but in her consciousness was the knowledge that she had something to perform. Yes. She had to meet Ralph and explain to him, send him off to his parents or to Ada. It was all so tragical, but then he would understand at once. She washed and did her hair. It was annoying that going to sleep in the afternoon made her so clumsy—she dropped her hairbrush and smashed the bottle of perfume she had just bought. Useless to be annoyed by trifles, especially when there was no time to waste. She felt too tired to change out of her office dress,

so tired she wastefully took a taxi to the station, but her
legs seemed to have become powerless.

There were quite a number of people waiting at the
barrier for the leave train, and Etta joined them patiently.
She found she was standing beside a couple of soldiers,
one of whom kept glancing at her. He said something to
his friend, who nodded, and then spoke to her:

"Beg pardon, miss, waitin' for someone off the leave
train?"

"Yes."

"Well, it's 'arf an hour late. No call for you to stand
here, you look fair knocked out, you do. You go and
sit there under the clock, and I'll come and tell you."

"Thank you, it's very kind, but I don't want to trouble . . ."

"No trouble at all, miss. Me and Joe here's waiting for
a pal, so it's all the same to us. We'll keep your place.
Here, I'll take you over. Don't let nobody pinch my place,
Joe."

The soldier took her arm very respectfully and led her
to the seat. He stood beside her a minute, hesitating, and
then said:

"Beggin' your pardon for the liberty, miss, your young
man on this train?"

"Yes."

" 'Struth! You don't look like it. 'Ad bad news from the
front like?"

"My brother is posted wounded and missing."

"Wounded and missin'? Gah! Don't you worry about
that. Why, I betcher 'e's safe in 'orspital a'ready, and
drinkin' old Jerry's beer. Don't you believe what the
newspapers say, miss, them 'Uns have got 'earts as big
as bullocks. I betcher they look after 'im a treat. Your

brother ain't 'arf clicked lucky, bleedin' war's over for 'im. Now, you just sit there and rest like, until I fetch you."

For a while Etta sat with her eyes closed. If only she could get over this awful feeling of weariness, she simply would have to be a little cheerful and alive for Ralph. The snorts of that engine going out were like cannon. Presently she opened her eyes and looked about. Opposite was a telegraph guichet, and Etta remembered she had forgotten to send any word to her father. She went over and sent:

DOING ALL I CAN WILL WIRE ANY NEWS ETTA.

She said nothing about Geneva or the War Office, afraid that the telegram might be held up for censorship.

It seemed a very long time that she had been sitting there, and she began to fear she had missed the train when the soldier suddenly appeared.

"Train signalled, miss. Come along."

Etta followed him, and the crowd, obedient to the uniform, allowed the soldier to place Etta very near the gate. People pushed against her in their excitement, and she heard a woman sobbing hysterically. Etta gazed down the platform and along the faint shining rails, but there was no train. They waited. Then came a sudden stir; voices said: "Here she comes," and a long train hissed slowly into the station, doors opening and men jumping out while it still moved. In a moment a bewildering stream was passing her eyes: faces, faces, faces, khaki, khaki, khaki. But no Ralph. Names and greetings were being shouted, and she saw women clinging close to their men and crying. Then, like magic, Ralph was in front of her, rather red-faced and large, with a slung haversack. He saluted her and took the hand she held out blindly to him.

"Hullo," he said.

"Hullo."

But he held her hand tight, tight, and Etta was swallowing something hard and dry in her throat. She had rather hoped he would put his arms round her as the soldiers were doing, but the hand grip made up for the disappointment. And she liked that "hullo," as if they'd just met casually after parting for a few hours. She liked the pride of it. The soldiers had vanished at the sight of the officer's uniform when she turned to thank them. Side by side she and Ralph walked from the station to find a taxi.

"I say," he exclaimed, "you look so lovely, Etta. I'd no idea a woman could be so beautiful. So fine and delicate. . . . Let's go and have dinner first, shall we? You must be hungry waiting all that time. I am. Isn't it all wonderful? I've been living for this moment."

Etta had meant to tell him at once, to get it over, but resolution failed her; she couldn't spoil his first moments, his first dinner at home after all those weary months. Besides, she did hope he would kiss her and comfort her a little before he left. Perhaps there'd be good news of Teddy within a week, after all, and then they could still have their own week together. So she let him take her to a taxi, and they sat there, Etta almost silent, and Ralph talking like mad, holding her hand in both of his. On an impulse she lifted his hand and kissed it, murmuring under her breath: "Ralph, Ralph, don't let me be lost."

The dinner was not easy for Etta, and once or twice she thought she was going to faint. She stopped the fainting by pinching the palm of her hand hard between her finger nails. Fortunately, Ralph was so much absorbed in his own happiness that he didn't observe her silence and pallor. Once he remarked she looked a little pale, but Etta said she was only tired. She knew she ought to have used that as an opening to tell him, but she funked it. He went on talking, and she saw him looking intently at her mouth and the round of her breasts under her blouse. At any other time how glad she would have been that Ralph should look at her amorously and find her desirable, but now her flesh shrank from his gaze. A voice in her seemed lamenting—if only things could have been different, if only that dead flesh were not between them. Ralph talked of the war, he was sure a big push was imminent. Presently she interrupted:

"Do you have many wounded and missing?"

"Not from our lot unless there's a big Hun attack. It's mostly the infantry, trench raids and counter attacks and that sort of thing."

"What happens to them?"

"Scuppered most of them, I'm afraid. But don't let's talk about that now."

"Don't any of them get saved?" she inisted.

"Oh, a few, I suppose. But, as I was saying . . ."

Etta scarcely heard what he was saying. Her ears went on repeating "Scuppered, most of them." And still she couldn't tell him. They finished the meal, which Etta had made a poor show of sharing, and then Ralph became rather shy, and she made conversation desperately. Finally he said:

"Shall we go? I'll get the bill."

And his eyes said very plainly: Now let us be lovers. Etta thought his face looked a little coarser than she remembered, and his eyes, rather hard even when he looked pleading and smiling at her, reminded her horribly of Robert's. She stopped him.

"Just one moment—there is something . . ."

"What?"

"Ralph, I've got to tell you. It's all so dreadful. Since last night I've suffered more than in all the rest of my life, and instead of utter happiness, it was agony to know you were coming this evening."

"Etta! What do you mean? Are you in love with someone else?"

"In love with . . . ? Oh, that! No, no. But you can't come back with me tonight. You see, my brother is wounded and missing, he may be dead."

"I'm awfully sorry," said Ralph rather carelessly. "But you mustn't get too worked up. I daresay he'll be all right. It's all in the day's work, you know."

"But you said just now most of them were scuppered."

"Did I? Well, some of them are, no doubt, but I feel sure your brother'll be all right. He's lucky. Let's go back to your place now—it *is* sweet of you to have me."

"No, Ralph." Etta shook her head. "I can't let you come."

"Why not?"

"Because, if you did, you'd want to love me, and it would be all the harder to send you away."

"But I don't see why you want to send me away," said Ralph frowning.

"You must see! It would be a profanation. My brother may be lying in agony, he may be dying, he may be lying unburied. Ralph, be kind. Go to your parents and Ada for your first week. The War Office have telegraphed to Geneva. Directly I get news, I'll wire you. If it's good news, you may come when you will. And even if—" her lips quivered—"even if he's—he's dead, I'll have mourned for him, I won't have profaned his death, and I won't refuse you then, even if it breaks my heart and violates me."

To her utter amazement Ralph turned angrily upon her, his face hard and his eyes furious.

"Do you really mean this?"

"Mean what?"

"That now, *now*, after all these months of waiting, you're going to refuse me, on this pretext?"

"But it isn't a pretext, it's *true*."

Etta felt the tears brimming in her eyes as she looked at him, but he paid no attention.

"Well, even if it is true, does it matter? Hundreds of men are dying daily. Do you eat or drink or live any the less gaily for that? And you don't even know he's dead."

"But he's my *brother*, Ralph."

"And the others are nothing, cannon fodder, eh? Suppose your brother is dead, he'll be no less dead in a week, a year, a hundred years. We're alive."

"Ralph!"

"You wrote me those letters, you promised me, and all these months I've thought of nobody but you, not even my mother. Now you want to put me off. Once before you did it, on some scruple or other, and now there's this new bit of prudery."

"Ralph! Please, please!"

"What a fool I've been. I thought before that you were merely flirting with me, and then, like an idiot, persuaded myself I'd misunderstood you. But now I know you're the kind of woman who likes to lead a man on and then amuse herself by throwing him over."

"Are you mad, Ralph? You mustn't speak to me like that! What possible motive could I have for——"

"How should I know? Perhaps you've got someone you like better, some civilian. Perhaps you like the sense of power and the fun of it. But, I can tell you, there are other girls in the world who wouldn't treat a man so rottenly. They aren't all moral prigs nowadays, thank God."

Etta stood up; it was impossible to argue. Hers had

been a long hard day, and she was very tired, and it was ignominious to sit there with her eyes full of tears. She noticed people at neighbouring tables were looking at them and whispering.

"Since you feel that, there is nothing more to be said." She spoke in an undertone. "I'll say good-bye and meet you again when you've had time to think."

"If you go now, it'll be the last good-bye," he said in loud angry tones.

"Hush, my dear, hush."

"I repeat, if you go now, it's good-bye, and you won't see me again."

"Then good-bye, and . . . and . . . I hope you'll . . . be happy."

The house was dark and silent after the noise of the streets where twilight still lingered. It seemed to Etta that she ought to be feeling a great deal, but in fact she only felt very tired. She could no longer be acutely anxious for Teddy—if he was gone, well, it must be so. Nor could she feel resentment or regret for Ralph, who was also lost. It was as if God had said to her heart: Let there be emptiness; and there was emptiness. Except that she felt very tired, very tired. For a long time she sat quite still in an armchair in the darkness. She heard other people return to the house, voices and footsteps on the stairs, faint noises overhead, and then again the darkness was silent. If she wanted anything, it was to be undressed and put to bed by some quite impersonal woman, a nurse or a servant.

At last she went to her bedroom, lit the gas, and began to undress. The alarm clock by her bed marked twelve-twenty, so she must have been sitting there for two or three hours. As she went to hang up her dress, she saw the two new dresses she had bought, soft and motionless on their hangers. She touched each in turn, pulled them a little towards her and let them fall back; then she opened the two drawers which held the other new things she had bought, and looked at them, saying to herself: He might have been here now. But it was all meaningless. There was nothing to do but to go to bed.

Next morning Etta stayed where she was, and when the woman came to clean the room, told her to bring some breakfast. She wrote a telegram to Vera, almost commanding her to return at once—Etta felt she couldn't stand another evening alone. And she scribbled a note to Reynolds, saying she would be at work the next day. When the woman had gone Etta remained in bed thinking, and the more she thought, the more her resentment against Ralph glowed up. She wished she could unsay the gentleness of her last words to him and that she had hurt him with bitter words as he had wounded her. How crude, how insensate Ralph had been, like another person. And rather vile. It was true that she believed that love should be desire and of the flesh, the consummation of the flesh, but not in that way. Ralph had behaved like a drunken sailor on shore leave, wanting a woman, any woman, and she had happened to be there—anyone else would have done. He had even said something insulting about other women.

Nevertheless, she found excuses for him. It wasn't really his fault, it wasn't the real Ralph. It was the fault of the war. They said that fighting made the men finer and better. What lies! They grew brutal and coarse—it was marked already on his face—growing coarse to escape suffering. But it was all irreparable. His fault or not, he had trampled over that small secret flower garden of devotion and desire she had tended for him, and nothing could bring it to life again.

Over and over the same thoughts revolved with the

same regrets, until—blessed relief—she heard Vera's steps
and voice, and found herself in Vera's arms, sobbing out
incoherent answers to Vera's equally, incoherent questions.

Several days later Etta put through a War Office call to
Reynolds. She saw him making notes, as if it were official
business, and started when he put down the receiver, and
said:

"Good news for you, Miss Morison."

Etta gazed stupidly at him, not understanding.

"Your brother—he'll be all right. He's a prisoner and
in a German hospital. Rather badly wounded, I'm afraid,
but he'll recover. I've taken down the address—you can
write and send parcels there, and they'll be forwarded.
I advise you to send parcels, the German rations are not
good."

"Thank you very much. I'm very grateful," Etta
answered, almost in official tones, though she was violently
trembling. "May I have the address now to wire to my
parents?"

PART III

IF IT WERE TRUE that the world of Ada and her like disappeared in 1914, it was also true that the world of the-
war's-a-splendid-lark smashed itself to pieces on the
Somme. But Etta was very far from perceiving this. Her
own life had splintered before the preliminary bombard-
ment began, and during most of the summer she merely
went through the motions of living. Nothing much seemed
worth while, and it was certainly no great enthusiasm
about the war which kept her going. But the fact that she
had to go on working kept her from complete apathy.
Somehow she stumbled through the routine of the colourless days.

In September she went to the country again with Vera.
They took long excursions on foot and talked; and what
with the air and the exercise and the discussions Etta began to recover her spirits and to replan her life. First and
foremost—no more men. Ralph had not only betrayed

and hurt her to the death, but had even cut her off from
Ada—there could be no more friendship with Ada now.
Etta and Vera would live together and be old maids. The
next thing was to get the war to end, but that was something which couldn't be compelled. They agreed that
they couldn't back out now, they'd have to see the thing
through; but they also agreed they had been fools not to
see from the beginning that it was a disaster. And then
what? Etta wasn't sure. Vera thought they might start
a business together, a hat shop or something like that.
Etta wanted to go to the country, the real country; at
least, she thought so, under the warm sunlight with a hazy
peace settling over the fields and woods. But they agreed
they must save money, to be ready when the time came.

Then back in London again, with nothing much happening. There was an ache in Etta when she thought of
Teddy, and something worse on the rarer and rarer occa-
sions when she thought of Ralph. She tried not to think
about all that—it made her petty and squalid to herself.
News came from Teddy: he was out of hospital and working at camp, but needed food. So a weekly parcel went
from Dortborough, and Etta sent one or two extra ones
each month. But the world had gone cruel. The harsh
winter of 1916-17 turned to a cruel spring. The Ministry
of Munitions grew larger and more active. Reynolds was
moved to a more responsible post, and Etta went with
him, and received an increase of salary. But by now she
had so come to take for granted that she could succeed
at her work that this gave her very little pleasure.

Gradually, after many exhortations and scoldings from
Vera, Etta ceased to live so solitary a life. She went out
to teas and parties, and if she made few friends she had
plenty of acquaintants. They were queer parties, mostly
of war workers and their friends, sometimes with a mixture

of soldiers on leave. In the evening there was generally
drink, and they danced to gramophone records. Rather
to her astonishment, Etta found she enjoyed the dancing,
and still more to her astonishment discovered that men
liked her. Some of them fell in love with her, sent her
flowers, and tried to kiss her. She repelled them, only
sorry that a rejected lover so seldom remains a friend.

Only once was she tempted to allow herself to drift
into one of the numerous facile "affairs" with young soldiers which she saw going on all round her. It was at the
farewell party given by a young man named Eric Marshall
the night before he went to the front. He was only nineteen, and it was his first time out. Etta had only known
him a few months and had not seen him half-a-dozen times,
but he fell exceedingly in love with her at the first meeting,
wrote her extravagant letters from his training camp, and
when on leave waited outside the Ministry to see her, and
had to be turned out of the "suite" when he was allowed to
call—he stayed so long. Etta liked him, perhaps because
of his clear eyes and pleasant innocence, perhaps because
those who admire us always have good taste. At any rate,
she had allowed him to hold her hand and to kiss her when
Vera was out of the room, but without much interest on
her part. She only wanted to be kind to the boy.

The party was large and rather drunken. One subaltern
made himself rather a nuisance by a truculent anti-femi-
nism, owing to his girl having turned him down. He kept
saying in a loud, intoxicated voice:

"What-I-wan'-know-is *why* there aren't—more women's corpses? Pleny-o'-men's."

His friends gathered round him, some trying to humour
him into calmness, others expostulating, others apologizing
to the women. Nobody minded, but under cover of this
tumult Eric drew Etta into a corner of the room and began

earnestly pleading with her—it was his last night, mightn't he please, please, spend it with her?

"But I live with Vera," said Etta, trying to put him off.

"Never mind that—we can go somewhere else—there are plenty of hotels."

"But, my dear," said Etta, "suppose I don't want to?"

"Don't be cruel, Etta, Etta, you know how much I love you. It's devouring me. I couldn't love you so much if you weren't really in love with me, too, inside, without knowing it. You think you're not, because you're good, and you've never been in love with anyone. I can tell that, because you're so calm. But you will be, you will love me, you must. Let us just be together tonight, I swear I won't do anything you don't want. I've asked you to marry me —you know I've got money—I can make you happy—do say you will, just tonight—if I have to go out not knowing whether you care or not I shall go all to pieces."

Etta was touched by his incoherent and naïve words. She looked at his flushed, desperate face and felt very, very sorry for him. As the drunken man again blurted out his crude phrase about women's corpses, Etta knew that the boy was afraid. What was it like to face one's own death hourly? But it wasn't a lover he wanted, it was a mother. He wanted to be mothered and comforted and sent out strengthened to his fate. Why shouldn't she mother him? Why not? What harm? Wasn't it the least they could do as a ransom for not being made corpses? But instead of saying Yes, she said No, and turned her back on him. It wasn't her business to comfort the troops; she wasn't going to give her sex out of mere pity, as motherly comfort. Let the boy's mother mother him, and if he hadn't a mother, let him be a man.

This social phase in Etta might be explained in conventional terms as providing the necessary compensation for the thwarting of her sexual instincts, a compensation which success with her work could no longer provide. But these generalized formulæ, which are supposed to explain everything, really explain little. The modern town dweller is often too complicated for such facile explanations. The specialized paper worker is peculiarly liable to take his sanction for living from the printed word, so that conduct and even feelings may be determined by ideas, or what pass as ideas. To say such people are a mistake and would be better dead no doubt gives the sayer a feeling of pleasurable superiority, but is not a helpful contribution towards understanding them. And to scream that they ought to put the solar plexus *en rapport* with the sun is at best a counsel of perfection in a foggy, cloudy, and smoky town.

Etta's nature was opposed to self-depreciatory hara-kiri, and she never thought of practising theosophical nudism. Instead, she cut her hair short in what was then the "advanced" fashion, dressed as well as she could on a little money, and went to parties. Etta liked being with other people. She was naturally sociable, and only circumstances had forced her to a solitary life. Dortborough people had repelled her by what she considered their sluggishness and miserable spite; and with Ada's friends she had always been conscious of her position as the dependent, the inferior. But now, an expanded example of the emancipated girl "on her own," Etta could assume the part of a woman of the world among people who had much the same interests as herself, people who had all fled from some personal Dortborough, and were "doing things."

It was pleasant to be liked and even rather petted by such people, to have a reputation with them for being "charming" and "witty." It was pleasant to be flattered by most of the men and even by a few of the prettier women, while receiving the homage of disapproval from the plain time-and-tide women who waited for no man because, alas, no man pursued them. But to receive these pleasures, it was necessary to please; and that involved taking on the attitude of those pleased. In this case it was the philosophy of "the latest thing," which is all very well so long as you recognize that it's usually the same old thing over again. But who is to say what *is* the latest thing? Who is the authority? Well, in this particular bunch the standard was mostly set by two people, both very friendly to Etta. One was Kate Mendip, a handsome woman whose husband was a very wealthy director of several companies; and the other was Francis Leigh, a successful barrister, a little over forty, who was already Recorder of a small town. It was a great offence to call Kate anything but Kitty; whereas, to call Francis Frank was an even more ghastly solecism.

One of the conventions of this society was to include the war among the "shop" topics which were to be discussed as little as possible. Of course, the war was just and necessary (some of them were doing pretty well out of it), but *their* task was to keep alive the fine flame of civilization in order to hand it on to the next generation, who (as we now know) received it with grateful acclamations. The present social comedy would not be so richly gratifying if all those in the war hadn't thought themselves the salt of the earth, while all those out of it for whatsoever cause found excellent reasons for arriving at the same conclusion about themselves. Which is the worse pack of fools history has not decided. At any rate, most of the males among Etta's new set were "indispensables," with the necessary outlook, i.e., those over military age were pretty hearty, thanks, and rather aggressive, while those under were all *the* most able men at their jobs.

Now Etta really enjoyed being one of the chief pets and admirations of this little set, but, by an odd twirk of complication, at the very moment when she had attained at least something of what London had to offer, she persuaded herself that she disliked it and wanted to get away. Memories of Dymcott and of summer holidays wove themselves into her reading of the not uncommon books which in various forms assert that the "only real life" is "on the land," and which present the peasant farmer as the ideal type of humanity. From all this she formed a picture of living with Vera in a country house (not too big) with a flower garden and a vegetable garden and fowls and animals. Life would be healthy and sane, and they would be creating something useful.

This reaction from the destructiveness of war and the essential futility of so much town society produced another complication. Among Etta's dreams there had always been a niche kept for having a baby "on her own." She did not presume, of course, to repeat the respectable mystery of parthenogenesis, but the idea was to have a child outside marriage, which legally would be entirely her own. Since the Ralph disaster, Etta had abandoned the idea of finding happiness with a lover, but believed she could be happy as a mother—"on her own," of course.

The great slaughter of the English males began with the Somme and reached its apex with Passchendaele in the autumn of 1917. Etta's unconscious reaction to the casualty lists was comprehensible and one that was fairly common. She became obsessed with the idea that she *ought* to have a child, not merely to help fill a numerical gap, but to register her individual protest as a life maker against all this life destruction. More and more, as she brooded over herself, she became convinced that the way out for her was to have this child with some carefully chosen father and then to retire with Vera to the country to bring it up. Isadora Duncan had shown the way. But not yet, not yet.

The war must end first; she must save enough money to ensure that the child be properly born and to install herself and Vera properly in the country. Moreover, there was the question of choosing the right father.

2

IT WOULD HAVE BEEN very nearly impossible for Etta to fit the exact time when she began to fall in love with Francis Leigh. Precisely those circumstances which, if she had thought of the possibility, would have made her certain she could never be in love with him most contributed to it. Though the breach with Ralph was final, Etta was convinced she would never be in love again—she was going to be an old maid, of a sort; and the baby idea was only an idea, there was no passionate impulse behind it. And then Francis for some time seemed to her quite an old man, since he was married, with two children. Etta would have thought it absurd to imagine she could fall in love with a man over thirty, let alone one over forty. Though she had fiercely cut Ralph out of herself, unconsciously she still thought of the young lover as the only one.

So the falling in love was a gradual process, not recognized as such, and in any case lacked the fresh sweetness and spontaneity of her feelings for Ralph. Now Francis Leigh was the most subtile of all the male beasts in that particular show; while Etta, overconfident in her new part of an agreeable but disillusioned woman of the world, was nearly as defenceless as a mouse against him. She thought she knew all about Francis Leigh, and she didn't. She knew about the wife and children, and she knew that Francis held "modern" views about the sexes; but she was completely deceived by the hypocrisy of respectability which is forced on men in any public position, especially a man of law who is ambitious and has rivals.

Francis Leigh was a tidy-looking man, not tall as Englishmen go, but with what is known as a good presence. He wasn't old enough to deserve the devastating compliment of "well preserved," but his slim figure made him look youngish, in spite of the slight grey at his temples and the evident thinness of the dark hair over his forehead. As a Junior his practice had been lucrative, and both he and his wife had private means. He was just too old for the war. Foreseeing the return of a horde of hungry Juniors after the war, Leigh had taken silk early and had made good. At forty-four he had excellent prospects, not indeed of the woolsack, but of a career as leader, with the possibility that he might end up as Mr. Justice Leigh. The exterior decorum was absolutely essential, therefore.

But, like some other men of ability, Mr. Francis Leigh (not yet Justice) was of an amorous temperament. Before marriage, he had followed the usual practice of his kind by "helping" various "little girls," whose wages were inadequate to their wishes. By concealing his name and taking furnished flats in unlikely parts of the town, and by never confiding in anyone, he had kept these voyages to Cythera entirely secret. After marriage, he had quickly tired of his wife; and while keeping up the façade of domestic felicity—even to her—he had returned to more exciting pursuits. He was careful to choose girls so poor that they had absolutely no contact with his own world, or women so placed that they must be completely silent for their own sakes. Thus nobody, Etta least of all, suspected his liaison with Kitty Mendip.

When Etta appeared on the scene, he was growing tired of Kitty Mendip. Directly he saw Etta, with her finely

shaped face and beautiful colouring, he was extremely
attracted. A good-tempered, intelligent girl, as well as
good-looking, and obviously quite inexperienced—such
was Mr. Leigh's judgment on Etta. He was too cautious
to proceed rapidly, but immediately began to withdraw
little by little from Kitty and to talk to Etta when Kitty
was not about. As to Mrs. Leigh, she hardly came into the
picture. Etta had heard him say with his air of being
original—at small expense:

"It's such a *mistake* for married people never to go out
socially except in pairs, as if they were Siamese twins.
It's disastrous to all the finer sensibilities. People never
seem to understand there may be a 'blunting of the fine
point of seldom pleasure.'"

How wise, Etta thought, how sensible. And she listened
to him with pleasure as he took up the theme of Shakespeare's Sonnets and refuted Wilde's absurd "Mr. W. H."
theory, as if Francis Leigh were the only person who had
seen through it—which indeed Etta was quite prepared to
believe.

Clever flattery and persuasion were the methods employed by Mr. Leigh to ingratiate himself with women. He
knew that flattery is always welcomed by women, but that
to succeed it must be indirect and seem sincere. Above all,
it must not be clumsy or fulsome. Flattery, he said, was
alien to his nature; he knew he sometimes gave pain by his
frankness, but he must speak his mind. Possessing that
cynical contempt for feminine intelligence so common in
lawyers, he always made a point of flattering a woman for
what he believed she hadn't got—intelligence. When he
talked to her, Etta received—she couldn't have said how—
the impression that he felt he had stepped to a higher level,
that at last he had found a woman to whom he need not
condescend. And his flattery by no means limited itself
to agreement. He would listen with well-affected deference

to a remark, and then break out with well-assumed honest candour:

"Oh, do you really think so? Forgive me if I seem stupid, but don't you think . . ."

It didn't matter a straw to him what point of view he was defending—it seldom does to those whose living depends on making the worse seem the better cause. What mattered was to give the impression that he was using all his mental faculties against a formidable opponent. Sometimes he would yield, as if baffled by a distributed middle; more often he urged his point with soft persuasion, knowing that women like to be convinced.

Thus, there came a time when Etta ceased to think of Francis Leigh as old. The mental picture gradually changed to that of an agreeable man of the world, experienced but tolerant, cultivated but without pose, eloquent but modest, the kind of man with whom one was *safe*. Above all, he "understood." As he told Etta, he had "immense respect" for the new type of woman who had achieved independence in the world. She was a "refreshing contrast" to the "bird-witted doll type." Soon they were "Francis" and "Etta." He sent her flowers on her birthday, and a tastefully bound copy of Marlowe's *Hero and Leander*. These were accompanied by gay friendly little notes, entirely uncompromising. Teddy in his prison camp became a dim figure, and Ralph at his battery was forgotten.

Mr. Leigh believed in the efficacy of the fine arts and literature as valuable aids to sapping the fortress of feminine resistance. While a certain amount of sentiment was needed, he didn't believe in pitching the note too high. The arts were a much better line of approach, and did not involve those forever-and-forever protestations which might be so inconvenient later. Besides, as he once pointed out to Etta, there was so much *pretension* and unconscious *hypocrisy* in love affairs. Perfectly ordinary people tried to persuade themselves that they felt the consuming passions of Abélard and Héloïse. Surely she would agree that even men and women like themselves, who, he ventured to say, were distinctly above the average, should keep within the limits of their feelings? Etta did agree.

So, in accordance with plan, and with his character as a "cultivated" man to keep up, Francis talked, almost gushed, about the "exquisite" quality of Japanese colour prints and the "subtle elegance" of eighteenth-century French engravings. And as he knew a good deal about them, and Etta knew very little, it wasn't hard for her to be impressed and "interested." From time to time he lent or gave her books: the Rubaiyat, to form the right atmosphere of modern hedonism; the Mardrus version of the Arabian Nights, containing the immemorial wisdom of the East about everything, especially sex; the *Aphrodite* of Pierre Louÿs, bringing in the old pagan blitheness, that *Heiterkeit* of which Pater has written so subtly; Marlowe's *Hero and Leander*, which introduced the splendid outspoken frankness of our own Renascence; and "modern French things." Absorbed in the reading of these books, Etta would scarcely have known there was a war on, but for the rations and air raids.

Soon they had a secret.

Francis was escorting Etta home from a tea. It was a quiet, rather misty day, towards the end of March, 1918, and the street noises seemed unusually loud. Francis spoke wearily and wistfully:

"How noisy these streets are—I can hardly hear your voice. There's an insistent *clamant* quality in modern life which frays the nerves, don't you think?"

"Yes," said Etta, "it *is* rather bad sometimes. I often

think I should like to live far away from it all, in a cottage somewhere."

"Oh, you mustn't exile yourself," said Francis quickly. "The modern woman, especially when highly sensitive and beautiful, needs the grace, the luxury of city life. I can't imagine you in tweeds, or even stroking a syllabub, as dear old Walton says. No, no, what I was regretting is the absence of quiet and privacy. How rarely one can be alone, how rarely enjoy the delight of intimate conversation with all its subtle play of thought and delicate feeling."

"Yes?" said Etta deferentially.

"You must have noticed that in a group, even one so charming as poor dear Kitty's, one can never be entirely oneself, never *reveal* oneself. Of course, it's very right and delightful that everyone should possess an agreeable social personality. But one grows weary of wearing a mask, and of seeing others in masks, however gracious—don't you think?"

"Yes," Etta confessed. "I have sometimes felt that. I don't like having to be on my guard, do you?"

"Not in the very least."

"And then even the nicest women can't help being a little treacherous and catty. Did you notice how Betty Westbury was trying to hear all we were saying this afternoon?"

"No, was she? How very silly of her! But there you are—none of us has any real intimacy. Do you know I've been wondering about you?"

"About *me?*"

"Yes, whether you could destroy another of the foolish old legends about women and keep a secret?"

"I think so," said Etta laughing in answer to his laugh. "Why not try me?"

"Oh, but it's very secret, and to me important."

"Now you have roused my curiosity," said Etta, laughing again.

"Shall I tell you? Yes, I think I will, but you must promise complete secrecy. I can't have my lovely secret profaned by the world."

"Of course I promise faithfully. Do tell me what it is."

Francis seemed to meditate and then to take a sudden resolution.

"Don't laugh at me and my precautions, but, you see, I have a secret 'den' to which I sometimes retire from the outer world, after a hard day in court, you know. In my profession, unfortunately, we see much of the worse side of humanity, and it's entirely necessary to have somewhere for peace and meditation and solitude."

"I think it's a lovely idea and worthy of you," said Etta, glancing at him admiringly. "But why couldn't it be in your own home?"

"Oh, that wouldn't be the same thing. One is never quite certain of absolute seclusion. The telephone, callers. And then poor dear Bunty can *never* learn to respect my solitude. No, my plan is the only one. There I have some of my choicest treasures, books and prints, and there I can smooth down the ruffled plumage of the spirit."

Francis made a mental note of congratulation on the Pateresque felicity of his last phrase—it might come in useful for a prose poem.

"I do most of my writing there," he added.

"Oh, I didn't know . . ."

"Only prose poems, composed for the happy few, as poor dear Stendhal says. I'll read them to you. But wouldn't it be very pleasant if you came there from time to time, when we are both weary of the fever and the fret, and we talked of higher things?"

And Etta, completely deceived, assented, feeling honoured.

Thus it came about that Etta made her first visit to Francis's "den." It was really only a flat, but Francis had worked hard to make it mysterious. Etta found herself in a room furnished with glazed rosewood bookcases, a couple of armchairs, an elegant writing table, and a very thick blue carpet. The windows were hung with heavy blue curtains, and blue hangings and a large Chinese screen concealed the entrance to the bedroom. Etta thought there was only the one room; and there was not even a couch or canapé to flutter the suspicious female mind. She sat in one of the large chairs before a small wood fire, and watched Francis as he moved about the room. He drew the curtains and lighted two large candles in painted wood stands, and then prepared tea from a samovar which took some time to warm up. The tea, he said, was specially imported from Russia, and he hoped the little popular disturbance there wouldn't prevent his getting more; at which drollery he laughed with the easy tolerance of those accustomed to foreign frivolities.

Over tea they talked, and then Francis read Etta some of his prose poems, which were symbolical but erotic, possibly reared in a hothouse of pomegranates. There was a lot about pomegranates and nenuphars and henna and scarlet sin and chrysoprases which Etta didn't quite grasp, but, as Francis pointed out, new movements in poetry are always baffling at first. He read these productions in a queer chanting voice, as if intoning the general confession. When Etta had given the prose poems the praise she was fully persuaded they deserved, Francis brought up a kind of lectern, cunningly illuminated, and displayed his prints. Some of the subjects startled Etta, but Francis discoursed on them with the detachment of the true artist. The subject, he said, was unimportant; what mattered was the treatment, the vision. He pointed out beauties of line and mass, which Etta tried to admire; and yet she couldn't help thinking there must be something in the subjects, or why should she feel flushed and a little embarrassed and yet both curious and interested?

On her next visit Etta was met at the door by Francis dressed in a blue-silk dressing gown; and joss sticks were burning before a bronze replica of Buddha. He kissed her with impetuous *bonhomie*, exclaiming:

"How charming of you to be so punctual, and how well you look!"

Once again they had tea and turned over French engravings, after which he talked amiably of *galanterie* and Madame du Barry. And before Etta departed, he kissed her again—oh, in no spirit of seduction, but because he was so spontaneous and exuberantly grateful for the intellectual charms of her conversation. Where was the harm? Etta still did not know there was a bedroom in the flat.

But a kiss is a kiss, a fact on which the most artless maiden meditates. Etta was a maiden, no doubt, but not so artless as to fail to guess whither all this was tending. Certain glances, certain phrases, the display of erotica showed quite plainly what was to be expected. What was she going to do about it?

3

THE MISERY OF THE LAST WAR YEAR oppressed Etta far less than many, but she was too sensitive to be able to ignore it. The rare letters she received from Teddy sounded depressed and a little mad, and Etta sometimes reproached herself for the contrast with her own life. Ada she never saw, but heard through Vera that Ralph had been wounded and then later sent to the East. Her intimate connection with the war was cut. Yet, though people were beginning to whisper that no victory could now atone for all that had been lost, Etta had to admit that her own material success was due to the war. She was promoted to a departmental post, where the salary and war bonus reached a figure she had scarcely hoped for. With horror she found herself feeling regret that the war must end some day.

At the same time she could not help being infected by the despairing recklessness of those days. Among its other conveniences Miss Millingham's house was situated in a bomb area. When any night she ran the risk of being blown to pieces Etta asked herself why she should not take what happiness she could with Francis, especially since all round her she saw examples. Why not? Why, after all, should she doom herself to a life of celibacy, merely from pique with Ralph? True, her feelings for Francis were tepid compared with the raptures and the agonies of the past; but if those alone were love, then love was too painful. There might be a better, quieter way, as Francis had said.

Oddly enough, the baby plan faded from her mind as completely as the resolution to live an old maid. She didn't think of Francis as the possible father. She thought of him as the wise, tolerant, kindly initiator, experienced and delicate about women. She was convinced that she understood him perfectly, and smiled even at his æsthetic affectations, which she dismissed as quite a lovable foible in a brilliant lawyer. After all, he might have been merely a business man out for money and the common pleasures, like most of his tribe. For the rest, she accepted him at his own valuation and was flattered that she had attracted him. She found herself depreciating her former passion for Ralph as "calf love." So much the better if she didn't feel "calf love" for Francis. This affair, if it happened, would be quite different, modern and mature. They would go into it as equals, understanding each other perfectly, and parting in perfect friendship, without rancour, at any time either of them wished. Thank God, *she* hadn't that awful possessiveness of some women.

With these dispositions on both sides, no long time elapsed before an entente was formed. Francis was quick enough to see that he need waste no more time in preparations and what he would have described "in court" as "cunning and abominable corruptions of innocence"; while Etta was far too frank and downright a person to play the old ridiculous part of the maiden who vowing she will ne'er consent consents. When Francis with much unnecessary eloquence came to the point, she accepted; and very shortly discovered that the æsthetic den possessed a comfortable bedroom annex.

The open world conspiracy against the female served Etta rather ill at this first experience. Having long ago rejected, on purely a priori grounds, the fretful warnings of the moral conspirators of impotence that such actions were extremely wicked, she very naturally formed the opinion that what was forbidden with such mumbo-jumbo terrors must be very pleasant indeed. Her own instincts told her so, and they in turn were confirmed by much that she heard and saw, not least by the works with which Francis had so carefully plied her.

It was disappointing as well as rather a shock to find herself shy, awkward, and cold, and terrifying to discover that a good deal of pain was accompanied by very little pleasure. Like everyone else brought up under our absurd and contradictory sexual customs, she was a tangle of inhibitions and was disgusted by the physical verities. Her first thought was the rhetorical question: Is *that* all it is? Her second was to wish she hadn't done it. There was none of the triumph, the ecstasy, the O altitudo, she had dreamed of so often and with such lazy rapture. As she lay with head averted and limbs still rigid with repulsion, Etta promised herself that she could never let this happen again.

Francis, however, was equal to the situation and read her mood perfectly. He was surprised and greatly flattered to find himself the pioneer, and he was not going to lose what he had taken such pains to obtain. He soothed and cosseted her, fetched champagne from a corner cupboard (which had Leda and the swan painted inside the door) and made her drink. He spoke rapturously of his "delight," and talked so eloquently of his gratitude for all she had given him that Etta was touched and already half reconciled. Forestalling her, he explained that her disappointment was natural and inevitable. But let her only trust in him, soon all would be well. Did she think she could become skilled in the most difficult of the arts in a few minutes? He talked so persuasively, so gratefully, treated her so caressingly, interpreted and explained her own feelings so correctly, that she did trust him. She went home, still rather upset, but more than half convinced that she would try again. Meeting Vera made Etta feel a little furtive and ashamed, but that was quickly lost in triumph. After all, *she* was now a woman, a charming man had found her desirable, while Vera—poor Vera—was nothing but a wretched old maid on the shelf.

And, as it turned out, Francis had been quite right. What had been painful at first soon became endurable, then pleasant, and suddenly one day soared to a thrilling delight. It was now Etta who was grateful to Francis. There was no longer any need for Francis to plead with her for another rendezvous; in fact, with the unconscious grasping of the satisfied woman it was now Etta who asked: When can we meet again? And it was Etta who felt disappointment when there had to be delay because of

"legal business" or the exigencies of "poor dear Bunty."
Etta tried not to think about Bunty and the children—
what had they to do with her and the delightful new world
into which Francis had initiated her?

As for Francis, his gratitude was genuine enough, but
he passed easily, if gradually, from the position of pleading
lover to dominant male. He delighted to play the refined
and experienced initiator, to watch the growing warmth
of Etta's response, to see how quickly she was transformed
from melancholy girlhood overprolonged to dazzling
womanhood. And it flattered the sexual vanity of the man
growing old to have captured so completely a human being
capable of so delightful a change. Really, he was growing
quite deeply attached to her; and he almost believed it
himself when he assured her that no woman had meant
so much to him. It was quite certain that he wanted to
keep her—on his own terms.

Francis's attachment, such as it was, remained a slight
thing in comparison with the swiftly deepening devotion
Etta felt for him. During those long months of 1918, her
life was cleft into two unequal portions. One, the more
intense and ecstatic, wholly given up to Francis; the other,
nonchalantly, to her everyday life and work, with a war
going on somewhere in the background, and a far-off
Teddy writing incomprehensibly and ridiculously about
his religious doubts and what consolation he found in the
Bible.

The affectations and æstheticism which once had almost
annoyed her and struck her as false now seemed rather
endearing. After all, Etta reflected, there is *some* truth in
the theory that men are big children—they must have
their playthings. And Francis's playthings showed his
fine sensitive nature. It was wonderful to have the desire
and affection of such a man, and wonderful to feel this new
elation and pride of life in herself. She respected Francis's

reiterated wishes, almost commands, to keep their relation an entire secret; but for herself she hardly saw the necessity. After all, they were both equal and free—well, Francis wasn't quite free, but then Bunty didn't really want him, and that could easily be arranged. Etta herself would have been quite ready to avow the situation and to dare the world. She was proud of Francis, of herself and of their relation. Of course, she was no exhibitionist, but she would have liked to share her happiness with others and to see them happy. Vera, for instance. Poor, nice, steady, reliable old Vera—why, she was being cheated of life.

Etta decided she really ought to "help" Vera. Respecting loyally her promise to Francis, she still managed to drop hints about unknown delights in store, and even suggested that various young men they both knew might be worth considering. One or other of them might easily be encouraged into an attitude more interesting and valuable to Vera than that of a mere acquaintance or so-called friend. At these hints Vera merely looked bewildered and a little frightened. Miss Millingham herself, in her moments of most misanthropic devotion to The Cause, could not have been more emphatic than Vera in disclaiming all intention or wish to become intimate with one of the worse half of the human species. Vera was quite certain she didn't want to marry anyone, and was scandalized when Etta suggested that St. Paul had omitted one obvious alternative. Etta shrugged her shoulders and said no more. If Vera must be a fool, let her be a fool.

4

THE END OF THE WAR provided Etta with a new crop of problems, complicated by the existence of Francis. What was to be done? For the moment she was still safe in her job, but obviously a superbloated Ministry of Munitions would not continue in peace time. It might be just possible that she would be taken on the permanent staff of civil servants in an inferior position at a smaller salary. But Etta was sick of what she now considered the "sterile" routine of offices. She yearned for something different, something she vaguely labelled "life." What on earth did she really mean by this quasi-mystical "life," which now was always coming up as the decisive argument in her discussions with Vera?

Life. It is really the most succulent metaphysical carrot ever dangled before the silly nose of the vast collective human donkey. Exploitation of that word is the basis of most magic and religion. At one time "life" meant fecundity and the earth's fruitfulness, which was at least sensible. Then the unfortunate idea occurred to somebody that he might go on living after he was dead. That discovery had big news value. The Prehistoric Mail ran big headlines: Sensational news from Egypt—Ruler claims secret of immortality found—Pisgah heights of patriotism —Pharaoh consents to live forever in best interests of nation—All hands to the pyramid—Roll up with your gold— Egypt expects every man to do his duty.

That lasted a long time. Heaven was democratized, and millions of suckers bought diuturnity for their mummied corpses. But Lincoln was right. Even that venerable gaff was blown after forty or fifty centuries—pretty smart of *sapiens* too. The ghost of Achilles remarked that it would rather be a slave among the living than king of the dead. But that didn't do. *Sapiens* wanted more life, and wanted it abundantly. *Sic itur ad astra.* Besides, the business properly run is a lucrative one, and only needed reorganization. Which it got. Believe senselessly in certain unprovable propositions, behave in a certain way, and yours is the kingdom of heaven. And there we so very much are, except that the wheel has gone full circle, and once more there is a very half-hearted waving of the phallus in the face of humanity. But it's still extremely uncertain what most people mean when they hanker after "life."

So it is not surprising that Etta was a little vague in her definitions of "life." She was not unique when she allowed it to be coloured by her preoccupations and interests of the moment. At the end of 1918 her relation with Francis not unnaturally impelled her towards the fruitfulness cycle of ideas and feelings. Etta had always possessed a healthy desire to do things, to make something. The destructiveness of the war appalled and revolted her. She decided that making dossiers was not *life*, was not *creative*. So once again the country cottage idea came well to the fore. She saw it all perfectly—working with Vera on their own bit of land, and growing food to help alleviate this dreadful shortage. Why, butter was seven shillings and sixpence a pound and almost unobtainable at that.

The only difficulty was Francis. Etta's idea was that Francis could spend every week-end and his vacations in the country with her, which would be so much better than snatched afternoons or evenings in the den. But Francis refused to be drawn into the scheme. He pointed out that such a proceeding would inevitably compromise Etta—meaning, of course, himself. And when she said she didn't care tuppence if she were compromised, Francis most unselfishly refused to accept the sacrifice. Moreover, he mocked at her agricultural ideals, and repeated his remarks about beautiful women being the product of town civilization.

"Of course," he added, "I don't see any reason why you shouldn't have a week-end cottage, if you can find one. And you'd need a little car. I'll gladly stand you a two-seater—I wish you'd let me. But don't ask me to come there. Believe me, it would be fatal. I know the world, and its prejudices must be respected."

And from this position he refused to budge, though they almost had a quarrel over it. Etta on her side refused the car. It was contrary to the whole code of being on one's own to accept anything from a lover. Disappointed and rather hurt, Etta brooded. In the four years of the war she had saved nearly four hundred pounds. On a smaller salary, Vera had saved nearly as much—but then she had her own income to live on. Surely with that amount of capital they could run a cottage and a few acres of ground, and really "live"? How very strange that Francis couldn't understand the position. Surely he didn't mean her to work in offices for the rest of her life in order to be near him.

The significance of that "for the rest of her life" escaped Etta. If questioned, she would have denied eloquently that she had changed in the least her attitude to Francis. Everything was still perfectly "modern and mature." If either wished to break off, the other was quite prepared for it; but why in heaven should they, when they suited each other perfectly? But, in fact, there was a great unconscious change in Etta. Wanting more "life" meant wanting more Francis, all Francis. Etta was convinced she wasn't possessive—the very idea was absurd—but the trouble lay, she felt, in that childishness of the male, which could be so engaging but might be tiresome. Francis ought to be able to see how "sterile" his legal work was. A fine gloriously physical man like him needed real "life." She could see him striding in from haymaking or ploughing, sunburned and earth-scented, sitting down to eat the food she had prepared (Vera had somehow disappeared from this picture), while "their" child sat with them in his high chair. Francis could have his study, and in the evenings they could look over his books and prints together. . . .

At this moment Etta recollected "poor dear Bunty" and the other children. That was certainly awkward. Etta had no feeling of animosity towards Bunty; on the contrary, she felt quite friendly towards her. The trouble was that Bunty was stupid—she simply could *not* see that she wasn't the woman for Francis. Really, the way that woman exploited Francis's good-nature would have been monstrous if it hadn't been pathetic. But for the children . . . Obviously, the children were the tie there. Francis was very fond of them, and Bunty thought of nothing else. She was in love with the children, not with Francis. It seemed awfully wrong and unfair that a man should have children with a woman he didn't care about, and not with his real mate. It was part of the whole disgusting hypocrisy of town life. Why shouldn't Etta have a child with Francis? It would really be wonderful, and then it would be such a *real* thing. It would make Francis understand how utterly she was devoted to him (without any sort of possessiveness) and show him where real "life" lay.

If, by any system of mental television, Mr. Leigh had been able to follow these meditations of Etta's, he would have fallen into a cold sweat of apprehension. They pointed to an event, a tangible, indisputable bit of evidence that his conduct had not been legally "respectable," which he was most sincerely anxious to avoid. One of the lines of his persuasive period a few months earlier had been that if Etta followed his instructions carefully there could be "no possible danger." At that time Etta had been very glad to carry out his instructions; and the event proved that here again Francis had been right.

Etta was quite unaware how often she had changed her mind and vacillated in her plans during the confusion of the war years. She was certainly pleased to know that Teddy had returned from captivity, but she excused herself from going to see him that Christmas. The children had whooping cough, so Bunty and Francis were staying in London. So, of course, Etta couldn't go. And the thought

that, if Ralph were still alive, he would be returning sooner
or later, never occurred to her. She was far too much
occupied with another situation.

A week or two after the Armistice, Etta had proceeded
so far as to give Francis a slight hint of her ambitions in
the maternity line. His opposition had been surprisingly
vigorous, even consternated. He begged Etta to abandon
all such foolish and unnatural notions. Her life would be
ruined—social disgrace—consider the legal disability of the
child—his own position, et cetera, et cetera. To quiet him,
Etta promised, sweetly and submissively, but with a Eu-
ripidean reservation. The tongue swore, but not the heart.
She saw the whole position so clearly. Francis was afraid
for her sake—as if *she* minded a little pain or the tattling
of social gossips. He didn't realize how the modern woman
was quite prepared for all that. Besides, he didn't realize
either how much she loved him. Once he had that proof,
she felt certain he would understand all she was striving
for in seeking "life" for them both.

Without saying anything more to him, Etta took her
own way. Francis had to be saved.

On a very wet Saturday afternoon towards the end of
February, 1919, Etta came out of the house of a woman
doctor she knew and stood waiting under her umbrella
for a taxi to take her to a rendezvous with Francis. The
doctor was nearly certain but not quite—at least, so she
said; but Etta was convinced that it had happened. She
felt solemn and uplifted as she stood waiting, and thought
that in her the mysterious life cycle was beginning once
again. Normally, she wouldn't have dreamed of taking a
taxi, even in rain, but now . . . The doctor had advised
good care of general health, but without fussing.

As the taxi squeegeed its tires over the wet streets,
Etta's thoughts darted about swiftly and rather incoher-

ently. She would have to do those exercises and walk every day but not catch cold. A good many of the clothes she could make herself. In a few weeks she would resign from the Ministry—the sooner the better, because that place in the country must be found. Would it be best to move there before or after? Francis must help her to decide that. She wondered what he would say when she told him the news. Probably a little upset and timid at first—men are like that—but all that was good in him would respond to the *fact*, however he might object to the *idea*. He would soon feel as proud of it as she did. After all, they couldn't bring the dead to life—which reminded her for some reason that she mustn't forget a present for Teddy when he married that Muriel Bates girl after Easter, a great mistake for the boy—but however much the dead were dead, life must go on. How marvellous to watch a new life growing, and how curious to think that one day a young man would be calling her "Mother." Seemed quite absurd, in a way, and yet, wasn't it the real solution? Etta didn't stop to enquire exactly how and why the problems of life are solved by producing someone else to face them.

Though Etta was longing to tell Francis, her whole instinct was against sailing in with a dramatic announcement. Far better to wait for a moment when the great and lovely news could come out easily and naturally. So she waited. . . .

Francis stirred beside her on the pillow, yawned, got up and wrapped himself in the blue dressing gown, and then took whisky and a siphon from the Leda and the swan cupboard. The champagne had been dropped for some time.

"Whisky and soda?" he asked.

"No, thanks, darling," said Etta sleepily.

"Liqueur, then. Which?"

"I won't have anything."

"Why not?"

Etta sat up and pulled the bedclothes to her chin. She smiled affectionately at him as she said:

"I've a particular reason for giving up all drink."

"What d'you mean? Is there anything wrong with your health?"

"Nothing whatever. I never felt better in my life. So guess again."

"I can't imagine any reason," said Francis, a little fretfully, letting the soda fizz out. "But then I never do try to find reasons for feminine whims."

"Shall I tell you?"

"If you like, but it's of no importance."

"I'm going to have a child, darling, yours and mine."

"*What!*" Francis stared at her with amazed horror. "What are you talking about?"

"It's quite true, my darling, and I'm so happy about it."

"How do you know?"

"My doctor says so."

"Good God!" exclaimed Francis, striding up and down the room. "What an appalling calamity! I can't believe it. Didn't you do what I told you?—it's infallible."

"Well, it wasn't infallible in this case," said Etta, sweetly dissimulating.

"I simply don't understand it. It can't possibly be mine."

"Francis! How dare you suggest that. It *is* yours. You're being cruel and insulting."

"I beg your pardon," said Francis, pausing in his ambulations, and trying to speak suavely. "This news upsets me dreadfully—for your sake more than mine, of course. What an awful position! How long has it . . . ?"

"Three months."

"Three months! Gracious heavens, why didn't you tell me sooner?"

"I wanted to be quite sure."

"You should have told me when you first suspected. Dear, dear, dear, what a misfortune, and coming at this particular time when it's so hard to get a passport. But don't worry, and above all don't tell anybody. I'll arrange everything. We can get it done in Paris. Leave everything to me. I know a very good medical man who will arrange it—in the strictest secrecy, of course. Let me impress that on you—complete secrecy is essential. There is no danger, I assure you, when it's carried out properly. Naturally, I shall pay for everything."

"But, Francis . . ."

"Etta, you must obey me, and let me deal with the situation. How it arose is a mystery which must be cleared up later. Today's Saturday, isn't it? You must be ready to leave on Monday or Tuesday."

"I'm not going, Francis."

"*What!* What do you mean?"

"I'm not going to have our child destroyed," said Etta, unconsciously folding her arms across her body as if defending something. "It's going to live. I want it and . . ."

"Don't talk such nonsense! Good heavens, don't you realize . . . ?"

"I realize everything, Francis, and I've had much more time to think this over than you have. It's useless for you to argue, because I've made up my mind. I know I'm right, and in good time you'll see it too."

"But, good heavens, woman, you don't mean to father me with a—an illegitimate child? You must be mad!"

"Pah!" Etta exclaimed contemptuously. "Do you think I'm to be frightened by those dead bogeys? There are realities outside laws and gossip. Believe me, I know what I'm doing."

"Forgive me, but I don't think you do," said Francis,

trying to control himself and speak calmly. "I understand
how you feel, and in a sense it's very creditable, but utterly
misguided. You think only of your own selfish desires in
the matter. What you propose is a sentimental schoolgirl's
dream. You don't consider that a child is something that
can't be hid. Everybody has to know. The life of an
illegitimate child in England is unthinkable—disabilities
and humiliations at every turn. Besides, if this were to be
known, my career would be ruined."

"If it's only that which worries you, I give you my
solemn word of honour nobody shall ever know it is yours."

"But a child has to be registered by law," Francis almost screamed at her. "Get that into your head to start
with."

Etta tried an appeal:

"Don't let us quarrel, my dear——"

"I'm not quarrelling, I'm trying to knock a little common sense into your obstinate lunacy."

"I'm not going to let you make me angry, Francis," said
Etta wistfully. "I love you, and you're the father of the
child I'm going to have."

"You're not!"

"I am! I've planned it all out. I shall go to the country
with Vera and the child and work there for it and bring it
up. When you see the child, you'll love him too, I know
you will. I shall have a room kept specially for you, and
you will be able to come down and see us whenever you
like. Nobody need know. And we can be together much
more happily than we ever could in London. I promise you
I won't be a bit possessive—you can come and go just as
you like. You can go on with your law work if you like,
but you have vacations, and I *know* it would do you good
to live a healthy life in the country, and I believe you'd
come to like it as much as I know I shall. So don't be cross

any more, darling, or say horrible things to me. I *know* it will make us both terribly happy. I'm very happy now, except that you don't quite understand. Come and kiss me, like a good boy, and say you want him too."

Francis listened to this in staring amazement, too angry and suspicious even to interrupt. So that was the little game, was it? Trying to blackmail him into divorce proceedings, and then to pin him down for the rest of time to this fatuous idea of life in a country cottage. Throw up a fat income and a career at the bar and on the bench for the sake of a wretched little girl out of an office who had contrived to get pregnant, probably by someone else. Luckily she hadn't a scrap of evidence or a single witness. It was merely her word against his, and in any case, an action for loss of service by the father wouldn't lie. An affiliation order could be defeated—a strenuous affidavit, a good counsel, and a word in the right quarter. But no doubt it needn't come to that. The point was to get rid of the little bitch without scandal.

"That sounds very idyllic," he said, unable to keep a sneer out of his voice. "But unfortunately it overlooks the facts of life. Don't you know that in the country everyone knows all about everybody else's affairs and a good deal more? Hasn't it occurred to you that I'm a married man with a family and a position to keep up? Can you seriously weigh your own reputation and chances in life, not to speak of mine, against this silly whim? But it's useless to argue with you while you're in this hysterical state. Try and come to your senses, Etta. Look here, I'm willing to be generous if you'll be sensible and follow my advice. Do what I ask, and I'll not only see it's done in the best possible way, regardless of expense, I'll give you a couple of hundred, there! That'll help you with the cottage—but don't ask me to come to it."

Make it an open "cash" cheque and then destroy the
cheque after it was paid, Francis thought; and, by Jove,
if she ever catches me alone with her again she'll be
lucky. It's a risk offering money, but it'll shut her up,
and if she tries for more I can threaten proceedings for
blackmail . . .

"What!" exclaimed Etta, flinging herself in fury from
the bed. "You offer me money, *money*, to destroy my
child's life? You think you can bribe me? It's mine,
and you shan't and can't destroy it! You cad, you miserable cad!"

They faced each other, Francis with a look of white
hatred and repulsion on his face which turned her indignation cold. It was quite horrible, so murderous and so full
of loathing for the very flesh she thought he loved. Without replying, Francis picked up his clothes and went into
the next room, shutting the door behind him. Etta stared
at the closed door and then threw herself face downwards
on the bed in an agony of despairing tears. How bitterly
cruel of him, how utterly selfish. And for something which
could be so beautiful, such a perfect culmination of desire
and life. And he had actually tried to bribe her to kill his
child; and looked as if he would have killed her, if he
hadn't been afraid.

Yet she still hoped—women always do. Her tears and
sobbing stopped; she got up quietly, washed and dressed
herself, and went quietly into the next room. Francis was
dressed and sitting sulkily in one of the armchairs.

"Francis!" Etta said softly. He took no notice.

"Francis! I'm sorry I said that to you just now. I
apologize. You see, I was very upset, and . . ."

"Are you prepared to do what I wish?" he asked, without looking at her.

"No, but Francis . . ."

"Then I think you'd better go," he said coldly.

5

THE END MR. LEIGH HAD PROPOSED in defiance of the law by Parliament enacted very nearly happened of itself owing to the effect on Etta's nerves of this somewhat brutal scene. She took to her bed for a couple of days to recover. Violent spasms of weeping alternated with long periods when she lay exhausted and dumbly miserable. The shock of Francis's abominable volte-face and evident desire to be rid of her was worse even than the utter collapse of her invented happy future. During the quieter intervals Etta did some hard thinking, and her sufferings were salutary to the extent that she became mentally adult. She admitted she had been duped, and that she had duped herself—which was far more serious. She had committed the fatal error of believing in what she wanted instead of realizing what was. She had invented a romantic Etta who had power over Francis, because she wanted the power. And she had equally invented the Francis she wanted him to be. With disastrous and shameful results.

In her distress Etta turned to Vera, the Vera she had been despising as a fool not so long before. Except that she concealed Francis's identity, Etta told her everything, confessed herself, accused herself, admitted her long tissue of self-deceptions. Etta expected Vera to be upset, helpless, and reproachful. But directly she learned that Etta was with child, Vera for once took command of the situation. She gave Etta the loyalty, the protection, the sense of confidence she needed. Though she thought Etta had been both foolish and immoral, Vera made no sign of disapproval and carefully hid the fact that she foresaw all kinds of difficulties for them.

Vera divided their functions—Etta was to concentrate entirely on her health, while Vera did the planning. And plan they did. Vera wangled Etta's immediate resignation from the Ministry and got her a handsome testimonial of good behaviour and efficiency. She saw the doctor and made Etta follow the proper régime of diet and exercise. She reserved a place in a nursing home. She talked cheerfully about how they would live in the country, and promised to find a place, though she knew how difficult it was at that time. She determined that Etta should spend the summer months on a farm.

Etta allowed Vera to take charge of her life for the time being with a docility which surprised herself. But something had gone from her forever; she had lost the confident *élan* of youth and looked forward to the future with no particular hope. Going into the country was now merely a refuge from a world which had hurt her; it wasn't an adventure any more. Already she began to surrender hope for her own life and transferred her hope to the life which was slowly growing within her body. In her distress she invented a God, who had no particular theological qualifications, except that he was strong and kind and Etta's friend. She felt that somewhere or other there must be a God who looks after all women heavy with child and sorrow. So she asked God to make the child a boy, because it is not good to live a woman's life.

It was quite true that Francis had killed what was young in her, and yet she couldn't quite believe that he was as brutal and selfish as he seemed. She excused him by blaming herself. In a hundred ways he had showed her the kind of man he was, and it was surely her fault if she had preferred not to see and had romanticized him. It was also her fault that she had played a kind of trick on him. After all, they had made a compact, and if she hadn't broken it, there would have been no breach. She hadn't played fair. Even in that last scene she had dissimulated by not admitting that she had deliberately allowed the child to happen. She wondered how on earth she could ever have imagined he would leave his wife and children and career for her, or that he would be touched by her pregnancy.

At any rate, Etta told herself, she wasn't going to ask him to suffer anything. Whatever penalty there was, she was going to pay. What hurt her, what was degrading, was his offering her money and their parting on terms of such violent hatred. Surely they could part friends, surely there wasn't any need for a complete break, surely, too, he'd want to hear about his child occasionally? She ought to get in touch with him, give him an explanation, and at least wipe out this hatred and double betrayal. She couldn't let the child be born, hating its father.

Here Etta examined her conscience closely. Could she be absolutely certain she wasn't tricking herself again? Was it really true that she only wanted to make a decent end, or was she unconsciously trying to make a reconciliation and somehow involve Francis in the fate she had brought on herself? Truthfully, yes, truthfully she didn't want to go back to the old relation, she didn't even want him in her life. After what had happened, after that terrible look in his face and the realization of what he was, she couldn't bear even to let him touch her again. But that explanation she must have.

So she wrote a short letter and sent it to the den. The letter came back marked "Not known." She ventured to ring up Francis's chambers, and as soon as she gave her name she was rung off. That was pretty insulting, but she tried to think it was a mistake. She decided it wouldn't be fair to write or go to his house, because it might involve him in trouble with his wife. In her despair she gave Vera the slip one afternoon and went down to the den at a time when she knew Francis was usually there. She knocked several times and got no reply. As she stood mournfully hesitating outside the door, still hoping that by some miracle Francis might open it, a woman in a sacking apron came up from the basement and called to her rudely.

" 'Ere! What d'you want?"

"Is Mr. Leigh in?"

"Leigh? Never 'eard of 'im. There was a bloke called Collins uster stop there, but 'e's gone, took all his furniture and everything."

"Do you know where he went?"

"No, I don't, and no more don't nobody else. And a good riddance, considerin' what went on by all reports."

Etta flushed scarlet and fled.

A few days later Etta forced herself to go to one of Kitty Mendip's parties. She was morbidly afraid people would guess her condition, and felt that everyone who glanced at her knew her secret—rather a different frame of mind from the bold frankness and composure she had meant to have. She learned that Francis had gone abroad, nobody quite knew where, nor when he would be back. From which she was forced to conclude that he had ratted on her completely, as a good many men invariably do under such circumstances.

Very soon it became impossible to conceal what was happening to her, even if she had wanted to do so. Etta fought hard against her own shyness and tried to be open about it. She couldn't help feeling important, a pioneer trying to establish a valuable right for women at whatever cost to herself. Etta told herself that she must be prepared for anger and reproach and the kind of disapproval which meets unconventional courage. It would do her acquaintances good, she thought, to be shocked out of their silly, frivolous lives by the sight of a woman doing what was real in defiance of obsolete customs. After all, somebody had to begin breaking down these old walls of prejudice in practice as well as in theory.

She was a good deal disconcerted to find that she was not allowed any of the honours of persecution and to find herself treated as a compound of a bore and a fool. Whatever they might do in practice, the disciples of the Latest Thing theoretically considered that Etta was crashing through an open door. *Everybody* has bastards nowadays. Who? Oh, well, I can't be bothered to think of names, but they do. So Etta was robbed of her glory. Among the women there was a feint at feminine solidarity, with a little patronizing "poor darling" compassion. The men were merely indifferent; nobody could make them pregnant, so what did it matter? The one thing which interested them all was trying to find out who the father was. When they had all failed to break through Etta's determination not to tell, they faded away. After all, pregnant girls are not very amusing.

So Etta was very glad to go to the country and get away from people. They made her feel squalid, belittled her experience which she was still convinced was something essential, tremendous even. It hadn't the spurious "originality" which people hunted with such simian eagerness. It was "original" to have strings of futile "affairs," but boring and even ridiculous to be a maker of life. She resented the public conspiracy of prudery which shoos pregnant women into seclusion, as if they were an indecent spectacle. In any event, Etta wasn't prepared to be an indecent spectacle to Dortborough at Teddy's wedding. She sent a present and wrote that she couldn't come; for which she was upbraided as an unnatural daughter and sister by her mother.

Vera took Etta down to the small place where she was to stay. As they waited for the local train on the platform of a small junction, Vera said diffidently:

"There's just one thing I have to tell you."

"What?"

"Well—I had to tell them you are Mrs. Morison."

"But why? Why did you do that?"

"Because they probably wouldn't have had you otherwise."

This was unanswerable. Etta said:

"I hate this miserable lying and subterfuge."

"It can't be helped. I told them your husband had been killed in the war."

"But won't they know that's false?"

"Very likely, but they won't care. All they're afraid of is the opinion of their neighbours. They want a story to tell, and I gave it to them."

"It was kind of you," said Etta, trying to feel grateful. How disgusting to have to pose as a war widow! How mean and beastly!

"I warned them not to speak of it, that it upset you to be reminded," Vera said apologetically.

Etta didn't answer. She felt rather sick.

The Browns were west country people, renting a small holding in one of the home counties. The idea was that Etta should try to learn all about running such a place while she stayed with them. The house delighted Etta at once. It was an old six-room cottage with barns and stables, which evidently had once gone with more land than the seven acres worked by Mr. Brown. The large kitchen, in which the Browns mostly lived, had an open fireplace where Mrs. Brown cooked, a plain brick floor, and raftered ceiling. The floors of the upper rooms undulated where the wood had warped. Mrs. Brown apologized for these defects, and evidently thought Vera and Etta were lying when they protested they liked such things.

"What a charming old place!" said Etta, when she was alone with Vera in her own bedroom. "And what a delicious old room this is. Look at that tallboy and those old ornaments and the lattice windows. But why must they have this dreadful wall paper and that hideous modern bed and carpet?"

"They have no real taste, you know," said Vera. "They have to buy what they can afford."

"Yes, but why are the old things all beautiful and the new ones all hideous?"

"I'm afraid they prefer the new ones. Mrs. Brown is very proud of that bed. She insisted you should have it instead of the old wooden one."

"What a pity! I wish we had this place, Vera. We could make it lovely."

"It's just possible we might be able to get it. Mr. Brown has applied for a grant of land in Canada—there's some scheme for giving it to ex-soldiers—and the reason they agreed to take you was because they want to get all the money they can. I've been hoping we might get it."

"How wonderful!" exclaimed Etta, clasping her hands. "If only we *could* get it. I should adore to live here. Come to the window. Just look at that garden—we could have more flowers as well as vegetables—and those meadows with the buttercups just coming out. Isn't it all heavenly?"

When they came down they were given tea in the parlour, which was decorated with a stringless piano and black, slippery horsehair furniture which was very cold to sit on. The empty fireplace was filled with cut evergreens, and the shelf above held mathematically grouped vases in despicable polychrome—the kind sold at fairs. The tea was very plain, because of the rationing orders, but after so many hasty office teas it seemed delicious to

Etta. After tea, they went out into the garden with Mr.
Brown, who was going to milk. Etta knelt down to smell
the white clove-scented pinks.

"How delicious!" she exclaimed. "Do come and smell,
Vera. Did you plant them, Mr. Brown?"

"Ess," said Mr. Brown indifferently. "Missus would
have they old clo' pinks. Neighbours'd say us wasn't respectable if us didn't have flowers."

They went into the large byre, smelling of hay and dung
and cows' breath, where only four of the twenty stalls
were occupied. Mr. Brown showed them how to milk, sending long spurts of milk drumming into the deep pails. Both
Etta and Vera tried, but were unable to extract a drop,
while the cow swished her tail and looked heavily round to
see what was wrong.

"Hey!" said Mr. Brown facetiously. "Don't ee go pulling th' udder off old Molly now. 'Tis done by kindness like.
Let me show ee agen."

But they couldn't do it, and tacitly agreed to postpone
the agricultural lesson for that day by leaving Mr. Brown
and climbing the rather steep meadow behind the house.
The grass was speckled with purple orchis, which Etta
gathered; and then they sat in the sun near the crest of
the hill, looking over the fields and watching the golden
evening sunlight throw long and longer shadows. Birds
sang from the fresh green copse behind them, and they saw
a hawk slowly circling in the distance. They heard the
scrape and clink of a shovel from the yard, and the occasional cluck and gabble of a hen. Otherwise there was a
gentle silence, except for the lowing of cows coming back
from pasture. They sat quite still, without speaking, and
Etta felt filled with a deep, almost ecstatic peace. This rich
land awake in full spring, the life of the animals and trees,
the Browns going quietly about their work—that was
what she wanted. They were friendly to her and the grow-

ing child; they wouldn't spoil her fruitfulness with nerves and superiorities and being smart. The peace of it, with the war over and her own office life finished and the thought of long happy years ahead with the child growing up. She turned to Vera with tears in her eyes:

"How sweet of you to find this place for me, Vera! How I wish we never had to leave it."

"Perhaps we can come back," said Vera, brightly trying to prevent Etta being emotional. "Leave that to me."

"You're so good, so kind to me, Vera," said Etta gratefully. "How lost I should have been without you, the only real friend I have."

"Nonsense!" said Vera, getting up. "You'd better come in now, Etta, this grass isn't too dry, and the air will be chilly soon."

"It's not nonsense," said Etta, clutching Vera's hand as she rose heavily to her feet. "But I do love this place. It's all perfect."

6

WITH SUCH DISPOSITIONS of goodwill Etta had not much difficulty in passing the time happily enough. If she got at all bored or impatient with the inconveniences of her surroundings, she had a complete excuse in her condition. Later on, she would be too busy to notice such things. The agricultural education did not progress very far or very rapidly. If Mrs. Brown saw Etta trying to do anything even moderately strenuous, such as weeding or trying to saw a tree bough into logs, she would rush out screaming shrilly:

"Don't ee go doing that now, 'twill bring ee on afore y' time like!"

So Etta had to abandon whatever she was doing, never quite certain whether Mrs. Brown was concerned for her health or only wished to prevent her from interfering.

However, she learned how and when to feed the fowls and where to look for the eggs, under the guidance of Mrs. Brown's Gladys, a small, solemn child, pallid from too much potatoes and pork. She learned to milk after a fashion, but had to give it up because of the strained position. Mrs. Brown showed her how to churn the butter, how to skim and scald the cream, and how to make what she called bag cheese—squeezing curds in a bag which hung from the pump handle in the scullery. Etta made some—it wasn't a good cheese, but still it was cheese. During these operations Mrs. Brown talked in her high Devonshire voice. She was fond of airing her contempt for the young generation of agriculturists.

"They young uns don't know what 'tis to work," she confided. "Born lazy, they be, and all for luxury. Up every morning at four, and sometimes three *I* was when I was dairymaid, making the cheese with me own hands—cut, cut, cut, until me arms was dropping off. Then walk to Tiverton market and back and work till 'twas dark. Now 'tis all done by a machine."

"But isn't it better people shouldn't have to work so hard?" asked Etta.

"Why, 'tis the ruination of they!" said Mrs. Brown shrilly. "They'm all for spending. They gets twice the wage us ever had, and never stops grumbling. Us hadn't but two or three fairings year-end to year-end, and now 'tis fairing every week. All for shop trash and such like, as if so be they was gentry."

Etta didn't try to argue the point. Mrs. Brown had immovable views about the gentry, and knew what real live people ought to do and what the gentry ought to do. Anybody who wore city clothes and didn't work was gentry to Mrs. Brown. Vainly Etta tried to plead that she wasn't gentry, that she and Vera both worked in London; but Mrs. Brown wouldn't have it. Who ever heard of a working woman taking three or four months' holiday merely because she was pregnant? So Etta had to be gentry, was refused permission to help Mrs. Brown with the washing up, and compelled to take her meals alone in the parlour. As Etta was rather squeamish about table manners, this was perhaps just as well, since Mr. Brown removed his boots before supper, ate with his knife, and belched heartily when he had finished. Etta put the finishing touch to her inferior position as one of the gentry by an unlucky remark in the dairy.

"I wonder why the butter is so pale?" she asked innocently, "with all those lovely golden buttercups."

Mrs. Brown laughed so much she had to put down the large bowl she was scouring.

"Dear, oh dear!" she gasped. "Do ee think as 'tis buttercups makes butter yellow?"

"I didn't know," Etta stammered.

"Why, 'tis a tale for babies! Cows, they won't touch buttercups—they'm so sharp as papper! 'Tis in they green seeds."

Etta tried one and found it was true.

For the time being Etta gave up trying to share in the day's routine, and watched with interest how the Browns worked their holding. At dawn she heard Mr. Brown get up and rekindle the kitchen fire before he went out. Then she could hear Mrs. Brown's voice scolding and reproving as she washed and dressed the children and began tidying up the house. And so they worked the whole day through, never hurrying, but going on persistently in a slow rhythm which Etta found very soothing. She envied their placidity and tried to imitate it. She wanted to be unhurrying and placid like that, unperturbed as the animals, for she believed her state of mind would influence the child. At first, she was distressed by the sudden sharp quarrels of the

Browns which occasionally disturbed the peace with oaths and cries, but they passed as suddenly as they arose, leaving everything as it had been. The Browns seemed to bear each other no grudge for scenes which, Etta felt, would have severed her from a man forever. At such moments she was very glad not to be married.

When the day was fine Etta spent the sunny hours sitting in a chair on the path under a hoary apple tree, trying to be placid. To some extent she succeeded, but her mind was too active. Try as she would to imitate the mindless nirvana of cows, she couldn't prevent herself from brooding over the past or thinking anxiously about the future. She had a small table brought out, and sat with the patterns and materials she had brought from London, sewing or knitting clothes for the baby. In six years how much had happened to her, how often she had changed, how many people who had been important in her life had gone out of it—her father and mother and Teddy now held to only by the slim thread of occasional letters, Drayton, Ada (what was Ada doing now?) and her husband, and Ralph, and the Admiralty and Munitions people, and Francis. From Dortborough days only Vera remained to her. Funny little Miss Millingham she still knew only because she was still her landlady, and soon she would be gone. And of all the other people only Kitty Mendip wrote to her and sent her things for the child.

Sometimes Etta was so restless and depressed that she would leave her sewing and walk up and down the path or out into the lane. She felt too burdened to walk far, but at these times she had to move about. There were moments when she even doubted whether she wanted to live in the country, whether she could ever work like the Browns or endure what they endured. Little things got on her nerves. When Mr. Brown methodically scraped from the styes the dung which, he told her with affection, was "almost so precious as goold," she had to fly from the overpowering stench. It hung in her nostrils all day and prevented her from eating, though she was often ashamed of her appetite. Again she was desperately upset and cried bitterly when a sow farrowed and ate half her litter before Mr. Brown could stop her. Etta agreed with Mr. Brown when he remarked "thikky owd zow be wickeder than Zatan hisself," but it didn't console her for the abomination.

Fortunately Vera came down faithfully for week-ends and diverted Etta's mind from these distresses and worrying about the fate of herself and the child. For there were days when Etta blamed herself ruthlessly and thought she was nearly as wicked as the sow, for having a child under such circumstances. Vera explained the depression as a natural result of her condition and attributed the restlessness to all the upset of the war. Etta tried to believe her and that all would be well when the child was born. Vera asked anxiously if she didn't love the child already; but no, Etta was obliged to confess, she didn't love it at all; in fact, she almost resented this occupancy of her person. Altogether, it was not the ideal pregnancy Etta had imagined, something quite different from the state of poise and contentment and soft radiance she had promised herself.

Nevertheless, she was sorry to leave when the time came, towards the end of July. The thought of London, of waiting in Miss Millingham's suite for the ordeal, and the ordeal itself, depressed her, seemed more than she could bear. She was afraid she would never learn to look after the child properly. The only consolation was that the Browns had received their grant of land in Canada and were leaving in September; and that after weeks of diplomacy Vera had succeeded in persuading the suspicious Mr. Brown to yield his stock at a fair valuation (he suspected some smart town trick) and had secured the cottage and land on an annual tenancy. In spite of this, Etta cried as they drove to the station.

"We shall be back in two months," said Vera comfortingly. "And then it'll be ours. Think what fun it'll be!"

But Etta shook her head in mournful silence; she had recently developed an apprehension that she would die in childbirth and there would be nobody to look after the infant. Also, she wanted to eat lobster salad as soon as they got to London, and Vera had utterly refused to consider the idea, on the absurd pretext that it would be bad for her.

Strangely enough, it was rather fun to be back in London. Etta quite enjoyed the drive from Paddington, the glimpse of the park as they passed Marble Arch, the red buses, the movement, the people sauntering along in summer clothes. She noticed that the darkened street lamps in Oxford Street were being changed, but there were still plenty of men in uniform. Miss Millingham met them at the door, presented Etta with a bunch of flowers and some tears, and made a little speech in which Etta's heroism in affronting lonely maternity was somehow mixed up with the triumph of the vote they had all won through the war.

Every day Etta waited for the symptoms she had been told to expect, but nothing happened. The child stirred and kicked vigorously enough, but appeared to be in no hurry to make its début on the world's stage. Etta spent most of the day in the large cool room with blinds drawn against the sunlight, putting last touches to the collection of clothes and making meals for herself and Vera. She supposed she ought to feel touched by the look of these baby clothes, but in fact they were rather distasteful, bringing back child memories of her mother struggling with Teddy,

and suggesting domestic servitudes. And still they were
not all done. Towards dusk she took a short walk with
Vera, and went to bed early, hoping to goodness the next
day would set her free from this heavy waiting.

One evening at the beginning of August, Vera left her
alone after coming back from the walk, to visit some
friends. Instead of going to bed, Etta lighted an old reading
lamp and sat sewing in its concentrated light. She had
managed to give up worrying about the money they were
spending and felt comparatively happy and at peace. She
sang softly to herself as she sewed and thought about the
child. There was a knock on the door, and one of the
numerous successors to the incompetent Gertrude of old
days blundered in, announcing:

"Gentleman to see you, mum."

Francis! thought Etta, and swiftly moved the lamp
so that she was left in darkness. She didn't want to be
seen by him. A man's voice—but not Francis's—said:

"I hope this isn't an intrusion, but I wanted so much to
see you."

Etta was puzzled and a bit frightened. Who was it?
Something in the voice was familiar, but she couldn't place
it. Peering into the half-darkness outside the arc of bright-
ness from the lamp she saw a tall, shadowy figure in khaki
—it couldn't be, it was! Etta shrank back in her chair with
a cry of terror.

"Ralph!"

"I didn't mean to startle you. I'm . . ."

He took a step towards her, holding out his hands, but
she huddled away from him.

"Don't come near me! Don't touch me! Go, go, please
go away. Why did you come?"

"Let me speak to you first, I must speak to you. May I
sit down?"

Etta was too terrified to answer. What did he mean by appearing suddenly before her like a ghost? The absurd thought came to her that Ralph was dead, that this was his ghost come to tell her she would die. She wanted to scream, and couldn't for very horror, as her heart pounded with the rush of blood. She saw the shadowy figure take a chair and bring it near the table and sit down.

"Please go away, please leave me."

"Etta, I can't—not until you've heard me. I'm so sorry if I frightened you. . . ."

She could see now that it was a live man and that the face was Ralph's, very thin and dark-looking. Her terror waned, but she still felt dazed.

"I don't understand. Why have you come? How did you know I was here?"

"Ada had this as your last address, and I came to try and trace you. I'm just back from Egypt. I didn't dream I should find you—the girl offered to bring me up—it seemed a miracle. If you prefer, I'll go now, and come to you again tomorrow."

He spoke very rapidly, and Etta scarcely understood the words, except about coming tomorrow. What! Let him see her by daylight in that state! She turned further from him, trying to conceal her figure with her arms and the folds of her gown. Now that her panic fear was going, she began to feel angry with him. She said:

"I don't understand. Why have you come to me now? You told me it was good-bye for always, didn't you? Why do you suddenly pounce on me like this and bring up bitter memories?"

"All you say is true and just and less than I deserve," Ralph said in a quick nervous voice, "but listen to me a moment. I've come to apologize, to humble myself to you. I know I behaved with unspeakable brutality, like a madman, a cad, anything you like. From your point of

view I was all that. I don't hope to make you understand
—I don't think any woman can—she can only imagine—
you see, for months I had lived solely for that meeting—
you were life. You—I can't tell you what the thought of
you, of loving you, meant to me. Your refusal seemed the
most awful treachery—a piece of silly cruelty—like tearing
the wings off a living bird. Oh, I know I was wrong. The
fault was mine. I should have known, I should have been
gentler, I should have seen your love was finer than mine.
If I hadn't been so young and selfish, I should have seen
that only a woman who could love greatly would have
mourned so tenderly for a dead brother."

"He didn't die," said Etta tonelessly. "He's back in
England and married."

Ralph drew a deep breath.

"I'm glad he came through," he said. "It was all a
queer tangle. But why didn't you tell me?"

Etta began to feel desperate. Ralph's presence, the old
pleading trick in his voice were more than she could bear.

"How could I, after you hurt me so much? Did you
think I was a thrashed dog to come crawling to you?"

"Etta, don't be so hard on me!"

"Hard! Who taught me to be hard? Do you think I
haven't learned the lesson? I was tender enough to you,
Ralph, I loved you. You failed me utterly, you crushed
out the real love and tenderness I had. At times I've hated
you since, I've even blamed you for sending my whole life
wrong. Now I neither hate nor love you. I just don't care.
I want you to go away, 'forever,' as you said yourself.
You can bring me nothing but pain."

"Etta! Can't you ever forgive me?"

"What does that mean? You say you are sorry, I was
more sorry."

"You are mistaken if you think I haven't suffered," said
Ralph quietly. "I have suffered. At first, I confess, I was

bitter against you and tried to forget you with other women. But it all turned to ashes in my mouth. I was wounded and then was sent to the East. I saw that in both of us pride was too quickly wounded, we were too self-willed to know how to be compassionate—and that I was the more to blame. I don't say I went through the war a love-sick Romeo, but I found all this out bit by bit, in the quiet patches. Sometimes I thought I'd write to you, but I knew we could only untangle this web of ourselves by being face to face."

Knowing him, Etta guessed how deeply he must feel to be able to humble himself like this; but she hardened herself.

"What is the good of all this? It's useless. I've let you say what you wanted to say. Won't you please go now?"

"It isn't all useless," Ralph pleaded. Etta tried not to listen. Why wouldn't he go? The bitterness and resentment, conscious and unconscious, which had grown up in her against Francis were turned against Ralph. She was half suffocating with anger for the selfishness of men, who wanted from women only their own pleasure and submissiveness to their wills. Let the woman choose *her* way, let her cease to be a pleasure-gadget, let her want a little disinterested affection and kindness, whew! *Va donc, bonjour! mais va-t-en, sale femelle!* When she thought her brother was dead and she asked only for a little kindness, a little restraint, Ralph abandoned her in brutal annoyance. Now he was at a loose end because the war was over for him, he wanted her back. Of course, he assumed she'd been meekly and chastely waiting for him. He'd had other women, he admitted it, assuming her acceptance. That was *quite* all right, of course. And she had only to stand up and let him see her figure, and there would be horror and indignation and reproach, and *sale femelle, va!* Men were hateful, really base.

Through all this she heard Ralph talking, talking, trying (she thought) to impose his will on her as of old.

"It seems to me there's still a chance for us to atone for past errors and misunderstandings," he said. "I've tried tonight—and I shall go on trying—to show you that I am different—wiser, I hope. I don't ask you to believe this now, but—give me the chance to prove it to you. I know I made us both suffer through my own self-will and impatience and silly pride—I bitterly regret it—but now we've got this one chance, don't you repeat my error. If I've remembered you through all these bitter years, I can't believe that you've forgotten me. What was between us was too deep for that. You know it. But I can see now what a difficult position you were in, how our little snobberies and posturings must have grated on you. That's all gone now, blown to smithereens with most other things. But you and I can salvage something from the wreck. And, anyway, there's always injustice to be fought in the world—why shouldn't we fight it together? You've had a bad time in life; but so, in my way, have I. You can give me a motive, a centre, something I believe is worth having. Couldn't I give you something—at any rate, an interesting enough life free from material anxieties? I didn't really mean to bring this up at first—it came out in spite of me—and I don't expect you to answer. . . ."

"Neither of them had heard Vera enter the room until she spoke.

"I beg your pardon—I didn't know you had a visitor."

Etta scrambled to her feet and stepped forward into the light.

"Vera! Look at him!" she said hysterically. "A major! Let me introduce him, Major Lawson of the Gunners! A soldier and a gentleman!"

"Etta!"

"Etta!"

"Look at him!" she raved, losing all control, laughing and sobbing hysterically. "And look at me! He says he loves me, the man who told me I was a moral prig because I wouldn't go to bed with him when I thought my brother was dead. He insulted me, he abandoned me—utterly—completely—for three years not a word—not a message—and now he wants me to marry him! Me! Look at me carefully, Ralph—do you still want to marry me . . . ?"

"Hush, hush!" Vera exclaimed, taking Etta in her arms. "Be quiet, Etta!"

Over her shoulder she said:

"Please go at once, Major Lawson. You've made her ill, and you can see she can't stand it."

And then to Etta:

"Hush, my darling, hush! Don't sob like that, *don't.*"

Two hours later Vera took her to the nursing home in a taxi, and the child was born about ten the next morning.

As Etta lay exhausted and broken from the grinding rhythm of childbirth pangs, she was told that it was a fine healthy child, over seven pounds, and a girl. She turned her face into the pillow as she murmured:

"I don't want to see it."

7

BUT THERE THE CHILD WAS, and, as Etta dismally reflected, there it would remain as a living example of how to conduct a really modern and sensible love affair. She watched the nurse undress, wash, and re-dress the wailing little creature with a feeling that she would never be half so efficient, and rather disliking the mixture of a clinic and a latrine which the operation involved.

She wondered whether the nurse really loved babies, or whether this boo-boo-ing and did-it-then-ing was one more bit of hypocrisy in the universal scheme of sentimentalizing life. Nor could she share the professional enthusiasm over the beauty of the child. In fact, she was a bit horrified when she saw her daughter—"it" looked so little and bird-like and wriggling. She couldn't honestly say she "loved" it—or rather her, for the baby was human, after all—she only wished the poor little beast hadn't such a fool for a mother.

The nurse plagued her to give the baby a name, and Etta couldn't think of one she really liked. Well, as "the father" had died for King and Country, didn't she think it ought to be called Mary Alexandra? But Etta said most certainly not. When Vera arrived, as she did every day, she consulted her.

"You see," Etta said, "you're the only person except Miss Millingham—and she's been a darling in her way —who's been kind to the poor little wretch. So I'd like to call her after you. But we can't have two Veras, can we? Haven't you got another name?"

"Yes, but it's Hermione. One can't call an innocent child that and have it shortened to Hermy at school. Why not call her Anne? It's quite simple and unpretentious."

So they called her Anne, and the baby didn't seem quite so remote now she was no longer "it." Even so, Etta couldn't quite get used to suckling Anne—it seemed a primitive performance better performed by a cow and a bottle. On the other hand, she had to admit to herself that it was rather touching to have a tiny little creature greedily sucking its dinner out of one. Absurd, of course, but, yes, touching.

A few nights after Anne's birth, Etta had occasion to revise her impression that she wasn't much interested in the child. She was awakened from sleep by the child crying, and it seemed to her that the cries were louder and more penetrating than she had heard, as if something were really wrong. There was only a night-light in the room, and Etta waited anxiously for someone to come. The cries went on, choking and desperate, and Etta suddenly lost her head—suppose the little thing should be dying! Trembling with anxiety, she switched on her light and rang the electric bell. Still nobody came, and her heart was pierced by the cries —they seemed to call to her very blood, such panting, agonized little cries of distress. She was sure Anne was dying, and no one came to help her. In spite of all their strict orders to the contrary, Etta threw back the bed-clothes and began to get out of bed just as the night nurse came in.

"Why, whatever are you doing?" she exclaimed severely. "Get back at once, you'll make yourself ill."

"I'm sure there's something wrong with her," said Etta, sinking back and trying to pull the bedclothes over herself.

"Just a little wind, I expect," said the nurse, picking up the vocalist and putting her face downwards on her lap and patting Anne's back. "There, my pet, there!"

"Poopf," Anne belched faintly, "poopf," and ceased crying.

"There!" said the nurse. "Did it have nasty old wind on its little tummy."

"I'm sure it's something worse than that, Nurse," said Etta. "She was in agony. Do let me have her a minute."

"Wait till I've changed her."

Etta watched the process with deep anxiety, feeling convinced that this heartless woman was *not* the person to be responsible for a child. She resented it, too, when, after being allowed to have Anne with her for a few minutes, she was told with maddening cheeriness:

"Time for her to go back to her cradle."

Interfering old brute. The nurse straightened Etta's bed and then took her temperature.

"Don't you dare try to get up again," she said severely.
"Lie still and try to go to sleep."

Which good advice did not prevent a feverish night.

Besides Vera, Etta had only two visitors—Miss Millingham and Kitty. Removed from the dim splendour of her
own setting, Miss Millingham looked small and red-nosed.
Her hat was peculiar, and her assumption of aristocratic
airs was not approved by the matron. Etta lost a bet with
Vera that Miss Millingham would say the baby was distinguished, but she delighted them with some remarks on
eugenics.

"Paradoxically enough," she said with great seriousness,
"we of the upper classes do *not* pay enough attention to
breeding. How many fine old families are becoming extinct
among all this modern riff-raff? I myself am the end of My
Line. You've done splendidly, Miss Morison, and how glad
you must be that it's a girl. So unpleasant for you otherwise. You make me feel that I've failed in my duty to my
Country and my Class."

Vera, whose bigoted suffrage views were now turning
to an equally bigoted left-wing socialism, attempted a
refutation, but Miss Millingham skipped off happily to
other topics. Etta found that her social stock with the matron fell very low after Miss Millingham, but it soared
up again when Kitty arrived with her Rolls and chauffeur
fashionably dressed, and bringing orchids. The matron
purred over these evidences of wealth. Kitty behaved very
nicely, but Etta felt shy with her. She was disconcerted
when Kitty said after looking closely at Anne:

"Do you ever see Francis now?"

"No."

"Neither do I. . . . Perhaps it's just as well."

She hesitated as if she were going to say something more
and then changed the subject. Etta wondered what she

meant, but was touched when Kitty took her hand at leaving and said:

"Don't let us lose sight of each other, Etta. May I come and see you in your cottage some day? And, remember, if you ever want to stay in London you must come to me. You know, I feel a little responsible for you."

"Why ever should you?" Etta laughed. "But thank you, and yes, we *will* keep in touch."

Etta was impatient to get away from the restraint and expense of the nursing home, but at the same time rather dreaded it. She couldn't believe that she would ever be able to look after Anne properly, and at the same time work. As they came down the steps to the waiting taxi, which had Etta's shabby luggage strapped on, it struck her they were a singularly forlorn and unpicturesque group—the temporary nurse carrying the baby, herself a little unsteady on Vera's arm. If birth were as imposing and important as they pretended, there ought to be a little bit of symbolical ritual for Anne's entrance into the world—not just this commonplace driving off. Perhaps if there had been a man with them. . . .

The Browns were leaving the cottage in a few days, but Vera refused to allow Etta to go down with her—she insisted that she must go on ahead, arrange for a man to look after the stock for the time being, and prepare the place for Etta. When everything was ready, Vera would come back and fetch her; and meanwhile Etta would have the temporary nurse to help with Anne. To all this Etta agreed rather helplessly, wondering how on earth she could have faced the situation alone. But for Vera she would have been lost. Yet why, after all, should Vera so unselfishly give up her life to Etta? It was something to remember that in distress only women were unselfish.

Two days before Vera left she brought Etta a bulky envelope, saying:

"This came for you some time ago. I know who it's from because he wrote to Miss Millingham, asking her to send it on if you were away. I've deliberately kept it back until you were stronger."

Ralph's letter was a long, involved, and—in Etta's opinion—priggish document, beginning with another string of apologies, repeating most of what he had said, and going over all their past. Quite a valuable essay on the theme of the course of true love never did run smooth, Etta thought sardonically. He wound up by repeating his offer of marriage and promising that the child should grow up as his. He pointed out that this would remove most of the disabilities, which Etta ought to consider; and, in any case, why shouldn't they forget all the unhappiness of the past and try to make something of life together? He would resign from the Foreign Office, and they could go abroad together, perhaps to the south of France, or anywhere she liked.

Now if Etta had heard this about other people, she would have said the man was being decent and generous. In her own case, she took quite a different view. She persuaded herself that the offer was not sincere. These returning soldiers grabbed at anything to give them a bit of stability, instead of waiting sensibly to find out what they really wanted—just as Teddy had plunged into marriage with Muriel. And then, even supposing the offer was sincere, what did it mean? That as soon as Ralph got over his first interest in her and they settled down to the realities of life together, she would be entirely and slavishly at his mercy. All her life she would feel that he had married her out of compassion, and she would have to endure anything from him for Anne's sake. And then he might be unkind to Anne. Besides, if she married Ralph, Etta would have to give up her own life (that didn't matter much now) and her chance of making something better for Anne—if she gave up working there'd be nothing for Anne but what Ralph chose to give her. And with that situation he had the audacity to plead that they "should come together entirely as equals"!

No! Etta deliberately tore the sheets of the letter into small fragments and held them in her hand, thinking: No! Much better work for her in the country, bring her up in good air and peacefulness, and see above all that she was educated to hold her own in the world. . . . Vera's voice brought her back:

"I hope that letter hasn't upset you?"

"Not a bit. It was only a proposal, my dear."

"A proposal! Of marriage? What are you going to answer?"

Etta held out her handful of torn paper.

"That's the answer," she said, bitterly.

8

AT THE END OF SEPTEMBER Etta was able to begin her long visualized life in the country, among the "realities." They left London in a grey fog which changed to heavy white mist as they emerged from the filth area. From the window of the carriage Etta could see dim gliding forms of yellow half-leafless trees, sodden green meadows, and the undulating telegraph wires dripping with moisture. It was not an auspicious beginning. Etta felt that she had broken down her bridges and that there could be no turning back. She was nervous about the future, but at the same time hopeful. They were going to a fine healthy life, and if there wouldn't be much money, there ought to be all the essentials. She had visions of winter evenings by the huge fireplace, the slow coming of spring, long warm summer days, and then the gentle English autumn with its calm and abundance. Through this recurring cycle, with always some change and something new to look at, the years of their lives would pass until Anne began to grow up. And then? Time enough to think of that when it happened. Meanwhile there would be long happy years when Anne would live only for her and she only for Anne.

Vera had performed wonders, Etta thought when they went over the house together. As they came up the garden path—which was a bit muddy and puddly and would have to be mended—they passed the cowherd trampling heavily round to the byres. He pulled his forelock to the missus and vanished sheepishly. There was a fire in the big kitchen, and one of the neighbours was preparing them some food. Her little girl dropped a curtsey, and Etta was so pleased with all the kindliness and the way Vera had rearranged the room that she didn't notice the damp stain coming out with autumn on the north wall. Upstairs one of the rooms had been freshly papered and painted for Etta and Anne. There was a coal fire with a proper child screen, a bed for Etta, and a large chair, so that she was able to sit down at once and to attend to Anne, and have her ready for sleep almost as soon as the cradle was brought up. The room looked clean and nicely coloured, but Etta fancied it was a wee bit chilly. Otherwise everything seemed perfect, down to the spirit stove to heat Anne's food, and the new primus stoves in the scullery.

"How nice it all is!" Etta said enthusiastically. "You've thought of everything."

"Well, it's not *quite* finished," said Vera hesitatingly. "You see, I haven't had time to get at the parlour and the other rooms, and we shall need some more carpet and one of those oil stoves for heating and . . ."

"Oh, we can soon get all that done," said Etta. "And

how happy we're going to be here. Tomorrow we'll really begin work."

Later that day, when Etta pumped water into the kettle for tea, she thought how much more fun it was to draw up water instead of just turning on a tap. It made you feel water was valuable. And after she had gone to bed, with Anne in her cradle near at hand, Etta lay and watched the firelight reflected on the old beams and said to herself that at last she had reached her haven.

Etta plunged zestfully and energetically into this new life and tried to ignore the inconveniences and difficulties which she discovered more or less speedily. Heavy rain fell in October, and the roof leaked, and the damp patch in the kitchen ran a race in spreading with the damp patch in the parlour, and the farmyard became a quagmire, and even the path was a mass of thick mud. The landlord, complained to, said he'd mend the roof, but at present it was impossible to get labour; and as to the path and yard, what did they expect in the country? So Vera bought them gum-boots, which they scrubbed with a broom at the scullery door, and they agreed that "later on" they would mend the path themselves.

They had meant to economize by getting rid of the cowherd at once, but a difficulty was that one of them had to be near Anne, so they could seldom work together. Etta went round with the boy, taking the mash to the chickens and carrying pails for the pigs, helping to fodder and litter down and milk the cows, and getting soaky green stuff for the rabbits they meant to breed from as an extra food supply. When she came back, with Anne to attend to at once, and more mash to be prepared, and a sack of bran to be ordered, and the milk to churn, and a dozen other things to be done, Etta decided that they would have to keep the boy. And then Anne was a dreadful tie, poor darling—she didn't mean to be. But there it was. It was all very well to say, "Let her cry," but Etta couldn't. And it was difficult to break off in the early morning, when her hands were black with building the nursery fire, and attend to Anne, or later in the day, when she was peeling vegetables or washing up. So they decided it would be more "economical" to have a girl in the house to do some of the rough work.

Moreover, there were hosts of little things Etta had scarcely noticed while she was with the Browns. For instance—the wood fire. Etta loved the wood fire but hadn't realized how it was fed. They omitted to shelter the wood pile properly, so it got soaked, and the logs hissed and smouldered instead of burning. Trying to saw logs with too much energy Etta strained herself inside and had to lie up for a day. Then came the question of a fresh supply of wood. Brown, they discovered, had paid so much for the right to cut down firewood in a copse about a mile away; but they had neither the strength, nor the tools, nor the time to do this. So they had to pay heavily to have wood cut and brought to them. Thus it happened with numbers of things—they had to pay out instead of getting in. There was the earth closet, for instance, which was in a little hut twenty yards from the house, in summer covered with roses. It had seemed engagingly primitive and picturesque then. But now it was a penance in wet weather, and then they couldn't find anyone to empty it, until reluctantly a neighbour consented to "oblige them"—for a shilling a week. They discovered that all odd jobs had to be contracted on the "oblige" principle.

There seemed to be no end to the problems which had to be coped with almost daily. Etta tried hard to organize their work on orthodox lines, and typed out schedules beginning "Rise at dawn," and laying down when everything was to be done. Unfortunately, as she discovered, even a

very small farm isn't an office, and you don't have to do
the same thing every day. Moreover, pigs, cows, chickens,
and rabbits can't be docketed "to be fed tomorrow" when
something else urgent crops up—they have to be fed today.
True, the cowherd, Tom, ploddingly looked after them, but
Etta was determined to learn herself, and staggered under
buckets of hog wash, and milked at the cows until her fingers swelled and she hated her animal sister-mother.

Honest as he was and hard-working, Tom was one of
those who get on with their own jobs and assume that
other people know theirs. He was accustomed to take orders and not to supplement the ignorance of others by tactful promptings. Thus, it was plain to him that one of the
cows had gone dry and would need the ministrations of a
bull; but Etta didn't discover this for some time, not indeed until she tried vainly to milk the unhappy and restive
beast. And then the cow's matrimonial future had to be
discussed with a farmer, who disliked having such matters
brought up by young women. It was equally plain to Tom
that the garden ought long ago to have been rough-dug
for the winter, whereas the bean poles and pea sticks had
not even been taken in. When Vera at last discovered this
through a hint from Mr. Crowder, an elderly neighbour of
benevolent intentions, she and Etta got bad blisters and
broken backs in digging together rather less than a fifth
of what Tom dug with no apparent effort.

"Oh, well," said Etta, trying to be cheerful, "this is real
work, you know. We're getting on."

"Yes," Vera agreed hopefully. "We're learning."

But she didn't mention that, as treasurer, she found her
weekly accounts sadly on the wrong side.

Later on, taking an impartial retrospective view, Etta
admitted that this first winter was hellish. The days grew

shorter and darker and wetter, the cottage leaked and was
increasingly difficult to keep up to their town standards
of warmth. They both got colds, and in spite of all Etta's
care, Anne got a sniffle cold too. Etta was alarmed by this
avant-garde to the many maladies which children seem to
take a perverse delight in having. She was ashamed later
of having called in a doctor.

Christmas was almost upon them when Etta recollected
that she had not written a single letter since August, and
that in her total self-absorption she had even forgotten
to write to her parents about Anne. Vera and Anne and
herself seemed a tiny world self-contained, better off when
isolated. It was a difficult letter to write, and Etta sat with
paper and ink in front of her in the lamplight for a long
time before she could begin. She noticed how swollen and
chapped her hands were and called Vera's attention to
them.

"You ought to be glad you haven't got chilblains as I
have," Vera replied unsympathetically.

"What a gale there is tonight!" said Etta. "I hope it
won't blow the roof off. Oh, Vera, this is an awful letter
to write—what am I to tell them?"

But Vera had no suggestions, and Etta tried to steer a
middle course between defiance and apology, humour and
a statement of the rights of women. She expected to be
denounced and cast off, and was pleasantly undeceived
by a long flowery grandmother letter from her mother and
a much shorter one from her father, enclosing £25 to start
a post-office banking account for Anne. Etta replied gratefully, and informed Vera that she was going to add another
£25 from her own savings—it would give Anne something
in the future. This provided Vera with an opening for an
awkward revelation.

"I think you're quite right, dear," she said. "But now

we're on the subject of money, would you mind looking over the accounts? We're nearly a hundred pounds down already."

"Impossible!" exclaimed Etta.

It proved to be not only possible but true. There followed a long discussion. Finally Etta said:

"There's only one possible course—we must get rid of Tom."

"But we can't do the dairy work ourselves."

"Then we must sell three of the cows—they're fetching good prices now—and keep only one for Anne's milk and our own. The cows are the chief bother. We must try to make up on the pigs and fowls and rabbits."

But it was a difficult struggle, what with an empty garden and fowls which unaccountably wouldn't lay and pigs which ate without growing fat. Life that winter was like a long rainy picnic after all the fun has gone out of it.

The days began to lengthen after Christmas, but you don't notice it at first even in the country. Going round the west side of the house in January, Etta saw some new green-blue shoots coming out of the soil under the shelter of the wall and brought Vera to see them.

"Look, the snowdrops are coming up," she said. "Soon the spring will be here."

How much she wanted the spring to come, when the mud and the mire would dry and the cottage not be so hard to keep warm, and there wouldn't be so much risk of chill for Anne, and they could plant the garden and have salads and fresh peas . . . what a pity they couldn't have ducks. Every day she went to look at the snowdrops, imperceptibly fighting their way up through poor hard soil and against nipping winds. Etta broke the hard crust of earth round them with a trowel—she liked so much to see frail beautiful things fighting bravely and winning.

She wanted to believe in something beneficent in the nature of things, something finer than violence and selfishness and greed. Snowdrops are just as real as the war, she thought, and a good bit more real than Francis. How strange that Francis had never seen his child, didn't even want to; but, then, that's how men are—they can get wildly excited about killing each other, and care nothing for a beautiful new life, fragile and brave as a flower. And so conceited about the superiority of their sex, when it's the women who have to undo patiently all the reckless evil men do.

When the first flower, like a small white Dutch cap, broke from the spindle-shaped bud, Etta was happy. She remembered how the early flowers along that awful Muncaster Road at home had consoled her, how trapped and imprisoned she had felt there, and how she had managed to escape Dortborough at last, as the flowers escaped from the grimy soil. One's life had to be renewed like the life of flowers, or it shrivelled. Now once again she had to struggle to escape, from war-frenzied London and its falsities, and all the suffering and mistakes with Francis. It was worth all the discomforts and hard work and the annoyances to feel that they were putting out new shoots of life, she and Anne.

More snowdrops flowered until there were snowy clusters under the wall, and farther along, after the soil was soaked with rain, crocus leaves pushed up like thin sharp green wires, and blunt daffodils among them. Enthusiastically Etta began to dig over the vegetable garden, and at night went to sleep over seed catalogues and a book on how to organize a garden. The affable Mr. Crowder, always ready for a crack, liked to lean on the wall and enjoy the spectacle of Etta's unhandy struggles.

"Diggin' up the garden like?" he suggested.

"Yes," said Etta, tugging away at some pestilentially

long roots of bindweed. "I want to get it started in good time."

"Shallots coming along?"

"Shallots? I haven't planted any. Ought I?"

"Maybe you don't care for pickled onions?" said Mr. Crowder apologetically. "Some ladies finds 'em strong, but I always says they goes tasty with a bit of bread and cheese. They says round here you plants shallots on the shortest day and pulls 'em on the longest, bit of superstition like. But it ain't too late to put 'em in."

"I wanted to grow some spinach."

"Ah, spinach, we gives that to the pigs here." This was crushing, and Etta didn't know what to say. Mr. Crowder went on:

"You can put your broad beans in soon, three inches deep and six inches apart, and don't forget to nip the top off when they're growed."

"Why do that?" asked Etta.

"Keeps that there black blight off. I see you don't care for artichokes no more than I do, always tas-tes like rotten potatoes to me," he added, pointing to a tangle of tall, withered stems bent at all angles by the wind.

"Artichokes?" said Etta looking round. "But they're sunflowers!"

"If you was to dig under them plants," said Mr. Crowder politely, "I shouldn't wonder if you found some artichokes. Begin to sprout again pretty soon, they will. Now, if I was you, I should lift them artichokes for the pigs and plant some of 'em back for next year—comes in useful, you might say, with the price of pig-feed bein' what it is, a 'issing and a reproach to a Christian gover'-ment."

Thus pleasantly did Mr. Crowder instruct his young neighbours in the rudiments of the ancient and difficult craft of making things grow. When he had departed Etta

took a fork and, half-doubting, dug up one of the stems.
Sure enough there was a mass of the knobbly tubers she
remembered seeing on the kitchen table at home. She
dug enthusiastically and carried baskets of them to store
in an outhouse. Give them to the pigs indeed, when they
would make lovely artichoke soup! She felt rich, if weary,
as she collected basket after basket of the apparently inexhaustible roots.

"Look!" she called to Vera. "Artichokes! *Masses* of
them! Why, we can live on the artichokes alone from this
garden."

"If we don't get sick of them," said Vera prosaically.

Etta was not to be discouraged. She liked this tussle
with the earth, in spite of aches and stiffness and blisters.
She wanted to grow things, and had her garden all planned
out. The whole of the right-hand patch was to be potatoes;
the other, all kinds of exciting things, with a border of
flowers all round. She had struggled nearly halfway
through the left-hand patch, after planting several rows
of broad beans—measuring the exact distances—when Mr.
Crowder again appeared. After a few remarks on the
weather, which he opined would turn cold, Mr. Crowder
proceeded:

"You ain't puttin' in no dung like?" he opened with
his usual gambit.

"Oh!" Etta exclaimed as usual. "Ought I to?"

"Brown," said Mr. Crowder reflectively, "was a mid-
dlin' smart feller. I watched 'im a-diggin' of this garden
last year. He knowed as he was leavin', and he didn't waste
no dung on *that* garden. Now, as I was comin' along I
see you got a lovely 'eap of pig's dung in your yard. If I
was you I should dig some of it in. If you wants a good
crop, you've got to feed it. Stands to reason, like. Crops
likes their bit of dung same's we like our bit of dinner."

Undeterred by this too vivid simile, Etta enquired anxiously:

"So you think I ought to re-dig all I've done and put manure in?"

"No, I wouldn't say that," Mr. Crowder replied judicially. "If I was you I'd plant the bit you've done with surface roots, onions and carrots and turnips, if so be you want 'em. No call to dung them. Poor land suits 'em best. Runs all to top and fandangles if you feeds 'em too much. Jest you mark this line with a bit of stick and dung all the rest."

"Thank you so much for telling me," said Etta gratefully. "I want to grow peas—should I put them in now?"

"Love-a-duck," said Mr. Crowder, scandalized. "If you was to put 'em in now they'd all be frosted. Mustn't plant peas till the frost-es is over. But I don't 'old with peas. What the field mice don't dig up, the birds gets, and anything they may 'appen to leave the snegs has. If I was you I'd plant runner beans—looks pretty and bears wonderful."

Etta laboured to carry out Mr. Crowder's instructions implicitly and ordered Vera about on the strength of the superior knowledge thus surreptitiously acquired. It was the more disappointing, therefore, when the wind veered to the northeast, bringing a blizzard and heavy frost, so that for days the whole garden was hard with frozen snow. Etta was terrified that Anne would catch a chill or pneumonia, for, with all their fires, the cottage was as cold as a tomb. She was sad to think that the snowdrops would be frozen. But both Anne and the snowdrops survived the thaw.

9

THEIR LIVES WERE LONELY and self-centred, especially during the winter months. They were an anomaly, puzzling to the village and by no means above suspicion. Two young women from London, one with a baby—and no man about—were enough to rouse the suspicions of anybody. "They two wenches up to where Brown usto be" were commented on acidly—if rich, why were they taking the bread out of honest people's mouths, and if poor, why messing about with good land they couldn't work? Nobody called on them, except the vicar—once, on an embarrassed duty visit. And hardly anybody talked to them, except the garrulous Mr. Crowder, who could not be kept silent. The people they knew in London seemed to have forgotten them wholly—until the warm weather came.

At Easter, the curiosity of Etta's parents overcame their moral sense and repugnance to travel, and they visited her. The stay was short, but to Etta rather shattering. She worked hard to have everything as nice for them as possible, and they evidently tried just as hard to be agreeable; but it failed to work. There was too wide a gulf between them. Mr. Morison, proud of his prosperity and obese with Dortborough comfort, couldn't understand why a girl who'd done well in offices should want to pig it in a miserable old farmhouse. Mrs. Morison, still immovable in high moral standards, couldn't think how a daughter of hers could have brought into the world a sweet little thing with a *stigma*.

Etta perceived that they no longer even hinted at her "coming home" to Dortborough and was surprised at her own cynicism in summing them up. They wanted to "do the right thing" by her, but the right thing could never be anything but what Dortborough opinion commended. That opinion required that an unmarried daughter should be "looked after" at home; but not an unmarried daughter with a baby. Among the many things she owed Anne was the certainty that she would never again be persecuted to "come home and settle down." True, they liked Anne

and were kind to her, but they didn't want her "stigma."
It wouldn't be good for business. Teddy's Muriel—Etta
learned—was "expecting," and that apparently was good
for business. Mrs. Morison lamented that Teddy was thin
and a bit queer in the head sometimes after his long captivity, but she was certain she and Muriel could bring
him round. Muriel was a nice domesticated girl, and a
"beautiful" cook. . . . Altogether, it was a relief when they
went.

Probably it was this visit and the astonishment at finding how much older they looked which caused Etta to
make a discovery about herself. Though the days might
seem long and monotonous, the years were moving more
swiftly and indistinctly. It wasn't that she felt at all old.
Indeed, as she approached thirty she felt much younger
than in the days when she had quaked over being too old
at twenty. But there could be no doubt that the months
were beginning to slip away more quickly and with fewer
memories. The summer came, and with it an occasional
visit from a London friend who remembered their existence
in the hot months when cheap week-ends are desirable.
Kitty sometimes came in her car for lunch or tea. But
with the autumn frosts these friends, even Kitty, let them
drop once more into oblivion.

Time, for Etta, was measured less by the calendar than
by the changing work brought by the different seasons
and by Anne's growth and illnesses. She remembered Anne
cutting her teeth, beginning to crawl, and then to walk
and speak; the frights she got when Anne had croup in
the autumn and something wrong with her tummy in the
hot weather. She rejoiced over the child's growth, connect-
ing it with the slow mysterious growth of trees and living
things, and brooded over her. Etta had many plans and
theories about bringing Anne up. There was to be no senti-

mentalism, but with patience and gentleness she tried to correct every tiny fault and exacted the most implicit obedience, until even Vera was moved to protest:

"Etta! Why are you always checking the child? It doesn't do any good, and you above all people ought to know how awful a persistent gentle nagging can be."

"I don't nag her," said Etta indignantly.

"Yes, you do. You've said 'don't do that, darling' at least eleven times in half an hour."

"Well, she must be trained."

"That's all right, but you seem to think she ought to be perfect."

"I don't."

"Yes, you do. You'd see it quick enough in anyone else. Why should Anne be perfect merely because she's your child?"

"Oh, Vera! How you exaggerate! You know how mischievous she can be. I don't want her to grow up naughty and self-willed."

"That's just what your mother thought about you, and see how grateful you are to her! You're pretty self-willed, so why shouldn't Anne be too? And as for mischief, all children *ought* to be mischievous. Let the child be human within reasonable limits."

"You are unkind, Vera," said Etta half crying. "Telling me I don't know how to look after my own child."

"Mother knows best!" Vera mocked her. "How cross you used to be with poor Mrs. Morison when she talked like that!"

"Oh, but this is different. How absurd you are."

"On the contrary, it's just the same, my dear. Your mother wanted you to be perfect, just like herself. You want Anne to be perfect, just like you. Drop it. You be Etta, and let her be Anne. Let her be mischievous when it doesn't matter. If she makes you angry, give her a slap."

"I shouldn't think of doing such a thing," said Etta loftily. Vera shrugged and said no more. But her remarks had their effect—Etta did try not to persecute Anne into perfection, but at the same time she worried. Even as a baby, Anne had a devil of a temper, and by the time she was two she had developed a will power which sometimes left Etta helpless and aghast. If Anne made up her mind she wasn't going to do something, nothing Etta could devise would make her. The child would scream herself into convulsions in refusing to take some medicine or food ordered by the doctor. And the supreme humiliation was that she would afterwards take them from Vera, still sobbing in that breathless way which went to Etta's heart and gazing at her mother with large teary eyes Etta felt were full of unjust reproach. Couldn't even a baby of two realize that her mother loved her better than anyone?

Besides possible vices in Anne's character, Etta had other worries. She had been prepared to make a loss at first, confident that as they gained experience they would eventually make good. But as time went on she had to admit that Mr. Crowder had been right when he remarked that "farmin' don't come easy like to Lunnoners, and no more it isn't women's work neither." The simple fact was that they steadily lost money. Etta tried every expedient —sublet the land they couldn't easily work, cut down everything to essentials, and tried to live as much as possible on what they produced themselves. She laboured heroically, but to small purpose. Anne ate little enough, but she was always needing things which had to be bought, and though Etta denied them even books and a daily newspaper and took nothing from the butcher but "pieces" and soup bones, she and Vera had to have clothes and shoes, and things were always being needed for the stock. Twice she wrote to her father for money, humiliating her pride for Anne's sake, but these subsidies gradually disappeared after her savings.

By the middle of 1922 they were living on Vera's private income. Everything they had saved during the war had been spent. Etta was in despair, and matters were made worse by the fact that nearly all their young chickens had died that year from a mysterious disease. It was a bad loss, and all the more disheartening since at Etta's suggestion they had bought a couple of incubators to increase their supply of fowls and eggs. Once again she wrote to her father, and in reply received a much smaller sum and a hint that no more cheques were to be expected. Soon that money was almost gone. Etta went about her work haggard and nervous. True, with Vera's income they could continue to exist, but how could Vera be expected to go on doing this forever? Especially as she was plainly getting tired of the farm. And what sort of future was there for Anne?

In her own bedroom Etta shed many tears over these distresses and nearly drove herself mad trying to think out some remedy. But for this money worry and the anxieties about Anne, how she loved the life! It would be horrible to have to go back to an office, and in any case, how could she manage it with Anne? Yet something had to be done.

Etta was in the worst depths of this mood of despair and uncertainty when Kitty Mendip arrived on one of her flying visits. There was the usual scurry to get something a little better for lunch, and in her nervousness Etta upset the omelette pan into the fire and wasted four eggs. It made her cry with vexation, and all through lunch she had to endure the wretched sensation that Kitty could see she had been crying. She almost wished Kitty wouldn't come, bringing with her the insolences of her husband's great new wealth and making Etta feel ashamed that Anne's clothes were so poor and all home-made.

After lunch Kitty invented a pretext to go out alone with Etta. They went up the hill at the back of the house and sat under the edge of the copse, where Etta had sat with Vera that first day and had planned so much happiness. For a time they talked of commonplaces, and then impulsively Kitty took Etta's hand, saying kindly:

"Don't think me intrusive, but I have a feeling things are not going well with you. Is there anything I can do to help? I should like to, if you'd let me."

This was said so gently and nicely that all Etta's resentment against Kitty for being rich disappeared. She tried to keep up the pretence that nothing was wrong, but under pressure gradually told the whole dismal story.

"It seems awfully hard, Kitty," she went on. "I've been working, and working so hard, for nine years. Nobody can say I've been extravagant, and, God knows, I've had little enough of the pleasures of life. And now I'm as penniless as when I started. I've worked like a nigger for Anne and me, and now I don't know where to turn. I know you'd give me money if I asked for it, but what's the use if the farm can't be made to pay? We should soon be back in the same state."

Etta bowed her head into her hands, trying to hide the tears of discouragement and weariness. Kitty patted her on the shoulder.

"I've been such a hopeless failure," Etta sobbed. "And I've tried so hard. When I started, there was so much I believed I could do, and I've failed in everything. Except with Anne. And even there I've failed, if I can't look after her and educate her properly."

Kitty talked to her soothingly and comfortingly until

Etta was calmer, and dried her tears and looked out despondently over the fields and trees she loved because of their beauty and hated because of the land's niggardliness.

"Etta!" said Kitty suddenly, as if taking a decision.

"Yes?"

"Do you remember that when Anne was born I said I felt a little responsible for you?"

"Yes."

"Did you ever wonder why?"

"I did at the time."

"Shall I tell you?"

"Why, yes," said Etta, wondering what was coming.

"I don't want to pry into a secret you've kept very nobly and without complaint all these years—but I believe I can guess who Anne's father is. . . ."

"Don't let's speak of that. . . ."

"If he's the man I think," Kitty insisted, "I know well how hard he can be with a woman. He treated me badly enough."

"You!"

"Before I met you he found out that I had a lover and —he did a beastly thing. He threatened to tell my husband if I didn't become his mistress. Oh, he did it all very gracefully and æsthetically. No open threats, just double-edged flatteries. I was panic-stricken, because I knew he could prove it if he wanted, and I gave way to him. Once I'd started I had to go on. It was dreadful slavery—you see, he could have ruined the man I was in love with as well as me."

"Poor Kitty!"

"I lived in agonies of self-reproach and fear. Imagine then how utterly relieved I was when I saw him going over to you. Of course, he tried to conceal it from me, but I saw what was going on. I was too happy that he left me alone to think of you. It was horribly selfish of me—I ought to have warned you—can you forgive me?"

"I don't think there's anything to forgive," said Etta reflectively. "Even if you had warned me, I shouldn't have believed you. Besides, I was in a mood when I wanted a lover, and . . . and he was very good about all that. If I hadn't had Anne, it would all have ended naturally, and nobody would have been a pin the worse."

"You don't feel resentful against me?"

"Good heavens, no! My dear Kitty, we don't belong to the betrayed maiden generation. I knew perfectly well what I was doing. And if I made a mess of life through it, that was entirely my fault. I don't even feel any resentment against—against him. I made a bargain with him and broke it. He had every right to be angry. I only feel that he was a lucky man to have two such nice women!"

"He ought to do something for Anne, though."

"No!" said Etta quickly. "Anne belongs to me. I wouldn't share her with him for anything."

"But you'd let me do something for you both?"

"What can you do?" said Etta despondently.

"More than you think, perhaps. You forget my husband is rich—I'm ashamed to think how rich—and correspondingly powerful. If I insist, he can do a lot for you. Will you let me try?"

"How can I refuse?"

"It would mean living in London again, I'm afraid."

Etta looked at the sky and meadows and down at the old farmhouse with the little curl of wood smoke still coming from the kitchen fire. She could see Vera and Anne playing together on a little patch of grass under the apple tree, and heard the girl singing as she washed up. Etta sighed.

"I don't want to leave it all, but if I must, I must!"

10

Not until after Kitty had gone did Etta recollect that
they had talked much more about Francis than about a
job for her. And she discovered that she was very little
interested in Francis. Astonishing how people come into
one's life, seem all important, and then pass, become indifferent. You could be utterly intimate with people, emotionally as with Ralph, physically as with Francis—and
in three or four years they were uninteresting memories.
If she had known about Kitty and Francis in 1918, what a
turmoil! And now it barely mattered, except to show up
Francis in a still less pleasing light. What mattered enor-
mously was to get hold of a decent job and stick to
it.

For the first time in her life Etta felt really beaten and
scared. She went cold as she imagined dreary fates for Anne
and herself. In her panic about Anne she caved in completely to the money concept of life. Nothing else mattered
so long as she had money, and as much of it as possible,
to keep Anne safe. She sneered to herself at Vera's socialism
—that sort of mawkish playing with "ideals" was a silly
luxury for people with incomes. And she sneered at her
own theories and ideals. After nearly ten years of life on
her own, Etta wasn't so certain that it had been worth
while. And what was the use of trying to live honourably,
when you were invariably punished for it? Cynically she
almost wished she had married Ralph after all. There
would have been money, anyway.

In that mood she wrote to Kitty, saying she wanted the
job desperately, but that it must be one where she could
make money, the more the better. As she wrote "Lady
Mendip" on the envelope, Etta envied Kitty for having
a husband who had been rich enough to buy a baron-
etcy.

There followed a brisk exchange of letters, and once more Etta took command of her life with energy and decision. By the end of September she had disposed of the cottage, arranged an auction of the stock and furniture, packed Vera off ruthlessly home to Dortborough, and was installed with Anne in Kitty's town house.

But for her experience with the Lawsons, Etta would have been bewildered by the change. Even so, everything at the Mendips' was on such a scale of luxury that she was a little awed by the spectacle of what money can do. It was so much more splendid than the house in which Kitty had lived during the war.

"Is Sir James very rich?" Etta asked.

"Very," said Kitty drily.

"It must be rather wonderful. I can't help envying you."

Kitty laughed:

"Do you? And I have often envied you the peace and independence of your cottage. Sometimes when I couldn't sleep I thought of you down there, working away so bravely for your child—and I envied you. I'm not a woman —I'm the financier's wife. I spend most of my life entertaining people I don't like for purposes I don't approve of. I can't do a thing without it's being noticed—why, if I merely go to Paris it's reported, or would be if we didn't pay to have our names kept out of newspapers. It's misery. The man who swore he loved me, that he'd die for me, fled to America because he was afraid Jim might find out and ruin him. Sometimes I think all this war-gotten money brought a curse with it. It has, so far as I'm concerned. Do you still envy me?"

"No," said Etta. "Not altogether. But why do you mind losing a lover so much?"

"I don't know, but I do."

"There's so much you could do with your wealth," Etta urged.

"What?"

"Start things going, help people."

"If I start anything, Jim says I'm not organizing it properly, takes it out of my hands, and makes it earn more money—that's the only success he can imagine. And I very seldom meet the people who really need help. I've tried again and again, and nearly always felt the money was wasted. What's the good of giving money to people who are supposed to be artists when they merely use it to be idle, come back for more, and are furious if they don't get it? Jim has a secretary whose sole occupation is to deal with begging letters. Most of them are frauds, and even he gets taken in occasionally. I suppose it doesn't really matter, but it makes one feel hopeless."

"Couldn't you go out in disguise and find things that need doing, like Haroun-al-Rashid?" said Etta romantically.

"Jim would be furious if he found out, and he'd think it was an intrigue. I can't move without the 'protection' of private detectives—I believe my chauffeur's one."

"How awful!"

"I don't ask you to pity the poor rich," said Kitty, laughing. "But you see some of the difficulties. That's why you're a godsend. I know you're genuine, and I know you need help, and I'm going to do what I can."

"It's terribly, terribly kind of you," said Etta. "How can I thank you?"

"By staying friends. Try not to hate me for anything I may do—most people resent being helped so much. They hate one for it. You won't do that, will you? I'm lonely— I've got so few real friends. Promise me you won't get like the others."

Etta promised, but her conscience was troubled by the thought that for years now she had neglected Ada Lawson, another benefactor she had promised herself never to forget.

The following days were a rush of excitement for Etta. Kitty hired a nurse for Anne, and then started eagerly on a campaign of "smartening up" Etta for London.

"If you're going to succeed in business," said Kitty, "you've got to begin by looking successful, and keep it up. Make a note of the names and addresses of the places I take you to—they'll be the smart ones."

"But how shall I be able to pay?"

"I shall pay now, and I shall see you have credit given you for the future. You want money. Very well, I shall give you a money standard to live up to."

Etta tried to protest, but Kitty whirled her away. Clothes first—one place for evening dresses, another for day dresses, others for underclothes, shoes, hats, perfumes, handbags, trinkets. At each shop Kitty's name was greeted with reverence and exuberant civility—the Rolls was at the door. And to every manager who hurried up, Kitty introduced Etta and said much the same thing:

"Miss Morison is a particular friend of mine. She's a business woman. You may be of use to each other in the future."

After the third or fourth time Etta ventured to ask:

"Why do you tell them I'm a business woman?"

"You'll see after you've talked to Jim," said Kitty. "I've got my idea. Now, have you made a note of that shop and the name of that slimy little toad of a manager?"

"Yes," said Etta, showing her notebook.

"Remember him," said Kitty, yawning slightly. "That business has an annual turnover of more than a million."

Then to the smartest obtainable hairdresser to get the most fashionable cut and wave of hair; and ditto manicurist. And everywhere, as Kitty left, she said to the manager:

"Don't forget Miss Morison. I want you to do anything you can for her—as a favour to me."

When Etta went up to dress that evening, she found her room a chaos of boxes and tissue paper, with a maid stowing clothes away in cupboards and drawers. It seemed a fantastic dream. And when she was dressed in a new evening gown and stood before the long mirror it seemed still more fantastic. Was it possible that elegant-looking creature had been feeding pigs and chickens, dressed in old tweeds, less than a week before? And what on earth was Kitty planning? Was it all a rich woman's freak, a new whim which would be forgotten in a month?

"Let me look at you," said Kitty when Etta appeared in the drawing room. Kitty inspected her minutely, from a distance and close at hand, altered her dress a little, and made her put on a ring taken from Kitty's own finger.

"You'll do," she said. "I wasn't mistaken."

"I don't know how to thank you," said Etta humbly. "You're spending an awful lot of money."

"I'm having an awful lot of fun," said Kitty. "I'm making an experiment. You're not going to be spoon-fed like this for long, Etta. You'll have to make good on your own. I believe you can do it."

"But what am I to do?"

"Wait till you've seen Jim."

The next day Sir James arrived back by airplane from Paris, and the whole house clicked into subservient awe of him. Even Kitty seemed to fall into the background. And yet there was nothing awesome about Sir James at a first glance. On the contrary, with his grey hair and fresh red complexion, he looked rather like a worldly bishop. Far from being overbearing, his manners were smooth, almost deferential, as if Etta were paying him a vast compliment by dining with him, as if he didn't know she was a pauper sponging on his wife. He talked simply, almost gaily, about familiar things, with not a word about business. And yet Etta was frightened of him, in spite of the seeming kindness. His eyes looked cruel and inhuman, like a leopard's, and the unconscious greed of his thin lips was insatiable. Etta ceased altogether to envy Kitty.

After dinner Etta had a long interview with Sir James, and in some ways it seemed about the most difficult ordeal she had ever faced. His manner was polite and even kindly, his tone of voice still deferential, but he watched her with an intense concentration which made her uneasy. Etta had a feeling that he was suspicious of her for some reason. At first he talked about business. Business was in a bad state, the government didn't understand it, the old primacy of British trade had been thrown away by vote catching and absurd concessions to unions. He gave instance after instance where some branch of trade had been lost or crippled by strikes. The war losses could never be made up.

Since Etta knew nothing about these things, she was unable to controvert what he said, even if she had thought it tactful to do so. She did venture to quote a remark of Vera's, to the effect that there would have to be some new standard of estimating the value of services and goods; but this he brushed away almost vehemently. Such ideas were disastrous folly, he said. As he went on talking, Etta got the impression that his interest in life was not money for its own sake or for the pleasures and privileges it could buy, but the excitement of the means by which money was made and, above all, the power it gave. He wanted the sense of dominion over others, and preferred that his power should be occult. The luxurious house, the handsome allowance to Kitty, were mere frills, the sort of thing expected of any moderately wealthy man. They gave him no pleasure, she decided. She noticed he neither smoked nor drank.

Cautiously but very cleverly he began to question Etta about her own life. Much as she disliked telling him, Etta saw that concealment would be useless. But why was he so suspicious of a person so humble and powerless? He questioned her very closely about her relations with Kitty and about the birth of Anne. Etta guessed where the suspicion lay. Quite beyond the usual rich man's instinctive thought: "What is this person trying to get out of me?" was the suspicion that Etta might have some hold over Kitty, might know something which Kitty was willing to pay her to keep secret. In a flash Etta saw that she would be doing herself and Kitty the greatest disservice if she mentioned Francis. Sir James would be on to that clue like lightning and would scent blackmail. He would never understand or believe the simple truth.

Etta made up her mind quickly. In everything about herself she told him the exact truth, but stuck to the story that Anne was a war-baby whose father had been killed. Within less than an hour he had learned almost everything there was to know about her. The mention of the Lawsons seemed to interest Sir James.

"Ah, Randolfe Lawson," he said, "I knew him. *Not* a successful man, too much wedded to old methods."

Too honourable and honest, you mean, Etta thought, but she said:

"I knew nothing about his business."

Sir James came back to Etta's family—was her father too poor to help her? No? Then why didn't he? What were her motives in running away? Etta tried to explain, but before his monumental cynicism her words seemed bald and foolish as her actions. Women's independence—life on one's own—doing work which was interesting in itself and of service to others—trying to prove that such a life could be happy and successful—not binding herself to inferiority by marriage—having her child entirely as her own. . . . She made a very poor case of it. Why wouldn't words come to express all the intangible things and feelings?

"And now," said Sir James suavely, "you want money?"

"Yes," said Etta; and felt as if she had betrayed her life. But didn't she want money? Hadn't she been telling herself she must do anything for it? Yes, but oh, not in his dreadful way.

"We all come to that sooner or later," Sir James went on. "I've never met anybody yet who could say sincerely he didn't want wealth."

"Artists?" Etta suggested tentatively.

"Quite cheap, cheaper than jockeys."

"Judges?"

Sir James glanced at her with an expression which made Etta terrified at her indiscretion.

"English judges are incorruptible," he said quietly. "They are the rock on which our liberties are built. But you need money. How do you propose to get it?"

Etta was nonplussed. She had expected the suggestions would come from him.

"I don't know," she said feebly. "I thought . . ."

"Have you any capital?"

"No," said Etta, thinking unhappily of the few pounds she had saved from the wreck of her country dream.

"Kitty wishes me to help you," he said gently, but bullying her with his eyes. "Would you like me to lend you —say—a hundred pounds?"

Etta was disappointed, staggered even by the meanness and inadequacy of the offer. She managed to stammer:

"I don't ask for money, Sir James. I want employment."

"What sort of employment?"

Etta didn't know how to reply. She was afraid to men-

tion Kitty's hints for fear of getting Kitty into trouble.
She said as boldly as she could:

"I need at least four hundred a year. I've earned more
than that in a government department, so I should be
worth that in business."

"They are different in their methods," he replied. "But
I'll think about it. Perhaps I may be able to give you a
letter. Now, shall we join Kitty?"

II

THERE WAS NO CHANCE for Etta to talk to Kitty that evening, and she spent a very unhappy night in consequence.
It looked as if Kitty had brought her up from the country
and lavished all that money to no purpose. Etta didn't
conceal from herself that she disliked Sir James even more
than she feared him—it was easy to understand now why
Kitty had so few real friends. For many sleepless hours
Etta was unable to forget her "quiet talk" with Sir James.
She felt—and yet couldn't have explained why—that she
had been forced to endure indignity and violation. The
manner in which he had made her feel his power was like
a moral rape. Somehow a merely physical brute would
have been less repulsive. Poor Kitty! No wonder she was
so unhappy at losing her lover; no wonder Francis had
been able to terrorize her.

The next morning, after Sir James had gone to his office,
Etta and Kitty discussed what had happened.

"Thank God you didn't say anything about Francis,"
said Kitty, with a look of hunted anxiety in her eyes. "I
ought to have warned you."

"I'm glad you didn't. I felt instinctively I oughtn't to,
and it was easier to go on my own intuition. If you'd
warned me, I might have felt self-conscious and have betrayed myself."

"He didn't promise you anything?"

"Only spoke vaguely about giving me a letter to someone unspecified."

"He never will commit himself, even in the smallest matter, if he can help it," said Kitty. "But I think he'll do what I asked. You see, it's not easy to find well-paid work for women, but my idea was that you could do well in one of the big advertising firms."

"But I don't know anything about it."

"You'll have to learn. I wasn't thinking of the more technical side of it for you. What they want is new ideas. They're willing to pay for them. Besides, where you could make money is by commissions on bringing them new business."

"How could I do that?" asked Etta, feeling that Kitty was setting her the impossible.

"By your wits," said Kitty decisively. "Look here, Etta, you thanked me very nicely for spending a little money on you. But you didn't mention a much more valuable service."

"What?"

"Introducing you to those managers, as a friend of mine —and of Jim's. All those people need to advertise. They have to. Why shouldn't you get hold of some of their contracts? It might be done."

"I see," said Etta slowly. "Yes, it might be done. I wish I knew more about the work and that I had more confidence in myself."

"You'll have to have confidence. Later on, if you're successful, you shall meet people whose business is on a still bigger scale. It'll be up to you to make use of it."

"It's a great opportunity," said Etta eagerly, "I see that. But, oh, Kitty, I'm afraid—afraid."

"Of what?"

"Myself, and all these people, and the way the world is run."

In spite of Kitty's hopefulness, Etta set out with misgiving to present Sir James's letter of introduction to Mr. Marshall Rhys, the managing director of the Universal Advertising Agency, at Universal House. And a chill of discouragement and repulsion came over her as she entered the huge steel and concrete building with its blank pseudo-marble inner walls, four lifts, mahogany notice boards covered with the names of firms painted in gold, and the impersonal people going in and out. The building seemed as inhuman as the people, who had no time to recognize each other as living creatures. To Etta, coming directly from the country, it seemed like a Wells's dream of the future without the interest and hope of Wells's enthusiasm. It was like the temple of a queer, ugly, inhuman god, the abstract Yahweh of Business, whose praises were hourly clicked by choirs of typists.

Etta sent in the letter with her card, and was received by a tall dark man wearing horn-rimmed spectacles, who rose to shake hands with her.

"Sit down," he said. "Sir James phoned me about you —thinks we can work together. Remarkable man, Sir James, one of *the* great geniuses of our time. I shall be very glad to oblige Sir James, if possible."

He emphasized the last words, as if to impress on her his importance in being able to oblige a genius like Sir James, and went on:

"Now then, let's see what we can do. By the way— know Sir James well?"

"I know Lady Mendip better."

"Not so good. Pity. Know anybody else socially?"

Etta mentioned the names of some of the people she had known.

"No good," he said. "Rotten, in fact. Lady Mendip's a good card, though. Know any business people?"

Feeling an awful liar, Etta ventured to name one or two of the managers to whom Kitty had introduced her. Mr. Rhys beamed.

"Not so bad, not so bad. Know 'em well?"

"Not very."

"Keep in with 'em. Now, Miss Morison, I'll give you an example of modern business methods and quick intuitional decision. When Sir James told me about you, I thought: That'll be Accounts Department, all a government servant's fit for. But now I've seen you, I've changed my mind. Contacts Department, Miss Morison, Contacts. No good putting you in the Art Department, you'd be wasted. And you haven't the experience for the Creative Department. Think you could handle Contacts from the Woman's Angle?"

"Certainly," said Etta, not having the slightest idea what he meant, "I should like it."

"Just what I thought myself," said Mr. Rhys complacently. "I placed you as soon as I saw you. Contacts Department, Woman's Angle, I said to myself. Pure intuition —that's how I run the Creative Department, on intuition. But I want you to be a free lance. We'll give you a desk here, and you can get on with the ordinary Contacts work, you know: Press, blocks, lay-out, and so on. Contact up with the press on that side, Miss Morison, and try to get stuff in as news. Indirect publicity. In my opinion worth twice as much as ordinary column space. What do you think?"

"I agree," said Etta, trying to keep cool.

"Hard to get, though," said Mr. Rhys despondently. "The journalists can be wangled, but the editors don't like it. Out-of-date fellows. Can't get it into their heads that all news is advertising and all advertising is news.

Now I'm a man with vision, and I tell you this—in twenty years' time all literature and art will be advertising and nothing but advertising."

"How interesting," Etta managed to say.

"Interesting? I should think it is! It's fascinating. Now, I can see you're intelligent, but you haven't yet got the right angle on advertising. Get it into your mind that advertising is going to be the religion of the future. What is life? Trade. What is trade? Selling things. What sells things? Advertising. We're going to employ the finest minds and the greatest brains, and pay 'em well. The G. B. Shaws and the Arnold Bennetts of the future won't worry about plays and novels—they'll be sitting in the Creative Department of this office. Advertising. Bring everything to the notice of everybody, make everybody buy everything. That's my ideal, and as I see it that's going to be the religion of the future."

"But government . . ." Etta ventured.

"Government? Sub-branch of Contacts. Leave it to us. We'll guarantee to bring the Empire before every business man in the world at his breakfast table. But about yourself." Mr. Rhys suddenly dropped from apocalyptic vision to practical affairs. "What we most want is new contracts. Go out and get us new contracts, Miss Morison. Two and a half per cent to you on all new contracts. Bring us a contract for a hundred thousand, and we'll gladly pay you two thousand five hundred. Money to be made there, Miss Morison. What about it?"

"I'll certainly try," said Etta hopefully, and feeling very unhopeful indeed.

"They're not so easy to get, though," said Mr. Rhys ruefully. "Very hard to convince, some of these business men are. Advertising's a big item on their balance sheet, and it's hard to persuade them that we can do better than other people for 'em, as of course we can. How's it to be done? I ask myself every night when I'm going to sleep. I had the Research sub-branch of Contacts on to that problem for months. And then I solved it myself, after all. Most of the real work in this business is done by me, the creative brain. And I thought of the way to get at business men."

Mr. Rhys paused very impressively, and Etta felt bound to ask:

"And that is?"

"Flattery!" said Mr. Rhys with tremendous emphasis. "Flattery. You can't lay it on too thick to a business man. Other people have a good opinion of themselves, but the business man tops the lot. I've seen it, I've watched it. Suggest ideas to 'em and then persuade 'em they've thought of it themselves and flatter 'em for doing it. *That's* the line."

When her interview with Mr. Rhys was over Etta left Universal House in a very confused state of mind. It seemed impossible that she could ever succeed in "contacting" the kind of people implied by Mr. Rhys's eloquence; and even if she did, how on earth was she to persuade them to spend large sums of money through her agency? Moreover, so far as salary was concerned, the largest amount she could get Mr. Rhys to promise for "formal Contact work" was £250 a year; and even that, he hinted very broadly, was only "to oblige Sir James." Anything else would have to be earned by commissions. Which seemed hopeless.

She had a long talk with Kitty, putting the position as truthfully and accurately as she could. And Kitty said:

"I can see it's by no means as easy as I thought. But try it. I still believe you can succeed, and I'll back you for six months. If you fail, we'll try something else. But you must

submit yourself, Etta, you must accept the business world
as it is. Don't try to fight against it. Believe in it. Will you
try—whole-heartedly?"

"I must," said Etta quietly; and added: "For Anne's
sake."

12

Now BEGAN FOR ETTA another and longer phase of life,
feverish and almost neurotic in its tensity. Through Kitty's
help she found a flat which she furnished (on credit) in
what was then the most "advanced" style of modern
furnishing; and installed Anne and her nurse. But she now
saw little of Anne. Etta was obsessed with the passion to
make money, and somehow this was identified with her
feelings for Anne. It was a constant pain to her to find how
little Anne cared about her; she was even jealous of Anne's
affection for the nurse. She wanted Anne to owe everything
to her, to think of Etta as her father as well as her mother.
And Etta suffered because there seemed to be something
impish and sardonic about the child's attitude to her, as
if Anne already knew she was in a false position in life and
blamed her mother for it. Impossible, Etta told herself.
And yet it was true that Anne didn't love her as she wanted
to be loved. Never mind. She would prove that she could
do for the child everything a father was supposed to do,
and when Anne grew up she would recognize it and be
grateful.

So Etta rushed eagerly into the hectic world to which
Kitty had introduced her, the world in which money is
made and spent. It was a world which oscillated between
champagne and short commons, where she might lunch at
the Savoy with a client, pass through a journalist's cocktail party at six, dine at home on scrambled eggs and a
brandy and soda, and go to a dance at ten in the hope of
meeting another client. Rather like a prostitute's life, Etta

told herself bitterly. And indeed, in her desperate anxiety
to make money, she was not above using her sex as a means
to that end; but carefully, calculatingly. She gave nothing
until she was well assured of a return, and soon found that
hopes were a better bait than realization.

As Mr. Rhys had hinted, it wasn't an easy job to persuade new contracts out of business men, who had a
devilish reluctance to spending money on anyone but
themselves. But for Kitty's help, Etta was certain she
would have failed entirely. It was Kitty who introduced
her to many of the people who were ultimately most
useful to her; Kitty who pushed her into the fringes
of what used to be known as Society; Kitty who helped
her to clinch a bargain by inviting the flattered client
to sit at the table of the great Sir James; and Kitty who
comforted her in days of discouragement. And her first
moderately large contract came from one of Kitty's
friends, a woman who ran a large fashionable clothes shop.
It wasn't an important contract, but Etta obtained £50
and a sense of confidence from it, and Mr. Rhys was
pleased.

"Not bad," he said. "Keep it up. Contacts. Contacts.
And don't forget to make her think she did it all herself."

Contacts. It was a very good description of her life,
Etta thought, for she hadn't much time for anything
else. She had to establish "contact" with the cocktail
pseudo-Bohemia of the commercial artists and journalists; with the caviare and would-be snob world of successful
business men and their wives; and with the younger
generation of impoverished aristocracy, who could be
used as publicity pawns, and who were very glad to sell the
snob appeal of their titles for a share of the caviare.

A queer world that money-spending, latest-smart-thing
set of the nineteen-twenties. Muy higgy-liffy, as the
Spaniards are alleged to say. A kind of Trimalchio's

feast, where Etta picked up some of the crumbs which fell from Trimalchio's table. For she did make money. Not very much at first or even in the first year, but more and more as time went on and she learned to play her part efficiently in her particular racket. By the time Anne was six and attending a "modern" school in Hampstead, Etta's income was much larger than she had ever dreamed of earning.

Thus Etta came to terms with the life of her time. Having snatched some very nice bones, she now rarely thought of Business as a dogfight. While she couldn't go all the way with Mr. Rhys in his enthusiasm for the art and religion of advertising, she didn't indulge herself in uncalled-for criticism. However, a good deal of the old Etta remained under the smart head of the Contacts Department of Universal Advertising. She still hankered after the "realities" of country life, and rented a small cottage in Sussex, where Anne spent most of the summer. There were still visions that she might one day come across a man in whom she could be interested for other than professional reasons. And the passion for saving money returned with a new sanction—Anne's future. Etta had to dress smartly, but she managed to do most of it on trade terms. Against his agonized protests, Mr. Rhys was forced to give her an entertainments' allowance— she threatened to go over to one of his rivals if he didn't. And she kept the expenses of her own establishment at a minimum—she was determined that Anne shouldn't start life with extravagant ideas.

Anne was the only disappointment and real worry in Etta's life. There could be no doubt she was a difficult child. Etta couldn't understand her—in some ways she was frighteningly precocious, and in others absurdly babyish. It was all very well to determine that Anne shouldn't be extravagant, but nothing could cure her of a wilful destruction and wastage of her toys. Anne seemed to have very little genuine affection for her mother, and Etta yearned for it. Sometimes Etta almost believed that the child was born wicked, and especially in a rather malevolent hostility to her mother. Etta happened to remark once at the cottage how beautiful the hyacinths were, and as soon as her back was turned Anne deliberately stamped on them. Again, Anne was given a puppy, "to make her kind to animals," and it had to be taken away because she tormented it. In vain did Anne's schoolmistress assure Etta that all children are little savages, that it was far better to allow such traits to come out than to repress them, that Anne would unconsciously learn better by imitation. Etta didn't believe it and was unreasonably angry with her. How could a woman like that understand a child as its own mother did?

In every other respect Etta's life was a full one. She had so many friends that she never had to eat alone or to spend a lonely evening unless she wanted to. Nearly always, she preferred to go out. Apart from a few of the latest novels everyone talked about, she no longer enjoyed reading; and she never went to a concert. A gramophone, with plenty of the newest dance records, was much more useful—people liked to have it playing while they talked. And she didn't neglect old friends. True, she failed to link up with Ada, and Miss Millingham was scarcely a possible acquaintance, but Etta occasionally asked Vera to stay at the cottage in Sussex. She wrote to her family and learned that Teddy and Muriel were adding steadily to the population. But she didn't go to Dortborough—the place was distasteful.

She was especially loyal to Kitty, to whom she owed so much; and though her work prevented her from seeing Kitty alone as much as she would have liked, she seldom missed one of Kitty's dinners. For Kitty's sake, she was particularly nice to Sir James—anything to make things easier for dear Kitty. And she succeeded so well that Sir James became quite fond of her, and showed his fondness in a substantial way by giving her valuable business hints about when to buy and sell on the Stock Exchange. "As Sir James Mendip says," became a familiar phrase with Etta in business discussions, and the quotations were always listened to with respect. As Sir James said, financial conditions were stringent, but we must all pull together. As Sir James said, nobody was ever ruined by making a profit. As Sir James said, the important thing in business is to know when to stop. Etta didn't quote what Sir James said about which shares to buy or sell, because she had promised faithfully not to; but she always said that, whatever some people might think, Sir James had a kind heart. . . .

Towards the end of 1925—in October, to be precise—Etta was called to the Art Department one morning to give her decision on a dispute which had arisen. She kept them waiting a few minutes on principle; for by this time Etta had pretty well established her dominion of Universal and exercised it relentlessly—even over Mr. Rhys. On her way she paused to look at the reception room which she had insisted should be redecorated in *dix-huitième* style with imitation Latour pastels—one of Etta's theories being that office furnishing styles should be civilized. Not a bad bit of business, Etta reflected, as she looked critically round the room—the decorators had smartened up the office at bare cost as an advertisement, and she could use the room as a demonstration to obtain orders. A good commission was promised on all orders she brought.

Feeling well pleased, Etta negligently pushed open the door labelled "Art Dept."

"Well, what is it?" she asked.

The elderly Scotsman who was responsible for the making of blocks handed her some drawings:

"Look a' that," he said sourly. "We're expected to pay forr stuff of that kind."

At once Etta saw what was wrong with the drawings. They had a noncommercial quality. Instead of concentrating on selling appeal, the artist had thought first of his design—within his limits he'd tried to make a work of art. Just the kind of work Etta was accustomed to turn down.

"Who made these drawings?" she enquired.

"Maurrice Rraymond, the young man yonderr," said the Scot.

Etta looked at the young man and perceived that his large brown eyes were appealing desperately to her. His worn clothes, his diffident manner, the mere fact that he had to do such work, showed he was poor. No doubt he needed the money badly. He didn't even venture to put his case to her, but awaited her verdict with pathetic fatalism—obviously a young man completely out of touch with the business life. There was a short silence while Etta pretended to look at the drawings again. Yes, the man was gifted. A sense of her own power came to her. They were waiting on her word. She was aware that Raymond was looking at her with respectful admiration, as something beautiful but inaccessible. It was a triumph to stand there confidently in her fine clothes, and to be in a position to decide by a word the fate of this handsome young man who had a gift for something besides advertising.

"I accept them," she said, putting the drawings down carelessly and enjoying the look of relief and gratitude in Raymond's face.

"But," exclaimed the Scot indignantly, "think o' the cost o' rreprroducing. . . ."

"I know that better than you do," Etta retorted sharply. "Put them in hand."

He went off muttering under his breath, something about "Southern hizzies," no doubt. Etta turned graciously to the young man:

"Do you do much work for us?"

"Not much," he confessed. "I don't seem able to hit off what they want."

"Perhaps I can help you there." She looked at her watch, a fine platinum oblong just "launched" by a French jeweller as a new line—Etta's was a free advertisement, of course. "Twelve. Can you lunch with me at twelve-thirty?"

"I . . ."

"At the firm's expense," Etta interrupted smiling, anticipating his thought. "We like to treat our artists well, you know. Will you wait for me in the reception room?"

She took him for lunch to Boulestin's, where she had an account in the firm's name. Strictly speaking, she was supposed to use this only for entertaining people from whom something substantial might be expected. It was not the firm's habit to waste expensive lunches on hack artists. But for some reason Etta wanted to impress Raymond, which made her overlook the irony of spending more on one meal for him than he could earn in a week. She took a table by the door, and noticed with amusement and some pleasure Raymond's look of surprise at the number of smartly dressed people who waved or spoke to Etta as they came in. She liked him to feel that she was important and powerful. He might have all the talent in the world, she thought, but he couldn't afford to take *her* to such a place for lunch.

Raymond was not wholly at ease in these luxurious surroundings, but Etta laughed and talked him into gaiety.

She felt she was communicating to him her own complete easiness and at-homeness in the place. It wasn't long before she got the essentials of his life out of him. The usual story—passion for art, family quarrels with an engineer father who thought art was rot, a year or two at the Slade, two or three years half-starving in Paris, and then back to one room in Chelsea trying to paint and at the same time to earn a living from hack work. No, he hadn't been in the war—he was only eighteen at the Armistice. This was the one thing he said which at all disconcerted Etta—it made her feel more than ever how swiftly the years were passing. A generation she had always thought of as children were now grown men and women. She wondered if he were in love with any girl of his own age and found herself sympathizing with the dowager who said: "I don't like young girls, I hate their horrid bloom."

Their intimacy progressed rapidly. Etta now made a point of being cynically frank with herself. She admitted that she liked Maurice very much indeed and wanted him. Unfortunately, he was very shy and unenterprising —almost indifferent to sex appeal, she thought. The advances had to come from her, but this was not altogether displeasing. Maurice was astonishingly malleable, and Etta greatly enjoyed the dominion she established over him. Setting aside his unrecognized talent, she held the superior position all along the line. Why, she was a godsend to him, the unhoped-for stroke of luck—a handsome woman, still young, with money and a legion of "friends," able to push him in the world. If he did what she wanted, she could give him a great deal; and she had little doubt that she could easily control him. What puzzled her was his gentleness and indifference. He didn't seem to resent the inferiority in which he was

kept by her, accepted it quite calmly. Even when they
were hopeless neurotics, she reflected, the men of her
own age were accustomed to command, to impose themselves. Maurice appeared to have no assertiveness. So
much the better.

Very soon, Maurice came frequently to Etta's flat.
She showed him how to make his commercial work more
effective and *willed* him to do it as she wanted. When he
had satisfied commercial requirements, it was easy enough
for her to get his designs accepted and paid for at the
higher rate. He brought her portfolios of his own work,
delicate line drawings of animals—leopards, deer, horses
—and sensitive nudes. Maurice happened to remark one
evening that he could rarely afford a life model, whereupon Etta insisted on sitting to him herself. Then occurred
the curious episode of the mistress of a modern flat standing naked under the electric light of her own drawing
room behind locked doors, while a young man gravely
and intently sketched her. Etta was quite aware that
her body was shapely and desirable, developed but not
in the least flabby; and she was piqued by Maurice's
purely abstract interest in her planes and contours. Some
little time, patience, and encouragement were needed to
bring him to the point.

They went about a good deal together, and, to avoid
uncomfortable feelings, Etta provided him with new
clothes including an evening suit, through a firm with
whom she had a pull. She howked him out of his squalid
little room and installed him in a small flat not far from
her own, where she could see him away from Anne and
her nurse. In the midst of other work she found time
and energy to arrange an exhibition of Maurice's paint-
ings and drawings, bullied her press friends into noticing

them, and cajoled a few people into buying. Gradually Etta became very, very fond of him, he was so docile and inexacting, so satisfactorily ready to carry out her promptings. Quite the ideal lover for her. He was even gentle and nice to Anne, who listened open-eyed when he told her magic stories (Etta herself rather disbelieved in them, besides she hadn't time), and was delighted to ecstasy when Maurice taught her how to make simple figures in plasticine.

"I 'dore Maurice," Anne said gravely one evening when Etta came to kiss her good-night.

"Do you, darling?" she said, amused. "Why?"

"He knows everything," said Anne, nodding her head emphatically. "He can do anything in the world."

"Can he!" said Etta satirically. "And what about Mummy?"

"Oh, *Mummy!*" said Anne scornfully.

Etta went away feeling a little jealous.

Quite suddenly "all London" (i.e., the few hundred people Etta knew) began to talk about her and Maurice; for it was the custom of that amiable society to pay no attention to the one-night or one-week affair, but to be scandalized by a duration which implied something more than disappointment. Nor did much time elapse before women, animated by the kindliest feelings of charity, put Etta *au fait*. She saw the danger at once. Damage to her reputation would give an opportunity to women trade rivals which they would exploit at once. It had been hard enough to live down the scandal of Anne, and float successfully the dead soldier-father fiction. So far as the Bohemian crowd was concerned, it didn't matter a hoot; but it wouldn't be so good with the business men—give them a chance to be impertinent—or with the alleged society people. Besides, Sir James wouldn't approve.

Etta acted decisively, after a sleepless night of reflection. She rang up Maurice, made him lunch with her in her own flat, and after lunch went direct to the point.

"Maurice! We're in a mess."

"How?"

"People are talking."

Maurice made a gesture with his hands, as if to say: Well, what can I do?

"It's no good being helpless," said Etta sharply. "We've got to deal with this situation at once. It may not matter to you, but it does to me: my living depends upon it. Anne's too. And yours, for the matter of that. So try to help me think what we can do."

"I really don't see what we can do," said Maurice despondently. "We can't *make* people stop talking, can we? Are you sure there's any danger in it, though? People always do talk."

"I know they do, and as a rule I pay no attention. But this happens to be a case where a good deal of harm will be done if the talk isn't stopped."

Maurice said nothing and looked carefully at his finger nails in a way which rather irritated Etta.

"Well?" she said aggressively.

"Well what?"

"Have you any suggestions?"

"No. I suppose we should be more careful?"

"That won't do," Etta retorted. "It's too late now. There are two alternatives. Either we must break off entirely and never see each other, so that I can give the lie to everyone, or . . ."

"Or what?" he asked, as she hesitated.

"Or we can be married."

Maurice was silent again, and Etta watched him intently.

"You feel certain that's all we can do?" he asked.

"Yes."

"Then why shouldn't we be married?" he asked calmly. "I'm quite ready if you are."

"That's decided, then," said Etta crisply, taking him at his word. "I think it's the best thing to do. It will be to your benefit, Maurice. I shall get one of those large studio flats. You can have the studio to yourself for your own work all day, and it will be useful to me for giving parties. I want you to do your own work —you know I believe in it—and only enough advertising work to bring you in pocket money. I've always wanted to give you a chance to do your best work, and here it is. I'll see that Anne and her nurse must have their own rooms and don't disturb you. We ought to be very happy."

"Yes."

"It won't cost much more than our present arrangement," said Etta, making mental calculations. "Perhaps a hundred a year or so. But when we're married I can push your commercial work more—you can easily make five hundred a year. Does the arrangement please you?"

"Yes."

"Well, come and give me a kiss, then! You ought to be quite excited."

How fish-like indifferent these younger men are, Etta thought; suppose this had been Ralph—what a flame of intense feeling there would have been between us! Obediently Maurice came over and kissed her.

"You're a nice, nice boy," said Etta, more moved than he was. "You won't regret this. I'll see you through. And if you're straight with me, I'll be straight with you."

"Of course," said Maurice tranquilly, and kissed her again. Etta fumbled in her handbag and produced a five-pound note.

"Now, listen, Maurice. Go this afternoon to the registrar's office of this district and arrange about the marriage.

Here's the money. You can find the address, can't you? No, you can't—you'll waste the whole afternoon looking and then not find it. I'll ring up."

Etta spent most of the afternoon and evening on the telephone, telling her friends—beginning with Kitty—that she was going to be married. The announcement of the engagement appeared in several morning newspapers.

Then followed three weeks of the kind of life Etta had come to love best—efficient bustle. Within forty-eight hours she found the studio flat she wanted, and had one of "her own" decorators at work on it immediately. She controlled the scheme of decoration herself. It was to be modern—bare floor with the new cubist rugs just launched in Paris, steel tube chairs, glass and metal tables, concealed lighting, severe walls with one impeccable Braque. The electric heating was in a sort of metal Venetian blind, and the bathroom was done entirely in different shades of green. As an afterthought, she added metal shelves to the studio for their books. It always looks well to have books about.

The new clothes she bought for Maurice and herself were very smart and in the best taste.

In accordance with the bride's wishes, the wedding ceremony was as simple as possible; and instead of the conventional white robe and orange blossom, she wore a new Worth creation. The witnesses were Sir James and Lady Mendip, Miss Vera Wraxall, and Mr. Marshall Rhys. After the wedding, Lady Mendip gave a small reception for the newly married pair, which four hundred people attended, plus reporters and gossip-column writers. Again in accordance with the bride's request, there was no conventional going away or honeymoon; after the reception, they slipped away quietly (in Lady Mendip's Rolls) to their quaint little cottage in Sussex.

Etta had all the morning papers sent down, and they sat looking them over after breakfast. Most of them published photographs, and two or three ran the romance as a story.

"I say!" Maurice exclaimed. "I thought you said we were to have a quiet wedding!"

"Well, so we did. We cut out all the conventional frills."

"But look at these newspapers!"

"What's wrong with them?" said Etta tartly. "It's all excellent publicity. How else am I to get your work known?"

13

BY FEBRUARY, 1926, they were all settled in the new flat—Etta absorbed in her business, Anne at school, and Maurice left alone most of the day to turn on his inspiration at will. Somehow not much of the "real work" got done, although Etta constantly expressed her interest in it. Unfortunately, Maurice was a slow worker, and then Etta was always coming across well-paid commercial work which it was a sin to give to the ordinary hacks when her husband was an artist of genius. Why on earth shouldn't Maurice have the benefit of it, Etta argued, especially since she could oversee it and make him do exactly what was needed? Maurice worked without any complaint, and to such good effect that his average earnings were soon nearer a thousand a year than the five hundred Etta had promised. As she said, who on earth could grumble at that? Besides, they could soon have a car. It was decided that Maurice should buy them a car as a joint wedding present as soon as he had earned three hundred pounds. Etta undertook to take charge of the money—Maurice was careless—and to see they got a good bargain. She said she would learn to drive it, so that it wouldn't be any bother to him.

The general strike of 1926 gave Etta a fright. If it had succeeded, it would have put the whole of smart London out of action, and then where would the luxury advertising trade have been? As it was, Universal did scarcely a stroke of business for a fortnight. As Etta put the matter to Maurice, it was all very well to try to get better conditions for the workers; she herself had worked her way up from the bottom of the ladder and had every sympathy with them; but this throwing out of gear of the whole of the national trade was sheer stark lunacy. Maurice made no comment on this, but began playing with Anne. Etta watched them. Anne kept making rushes at Maurice as he sat in his armchair, leaped on his knee, and shrieked with joy when she was able to tug his hair. Maurice laughed and struggled and pushed her off; and then Anne leaped at him again.

"I'm a tiger!" she screamed. "I'm going to eat you up, Maurice."

It was a comfort to Etta that Maurice got on so nicely with Anne, but she couldn't help thinking it showed something wrong—a rather unhealthy trait—in the child that she preferred a comparative stranger to her own mother. There could be no doubt about the preference—if Anne were unwell she always whined for "Maurice." A pity that Maurice would encourage the child to be rough.

"Don't make such a noise, Anne," she said aloud. "Leave Maurice alone."

"But he *likes* it!" Anne panted, rebelliously.

"No, he doesn't. He's got important work to do. Now,

do as Mummy says and go to your Nanny. It's time for your walk."

"I hate walks," said Anne. "We always go the same old beastly way."

"Now, now! I won't have you speak that way. Go to Nanny this instant!"

Anne obeyed, but made an ugly face as she looked back from the door.

"Don't spoil the child," said Etta when she had gone. "You're awfully sweet to her, Maurice, and I love you for it. But she's such a wild little thing, she's got to be tamed."

"Oh, she's all right," replied Maurice, going over to his drawing board.

During the strike Etta received a telegram, and then a letter from Teddy, containing the startling news that their father was dead. Mr. Morison had been greatly excited about the strike and in fear of undefined disasters. After a hastily eaten lunch he had hurried back to his office on foot—no trams running—and had collapsed ten minutes later from heart failure.

Etta was very much upset and wept alone for a long time. Poor Daddy! Terrible that she could never make him hear her voice again. How that word "dead" altered everything, so that many years of resentment slid away into nothingness, and she thought of him only as she had loved and idealized him in babyhood. She wished she could tell him that now there was nothing hostile between them. Perhaps he understood—she was sure he must understand. . . . Then came the problem of what she was to do. She went to Maurice, who was at work in the studio, and showed him the letter.

"You see they want me to go to the funeral," she said. "What ought I to do?"

"What do you want to do?" asked Maurice cautiously.

"It's not a question of what I want to do, but what I can do," said Etta impatiently. "How can I go down there while all this upset is on? It's very dangerous to travel. Only yesterday I saw a car with its wind-screen smashed by stones. I don't want to risk that. And these volunteer train drivers—I don't believe in them. Suppose some of these dreadful anarchists derailed the train?"

"Perhaps you'd better not go until the strike's over," Maurice suggested.

"Do you really think so?" Etta appeared to hesitate. "Well, after all, it isn't as if I could *do* anything for him, is it? If he were ill and needed nursing, I'd go at once. Merely being at the funeral means nothing."

"I really think you'd better wait," said Maurice.

"I will, yes, I will. I'll send them a telegram. There's no point in risking trouble going to a mere ceremony. Besides, my duty is with Anne and you—we can't tell whether something awful mayn't happen."

The week-end after the strike was over Etta drove herself down to Dortborough in the new car. There had been some difficulty in getting mourning, but she had succeeded—a very simple dress but beautifully draped.

It was an interesting sensation for Etta to drive through Dortborough and along the Muncaster Road in her own car. How quickly that dismal stretch of buildings glided past! Almost before she knew it she was turning the corner by the pillar box. Dortborough looked shrunken, more insignificant than ever, but its ugliness had ceased to afflict her. Etta wondered why it had once seemed to matter so much.

Her arrival in the house provoked a dismal scene. Mrs. Morison—strangely feeble and unimpressive to Etta now—fell on her daughter's neck and shed unavailing tears. This started Muriel crying, and the children howled in sympathy. It was a pandemonium, which Etta and Teddy tried in vain to quell. At last comparative quiet was established, and they all sat down. Etta noticed that Muriel was impressed by her discreetly elegant mourning.

"I wish you had been here for the funeral," said Mrs. Morison, with a decent sniffling of woe. "It was so beautifully arranged, and everybody wanted to honour him. There were twelve wreaths, one from the Mayor and Corporation, and nine carriages, and the Mayor came to the cemetery."

Teddy tried to divert his mother from these macabre recollections by talking about the will. A thousand pounds were left to Etta in trust for Anne; the business went to Teddy; everything else, the house and furniture and the interest on about four thousand pounds, was left to Mrs. Morison for life, and then to Teddy and Muriel and their children. Etta was touched that he had remembered her, but above all that he had thought of Anne. She lost track of the conversation for a minute or so, as she debated with herself on how she could best use the money for Anne's advantage. She would have to ask Sir James. Used judiciously, it might be raised to three or four thousand by the time Anne was of age. She enquired casually whether "Anne's little legacy" was free of duty. . . .

Before the shops shut Etta went out and bought the finest wreath obtainable at the best florist's in Dortborough, and on Sunday morning went with her mother and Teddy to lay it on the grave. They were all upset, Etta especially, by the spectacle of the mound of bare earth, on which the earlier wreaths were already withering. Etta laid hers at the foot, and stood crying into her handkerchief. Here was the last reality from which there is no escape. She thought with pain of how Anne would one day stand at the foot of her grave, and perhaps pass judgment upon her, as she was tempted to judge her father. Etta refrained from judgment, saying to herself: Let him be at peace. And then found herself wondering whether one's grief and tears at a grave are truly sorrow for the dead person or only an expression of terror for one's own fate.

Etta dreaded returning to the house and wished she had not said she would stay till Monday morning. Muriel and Teddy had three children—a boy about Anne's age, a girl two years younger, and a baby girl of about ten months. Muriel, dowdy and harassed, managed badly, so that the whole house was like an untidy nursery. Mrs. Morison did nothing to help, except to offer unasked and acrimonious advice; and Teddy seemed quite helpless. Etta was dismayed to see how he had degenerated. He was flabby and pale, with the beginnings of a pot-belly before he was thirty—a rather bloated neurotic who moved jerkily and occasionally twitched his cheek, and drank a good deal. Etta was sorry for Muriel and tried to be nice to her, but Muriel wouldn't accept her—Etta could see the "poor creature" was envious of her sister-in-law's success and comparative opulence and freedom. As if Etta hadn't suffered and worked for them! Poor creature, Etta thought contemptuously; and in the afternoon took Muriel and the two elder children for a drive. It was annoying, however, that the boy—Muriel seemed to have no control over him whatever—tore down the metal flower-holder and spilt water all over the cushions.

There was peace in the evening after the children had gone to bed, but the hours passed slowly indeed for Etta, who was longing to get away from these dreary surroundings to her own more animated life. She thanked whatever powers may be that with all her mistakes and follies she had never let herself in for this sort of domestic hell. It was an immense comfort to know that she had only Anne to worry about, and that Maurice luckily didn't want children. For the matter of that, Etta wouldn't have consented—she couldn't afford the time. With deep satisfaction she counted up her own safeguards against falling into a life like Teddy's and Muriel's— nearly five thousand in good Sir-James-recommended shares, her own fifteen hundred to three thousand a year, Maurice's seven to nine hundred (she must see he didn't neglect the bread-and-butter work) and Anne's thousand. . . . How all-important money is!

Muriel and her mother-in-law went to bed early; and Etta was about to follow them when Teddy asked if she wouldn't mind his talking a little; and she couldn't well refuse. Teddy sat opposite her in an armchair, chain-smoking gaspers, and drinking whisky and water. They talked for some time about their father and the disposal of the estate. Teddy hinted that the thousand pounds should be left with him, but Etta firmly refused—she had a duty to her child; if it had been her own money that would be a different matter; but in this case she regarded herself as trustee for Anne. Teddy sighed, and was silent for a little, and the twitching in his face became more frequent. Presently he said awkwardly:

"I hope you won't mind if I ask you something, Etta? It ought by rights to be Muriel, but she won't ask you herself."

"Certainly, what is it?"

"Well—it's like this—I—you see—the fact is, we don't want any more children," he blurted out, going very red. "And I thought you might tell Muriel what to do."

"Of course," said Etta briskly. "I'll talk to her tomorrow morning, and I'll send her what's necessary from London. Let me make a note of it."

She scribbled a few words with her gold pencil in the slim gold-covered notebook in which she marked her appointments. "Monday, 12:45, lunch Savoy, Sir E. Mander," she read—mustn't be late for that, an important contract.

"You see," she heard Teddy saying, "we've got three, and they're too much for Muriel. Besides, the expense is terrible, Etta. And then we can very seldom go out together. Muriel doesn't trust the girl we have, and Mother's too old. If we have another child, it'd be complete disaster."

"Don't worry, I'll see to it. But Muriel must do what I tell her."

"I was thinking the other day of what you said years ago about marrying and children," said Teddy, twitching. "And I'm now damn sure you were right. I was a fool. What on earth am I to do with these kids?"

"Bring them up as well as you can," said Etta brightly. "You wouldn't wish them away, would you? I'm a mother, and I know that. But three's quite enough. Don't have any more, and do your best for these."

"It's an awful burden. I wish I hadn't married so young."

"Well, you did, so you must make the best of it. You get on well enough with Muriel, don't you?"

"Yes, in a way, but it's not what it was at first. Sometimes I want to get away from it all, the worry and the same old day-in, day-out. I've seen nothing of the world but Dortborough and a German prison camp. You know, when I came back, they thought I wasn't quite right in my head. That's all rot, but I do find office work difficult. I should like an open-air life, or at any rate a job where I could make money."

"Isn't the business paying?" Etta asked apprehensively.

"Yes, it pays up to a point, but you know, business generally is bad in Dortborough. Seems to decline steadily, and heaven knows what the result of this strike'll be. You're lucky to be in London."

"We're hit badly enough," said Etta quickly.

"Are you? I was hoping, I was wondering if—if there was anything—better than this—you could help me to in London?"

Etta was alarmed—she wasn't prepared to take on this kind of responsibility.

"I don't know what I can do," she said quietly. "And I can't think of any opening in London which would justify your giving up here. After all, Teddy, you always wanted to go into Daddy's business, and now it belongs to you. Surely you'd do better by trying to modernize it— why not have it redecorated?—and make it a success. It's a great thing to be one's own master in life."

"Am I my own master?" said Teddy bitterly. "It strikes me I merely exist to provide for Mother and Muriel and the children."

"Mother has her own income."

"I know, but the responsibility for her life is on me. You got out of all that pretty easily, Etta."

"Well!" exclaimed Etta angrily, "I like that! Why didn't you get out? You chose to stay on and inherit, and now you grumble because I had the guts to make my own life. I took a big risk. Suppose I'd failed? What would you have done?"

"Don't let's quarrel, Sis," said Teddy humbly. "I'm sorry if I've offended you. But sometimes I get completely fed up with my life. You remember you gave me a warning once, long ago. I thought you'd sympathize."

"I do sympathize, but it's no good going off on wild-cat schemes, Teddy. You've got to make the best of what you've got, which isn't too bad. Think of the thousands of ex-service men who are tramping the streets."

"I do think of them," said Teddy grimly. "And it makes me wild. I'd like to kill the swine who exploited them. . . ."

"Well," said Etta, yawning, "if you've nothing else to say, I'll go to bed. I've got to get off early tomorrow. Tell Muriel to come to my room about eight and I'll talk to her. Good-night."

"Good-night."

She kissed him and left him seated in the armchair, reaching out his arm to pour more whisky in his glass.

14

CERTAIN EVENTS IN LIFE have a delay action. Once the immediate shock of her father's death had passed, Etta thought she had settled down again to her own life and that she was still perfectly satisfied with its aims. And yet, though she tried not to see it, from time to time a feeling of dissatisfaction came over her. What was wrong? She couldn't discover. Nobody could say she was losing energy, for she worked harder than ever; and it was an intense satisfaction to be adding continually to her investments, with Sir James to advise. Her sex life was all right; for if Maurice wasn't a thrilling husband he never gave her any trouble. Even Anne was beginning to be a little more satisfactory. . . . The fact remained that some time after that last visit to Dortborough she began to feel unsettled.

Taking the matter in hand, Etta came to the conclusion that she needed change and recreation. She arranged that the firm send her more frequently to Paris and Cannes —to make fresh contacts and to pick up new ideas. In London she went to the theatre more often. As Maurice seemed to get great satisfaction out of books, Etta took

up reading again. But, as she complained, there are so
few good books; and then she needed something more
lively. So she went in very energetically for dancing—
good wholesome exercise which took one's mind right
away from worries. Even at the cottage during week-ends
she liked to bring out the gramophone and have dancing
on the lawn. As Etta explained to her friends, she *had*
to be doing something—just taking walks or sitting about
was too boring. Golf? No, she didn't care for it; but dancing on the lawn in the open air always made her feel fit.

For more than two years Etta continued to cheat herself
in this manner. If at any time she was inclined to look
for the cause of her dissatisfaction in herself, she quickly
repressed the impulse. As she put it, she couldn't afford
to sap her energies by the futile introspection some people
thought it clever to indulge in. *She* was all right—it was
the constant struggle with the world to provide for Anne
and Maurice which took it out of her. . . . Then, all at
once, she discovered what was missing in her life. . . .
A few days after she returned from her summer holiday
in 1928, Etta saw an advertisement announcing that
Dymcott, with or without its contents, was for sale by
private treaty. A photograph showed that it was the right
Dymcott, *her* Dymcott.

The realization came to her immediately. *That* was
what she had been wanting. Dymcott. The one place
on earth where she had been really happy and could be
happy again. How long ago was it? Fourteen years.
Whatever else she had forgotten, she hadn't forgotten
Dymcott—that exquisite view from the library, the two
terraces above the river, the bathing pool. . . . For several
minutes she stood motionless, both her hands pressed
heavily on her desk, staring at the newspaper. Dymcott
on the market. A thrill went through her at the thought:

You can buy it if you want. An extravagance? Well, hadn't Sir James been telling her that, with a heavily over-valued stock market, house property was the thing to buy? And what a gorgeous inheritance for Anne!

She sat down and began making calculations on the back of an envelope, and then walked up and down the room, biting her lip in perplexity. She wanted Dymcott badly, but just as badly she didn't want to spend all that good money. Yet, if she missed this opportunity Dymcott would be lost, probably forever. Thirty-five hundred pounds was a lot of money, though. Suddenly Etta made up her mind, and went to the telephone. The bank mana-ger listened to her and said, Yes, if the property was ap-proved, he had no doubt that a mortgage for a thousand of even fifteen hundred could be arranged. He advised her to have the place carefully surveyed before making an offer—a lot of country property was in a bad state of repair nowadays.

Now that she had made the first step, Etta was too excited to be prudent. Her heart was set on having Dymcott, and her only fear was that somebody would get ahead of her. But just as she was on the point of ringing up the agent, she paused. Presumably Dymcott still belonged to the Lawsons. If Ada was in London, wouldn't it be better to see her first? The telephone book. Etta ran impatiently down the column and—there it was!—Lawson, Mrs. Randolfe, with an address in West Kensington. Instead of ringing up, Etta put on her coat and hat, left a message to Rhys that she was out on important business and would be back in an hour, and went straight down for a taxi. It was worth the chance—if she could see Ada and come to an agreement. . . . Etta gnawed at her handkerchief with impatience.

The taxi drew up in front of one of a row of small, rather mean houses in a side street. For a moment Etta hesitated. Could it be that Ada was living here, or wasn't it more likely someone else of the same name? She took out her card, pencilled out "Universal Advertising," and underneath "Mrs. Maurice Raymond" wrote, "I want to see you urgently, Etta." Then rang the bell. Etta was shown into a small front parlour. Directly she entered the room she knew she was on the right track—the furniture, looking oddly out of place and large in such a room, was from the old Knightsbridge home. To see them again stirred many old memories. . . . But Ada must be poor to live in such a house—probably her husband was dead. Etta leaned forward and peered into one of the rosewood cabinets, recognizing some of the ivory figures Ada loved so much.

The noise of someone coming into the room made her look round; and she gasped with astonishment. Could that be Ada, that white-haired woman, lined and pouched, squat-figured in mourning? Etta went to her swiftly.

"Ada! You haven't forgotten me?"

"So it *is* you, Etta!" The old-sounding quaver in her voice smote Etta to the heart. Impulsively she threw her arms round Ada and kissed her.

"You've heard?" said Ada, her eyes filling with tears.

"About . . ."

"About Randolfe, yes. You know he died about a year ago?"

"I'm so sorry, so very sorry," said Etta, feeling rather disgustingly hypocritical.

"It was nice of you to come," said Ada, drying her eyes. "But do sit down, won't you?"

They sat down in armchairs, facing each other, and Ada talked in an old-lady voice which to Etta was poignant from its contrast with the vivacity of old days:

"Yes, nearly a year ago. He never really recovered from Robert's death, you know. He was so fond of Robert.

We went to see Robert's grave after the war. It was a very beautiful cemetery. There were flowers. At Ypres. The Belgians still blow the Last Past every evening. We were both glad that he should rest in such peace among his own men, with his own bugles sounding every night over him. But life was never the same after Robert was killed."

"No," said Etta, swallowing a lump. "It couldn't be. And then did you come to live here?"

"No, we were nearly always at Dymcott, except in the winter when we went abroad because of Randolfe's chest. He gave up business, you know, soon after the war was over. He was always gentle and sweet, but he seemed to lose heart. I think he was glad to die. But, there, I mustn't trouble you with all this, must I? Now about yourself? You look very well. Are you happy?"

Etta was conscious of the contrast between them as she answered:

"Yes, as happy as one can expect."

"I see you are married."

"Yes, my husband is an artist, and I am a director of an advertising company."

Ada seemed either not to hear or not to understand Etta's last words.

"I always believed you should marry," she quavered. "More than once I said so to Randolfe. And he agreed with me. I hope you won't mind if I refer to it, my dear, but we could never understand why you didn't marry my nephew Ralph."

"I . . ." Etta began, and then couldn't proceed for the tears in her voice.

"It seemed so strange to us. I could see you were both in love, and Ralph wrote to me from Egypt that he wanted to devote his life to you. I don't deny that I was against it at first, but after Robert died I felt it would make me very happy if you and Ralph were to marry.

You were such a charming girl in those days. Randolfe thought so too. We were fond of you, and you had such courage, such a sense of honour. We thought Ralph could not have chosen better."

"We—we made mistakes," said Etta, fighting against the suffocation of her voice. "Where is Ralph now? Is he married?"

"Yes, he married an American girl about three years ago, when he was attached to our embassy in Paris. He's in Buenos Aires now, and likes South America so much. They have a son they're very fond of. Have you any children?"

"One. A daughter. How is Edith?"

"It was against Randolfe's wishes, but she would go on the stage. She calls herself Elspeth Montacute. Last year she had quite a good part, they tell me. I expect you will know."

"Yes, of course, Elspeth Montacute," said Etta, who had never heard the name. "What is she playing in now?"

"I don't think she's playing in anything, but she may be—she's usually so busy that I see very little of her."

There was a short silence. Etta pulled herself together. A glance at her watch showed her that she couldn't afford to waste time—she had an appointment to keep. She cleared her throat.

"Now I'm here, Ada, there's something else I'd like to discuss."

"Yes?"

"Dymcott is for sale, isn't it?"

"The solicitor said I couldn't afford to keep it. Randolfe lost a lot of his money, you know. He hadn't the heart for such things after Robert died. And the solicitor thought I should be better off in London, where I still have a few friends. But it's very sad to have to lose Dymcott. I shall miss it dreadfully."

"Now, listen, Ada," said Etta in her business-impressive voice. "You have to sell Dymcott. It's a shame, but you have to face it. Now, instead of selling it to a stranger, wouldn't you rather sell it to a friend, someone you know, someone who likes you so much that if this person bought Dymcott a room would always be kept for you to go there whenever you like?"

"I don't understand," said Ada uncertainly. "Do I know anyone who would do that?"

"I will."

"You! But the solicitor says that with the furniture it's worth three thousand pounds."

Etta pounced on the words—so she had been right in thinking the price too high.

"Three thousand?" she said. "Very well. If you agree, and the title deeds are satisfactory, as I assume they are, I'll pay three thousand. Is it a bargain?"

"I don't understand," said Ada, passing her fingers over her eyes. "Can you afford three thousand pounds?"

"Of course I can," Etta retorted. "I can give you a banker's draft for it tomorrow, if you want. There's no question about my having the money. The point is —do you accept my offer?"

"I must ask Randolfe's solicitor——"

"Why should you do that? You are mistress of your own property. My money is as good as anybody's. You know how I loved Dymcott. And then, you won't really be losing it. I promise you that you will always be welcome there."

"You are very kind, but I don't think I could bear to go back now—without Randolfe."

"Well, but will you accept my offer?"

"The solicitor——"

"Write to the solicitor now, and tell him you have this offer from an old friend. Surely you won't refuse me this, Ada?"

In her impatience, Etta dragged a small table in front
of Ada, found pen, ink, and paper, hunted for Ada's
glasses, and then dictated a letter to the solicitor, telling
him that she had accepted Etta's offer.

"Good," said Etta triumphantly. "Now give me the
pen."

She wrote Ada a formal offer and then made her write
an acceptance.

"I don't know what Mr. Bucknall will say——" Ada
began tremulously.

"Leave him to me," Etta interrupted. "I'll deal with
him. You'll have your three thousand as soon as the
formalities are completed, and—— Good heavens, I must
fly! I'm already late for an appointment. Do come and
see me sometime—here's my home address. Good-bye,
my dear, and thank you. Yes, I'll come and see you.
But I mustn't miss my appointment. Business, you know.
Good-bye, good-bye. . . ."

15

THE EXCITEMENT OF THIS PURCHASE gave Etta back the
energy and zest she had lost. The fact that she had bought
Dymcott on her own was not likely to lessen her pleasure.
Maurice's feeble protests against the extravagance were
brushed away, and Etta even found the audacity to main-
tain obstinately that it was a good investment to a sardonic
Sir James. With Kitty, Etta took the line that it was
above all things necessary that Anne should grow up in
beautiful surroundings. Not to any of them and scarcely
even to herself did she admit the plain truth—that she
wanted Dymcott for herself. It was at once the symbol
and the solid proof of her success in life—a point on
which she needed reassurance. But wasn't this triumph?
To go back to Dymcott from which she had fled as an
unhappy dependent would have been wretched if she had

returned under similar cicumstances. But to return as its owner, in her own car, with her own child and her own husband—that was triumph. How right it was, too, that she should help Ada by making this purchase just when poor Ada needed money. There is a deep satisfaction in being able to repay benefits. And it was fortunate that Etta had acted so promptly—not forty-eight hours after the conveyances were signed Ralph cabled that he would buy Dymcott and give the life tenancy to Ada. With the title deeds in her possession, Etta could snap her fingers at such an offer; especially since Ada would always be welcome there—she could have that charming room Etta herself had had and liked so much.

Naturally, there had to be one fly in this otherwise delicious ointment. Mr. Rhys was on holiday, and until he came back Etta couldn't leave London to take formal possession. She wanted everything arranged so that she could go straight in and live at Dymcott as if there had been no break, to savour the contrast to the full. At one time she thought of sending Maurice down, but Maurice —poor darling!—was very incompetent in all practical details, and besides, he had his work to do. In this dilemma Etta thought of Vera. Now, Vera had been a real brick (Etta always said so) through all the unhappy periods of Etta's life. Wouldn't it be a graceful act to associate her with the triumph? Vera was the one person in the world who would thoroughly understand and sympathize. To have her there when Etta entered her little Valhalla would give the right dramatic touch. Anne naturally couldn't know, Maurice wouldn't understand what it meant to her, but Vera would.

A trunk call to Dortborough summoned Vera to London. At first Vera didn't want to go, pleading engagements and her mother's health—she oughtn't to leave Dortborough for any length of time. But Etta pleaded and cajoled and willed her into obedience. As she pointed out, Dymcott was going to be Anne's, and it was tremendously important that the child's first impression of the place should be favourable. It would be lovely if she could see it first in mid-September. At last Vera reluctantly agreed; and was despatched with housekeeping money, detailed instructions about servants and supplies, and many recommendations about seeing that Anne didn't catch cold and get into mischief.

"Don't talk to her about it, but let her come under the influence of the place," said Etta. "And hint that if she behaves herself and does what Mummy knows is right for her, it'll one day belong to her. Take her out on the river if the weather's fine and the water isn't in flood, and let her rove about the gardens and orchard. Oh, and don't forget to have the garage cleared—Ada tells me they've been using it as a store for old junk. You can get a man from the village. And if the garden needs attention, get a gardener to work on it."

Not until the very end of the month was Etta able to get away from London. There were so many last-minute things to be done that it was long past eleven when they started. Etta telegraphed that they would lunch on the way. She made Maurice drive because she wanted to be quite free to enjoy every minute of the journey. She made a note of the exact time they left—11:27—so as to know precisely how long the journey took by car, for she had set her heart on spending the next spring and summer at Dymcott and coming up to London every day. As if to please her, the day was unexpectedly fine and warm, one of those autumn days when the sun chooses to give a reminder that it has not yet lost power. There was a faint haze over the landscape as they drove along, but the trees were unexpectedly green. Only here and there under horse chestnuts and elms a thin circle of yellow showed that the fall of the leaf had started.

They shared a hasty meal of sandwiches with the servant from the flat, whom Etta was bringing down to help over the week-end; and then pushed on again. Etta found she had forgotten most of the road; it seemed much more urbanized than she remembered. In fact, she hardly recognized anything until they abruptly turned into the village of Dymcott, and Maurice slowed down to ask her which road to follow to the house. The road forked into two lanes, one tarred and the other plain macadam. Etta sat in the stationary car staring at them, while Maurice stared impatiently at her. For the life of her she couldn't remember whether to take the right or the left; and finally they had to ask. It seemed horrible that she had forgotten to that extent.

The car ran up the rather steep winding hill between hedges, and then, as they came to the crest, Etta recognized it all in a flash, the long stretch of gleaming water, the wooded meadows stretching to the misty horizon, the beech woods, the orchard, and then the roof of the house. With this recognition came an utterly unexpected flood of memories, sweeping away her mood of exultant possessiveness. For the first time she realized that she had bought something more than Dymcott itself—the obligation to confront the ghost of her own youth and to render an account of what she had done with it. The car ran slowly up the wide gravel entrance and stopped before the door —it still had its climbing rose with one or two autumn blossoms.

"Is that it?" said Maurice. "What a lovely old place."

For a moment Etta could not move or speak, as she struggled to dominate her emotions. What was the matter with her? Why this curious difficulty to avoid breaking into tears?

"This is Dymcott," she said at last in a stifled voice. "Quite unchanged."

Now that she had spoken, she was able to move and get out of the car. She had a great desire to be alone. Leaning against the car, she gave the servant directions for getting in the baggage.

"Will you put the car in?" Etta said to Maurice. "And see that the engine is all right before you leave it. We can't afford to be late on Monday."

"All right," said Maurice.

"And then you'd better change, dear." She tried to smile. "You'll be so much more comfortable in country clothes."

Maurice nodded, and started manœuvring the car into the garage. Etta went into the house and was immediately impressed by its complete silence. Hardly any of the furniture had been changed. She went quickly up the stairs and entered the bedroom she had slept in and stood looking at it, with an intolerable sense of wistfulness and loss. The room was unoccupied, and the mattress rolled up on the bed; the old chintzes had gone, and there was new wall paper; but otherwise everything was the same, down to the two vases in which she had put wild flowers. She lifted one of the empty vases and gazed at it until the image went blurred with her tears, then swiftly set it down and went to the other rooms. Anne had Robert's room, and Vera was in Ralph's—it was very odd to see a woman's belongings strewn about Ralph's room. Then she went into the large bedroom which had been Ada's and saw that Vera had prepared it for Maurice and herself. On the mantelpiece still stood one of Ada's most treasured ivories, a small seated Buddha, smiling and serene, gazing from untroubled Nirvana on the new owner, who for some strange reason walked up and down wringing her hands, with tears falling down her cheeks.

Etta heard steps coming up and Maurice's voice asking which was his room. Instinctively she ran into the dressing room, and then, when Maurice and the servant reached the bedroom, went out through another door onto the staircase and down into the garden. She must have a few minutes alone to look round the garden—to see if anything needed to be done there urgently. Under the shelter of the side of the house she stopped to dry her eyes and took the pocket mirror from her handbag to make herself look a little decent with powder. She went on, and almost before she knew it found herself on the lower terrace where the green grass was half-hidden under fallen leaves. A double bench had been placed at each end. Vera was sitting reading on the one which overlooked the bathing pool, and Anne, barelegged and bareheaded, was playing intently some game of her own at the edge of the lawn.

"Oh," exclaimed Vera, standing up. "I didn't expect you so soon! You wired . . ."

"We made a fast run," said Etta, and then called: "Anne! Anne! Come to Mummy!"

Anne looked up and then came towards her, jigging along sideways. Etta embraced her emotionally.

"My darling! Are you happy here? Do you like the beautiful house Mummy has bought for her pet?"

"I'm c'lecting snails," said Anne, wriggling free.

"*Snails*, darling? Why do you want such horrid things?"

"They're lovely," said Anne, showing a dirty little hand full of the small black and white striped snails which swarm on chalk.

"I wouldn't collect those," said Etta. "They're dirty things. Look at the lovely chrysanthemums, don't you like them?"

"I want to c'lect snails," said Anne, whimpering.

"Oh, well, if you must . . ."

"May I?" said Anne, brightening immediately. "You keep those, Mummy, and I'll get some more. Don't lose them. I want to have a perfectly *huge* c'lection."

And off she went. Etta sank down on the bench beside Vera and closed her eyes.

"Are you tired?" Vera asked solicitously.

"No. Only . . . only a little . . . dizzy from the drive, you know."

Etta opened her eyes and looked about her. If she looked to the right she saw the ghosts of a girl and a young man walking up and down the terrace and then standing in passionate debate in the heavy shadows of the tall rhododendrons. If she looked to the left she saw the trees on the islet, a glimpse of the curved bridge, and knew that from the bathing pool the white ghost of a naked girl was holding out her arms entreatingly and despairingly to the house. The soft moist smell of the river and of roses came to her nostrils through the heavy autumn scents, and awoke a vague desperate yearning, an unappeasable nostalgia.

"Do you like Dymcott?" she asked, feeling she must say something.

"I think it's charming," said Vera enthusiastically. "I understand why you wanted it so much. It must be an intense satisfaction to you to own it—I remember how often you used to say how much you longed to have Dymcott."

"Yes," said Etta. And then, after a short pause: "How has Anne been?"

"Oh, naughty sometimes, but good most of the time."

"She's a great worry to me," said Etta sighing and looking towards Anne who was intently groping in a thicket of periwinkle leaves for her beloved snails.

"I don't see why."

"She's so childish and self-willed, and I can't get her

to learn. Do you know, she can scarcely read yet? And I want her to have a first-class education."

"It's early for that yet."

"I don't think so, one must begin to plan early. But she's far below the average of her age in most things, except the drawing she's picked up from Maurice. And that's of no importance. I want her to train seriously for some purpose in life. I want her to have a career which will satisfy her. She's not going to be turned out uneducated and hampered at every turn, as I was. If only I could think of the right career for her . . ."

"She may want to marry when she grows up," Vera suggested.

"Let me catch any man tampering with her until she's had some experience of the world and knows her mind, and I'll . . . I'll kill him!" Etta said fiercely.

"I thought you believed in sexual freedom. . . ."

"Anne won't be kept in chains nor in ignorance. When the time comes, I shall see that she knows everything she ought to know. And I shall warn her what to expect from men. Her best defence against them will be to have her own career, as well as the little I may be able to leave her."

"I wonder what she *will* do?" said Vera reflectively. Anne came running towards them with another handful of her little snails which she poured into Etta's lap.

"Take care of them, Mummy," she exclaimed excitedly, pulling Etta's hand down. "Don't let them fall. I'm going to give some to Maurice."

And off she went again.

"I don't know," said Etta, answering Vera's half question. "Nothing silly, if I can help it. You know how I've worked and scraped for that child. I've given up the hope that she'll ever be grateful. Children nowadays seem to have no feelings. But, all the same, I'm willing to go on working and scraping for the rest of my days, so long as I can save her from the kind of life I've had."

"But, Etta, what's wrong with your life? You always wanted to be independent, and you are. I know you had bad times, and we made that mistake of trying to live by farming. . . . Do you remember how amusing old Crowder was? . . . But since then you've been very successful."

"Yes—at advertising, one of the most futile of human occupations," said Etta bitterly. "Oh, I know it's treated me well enough, but just now, when I entered this house and remembered what I was when I lived here and what life there was, I hated advertising. I had a feeling that I'd betrayed something."

"That's rather foolish," said Vera, trying to soothe Etta's excitement. "After all, none of us lives the ideal life. And I must say I often envy all you've achieved. I think now that my little fixed income has been a clog to me—if I hadn't inherited it, I might have done something in the world."

"And what have I done? Nothing worth doing. I think I could have been something better than a commercial tout, if the world had let me. But I never had a chance, Vera. I had to use so much energy merely getting free and then merely keeping alive when I had broken away that I've never had time to develop. That's why I intend that Anne shall have every chance of a fine life. I can't go any farther, but she can start where I leave off. She's *got* to do something worth doing in the world. As for me—why, my real life ended long ago."

Etta was so much absorbed she scarcely noticed the child when Anne toiled over with another handful of shells. Unconsciously Etta gathered them together in her lap. Vera hardly knew what to say, and they remained silent, each following a train of thought about Anne. There was a low, droning sound in the air—three military airplanes flying very high towards the west. Etta didn't notice it, deep in bitter reverie. She startled Vera by saying abruptly:

"Do you think everyone at our age feels as I do—that somehow one has missed the essential?"

"I don't think so," said Vera, trying to laugh. "I don't, for one, and I don't believe you do, either."

"Were you ever in love?"

"No."

"But, Vera, haven't you ever had an affair with a man?"

"No, certainly not," said Vera primly and going rather red.

"It seems curious," said Etta slowly. "Very curious. I suppose . . ."

"When you say you've missed the essential," Vera interrupted, wanting to turn the talk away from this topic, "I think you're being very ungrateful. Years ago, I remember we talked about what you wanted, and it seems to me you've got everything. You've made money, and you've got Dymcott. I remember you said you wanted to have a child which would be entirely yours——"

"Not with the wrong father," said Etta.

"—And that you wanted to live here with a man you loved. And you have Maurice."

"Yes, I have Maurice," Etta said, unconsciously sighing.

"Don't you love him? I've always thought he suited you so well, that you were such a happy pair."

"Oh, yes, we're quite happy."

"Well, then, I don't see what's wrong or what you have to complain about. It seems to me that you've not only attained everything you set out to get, but everything any woman could possibly desire. Don't you think you're ungrateful?"

"Yes," said Etta, standing up and letting the shells

drop. She was staring intently at a young man's figure in white flannels coming down the steps at the other end of the terrace. . . .

"Maurice!" Anne shouted happily as he walked towards them. "Maurice! Hurray! Look what I've got, such lovely snails!" She grabbed his hand and dragged him along. "*Do* look at them, Maurice, aren't they fun?"

To please her, Maurice carefully examined the handful she presented.

"They're nearly all a little different, aren't they?" he said. "We might try drawing them."

"Oh, Mummy!" said Anne, stamping her foot. "You've spilled all my *lovely* snails on the grass!"

"We can pick 'em up," said Maurice. "Come on."

Etta moved a few steps away and stood with her back to them, looking out over the blurred meadows, while Vera helped the others to pick up Anne's treasure.

"Tea's ready," said Maurice, still crouching. "Would you like it out here, darling?"

"No, thanks," said Etta. "You go in and start. I want to go down and look at the boathouse. I'll follow you in a minute. Don't wait."

"Don't drop them," said Maurice to Anne, giving her the shells in his handkerchief. "And if you don't wash those hands before tea there'll be trouble."

If only they'd go, Etta said desperately to herself, if only they'd go and leave me alone just for a minute, one little minute.

"By the way, Etta," Maurice called over his shoulder, "would you like me to bring the gramophone down later on to dance?"

"To dance!" Etta exclaimed in a high hysterical voice which made Vera and Maurice stare at each other. "We can't dance here. There are too many dead leaves."